To Rich —

A dear friend of

John Clark & Arvo also

of mine!

Enjoy this "first run" edition!

All the best —

Jeanette

Vaughan

Flying Solo
An Unconventional Aviatrix Navigates Turbulence in Life

Jeanette Vaughan

AgeView Press

Blue Ridge, TX MMXII

DEDICATION

This book was written to celebrate the escapades of intrepid women everywhere who challenge the norm; for they are the true pioneers and heroes. – especially my daughter Paige.

ACKNOWLEDGMENTS

Writing a book based on a true story isn't easy. Sometimes feelings get hurt when events experienced by others are perceived through a different lens. I would like to acknowledge the woman who was brave enough to share this wonderful adventure. She was formidable enough to survive the highs and lows that life threw in her path. She was forthright enough to make decisions that challenged the norm. Some with good outcomes, some not. I admired her independence and her esprit de corps. It is with her permission that I share her powerful story. Many of the events described within occurred exactly as written, others did not. Lots of hours were spent over shared cups of coffee as she related this piece and that. Ultimately, she sacrificed her own wants to give the greatest gift possible, life. She will always remain an inspiration to me, a beacon toward the pursuit of individuality. In addition I would especially like to thank my group of test readers. They took their time to make suggestions to my early scribblings. Some of them are my sister, Susan and her partner Lori; as well as my friends and colleagues John, Carole, Steve, Amy, Beth, and Gary. I would like to honor, acknowledge and thank Gary W. Arthur for his aviation expertise. As a flight engineer and pilot himself, he spent countless hours assisting with the historical and technical components of how to fly a plane. For that, I am truly grateful. His guidance helped to make this powerful story accurate.

Flying Solo

Chapter One
∞ September, 1961 ∞

The blue Slimline phone was ringing incessantly. Ringing and ringing and ringing. Unanswered. It seemed like no one would pick it up.

"Keep your pants on," Nora screamed as she quickly darted through the living room of her 1960s bungalow. Early morning Mississippi tug boat whistles were barely audible in the heart of suburban New Orleans.

"Damn it to hell! I'm coming," as if the phone could hear her. Nora nearly took a face-plant as her foot slipped on some Lincoln Logs. She hopped over a basket of unfolded laundry laying there and toys that were strewn around the living room. Long legs lunging; she dove for the receiver.

"Hello?" she answered in her silky, albeit breathless voice. "Hello."

"Oh, good morning, Mrs. Greenwood. This is Dr. Joseph's office calling with your lab results."

"Yes. Go on." Nora waited.

"Congratulations! The rabbit died. Oh you've got to be terribly excited," gushed the chirpy office nurse.

Nora couldn't believe what she heard echoing through the phone line. In that instant, shivers went down her spine. Oh holy Jesus. I'm pregnant, she panicked.

"Mrs. Greenwood?" the nurse questioned, not sure she was heard.

However, Nora was still in shock and initially lost for words. Seconds ticked by. "Oh, yes," she recovered. "Thank you for calling."

"What a happy day. Congratulations again, Mrs. Greenwood. I guess you will be making your pre-natal appointment now?"

"Um. No. I will . . . I will call you back later. When I can think. I am just so . . ."

"Surprised?" the little perky nurse interjected.

"Yes. Surprised," Nora's voice was flat. That was a contradiction. A wave of nausea suddenly overcame her. She quickly replaced the receiver and bounded for the bathroom.

What she didn't realize was that in another room, there was a second click. Her daughter, Kayce, had been listening in on the other end. Kayce was furious. Another baby? Ugh. Couldn't her mother and father keep their hands off one another? The thought just grossed her out. If they weren't arguing, she guessed they were screwing. Almost a teen, at twelve, she knew the about the birds and the bees, as her mother referred to sex. Baby number five? The thought of it just made her skin crawl.

Nora had no idea that Kayce had been eavesdropping. Before she could even collect her thoughts, Kayce barged into the hall bathroom oblivious to her mother's retching.

"Another baby? You're having another baby?" she exclaimed with disgust.

"What are you talking about?" Nora tried to deny.

"Don't act naive, Mother. I heard you." Out she flounced. Nora could hear her yelling as she stomped down the hallway.

"I can't believe it. It's outrageous that you're having another baby. Another stupid baby for me to take care of. It was bad enough with Iggy," she screamed, referring to her little four year old brother. Bang. She slammed her bedroom door.

Nora ignored her daughter's rants. It was all she could do to raise her chin up after hugging the porcelain bowl. It wasn't that she was pregnant with another baby. It was the fact that she knew this baby was not her husband's.

Nerves shook her body again violently. Nora began to weep. "Oh what have I done?" she chastised. She was drenched in a frigid, clammy sweat. Cold. She felt very cold dressed in only a long t-shirt and panties.

Nora had to get it together. She had to collect herself. Her thoughts went to her family. Her beloved children.

Not only was Kayce going to hate her for being pregnant, but she would be mortified if she realized her mother was having an affair with a married man. A married man who also had children. How could she have let this happen, she fretted?

But she knew. She knew the exact moment when it must have happened. Visions of slow, steamy sex with her instructor pilot, Steve Novak, brought a hot flash to her groin. With the tumultuous climaxes he brought her to and as easily as she conceived; she wasn't surprised. It didn't take much to get Nora pregnant. Fertile Myrtle, her ubiquitously Catholic mother called her. But another man's baby? In the present moment, she was at a total loss about what to do.

Ever the plotter, she pulled herself together. She had been through rough spots before. A mish-mash of thoughts were whirring in her head. Nora feared this potential outcome when she started the affair, she rebuked. Or least the possibility of it anyway. She could do this. She was a survivor, she pep talked herself.

Nora just needed time to figure it out. She momentarily freaked when she heard the multitude of voices from her other three children clambering down the hall. Ignatius, Cathy and Leisel were all hustling to get ready for school. She had to get them in the car before they were late again. One parent conference per semester with Sister Margaret, principal of St. Francis Xavier was enough.

Pulling herself up off the bathroom floor, she wiped the tears off her face, put on some lipstick and smoothed her hair. Resolutely, she looked into the mirror; applying a little bit of hair spray to her auburn and chestnut, swept-up bee hive.

Christ, what an absolute mess. But she couldn't think about it now. Quickly, she donned some Capri pants and black loafers, grabbed her keys and coat and headed out to take the kids to school. No bra today.

She left the door open for the maid, Mabel. All four children were already in the station wagon, bundled up with sweaters over their school uniforms. The September air was crisp, even for New Orleans. Their chatty, happy voices were oblivious to the fact that within a few short weeks, their lives would be changed forever. Well, all but one.

During the car ride, Kayce spoke not one word to Nora. She simply stared out the window. Her strawberry blonde, curly, hair and round face were stark contrasts to Nora's dark French looks. She clearly took after her father. Her pale skin was dotted with a hundred freckles. She was cute enough, despite being way too savvy for her age.

The rebellious teenage years had come early to Kayce. Nora knew she could no longer get anything past her. Her eldest was nosey about everything. Kayce Greenwood, the pre-teen, social butterfly. Daughter of Franklin Greenwood, of the country club set. Scandal simply would not do.

It was about image and fitting in. Kayce mused. Her parent's marriage wasn't perfect, and she knew they fought like cats and dogs, but there was no way they would ever divorce. They were Catholics. In the sixties, especially in the South, it just wasn't done.

Another baby, Kayce miffed. Another screaming, crying, snotty little brat. Her parents had been excited when Iggy, that's what they called Ignatius for short, was born four years ago. She knew her mother adored her only son. Kayce had been keen to help at first. But the days of changing diapers and watching babies while her mother did her nails or made lunch appointments to go to the club were over. At least as far as she was concerned.

Neither Kayce, nor Nora, saw the oncoming car approaching on Metairie Blvd. as Nora ran the stop sign. A large, green Buick honked its horn and swerved to miss them.

"Mama! Watch out!" Cathy screamed. Their '61, wood paneled, Ford Country Squire station wagon careened up onto the curb, smashing some garbage cans and barely missing a huge oak tree.

Nora was catapulted back into reality. "Oh my God. I'm sorry kiddos." Gripping the large steering wheel, she maneuvered the wagon off the curb and back into the traffic. She had to focus. At least long enough to get them safely to school. Enough Scarlett O'Hara thinking for now. Later, she could actually process the disaster she was facing.

Chapter 2
∞ December, 1947 ∞

Nora would marry way too young. She was the daughter of New Orleans natives, Nellie Shryock and the late Jack Broussard. As a young girl, Nora spent many an afternoon riding the streetcars up and down Carrollton Avenue while her mother, worked at Hotel Dieu, the charity hospital. After putting in her nickel and two cents, she would sip on her sassafras soda and ride the rails amidst the tall live oaks. Her daydreams often were about the adventures she imagined her gypsy-like, Cajun father must have had riding the riverboats up the Mississippi.

To some, Jack Broussard was considered quite a rogue. An entrepreneurial jack-of-all-trades, he was often gone for months at a time. He was a clever innovator, investing in this scheme or that. There was nothing he wouldn't try once. Many thought he was purely a gambler, but that wasn't true. Jack just knew when to capitalize on an opportunity, whether it was gambling or business. He made scads of money and also lost mini-fortunes while traversing the dark swirls of the Mississippi. He was killed in a gun fight aboard the *Delta Queen*. Rumor had it, over a *belle jolie catin*.

Her mother wouldn't speak about it. But Nora remembers an exquisite, exotic woman, covered in a long, lace, black veil and cloak among the mourners at St. Louis cemetery. Nora was seven.

She noticed her while clutching Nellie's hand as they stood near the grey, granite, above ground crypt of the

Broussard family. It was the only thing she did remember about that monstrous day. The vision of that woman momentarily broke through Nora's unfathomable grief. She had simply adored her father. Nora knew she would be distraught without her kindred spirit.

Nora was the spitting image of him. Her dark complexion with olive skin. Her haunting, large, chocolate eyes. Thick, curly hair. Prominent, but regal nose and the high, trademark cheekbones which belied their Native American-Cajun roots. She was twenty-five percent Coushatta Indian.

Nellie was anything but. Prim, proper, fair skinned and relatively plain. She wondered what her father, Jack, had ever seen in her. Maybe she had been prettier in her younger days. It was possible, with Jack's prodigal behavior; he had been attracted to the simple charms of Nellie's pious goodness. Her parents met on Canal Street, as Nellie was coming out of Morning Call with fresh *beignets*. After a brief romance, they were married at St. Mary's Assumption on Constance St. off of Magazine.

Nora was every bit Jack Broussard's daughter. Vivacious. Charmingly irresistible. Precocious and daring. Like her father, there was just about nothing she feared.

After Jack's death, Nellie was nearly broke. She had moved Nora, her only child, into a small apartment near The French Quarter within walking distance of Hotel Dieu. Nora started second grade at Ursuline Academy for girls, mostly on scholarship. Nellie wanted only the very best, feeling that the discipline, piety and rigor of the school would squelch any remaining wayward Cajun tendencies in her daughter.

But it didn't. By the time Nora was a teenager, she and Nellie would do battle. She sought more and more adventure outside the confines of Nellie's protective mothering. Nora would often skip out during the night following one of Nellie's exhausting hospital shifts.

While her mother was sound asleep, Nora would scrap her school uniform, put on a party dress and head out to one of the jazz clubs in The Quarter. The bluesy melodies stirred her soul. She looked much older than her sixteen. Wearing some bright red lipstick and rouge, smoking her long cigarettes, she could pass for a young Ava Gardner.

No one in The Quarter seemed to care anyway.

It was much to the relief of Nellie that Franklin Charles Greenwood had come fortuitously into Nora's life. The Greenwoods were a well known family in New Orleans. Rich. Established. Just the sort of lineage that would upgrade her daughter's pedigree. Their money had come from oil and natural gas. They owned a large, stately home on St. Charles Avenue.

Franklin had met Nora at an Ursuline-Jesuit Mardi Gras dance. Nora was only eighteen and in her senior year at Ursuline. Franklin was attending Loyola School of Law. He was suave and handsome with light brown, sandy hair. Several years older than Nora; he was short, at five foot nine, but had an athletic build. He was taken aback by Nora's dark and alluring eyes. One sultry slow dance and a cop of Nora's tight ass was all it had taken for him to fall completely under her spell.

Within weeks, he was seeing her almost exclusively. For Nora, it was chance to experience things she had only dreamed. She was happy to trade her long grey kilt Ursuline skirts and saddle oxfords for high heels, a flouncy blouse, and a tight skirt. There was Sunday brunch at Brennan's. Tickets to the Bacchus ball during Mardi Gras. Dinner at Metairie Country Club. This was a life she in which she could see possibilities.

So he wasn't the best kisser. On their dates, he groped her incessantly, but she wouldn't let him go all the way. Touching her breasts on the outside of her scoop necked sweaters was enough to drive him wild and she held him at that.

He was crazy about her. Before she knew it, in uptown Audubon Park on her birthday in May, he had proposed. Nellie was over the moon. Her hard work, calloused hands from nursing, and prayers had paid off. She had to labor many a shift to pay the tuition at Ursuline, but it had been worth the effort. It had put her daughter into a position to marry up. Nora would now join the ranks of the New Orleans' upper crust.

Anxious to tie the knot and escape Nellie's constraint, Nora planned a summer nuptial. There wasn't time to plan a huge New Orleans wedding. Most churches were booked. Much to her mother's disappointment, she and

JEANETTE VAUGHAN

Franklin were married in a simple ceremony in the living room of his parents' home on St. Charles. The reception was a *Fais do do* in the garden behind. Although Nora was dressed in a designer suit, there was no big white dress. No bridesmaids. She carried a small bouquet of white roses and stephanotis. Simple and elegant, it was over far too quick. One final sign of the cross, a kiss from her groom and bam. On June 11, 1948, Nora was wed.

As a married woman, she felt all grown up. Her triumphant new life as Nora Greenwood had begun. But all Nora could think about was her wedding night. What would it feel like to have a man inside her? What would it be like to lie naked together, spent from ravenous sex? She had seen pictures of men's privates, but certainly had never touched them. The thought made her almost giddy with anticipation.

Chapter 3
∞ June, 1948 ∞

Franklin and Nora bid farewell to their guests and sped off in a limousine toward Moisant Field. Free. She was finally free from Nellie. And married. She looked down at her half carat princess cut diamond on a slim platinum band. Franklin had good taste. Or at least Adler's, the family jewelers, did.

Frank, as Nora called him, was taking her to New York for their honeymoon. Still dressed in her Chanel, mint green wedding suit, they prepared to board a Delta DC-3. This was her first experience with air travel. But she wasn't nervous, she was thrilled.

A couple of drop-dead, gorgeous pilots strutted past her and out onto the tarmac. Dreamy in their dark blue uniforms and wings. She was quite sure one of them winked at her. They were followed by a covey of smartly dressed stewardesses. Next, it was their turn to climb the stairs and board. Nora steadied her pillbox hat from the breeze.

She listened to the instructions on how to fasten her seatbelt. As the propellers whirled and the aircraft taxied, she tried to imagine what it would be like to be up in the air. Within seconds she knew. Engines whirred. The nose of the plane lifted. They were up.

"I wonder what it would be like to fly one of these?" she asked Frank.

"Women don't fly, Nora. You silly girl. That's a man's job," he squeezed her thigh.

Little did Nora realize, but that exchange was a metaphoric glimpse of what her life with Frank would become. Tempestuous Nora in the staid, conservative, rigid life of the Greenwoods. And it was only day one.

Nora peered out the tiny window and saw her crescent shaped city like she had never viewed. The huge, mighty Mississippi wrapped around and cradled the tightly packed neighborhoods. People looked like ants and cars became toy-like. Before long, they soared up into the clouds. The soft, wispy, white looked like spun cotton candy. It was magical.

An attractive and perky stewardess came around to first class with a tray of cocktails. "Champagne?"

"Oh, yes. Please," Nora obliged. So this was the life of a socialite. She liked it.

Even though she was exhausted from the wedding foray, she slept not a wink. Every bounce of turbulence as they ascended ever higher into the clouds electrified her. New York was a five hour flight and she adored every minute in the air. "One day, I am going to fly a plane myself," she envisioned. "One day, Franklin Charles Greenwood, you just wait and see."

At almost dusk, the skyscrapers of New York came into view. She thought New Orleans was crowded. But New York? It was bustling and brilliant. Scads of inviting, snugly packed buildings were crammed onto the narrow island of Manhattan.

"Look Frank," she pointed out. "The Empire State building."

"Yeah. It's pretty impressive to see it the first time," he said nonchalantly. His less than enthusiastic response didn't dampen Nora's exhilaration. She couldn't wait to land and explore.

They caught a taxi to the brand new Waldorf Astoria and checked into their honeymoon suite. It was plush and impeccable. Nora had almost forgotten what was solely on Frank's mind. Sex. Sex with a virgin. His wife.

Before she could even sit her green, alligator bag down, he grabbed her from behind. "Finally. After all your stalling, you are mine." He ripped away her jacket and tore open her satin blouse. His hot wet kisses to her neck were tantalizing to her skin at first. But his lips were coarse. His hands grabbed her breasts roughly. "God I've wanted to screw you," he moaned.

Spinning her around, he forcibly shoved his hands under her skirt ripping down her nylons. He wrenched off her bra. Before she knew it, his mouth was all over her nipples. Biting. Sucking. It hurt.

"Frank. Slow down," she encouraged.

"There's nothing that's gonna slow me down, Nora. Now that you're my wife, I am gonna fuck you until you can't walk." He removed his belt and within seconds stood naked before her.

Nora shuddered at his words. She had never heard him talk to her like that. Brutal and gruff. He threw her down on the bed and hiked up her slim skirt. He pushed aside her laced panties and shoved himself inside her. Thrusting and pounding he ripped through her hymen.

"Ohhh," she whimpered. Her virginity was now taken.

He was mechanical in his motions. His thrusts were rapid and jerky. She felt herself being pried open. Pounding her harder and harder until all at once, he cried out, "Gahhhh . . ahhhh . . ." and into her he came.

The experience for which she had waited. Nora's first time making love. That was it?

He pulled himself out of her and rolled over onto the bed. "So how was it? My virgin bride," he sneered, vainly pleased with himself.

Nora was revolted. Hurt. She felt violated. Almost raped. She hurried into the bathroom, too proud to let him see her cry. Tears streaked the perfect makeup of her wedding day. There was blood on her torn lace panties. She looked in the mirror and was frightened at what she saw there.

Christ almighty, what had she done? She looked down at her ring. She was only eighteen and married. Married to a man who made love to her like she was a whore. A cunt, nothing more.

She dabbed away her tears and blew her nose. Her body quivered with a cold shudder. The thought of getting into bed with him again made her almost wretch. How could she have been so wrong?

He was so different when they dated. His kisses had been tight lipped and unromantic, but she thought it was because he was nervous to be around her. She had kissed other boys and it certainly had been different. Running her finger along her lips, she thought of the smooth, sensuous times a mouth had caressed hers.

She changed into her negligee. Her honeymoon ensemble was a lovely, soft pink with lace over the bodice. Almost sheer. It was what she planned to wear as her new husband made love to her the very first time, she thought sadly. Was this married life? Was what she had just experienced sex?

Nora thought of all the romances she had read. About the gallant Romeos and how they caressed their lovers into libidinous bliss. That was what she dreamed it would be like. Waves of passion and arduous kisses. Suckling her, nurturing her, gently taking her into ecstasy.

Maybe she had jumped to conclusions about Frank. Maybe he was just anxious to take her. Maybe next time it would be different. It had to be. She bit her lip. She was married for life.

"Nora," he called out. "Get your tight little Cajun ass to bed. It's late," he bellowed.

Chapter 4

Nora couldn't think about the night before. It was just too awful. She woke early and dressed in a smart, burgundy Dior suit that outlined her hourglass figure. She was tall and Dior's lines befit her well. The bell hop had brought up breakfast and she poured over *The New Yorker* and a subway map to plot out her day.

"What're your plans?" Frank queried.

Without looking up, she answered. "I thought we would take in some of the sites. You know, like the Empire State building and Central Park."

"I've seen all that stuff Nora. But if you wanna go. Go. Here," he tossed a hundred dollar bill on the table. "Go buy a sexy corset and stockings at Macy's."

"They don't sell that kind of stuff at Macy's," she said embarrassed.

He came over to her and gave her a peck on the lips. "Well buy something nice that I can screw your brains out in tonight. I'm gonna see if I can score us some Yankee tickets."

The Yankees. Baseball on her honeymoon? Typical Frank. He had been quite the jock at Tulane before law school.

"Alright. I am sure I can find something to do." She was actually glad to spend time away from him after last night. She grabbed another bite of her toast and headed out the door.

New York was amazing. The doorman, amazing. High

rises, amazing. Spritely, busy streets. Couture and culture everywhere you looked. Nora immersed herself into the crowded street, hurrying up Park Avenue. She planned to shop until she dropped. Balenciaga. Pierre Balmain. Tiffany's. Bergdorf Goodman. She was in heaven.

After making several purchases, she popped into Chock Full O' Nuts with her designer bags for some coffee. "Espresso with a pinch of milk," she ordered. "And an éclair."

"Milk. In Espresso?" a deep, sexy voice said behind her.

Nora whipped around to see a tall, striking man in a pilot's uniform. The site of him took her breath away. His cerulean blue eyes caught her off guard. "Yes. That's the way all French girls like their coffee," she answered defensively.

"Is that so? Not in Paris," he challenged.

"Well maybe not, but I'm not from Paris."

"Ya don't say," he mocked her Southern 'Nawlins accent.

Nora smiled, catching the joke.

"What brings you to New York?"

Taking her coffee and pastry from the clerk, she wondered if she should answer. "My honeymoon."

"Oh, I see." He looked crushed. "Guess I am outta luck then. I was going to ask you to dinner."

Nora blushed and looked down at her ring, almost spilling her coffee.

"Careful there," he blotted her wrist with a napkin.

Just his touch sent thrills to her toes. Who was this guy? Stop it, Nora. You are off the market. Married. Day two. "Thank you, but I have to go."

Quickly, she left the café and walked towards Central Park. She was a wife now, no longer single. How could such a brief encounter have sent her into such a tail spin? Nora found an unoccupied bench and sat alone with her thoughts.

Across the boulevard, still in the café, Steve Novak felt like he had just seen a Goddess. He was engaged, but hell, he could look. Who couldn't help but look at her? The chestnut hair. Her curvy figure. Those captivating, large eyes. She was a site to behold.

Back at the hotel, her husband Frank was waiting for her. She entered, arms full of packages. "Shopping success I see," he smirked.

"Yes. I had a lovely time. New York is just marvelous. I met so many interesting people. From seemingly everywhere in the world." Nora started to take out her precious purchases.

"I was hoping you wouldn't be gone too long. I got us the tickets. Second row, just along first base," he proudly beamed.

"Great," she lied.

"But first, I want to fuck you again." He moved toward her and she hoped he didn't see her flinch. It was her honeymoon. Intercourse was mandatory. She really had no choice. But this time, she tried to get him to take it slow.

Nora took Frank's face and held it. She kissed him slowly and ardently. She slipped her tongue into his mouth and caressed his. This time, she would take the lead.

Her advances seemed to turn him on. He was moaning and pressed his hard cock against her. She moved against him, stroking him with her mound. He grabbed her hair and pulled back her head. Hungrily, he began to kiss her neck. Quick, hard, rough kisses.

To avoid a hiccie from his sucks, she guided his head to her suit lapels. She unbuttoned them. Slowly. Hoping he would take the hint. But he quickly undid all of them, defrocking her to a bra and matching panties.

"Get into bed," he commanded. "I want to take you from behind."

Nora was shocked. But she obeyed.

"Here. Like this." He turned her over, pulled down her panties and raised her hips. With one motion, he plunged himself inside her. Somehow, it felt deeper. Even more brutal than before.

Her face was buried into the pillow. He pushed and thrust. Over and over and over in the same motion. He reached up under her and grabbed her tits, twisting the nipples painfully.

"Frank. I . . ."

"You what? Want more of your husband in your

pussy?"

Harder and harder he pounded her. After what seemed like eternity, but was only minutes, he again cried out with the same, "Gaahhhhh . . . ahhh . . . oh yeah baby. Fucking tight. Fucking mine."

And then it was over. Love making round two. But was it making love? Nora didn't think so. It felt nasty. She was sore all over again. After he came, he withdrew from her quickly and got into the shower, leaving her there in the bed. No kisses. No cuddles. Nora felt empty and drew her knees up to her chest in the fetal position. She hated how dirty he spoke to her.

This time she had tried. She tried to seduce and make love to her husband. Why couldn't he let her? Why weren't her feelings important to him? She just didn't understand it.

"Nora. Come on," Frank yelled and poked his head from the bathroom door. "Get dressed for God's sake. We're gonna miss the first pitch. Yogi Berra's the catcher tonight."

She put on her full plaid skirt and new pearled white blouse. Stepping into her flats, she winced in pain. Her twat actually hurt.

"Buck up girl. There'll be plenty more where that came from." Frank slapped her behind. Yet again, in some chauvinistic, depraved way, he seemed proud of himself.

Yankee stadium was a site to see. Roaring crowds cheered. The Yankees were playing the Boston Red Sox. Whitey Ford pitched a shutout. Nora sipped on her beer. It was bitter and not like the Falstaff from home, but thankfully something to numb her nerve endings. Home. She wanted to just go home. Back to New Orleans. To start her new life. With Frank in law school, hopefully he would be too busy studying and too tired to want to have sex with her two times a day. Four more days. Just four more days and her honeymoon nightmare would be over.

Chapter 5
∞ July, 1949 ∞

Once back in New Orleans, Frank moved Nora's things into his large bedroom on the third floor of his parent's home. They pretty much had the entire floor of the house to themselves. The elder Greenwoods lived on the second floor. Formal drawing rooms, a magnificent dining room, the library, kitchen and a den occupied the elevated first floor. The house was built up on piers with only storage on the ground floor. The city of New Orleans was six feet under sea level. In uptown, even the most expensive homes often flooded.

Nora spent her time exploring the house. It was vast. The huge, wrapping, mahogany staircase looked like the one from *Gone with the Wind*. There were superb, Austrian crystal chandeliers. Thick, maroon, velvet draperies with large, gold tassels. Plush, Persian rugs. It was splendid. Frank seemed to take it all for granted. The home had been in his family since the early 1800s.

Her favorite rooms were the library and kitchen. During the day she would browse through walls of leather bound classics. *The Grapes of Wrath. Madame Bovary. The Scarlet Letter. Moby Dick. Lady Chatterley's Lover.* She was never without fabulous reading material. *Gone with the Wind* was one of Nora's favorite books. Many days, she felt like Scarlett O'Hara scoping out her next adventure.

Frank's father worked the family's oil business on Canal St. His mother was often away at church or volunteering at La Salle School for the Blind. But Nora didn't mind. With only herself and the maids there, she could pretend that the house was all hers. She thought about enrolling in Newcombe College, the female side of Tulane, but Frank had discouraged her. She didn't need a career, he told her. She was his wife.

She was his wife. She was his wife. If she heard it again, she thought she would scream. Nora was only weeks into her marriage and it already felt like a prison. She married Frank to be free of Nellie, but what she got in exchange was entombment of another kind.

When she tried to express her wishes, her dreams and desires, Frank just blew her off. It seemed, now that he had a wife and someone to screw, he really didn't care at all about what she thought or felt. Pretty much about anything. She wondered if he even loved her.

The sex hadn't improved. Nora had just gotten more used to it. He simply wasn't very good in bed. Now that they were home, however, she was relegated to his advances only about once a week. Thank God for that.

Nora's only other enjoyment was sitting in the kitchen, listening to the maids sing their deep spirituals as they prepared the dishes that made New Orleans famous. The Greenwoods ate only the most succulent shrimp, crawfish, and *boudain*. They dressed formally for dinner, only to sit down and chow on a bowl of gumbo or red beans and rice.

The spicy aromas coming from the kitchen were divine. Wafting through Nora's nose, it only took a whiff to draw her away from her books to the kitchen in no time. She had made friends with the help. Justine and Mabel seemed tickled that she paid them attention.

But Nora loved hearing their stories. Justine's family had been workers on a sugar cane plantation up the river road at Vacherie. When she was younger, Justine aspired to be a jazz singer in the clubs of The Quarter. She was too, until she got pregnant by a trumpet player. Unmarried and expecting, she was banned from the nightclubs. Adrift in New Orleans, she had no choice but to enter into domestic service. Dashed were her dreams of fame, but not her velvet voice which rang through the iron pot racks of the kitchen on St. Charles.

Mabel's family lived just outside *Vieux Carre*. She had a strong, Creole Haitian accent and many times Nora could barely understand her. Almost toothless and rotund, her dark, black skin was rich and warm. She had a big heart and a bigger body, but loved to sing with Justine as they made their dark *roux* for *etouffee* and gumbo.

It was in this kitchen that Nora learned to love cooking. At first she just watched, but soon, she joined in cutting up the onions, garlic, celery and green peppers to make the delicious meals. She mastered the secrets of making a perfect, dark chocolate colored *roux*. Frank considered her a bit daft to hang out with the help, but Nora didn't care. Justine and Mabel became her quasi friends and confidants. Nora talked to them about anything and everything. Even though she knew she shouldn't. It wasn't her place. But to hell with place, they were real and fun.

Hour after hour Nora spent in the kitchen becoming quite a chef. She loved her time there. Justine and Mabel made her feel accepted. Nora didn't see color. She saw women. Strong, self-reliant women.

Nellie came around about once a month. Pleased that her daughter had married well, she graciously accepted the Sunday lunch invitations sent by the Greenwoods. Since the upgraded status of her daughter had no bearing on her own economic situation, she still continued to nurse. Hotel Dieu was never lacking patients. Her concerns about Nora were not over, however. With her daughter in such lavish, need free, albeit sedate surroundings; she worried that passionate Nora would soon become bored.

But one Sunday, Mrs. Greenwood made a hopeful announcement. It seemed that through her connections, she wrangled an invitation for Nora to be sponsored into the Junior League. Nellie was elated. Nora looked perplexed. The Junior League? A bunch of uppity, ex-sorority girls volunteering their time for worthy causes? There not to make a difference, but to look good?

"Oh, what a lovely gesture," her mother gushed. "I am sure Nora would be pleased to accept."

Nora glared at Nellie. "Why yes, Mrs. Greenwood." She still couldn't call her mother in law *Mere*, as Mother Greenwood wished. "I would be delighted."

And so began Nora's introduction to the other side of

upper crust life. Volunteering for everything because one did not have a real job. Aiding the needy. Working the soup kitchen. Reading to the illiterate. Helping to raise funds for the cause. Whatever cause was going at the moment. Whatever was required of the Junior League participant. Giving back to society was a worthy endeavor, but to Nora it was *lagniappe*. She wanted to do something exciting. A career or technical vocation maybe.

The only good thing that came out of it was the friend that she made in Charlene. Charlene Hebert was the first real friend, besides Mabel and Justine, which Nora had since grade school. They fast became chums. At last it was somebody to share lunch. Somebody to talk about clothes. Somebody to attend the Endymion and Bacchus parade balls with at Mardi Gras. Charlene was a Godsend.

She was a few years older than Nora. She too had married into money. A Dominican high school graduate, she attended Newcombe College, which was why Nora had never met her. Dominican was Ursuline's rival. Charlene also married rather young, right out of college. Although she never got a chance to use her degree in education or have a career, she seemed to have an easier time adjusting to it all. Nora wondered; either Charlene had the patience of Job or had done a much better job at selecting a man to marry.

Chapter 6
∞ January, 1961 ∞

Several years and several children later, during one of the League's cotillion lunches at Metairie Country Club, Nora saw an intriguing flier posted on the current events board. It was an advertisement for flying lessons, sponsored by a member from the club. The flier was intriguing. Unbeknownst to Nora, its enticement would rock the world as she knew it.

From the moment Nora first flew, that time on her honeymoon, she had been hooked. Every time she got the chance, she booked an airline trip for her and Frank to get away for a weekend. Passenger planes had advanced from propeller to jet engines. Charlene had taken to calling her part of the jet set. The Greenwoods now even owned their own plane.

For Nora, flying was an escape. In some weird way, when she was up in the clouds, it was like living out some of the gypsy travels of her father, Jack. Aviation fueled her independent spirit. It was elitist. It was daring. It was modern. Hell, it was fun.

"What are you looking at now Nora?" Charlene beckoned. She knew that glint in Nora's eyes. She had barely crocheted a stitch on the baby booties they were making for the League's latest project.

"Have you ever thought of taking flying lessons?" Nora asked out of the blue.

"Are you kidding me? I didn't even like taking driving lessons." Charlene laughed. "Nora, surely you aren't serious? Frank barely lets you drive his car. Do you really think he would let you fly his family's plane? I would forget about that crazy idea. Before it gets your pretty little arse into trouble."

"Maybe," Nora answered unconvincingly. Charlene wasn't buying it. She knew what happened when Nora got an idea into her head.

"I'll be back. I'm gonna go see if Max made the list for the Endymion krewe." Krewes were the volunteers that dressed up in costumes and rode the floats at Mardi Gras. They threw the famous beads and doubloons. This year, Mardi Gras was early, in only a few weeks. It fell on February, 14 Valentine's Day. "You go turn in the booties we've finished."

Nora sat for a moment, waxing nostalgic. She looked down at the blue and pink crocheted baby booties they had made for the Catholic Charities drive. Making something useful validated her worthiness. Nonetheless, she couldn't stop thinking about the lessons.

Once Nora made her mind up to do something, there was just about no stopping her. Charlene lived through Nora vicariously. In the past, they had taken ski trips to Aspen. Once they had canoed Snake River canyon. Adventure travel was the name of the game on their joint family vacations. Those trips provided the excitement Nora desperately sought. Over the years, Frank and Charlene's husband, Max, had become friends and golf partners. Which was just fine for Charlene and Nora because it meant they could spend even more time together. Charlene had become a pseudo-sister to Nora. She was the only person who kept her from losing her mind in her loser marriage.

Charlene had been there when Nora became pregnant within her first wedded year. She was at the hospital when Nora's first born daughter, Kayce was delivered. She helped Nora learn how to breast feed. She helped organize Kayce's first birthday. Charlene helped Nora find her first real home. A good distance away from the Greenwoods, the home was just down the road from the club.

After the birth of Kayce, things on the third floor of the St. Charles Street mansion had become too close for comfort. As Frank finished school and entered a law internship for a big practice downtown, the stress had boiled over. While studying to pass the bar, he had been an absolute ogre.

His late night rants and drinking binges ignited numerous arguments. The vase smashing, knockdown, drag outs were just too much with which the anesthetized Greenwoods could cope. In her ever-so-polite manner, Mrs. Greenwood gave Nora a large check for a down payment on a home. Presented as a gift to Nora, to celebrate the birth of their first grandchild; in reality it was mostly a bequest to her son. It was time for them to get out on their own.

Nora was ecstatic. The home on St. Charles was lovely, but her own home? That she could decorate anyway she wanted? Her own four walls? It would bring independence and harmony. She just knew it.

Charlene and she had scoured the ads and taken numerous excursions with the real estate agent. They finally found the home of Nora's dreams. The house was a large sprawling one story with tall Georgian columns. It had hardwood floors and a tile entry. Four bedrooms, including an en suite bathroom. It even had a pool in the back. For Nora, it was Shangri-la. Tall towering oak trees surrounded the circular drive at 462 Woodvine. The gardens that wrapped the house were well established with huge azalea bushes and camellias. Plus, it was right around the corner from Charlene's on Iola.

Shopping for furniture had been a joy. Nora went all modern with sleek couches and sharp, edged coffee and end tables. Only the best from Maison Blanche. In the master bedroom, she decked it out in velvet patterned wall paper with a bamboo pattern. There was a large four poster bed. The one antique she allowed was the vibrantly patterned quilt that her father had given her, imported from India. *That*, she treasured.

Before she knew it, Nora had given birth to three children. All daughters. Kayce, Cathryn, and Leisel were all two years a part. Just like clockwork, when breast feeding was over at a year, shazam. She was knocked up again.

Outwardly, Nora epitomized the typical, good Catholic wife. Mother Greenwood was elated. So was Nellie. But

Frank wanted a boy. He was adamant to have his family namesake and legacy.

For Nora, that only meant one thing. More sexual attacks from her husband. For that is what they were. They had never become anything else. She was almost relieved when pregnant so early with Kayce, for it was an excuse not to have sex. Once she started showing, Frank wanted nothing to do with her. He called her fat and made her feel unattractive. Even though she could still squeeze into her jeans and skinny pants until she was almost five months, he was repulsed by her shape.

When expecting, Nora never looked more radiant. It drove Frank insane, because he needed her sexually. But there were two times he would never attempt to shag her, when she was on her period and when she was knocked up.

Nora loved being pregnant. Her morning sickness lasted only the first few weeks, then the hormones made her feel energized. Eating for two was fun. She could eat whatever she wanted. No more salads and hard boiled eggs to maintain her figure. It was gumbo and *beignets* all the way. She felt lucky, for her poor friend Charlene, it was just the opposite.

Charlene lived with her head in the toilet for almost the entire nine months of pregnancy. During the first trimester, she lost weight not gained. Nora had been there diligently to help her best friend through. She wouldn't have had it any other way.

For a few years after having Leisel, Frank had been pre-occupied with work. Needing more money to support his growing country club brood, he became the attorney for the family business, Greenwood Oil. The stress of that endeavor meant that in the evenings, if he wasn't out watching sports with the guys; he drank himself into a stupor. Their vitriolic clashes had not ceased once moving into their own home. If anything, they had gotten worse. At one point, the battles became physical. Frank had shoved Nora down on the bed so hard, she lost her balance and smacked her face on an end table.

Charlene was convinced that Frank was abusing Nora. But Nora denied it. She was tough. She could handle herself with Frank. However, with both their tempers,

Charlene wasn't so sure.

Nora happily kept a ready supply of Kentucky bourbon and brandy in the bar in their living room. For the more she let Frank drink, the less libido he had to bang her.

The temporary stay from sex was short-lived, however. Lately, Frank's determination to have a boy had worked him up into a randy, raging, sex-a-holic. Night after night, he wanted her and took her savagely. He was driven to conceive a son.

Luckily for Nora, conception came within weeks of his resumption to fornicate. She was pregnant again. Baby number four. She prayed it was a boy.

On August 8, 1957, Nora gave birth to a son. Finally. She named him Ignatius Jack Greenwood, after her father. They called him Iggy, for short. He looked nothing like his namesake, with his red hair, olive skin and green eyes. But Nora didn't care. She had a son. Proudly, she produced the legacy. Her little boy brought her another reprieve from her husband's need for her. And that was blessed.

* * * * *

"Nora . . . Nora," Charlene finally got her attention. "Girl, you were lost in that head of yours."

"Oh, Charlene. I am so sorry. I didn't even turn in the booties."

"I'm used to it. Once you get those cogs turning, Katy bar the door. I know you're gonna figure out a way to get Frank to let you take those damned lessons. I just know it."

"It's all I can think about. Some cosmic force driving the idea. Like it was just meant to be."

"Sorry, I was gone so long. Wendel, the concierge, gave me this to give back to you," her friend handed her a red and black Hermes scarf. "He said that you left it behind when you had dinner with Frank last week."

"What?" Nora was confused. She looked at the scarf and didn't recognize it. "Frank and I haven't been to dinner at the club for eons."

"Really? Wendel was sure it was yours. He said he saw

Frank on Wednesday night with a brunette."

"Evidently, that brunette wasn't me." Nora was fuming as she ran her fingers over the scarf. Damn it, Frank. She had suspected he cheated, but to do it at the club? People knew her here.

"Nora. I'm so sorry. You know I would never have brought it to you had I known. Frank's such an ass."

"It's not your fault."

"Well, hell. It's Hermes. Her loss." That made Nora smile. Charlene wanted to cheer her up. "Come on Amelia Earhart. We don't have much time before the kids get outta school. Let's go call about this flying stuff and check it out."

Before Nora could say no, Charlene grabbed their purses and took off for the phone booth. After getting some general instructions on location, Charlene and Nora hopped into Charlene's sleek, new, baby blue, Cadillac Coupe De Ville and drove out to the shores of Lake Ponchartrain to Lakefront Airport.

Chapter 7

Lakefront Airport was a gorgeous art deco terminal building with a couple of landing strips that been built jutting out into Lake Ponchartrain. It sat adjacent to the Industrial Canal, on a man-made arrow-head peninsula. To make land available for this elaborate project, the Orleans Levee Board drove a 10,000 foot retaining wall into Lake Pontchartrain and pumped in six million cubic yards of hydraulic fill to raise the field above the water.

The convertible, blue Cadillac pulled into the parking lot outside the terminal. "You know, the Greenwoods have their plane out here," said Nora sipping on her Coca-cola.

"Well that outta make it real convenient for you to have something to fly when know how, honey." Charlene was trying to be supportive. "Does Frank fly?"

"No. Not that I know of. I don't think he was ever interested in taking lessons. They mostly use it for company trips and usually hire a pilot."

"Oh, well that makes sense. They can sure afford it."

Now that they were here, Nora was getting butterflies in her stomach. Maybe she wasn't cut out to be Amelia Earhart after all. But then, as they were getting out of the car, she saw him.

Tall, arresting. Nora couldn't believe it. She was sure it was the pilot she had seen in New York. She never forgot a face. And no one could ever forget those deep, azure blue eyes. Nora stopped short in her tracks.

Suddenly, Charlene looked up. "Who in the hell is

that? Kiss my grits that is a fine specimen."

"Sssshh," Nora grabbed her arm. "He might hear you."

"Well, I'm sure he's heard many a cat call before. Lord have mercy, he is bee-uw-tee-ful. Stop my beatin' heart."

"Charlene," Nora gasped as he approached.

"How'd do ladies. Coming out for a flight?" His baritone, smokey voice nearly made them both faint.

Charlene stuck out the flier. "No. We, uh . . . well *she* is here to check on some flying lessons." She shoved Nora forward. It was only then that Nora took off her sunglasses and looked the pilot in the face.

"What the heck?" the pilot looked bemused. "I can't believe it. The girl with the chocolate, brown eyes."

Charlene looked confused. "Did I miss something? Do you two know each other?"

For once, Nora was lost for words. Lost in his look. His smile. His ever-so-sexy voice. Normally, she wasn't the blushing type, but she sure was today.

"Not really," the pilot explained. "You could say that we shared a cup of coffee. Almost. A very long time ago."

"Yes. A very long time ago. In New York." How well Nora remembered.

Charlene couldn't wait to hear that story. New York. How many times had Nora been to New York? Her honeymoon? On Nora's honeymoon she meets this dream boat? Why in the heck was she still married to Frank? This was just too good.

"Why don't you ladies allow me to introduce myself? I'm Steve Novak. It's my flying service that's offering the lessons. I'm also one of the instructors."

Nora thought she felt her heart skip a beat. She knew it was racing. She felt her face grow hot. Oh my God. The pilot from New York. The Adonis now standing before her was going to be her instructor?

Charlene dug her fingernails into Nora's arm. Steadying her friend, she propelled her towards the lobby. "Well sugar, let's just hear all about it."

They followed the drop-dead, dreamy, steamy Steve Novak into the airport lounge. Thank goodness Nora had listened to Charlene to wear their high heels to lunch today.

"Would you ladies like a couple of drinks?"

"Why sure, honey. I'll have a white wine. What about you Nora?"

Nora couldn't take her eyes off him. He was still as handsome as ever. "Um. Um . . ." she stammered.

"She'll have a white wine too, thanks," Charlene covered for her. Whispering to her friend once Steve left for the bar, Charlene tried to get Nora to pull herself together. "What's the matter with you? I've never seen you like this."

"What about you? Ordering all these drinks before five?"

"A glass of wine on top of a mimosa from the club ain't nothing. You know they water 'em down. I'm waiting."

I dunno. I'm just sitting here kind of in a daze. He is the most attractive man I have ever seen. Or rather, re-seen."

"Well do tell."

Nora explained how they had run into each other during her honeymoon. At the coffee shop. How when he dabbed her arm, his touch had set her on fire. It happened so long ago, but just seeing him again brought it all back like it was yesterday. Suddenly, Nora was self conscious. Had it been eleven years? Eleven years since she had seen him there. She had given birth to four kids since then.

When last she saw him, she was merely eighteen. Fresh skin. Slim frame. No stretch marks. "Stop it, Nora," she scorned herself inside her head. "You are a married woman. What difference does it make?"

"Here are your drinks ladies." He served them both. As he lowered the wine glass in front of Nora, his arm brushed hers. Electric. There went her pulse again.

Steve looked at his watch, "If you will excuse me, I have a lesson scheduled and the student is probably waiting. By the way, the lessons are taught out of the FBO, which is one building over."

"FBO?" Nora asked confused.

"Fixed base operators building for general aviation. Feel free to look around both here and there. There are some amazing murals on the walls. Just talk to my secretary about the lessons. I'm sure you would have a lot of fun."

Fun. Nora was quite convinced she would have lots more than fun. But she wasn't sure she could learn anything from this instructor. For every time he spoke, she got lost in her fantasies of making love to him.

Chapter 8

"Well I declare," Charlene hooted once they were back in the Cadillac. "Talk about afternoon delight." Her shrill voice shrieked with laughter. "Why, for gosh sakes has my best friend never told me about *that* story?"

"Oh, Charlene." Nora's knees still felt weak. "It happened so long ago. Just a brief encounter with a stranger. I never gave it a second thought."

But discerning Charlene knew her friend better than that. "Whatever you say, darlin."

Nora realized Charlene doubted her story. It was written all over her face. She had never been able to lie or hide her emotions.

"All I want to know is, when in the heck are you gonna sign up? And when do I get to come with you? Lord have mercy!"

Nora doubted she could ever sign up now. Her feelings for him were too powerful. Too strong. It would spell trouble. She could foresee that.

"I am having second thoughts."

"Nora Jean Broussard Greenwood. To Hades with that. I am going to fill out the form for ya. I'll even write the check. I haven't seen you look like that in ages."

Nora wondered if it showed that much. Of course it did. She knew when she picked up her children; Kayce would wonder why she was so distracted. Nora's face always belied her emotions. The blue caddy sped back towards Metairie. Despite the breeze from Charlene's lead footed driving, Nora was perspiring. Pulling out her ivory fan, Nora began to flap it near her face.

* * * * *

The next morning, Nora sat at her kitchen table with her cup of coffee. She thumbed the brochure with Novak Aviation Services printed on the front. The children had been packed off to school. Blessed be the months from September through May. She loved her children dearly, but was grateful for the alone time from eight until three. Before she had taken her next sip, her phone was ringing. She correctly guessed it was Charlene.

"Well? When are we sailing into the blue yonder?" she cackled.

"I've changed my mind. I don't think I am going to do it."

"Listen, Nora. I'm sorry I teased you so much yesterday. But he was dreamy, you have to admit. I just was tickled at seeing him rattle your cage so. You shouldn't give up on your dream just because of a hot instructor pilot. After all, he's married. He had on a ring."

Nora hadn't even noticed. She had been so lost in his smile; she had never looked away from his face. "He did?"

"Yessiree. Off the market, honey. And so are you. So, call him. I am sure it will be fine."

Nora thought about it all morning. At about noon, she put on a slim brown skirt and an orange blouse. She tied a brown and orange sash in her chestnut hair and put on her Jackie Kennedy sunglasses. Slipping into her brown ballet flats, she headed out the door. In her station wagon, she didn't feel quite as sexy as she did the day before in the Cadillac. Nor did she have the mimosa cocktails on board that she and Charlene had shared at the club.

As she approached Lakefront Airport, she felt her insides turn over. Nora Greenwood was shaky. She hadn't been that nervous on her own wedding night. "Stop it, Nora. Stop it."

She drove past the terminal and parked in front of Novak Aviation. As she entered the general aviation FBO, she felt like everyone was staring at her. They weren't.

But it felt like it.

"Well, hello there." Steve approached her. "I wasn't sure would come back. Where's your friend?"

"Oh, Charlene. She, um. Had a hair appointment. It's just me." She suddenly dropped her purse. Steve bent down at the same time she did to help her and their heads bumped. "Oh, I'm terribly sorry," Nora effused.

"No. It was me. Trying to be gallant."

They both laughed. He guided her up with his arms on hers. For a moment they just stood and stared at one another.

"Right. Well, I've come to sign up for those lessons. The ones offered at the club?"

"Sure. No problem. Just follow me."

In a few minutes, she had filled out the paperwork. She pulled out her checkbook and wrote a check for the balance.

He took it from her. "Thank you, Mrs. Greenwood."

Was it her imagination? Or did he emphasize the word *Mrs.* "Yes. I am married to . . ."

"The Greenwoods," he interrupted her. "The ones who own that nifty, little Piper Aztec out there." He pointed to one of the hangars.

"Is that right? I wouldn't know it if I saw it." Nora had never been up in the company plane.

"Does your husband fly?"

"No. Actually, I think his family owns the plane."

"I see. It's quite a beauty. Fuel injected engines. Purrs like a kitten."

Nora really wasn't paying attention. She was taking him all in. Soft, wavy brown hair. Luminous, blue eyes. Toned, tan forearms. Impeccable grooming. Wide, full chest.

"Mrs. Greenwood?"

"Yes?"

"When would you want to start?"

Start making love to you, she wondered? "Oh, right. The lessons." Nora felt herself blush. God her thoughts were wicked with this man. "I am not sure."

"Well, now's a good time as any."

"Now. As in right now? Today?"

"Sure. I'll take you up before I cash this check. I just wanna make sure you know what you are getting into." He reached out for her hand. "Here, follow me." He held it for only the briefest moment, to guide her towards the door.

When he released it, Nora felt like she was going to pass out. She brought her hand up to her nose. She could smell the scent of leather from his bomber jacket. Musky leather. It turned her on.

They strolled out of the terminal and onto the tarmac. He brought her over to his training plane. It was white Cessna 150 with red and black highlight painting. He was walking around it giving it a quick visual.

"There she is. Your wings to the sky. It's what you will be learning in. Here, let me help you aboard." Steve opened the door and again reached for her hand. The wing was overhead and she had to briefly duck.

Her slim skirt made it difficult to get up.

"Hold up, I'll give you a boost." He put his hands on her hips and helped her aboard. "Maybe next time, you should wear pants."

Embarrassed, she blushed. "Yeah. Next time."

Steve fired up the engine. As the propeller began to whirl, he did a quick instrument scan. Being inside a personal aircraft was so different than flying commercial. It was small and snug, putting her in very close proximity to Steve's arms on the controls. The propeller hummed as they began roll out to the runway.

He radioed ground and then the tower some garble-de-goop flight lingo and they were off. "Ready?" he looked over and smiled.

"Ready." Nora had never been more ready.

The plane picked up speed. Faster. Faster. And before she knew it, lift off. Right over Lake Ponchartrain. Nora looked out and all she saw was water. Higher and higher they flew.

"Doing okay?" Steve checked on her. Nora thought it was so sweet that he was worried. But she was fine. Mighty fine. She adored it. Flying in the Cessna was so much more thrilling than in commercial planes.

Suddenly he banked hard left. "Hold on."

Nora was jolted into him. She nervously pushed herself off him.

"Sorry 'bout that. Gotta avoid the Naval Air Station."

"No worries." Nora peered down to see NAS New Orleans. She forgot it was even there.

They flew southward over the Gulf. It was resplendent. He showed her the mouth of the Mississippi, where the muddy water mixed with the warm waters of the sea. Then they flew east. He took her past Slidell along the beaches of Mississippi. She remembered playing there in the sand as a young girl. Next, he turned north and flew down low over the swamps.

It gave him a charge that no matter how steeply he banked, no matter how dramatically he climbed, Nora seemed only more excited. She had not one fright in her bones. He loved it.

"Here. Now, you. Take the controls."

He grabbed her hands and put them on the yoke. Oh my God. She was flying. Nora was flying a plane. Of course Steve had his hands on top of hers, but she was flying.

After about an hour, he turned the plane back towards the airport. With a landing smooth as silk, the plane came to a stop.

"Whatcha think? Is this for you?"

"Ab-so-lutely." Nora was beaming.

"Great. Well as soon as you complete the ground school, you will be up, up and away."

"Ground school?" Nora looked surprised. She followed him back on the tarmac to his office. From the filing cabinet, he pulled out some papers. From the bookshelf, a stack of books.

"Yep. Just study these." Into her arms he dumped the bundle.

"All these?"

"Yep. That will get 'cha started. You can do them at your own pace. There are quizzes in class that I will give you along the way. Once you pass those, then you can do some simulator time."

"Simulators?" Nora asked.

"Yep. They are the latest thing. Practicing with the instruments at a console before you get into the plane," Steve explained.

"Righto." Nora wasn't sure she could pass. She hadn't been in school in quite some time. But she was determined. "Okay then. Um, see you next Tuesday?"

"Sure thing, doll. Next Tuesday it is. I'll be looking forward to it." He flashed her with his smile. It was then she noticed the gold wedding band. Charlene was right. He was married. What was she thinking?

Chapter 9
∞ February, 1961 ∞

Nora could hardly wait for the next Tuesday, and neither could Steve. She had taken his instructions seriously and poured over all of the books and readings to prepare. Thrust, lift, ailerons. She let out a big sigh. She hoped she was ready.

It wasn't only her head she prepared. Nora literally went through five sets of clothes before she decided what she should wear. He had told her to wear pants for flying, but today was classroom only. It was a bit reckless, but she decided to wear a snugly fitting skirt and v-neck pullover which accentuated her hips and bustline. The skirt was army green and had a tiny slit up the back. Her sweater was goldenrod. The color accentuated her olive skin and hair.

Today, she left her hair down and it hung several inches below her shoulders. She put in an army green, fabric headband and let a few bangs dangle. She wore some flesh colored silk stockings and brown low heeled pumps. Taking a last look in her dressing room mirror, she liked what she saw.

* * * * *

Parking the station wagon at Lakefront, she again had second thoughts. For a split second, she hoped she made the right decision. Frank would have a stroke if he knew she had signed up to learn how to fly. Grabbing the satchel with her books, she gave her lipstick a last check in the rear view mirror.

What she couldn't see was that Steve had noticed her arrival. He grinned from ear to ear when he saw her get out of the wagon. A suburban, aviator wanna-be. He admired her tenacity.

Entering the classroom off his office she greeted him. "I'm ready to get started," she excitedly proclaimed. It was only then that she noticed she wasn't alone. There were three other students in the class, all male. One of them gave a low whistle, getting a reproachable stare from Steve.

"Oh, excuse me," Nora apologized. "I didn't realize you already started class."

"We haven't. Just getting materials handed out." Steve handed her a leather bound flight log. Nora took a seat towards the back of the small classroom. This way, the other guys in class would be in front of her and she could avoid their stares.

"Welcome to ground school everyone," Steve began. He started his lecture explaining the objectives of introductory flight training and simulator training covering the required hours. Nora kept her eyes on the text as he talked. When she wasn't looking at her notes, she was noticing all of the pictures of military planes and aviation photos he had on the walls.

But Steve had eyes only for her. It was very difficult for him to concentrate on his lecture that day, even though he had delivered it many times before. For each time he looked at her, he lost his train of thought. Nora wondered if he was always this distracted.

At the first break, she headed for coffee. As she put her coins into the machine, he approached her, trying to act casual. "So how are you finding the content? Heard enough of thrust and lift?"

"Actually no, I find it quite fascinating." What she also found quite fascinating was his voice. She could listen to him talk about under water basket weaving for that matter.

"Nora, if you don't mind, I would like you to stay a few minutes after class. I want to show you something."

"Sure, I would be glad too." It was doubtless more checklists for her to study. She stirred the creamer into her coffee. As she turned around, she barely missed his arm leaning on the machine.

"No spilling today," he joked with her.

"No," she blushed, remembering his touch.

Steve finished the first day's lecture at about 12:30 PM. After answering some questions for the other students and giving them their reading for the next class, they were alone in the classroom.

"I was wondering if you could help me understand this formula," she asked. Before answering her, he moved to the door and closed it. He drew down the shade.

"I can answer anything you like."

At first Nora was puzzled by his actions. He approached her desk, happy for the excuse to be closer to her.

"It's the physics," she said. "I was having trouble making sense of the alphabet soup."

"Here, let me show you." He drew out a sketch on her notepad. Just the scent of him so near her was driving her mad. "See, here's how you figure the altitude and torque." His hand lingered as he handed her the pencil.

She took it from him and put the end in her mouth trying to figure out the schematic. But when she looked up at him, she knew their day dreams had been on the same wave length. She dropped the pencil, but neither of them noticed.

As she stood up, he pulled her to him, wrapping his arms around her waist. Without warning, he kissed her. He was sure he felt her lips part slightly. Self-conscious about his actions, he drew back from her. "I'm so sorry. I . . ." he stammered.

But she reached up to touch his lips. "Don't be. I've been waiting to do that all day."

Her acquiescence was all he needed. Pulling her close he began to kiss her ardently. Long, sweet, slow kisses. His lips were full and gentle. She was overcome with waves of passion.

Backing her up against the wall of the class room, he tilted her head and began to kiss down her neck, hearing her moan. Their mutual desire for one another was evident. The door blinds rattled slightly with their bodies pressed up again them. "We . . . can't. . ." he said between kisses ". . . do this," he pulled away.

She looked crushed.

"Not here, I mean. Someone might walk in at any moment."

Nora nodded her head in agreement. "You're right." It dawned on her that she had just kissed another man. Another man besides her husband Frank. But she felt no guilt.

However, Steve did. Despite the fact that they were consumed with the cosmic chemistry between them. For a moment, she remained in his arms.

"Again, I apologize. I just don't know what came over me. You are . . . just lovely. I really lost control, I shouldn't have." He suddenly seemed embarrassed. "I hope you won't let my actions discourage you from continuing your studies. It won't happen again."

"No. I am sorry if I gave you the wrong idea. That is not why I am here. I definitely plan to see this through. It's my dream to fly," she justified.

He smiled at her. "Good. Then, we should just carry on." Steve was still shocked at his behavior. He hadn't kissed another woman since he and his wife became engaged a decade ago. He was quite shaken.

Reading his thoughts, Nora quickly packed her satchel and proceeded to her car. She could still taste him on her lips. Spark, there were those feelings again. She quickened her steps. She had to get home.

Chapter 10

Nora was at the sewing machine when the Charlene dropped off the kids from school. It was Charlene's carpool week and she let herself in through the back door. "So, how was your lesson? Did you go?"

Nora looked up from the girl's dress she was making. She had started early on the children's matching Christmas clothes. "Yes. I went." She continued to sew on the black velvet bodice.

"Okay, Nora Greenwood. You are not going to get off that easy. I saw how he looked at you and vice versa. Out with it." Charlene stood over her with her hands on her hips.

Nora took in a deep breath and checked to see if her children were out of hearing range. "It was fine. Class was harder than I thought. And yes, he was just as dreamy teaching class," she gushed.

"I knew it. You have a crush on him. Well, he is pretty stellar. Did he flirt with you?"

At first Nora didn't respond. But she knew Charlene would see through her if she fibbed. "Yes. I think so. He kept staring at me during class, but I kept my eyes down."

"Oh, do go on." Charlene poured herself a cup of Community and added some cream.

"That's it," Nora avoided her glance, focusing on the hem she was sewing. "Nothing more to tell. I have class again next Tuesday. We start with the simulators." Her foot pressed the pedal of her Singer and it began to whir. "There is one more thing. He has a lot of pictures of military aircraft on the wall. I wonder if he flew for the service?"

"Oh, I bet he is just extra handsome in a uniform. There's nothing like a man in military stuff. Are you the only student?"

"Actually there are three other men in the class. They all look pretty young. One of them cat-called me." Nora looked perturbed.

"Honey, take all the compliments you can get. Heavens knows we don't get noticed enough by our hubbies."

About that time, Kayce interrupted them. She had gone out to get the mail. "Mom, look. I was nominated as a junior princess! For next year's Bacchus parade," Kayce proudly clutched a yellow paper. Nora looked up to see what she was talking about.

Charlene beat her to the punch. "Well, I'll be. Mother Greenwood put her up. Lookee there," she exclaimed bringing the envelope and document to Nora to see.

"Well, Kayce. You lucky girl. What an honor." Nora rose to hug her daughter.

Kayce was beaming from ear to ear. She began to dance a waltz around the room. "A princess. I'm going to be a princess. Oh, I can't wait to tell Daddy." She stopped short. "Mother, whatever am I going to wear?"

"I don't know. Maybe we can get you something from Maison Blanche," Nora offered.

However, Charlene jumped in, "Oh, no Nora. The girls all wear the same gown. Only the queen is dressed differently. You'll presumably get the instructions in the mail soon. They start planning the costuming and theme right after this year's ball is over. But don't worry; I'll help you make it. It's usually some beaded something or other. Hey listen, toots. I have to run. Bye now. And call me with any further installments." She winked at Nora.

For once, Kayce was oblivious to their gossip. She was high as a kite about her Bacchus nomination. Bacchus was a New Orleans institution; one of the richest and most elite of the Mardi Gras parades. It was the *coup de gras*. Only the best families were asked and could afford to participate. As Nora was about to return to her sewing, the phone rang.

"What'd you forget now, Char," she spoke into the receiver before hearing who was on the other end.

"Nora. Is that you?" Steve asked urgently.

Feeling transparent, like her children could hear his voice, at first she didn't respond.

"I'm sorry. I must have the wrong number," he apologized.

"No. Steve. I mean, yes. Yes. It's Nora," she answered nervously. Her hands were shaking. Her heart beating ninety-to-nothing.

"I'm sorry to phone you at home, but . . . ." There was the longest pause. "I just have to see you."

"Well, I'll be there. Next week. I told you I was coming back."

"That's not what I mean. I . . . I was wondering if you would like to meet me. Maybe to have a drink or something?"

For what seemed the longest time, Nora hesitated. It was decision time. The fantasy was over. The most splendid man she had ever seen in her life was asking to see her outside of class. She should have, at that very moment, contemplated the implications of her answer. Refusing to, she answered quickly.

"Yes, I think I can make it. When?"

He was waiting with the sweet anticipation of a puppy. Although she couldn't see it, his face broke into wide smile, elated that he had not offended her previously with his bold actions. "Great. That's wonderful. When are you free?"

"Let me think," she wanted to exclaim "now" but speculated. "How about tomorrow? At around one?"

"One's great. Where?"

Knowing that it had to be somewhere far from Metairie, she thought of The Quarter. They suggested it at the same time.

"What about The Quarter?" They both giggled.

"Jinx, you owe me a drink. How about Pat O's?" he suggested referring to Pat O'Brien's.

But Nora knew better. "No, too many locals there," she replied cautiously. "I have a better idea. Have you heard of Lafitte's Blacksmith Shop?" Nora knew it as a small, dark, historic tavern. Dim, secluded and most likely deserted during the early afternoon. "It's on the corner of Bourbon and St. Phillip."

"No, but I'm sure I can find it."

Nora rechecked her calendar. Charlene had carpool one more day. As long as Charlene could pick up her children at school, Nora would be free for the remainder of the afternoon.

"I'll see you then," she replied and replaced the receiver. It was done. She had made a date with another man. Good Lord.

Steve was still holding his. He knew they were treading into dangerous waters. He hoped he knew what he was doing.

Chapter 11

Nora could hardly sleep a wink that night. She tossed and turned thinking about her plans for the next day. At breakfast, she was almost giddy. She served her children pancakes, kissed them and sent them packing for school. From her front porch, still in her nightgown, she waved to Charlene.

Frank passed her on his way out. "Nora, get a robe on. The neighbors don't need to see my wife's tits." Some things never changed.

Handing him his newspaper, she wished him well. "Have a good day Frank."

As he got into his car, he called out to her, "And Nora. Tell Mabel that she needs to re-polish my shoes. She just isn't getting the shine on them like she used to. Damned darky."

Nora ignored him. She hated the way he treated Mabel and Negros in general. Normally, his statements would have made her pot boil over, but today, she had an agenda.

Once she closed the door, she scampered back to her bathroom and ran a hot bath. She lingered in the tub and wondered if Steve was filled with as much anticipation as she was. Nora then washed her hair and put it up in extra large rollers. Next, she did her nails. Five more hours to go. She could hardly wait.

Later, at her vanity, Nora carefully applied another layer of shadow to her eyes, accentuating their depth. She put on her dark, black, trademark eyeliner. Perusing her wardrobe, she tried to decide what to wear. It had been a decade since she had dressed for a date. Pushing the hangers forward in rejection she mumbled to herself, "No. No. Definitely not," before arriving at just the right choice.

It was a one piece, double knit, clingy, navy blue sheath with a narrow matching white belt. Perfect. She selected a pair of blue and white spectator pumps and a matching white and navy purse. Around her shoulders she draped a blue scarf with gold anchors. She attached it with a broach. She put a matching navy velvet small bow in her upswept do. Applying a last swipe of her lipstick, she dashed out the door.

She had no trouble making it to The Quarter; she knew it like the back of her hand. She parked around the corner, several blocks down on Dauphine, just in case on the off chance, she ran into someone she knew. Putting several coins into the meter, she strode towards the tiny bar. When she entered, it took her eyes a moment to focus.

It was quite shadowy. She could hear the sweet, savory sounds of a saxophonist playing. He was the lone musician. Once her eyes became accustomed to the dark, she saw him. He was seated at a secluded table for two near the back. Steve stood as she approached him. "You look lovely, Nora." She was flattered. He pulled out her chair for her, like a true Southern gentleman and seated himself across from her.

"I ordered us a couple of drinks. Great tune," he remarked.

"Yes. I've always loved jazz. I believe it's *I can't give you anything but love, baby.*" Nora then caught the double entendre.

Steve was impressed. There weren't many women who knew jazz. But then, how many women took flying lessons? Nora was a rare creature indeed. Her verve for life was intoxicating.

Nervous to be alone with him, she took out a cigarette. "I hope you don't mind if I smoke."

"Not at all, I will join you." He lit her cigarette with a unique silver lighter. After taking a puff, she reached for it from his hand.

"That's quite lovely." She noted the Naval crest of pilot's wings on the side.

"It's from my years in the Navy. I flew combat missions in the Korean War," he explained. "The Vought AU-1 Corsair."

"I'd love to hear about it," she said in her sultry voice. She took another long slow drag.

As the waiter served their Seven and Sevens, he began telling her about his time in Korea. The missions he flew. She was enamored. Her expressive eyes continued to take him in whilst he talked.

They discussed New Orleans and their families. He was originally from Chicago, but had stayed on in New Orleans after his stint with the Naval Air Station there. She told him about her father, Jack. He was intrigued by her Cajun and Indian ancestry. They must have conversed for over an hour. He ordered another round of drinks.

"Bloody Mary for me this time, thanks. I'll be back in a jiff," she excused herself to the ladies room.

When she came out into hallway, he was waiting for her. There was a curtain, partially obstructing their view from the bar. He reached for her face with his hands and placed a slow, long, kiss to her lips. This time, her lips parted. She felt him slip his tongue inside. Tasting her. She responded. They kissed for several minutes, their tongues exploring one another like serpents in heat.

Breathless, he was the first to speak. "I couldn't wait any longer. I had to kiss you."

"I know what you mean. I wanted you to."

He began to kiss her more passionately, moving to her neck. Small kisses to her ear lobe, a slow descent down her neck. His lips were supple and caressing. His hand moved from the small of her back around to her right breast. He cupped her gently. Hearing her moan, he gently massaged her there.

Just kissing her, touching her even through her clothes, brought him to arousal. He pulled her hips closer to his. Nora felt his cock against her. She was sure he had a hard-on. She reached down and touched him and he groaned in delight. Feeling him, she could tell he was huge. Much larger than Frank. She gently encircled his clothed penis in her hand and he began to move against her as they kissed.

"Oh God, Nora. I want you so badly," he whispered in her ear. "But I know it's not possible."

She continued to kiss him passionately. "I want you too. So much."

Abruptly, they stopped as a gentlemen came around the curtain. For a moment, they were flustered until they realized he paid them no mind. Lovers in The Quarter were no novelty. Collecting themselves, they returned to their table.

"Are you sure?" she questioned. "I mean. I'm married." She looked down and reached for his left hand. "You're married. It could be disastrous."

"I know. I realize that. I've never done anything like this before. Never cheated on my wife, I mean."

Nora wasn't surprised. "Neither have I. Never," she attested. "But I just can't help it, Steve. You take my breath away."

He picked up her hand and kissed it gently. She knew in that moment, his feelings for her were sincere. They finished their drinks quietly, letting the moment and the music wash over them.

After while, she noted the time. "I have to go. My friend, Charlene, the one . . ."

"The one from that very first day," he interrupted her.

"Yes. That's right. She's watching my children."

"Nora, I would like to see you again."

She almost retorted that he would next Tuesday in class, but didn't. "I want that too, Steve. I do. But I am just not sure it is wise." She rose to leave and he stood. She leaned over and kissed him on the cheek. "Call me. I'll let you know if I can." And with that, she headed for the door.

Steve was gobsmacked. The power of the desire she brought out in him was stunning. He had never met anyone like her. He wondered where it would all lead.

Chapter 12

Nora prattled through the next week. Homework. A club luncheon. Shopping for more fabric to complete the Easter outfits and Kayce's Bacchus gown. Studying her introductory flight materials. All she could do was mark time until the following Tuesday.

Housekeeping was not one of Nora's strengths. Thank God, for Mabel. But Nora loved to cook, sew, sing and read. She busied herself through the endless week. Nora had driven carpool.

Charlene popped in for an afternoon coffee. She brought fresh *beignets* from Café Du Monde off Jackson Square in The Quarter. "Is there a reason that Iggy was outside on the back porch naked?"

"What?" Nora looked up to see Charlene holding the hand of Nora's precious boy wearing underwear only. "Whatever were you doing out there?"

"Cathy and Leisel did it."

"Cathryn, Leisel. March yourselves in here," Nora yelled. She rolled her eyes at Charlene who understood totally. The girls entered and had looks on their faces as though they were hiding something.

"Stand here. And give me your best explanation for why your little brother was out on the porch with no clothes on?"

They exchanged glances, each daring the other to speak first.

"He wanted to be out there," Leisel offered.

Nora shook her head. "Try again."

"He asked for it, he was taking our game pieces for

Trouble. We warned him to stop it, but he started throwing them. So, he crossed the line."

"Is that so? And therefore he made you take his clothes off and put him out there," Nora offered.

"Yep. Sounds about right," Cathy said shaking her head. Leisel was crinkling up her nose wondering if her mother would buy it.

"I see. Well, number one it warrants a trip to the confessional and an apology to your brother. Number two, no TV tonight for either one of you."

"Mom, that's not fair," Cathy complained.

"Yeah. *Fury* is on. I have to watch *Fury*," piped in Leisel.

"Well, you have given up that option by being mean to your brother." Iggy stuck his tongue out at them. "That'll be enough out of you," Nora shook her finger at him. "Or they'll get you again. Now all of you scoot and get his clothes back on him."

Charlene clapped her hands in applause. "Well done, Mama Greenwood."

Nora gave her a smirk. "Thanks for the goodies. What were you doing in The Quarter?" Nora was curious, taking one of the *beignets*.

"Just dropping Max at work. His car is on the blink," she said mouth full of dough.

Nora had forgotten that Max worked near St. Louis Cathedral and Jackson Square in the Pontalba Building. It was only a couple of blocks from Lafitte's. Her paranoia kicked in.

"What're the plans for Kayce's debut? At Bacchus," asked Charlene sipping her *café au lait*.

Nora got out her fabric and the pattern. It was a soft, creamy, yellow chiffon, with a sateen underlay. There were several sections requiring beading. Charlene was a brilliant seamstress. She chatted on about when they could get started. Nora's phone was ringing.

"You gonna get that?" Charlene reached for the phone.

Nora lunged. "Yeah. Hold your pants on." She reached it first, guessing who would be calling her. "Hello?"

"Nora, Steve here."

"Well, hi there. Long time no talk too." Nora pointed

to the phone and mouthed the word 'Nellie.'

"What?" But then Steve understood. "Oh, can't talk. Gotcha. Listen, I just wanted to tell you, I just got the strangest phone call."

"Oh?"

"Yeah. It was from your husband Frank."

Nora turned pale. "Frank? Why in the heck was he calling you? Hold on. I am going to change phones." Nora sat down the receiver and went to the bedroom phone. "Got it, Charlene."

"Righto," Charlene replaced the kitchen line.

"So, Steve what is the deal?"

"I'm not sure. He called today saying that he had seen my flyer at the club and wanted to sign up. Mentioned something about wanting to fly the Piper."

"You have got to be kidding me? Your advertising is working a bit too well. Oh, God. He'll ruin everything." Nora began to fret.

"Don't worry Nora. It should be okay. He said he's gonna be coming on Saturday mornings. Your paths should never cross. Besides, you are a class ahead of him. He won't start for a couple of weeks."

"Are you sure?" she needed reassurance.

"Should be. Besides, I went ahead and changed your name on your registration form. I used your middle and maiden name, Jean Broussard."

Gosh she was thankful that Steve was so clever. "Great idea."

"I'll let you go. I can't wait to see you. Study up for your exam. If you pass, I'll take you up for your first guided solo."

"I'll be ready. Thanks for calling." Nora felt terrible about telling another fib to Charlene, but she just wasn't ready to reveal her indiscretions with Steve.

* * * * *

Nora fumed the rest of the day. Frank. Flying lessons. Why was he always raining on her parade? Couldn't she have one activity, just one, that didn't involve him or one of his family members? She was putting a pot of crawfish on the boil when she heard him walk in.

"What's for supper? I'm starved," he peered into the kitchen. "Cajun delights I see." Frank never missed an opportunity to put down her roots, even though he liked crawfish himself. "Say, I have a bit of news. My Dad is giving me quite a birthday present."

"What's that?" Nora feigned interest.

"You know that plane, out at Lakefront? The one the company owns?"

"Yeah. I've heard you speak of it."

"Well, you're lookin' at its new owner."

Nora was incredulous. What a damned silver spoon he had in his mouth. She was seething. "What would you want with a plane, Frank? You don't even know how to fly."

"Not yet, Nora. Not yet. But I saw a flyer at the club and rang the guy up. I start in a coupla weeks. On Saturdays." He tore off a piece of the baguette on the counter and shoved it into his mouth. Nora wished he would choke on it.

"That's nice Frank. I am glad to see you put it to use." Clearly, Frank was unmindful of the fact that just a few years ago, it was Nora who wanted to learn to fly. But she didn't care. Her books and notes were hidden in her sewing basket. She had studying to do later that evening.

Knowing that she needed time to herself to study, she offered him another drink. She was taking the course, too, and he was none the wiser. The thought of that made her smile.

Chapter 13

The first few quizzes for ground school had been challenging, but Nora aced them. In addition, she did well in the simulator during the next couple of weeks. She hadn't gotten much sewing done, but she knew her aviation material well. Nora was determined to outdo Frank, when it came to her dream.

Mabel was at their house several days a week. Her children were curious as to why, when their mother was home, she always had her nose in a book. The books she was reading lately didn't look like her usual novels from the library. Studying left Nora no time to prepare one of her delicious dinners. One more night of Ragu and noodles. Her big test was tomorrow.

She stayed up most of the night studying. Once Frank was out, she snuck to the den and pulled her books from their hiding place. By flashlight, she reviewed all the material practically pulling an all nighter. Bags under her eyes and all, she was ready to sit the test.

Nora was the first person in class on exam day. Steve capitalized on the chance to talk to her alone, since no one else had yet arrived. "How's it cooking babe? Ready to shine?"

"Ready as I'll ever be." Nora knew he missed that double meaning. When Steve taught class, he mostly was all business. Which is what made him the best.

"You can start whenever you like, no need to wait for the others," he placed the exam on her desk. Nora took her time before opening it. Her anxiety was high level and she tried to calm herself. Focus. Focus.

Steve walked behind her and began to massage her shoulders. "Loosen up, babe. You can do this. I believe in you." Nora was comforted. "Besides, I am a great teacher," he boasted affably.

Nora snickered, breaking her tension. Steve could always make her laugh. She took a deep breath and began. She was determined to show him what she could do.

While Nora tested, the other three came in and began. Steve walked the room and ensured no one was borrowing answers. As he passed Nora's desk he dropped an envelope in her lap. There were two notes. The first was a poem.

High Flight
Oh, I have slipped the surly bonds of earth
And danced the skies on laughter-silvered wings;
Sunward I've climbed, and joined the tumbling mirth
Of sun-split clouds...and done a hundred things
You have not dreamed of...wheeled and soared and swung
High in the sunlit silence. Hov'ring there,
I've chased the shouting wind along, and flung
My eager craft through footless halls of air.
Up, up the long, delirious, burning blue
I've topped the windswept heights with easy grace
Where never lark, or even eagle flew.
And, while with silent, lifting mind I've trod
The high untrespassed sanctity of space
Put out my hand, and touched the face of God.

by John Gillespie Magee, WWII pilot

The poem brought tears to Nora's eyes. It was how she had always imagined the glory of flight to be. It was how she felt the first time he took her into the skies. The second note read, *Come celebrate with me. Hotel Provincial 3 pm.*

The remaining students had finished. Steve was grading their results. Two passed. The other, you could tell by his expression, did not.

Thankfully, Nora was on her last question. They had both avoided any further personal contact. For obvious reasons. Now this note. Rereading it, she contemplated what to do, then penned a response to Steve. On the back she wrote one simple word, *Yes*. She turned the note in with her exam.

When the other student pilots left, Nora, as had become a pattern, lingered. Steve gave her feedback and pointers on her progress. But today, she was anxious to find out her scores. As she sat outside the classroom, her knees were shaking, awaiting the results. She knew she would be able to tell by the expression on Steve's face. Her hopeful eyes darted when she heard the classroom door open. Steve was beaming.

"Good heavens. I passed," she jubilantly jumped into his arms.

He squeezed her tightly and swung her around. "The sky's the limit, Nora," he whispered, nuzzling into her neck. She smelled fantastic. "Remember what I promised you?"

"A guided solo? Precisely. Let's go."

"Something even better. A ride in my plane." Steve put on his leather bomber jacket and strode with Nora in tow to the hangar. "Gas up the Corsair today, Joey. I'm taking her up for a spin."

He was referring to his personal plane that he had saved for years to purchase. It had been taken off the military flight line and sold. He bought it in auction, had it serviced and repainted. He also enlarged the cockpit to put a small jump seat behind. It was his pride and joy.

Elation covered Nora's face. The hotel could wait. She knew this plane flew higher and faster than the trainer aircraft he had flown her in a few weeks back. Anxiously, she waited until his preflight inspection was complete.

Steve extended his arm. "Ready to touch the face of an angel?" he asked. His pride was evident.

"You bet. Let's do it."

He assisted her up the short step ladder and onto the wing. He popped open the canopy. She knew she would be sitting behind him. Luckily, she had worn her slacks today. Stretching her leg over, she slid down into the seat. He buckled her in snuggly. Then he helped her on with her helmet, a set of goggles, and a radio head set. Steve took his place in front, and put on the same. He explained that she would have to use the radio switch for him to hear her if need be. Steve was beaming. It charged him up that Nora was so fearless.

Wing flaps up. Carburetor heat cool. Throttle full open. Once the pre-takeoff checklist was complete, they were ready to go. Clearing ground control, Steve radioed the tower for takeoff. "Lakefront tower Corsair six, three, three, five Charlie requesting permission for takeoff runway two seven. It'll be a right turn out to the south, Lakefront. Over."

"Six, three, three, five, Charlie. Clear for takeoff runway two seven," the tower called back.

Nora could feel the difference in this craft as Steve pushed forward on the throttle. He rapidly reached a hundred twenty knots and began to climb upward. Within seconds they were out over the lake and headed for the Gulf. The plane's large engine purred but was much louder than the Cessna.

"Okay back there?" Steve checked on her.

"Doing fine," she answered confidently. And she was. Nora was in heaven, literally. Steve climbed to six thousand feet within a few minutes. He was out over the water amidst the puffy, white clouds. He banked and turned such that Nora could see the coast and the water below. It was magnificent.

"Ready for some fun?" he challenged.

"At the ready." Nora was game.

Steve barrel rolled the plane not once, but three times as he soared higher into the sky. Nora lost all sense of ground orientation, but she wasn't fazed. She felt the blood rush to her head.

"When you get a head rush," he radioed, "just bear down and sorta grunt. It'll help you with the G-forces and keep ya with me." Ever watching out for Nora.

"Roger that," she answered.

Their flight in the Corsair lasted about an hour. Nora had the time of her life. She was so taken with Steve's brilliance. With his interest in her. Heart full, she was falling hard for him.

When they returned to the hangar stimulated beyond belief, they could hardly keep their hands off one another. Doing a quick look-see to ensure that they were alone, as soon as Steve took off her helmet, he planted a kiss on her lips. She wrapped her arms around his waist.

"You're pretty damned incredible, Steve Novak."

"I could say the same about you. I've never taken a gal up like that."

Nora beamed with pride at the thought that she was his first female co-pilot. "Really?"

"Really and truly." He bent his head to kiss her once more. "Come on," he grabbed her hand. "We have a hotel suite waiting."

The flight was so mind-blowing, Nora had almost forgotten about his note. Grasping his hand tightly, she followed him out to his car. Steve had a red Mustang hard top with spoke wheels. It suited him well. He turned on the radio as they drove towards the Causeway. It was playing *Smoke Gets in Your Eyes* by the Platters.

Arriving at The Quarter, Steve parked on Rue Chartres. Knowing they did not want to be seen entering together, he suggested that she wait at a corner bar for about twenty minutes until he had checked in. Then, she could meet him on the second floor. Nora agreed. It would give her chance to call Charlene. Her gig was up. It was time Charlene knew her whereabouts, since she anticipated that she wouldn't be coming home until late in the evening.

She found a pay phone on the corner. "Charlene?"

"Nora, heavens to Betsy, are you okay? I was worried sick."

"Are the kids alright?" the concerned mother came out.

"Your kiddos are fine. Kayce is a bit ticked, since you missed her Junior Princess meeting." Nora had completely overlooked the meeting. "But don't worry about that now. Where are you?"

It was now or never. "I'm with Steve," she blurted. "Char, I'm seeing him."

"Hells bells, Nora," Charlene was stunned but tried to be supportive. "Sweetie, be careful. Okay? Frank would kill you if he found out."

"I know. I know. I have to go. I'll tell you all about it later, alright? Just give the kids a hug for me."

"They can spend the night. I'll make up something to

tell Frank. Just . . . be careful, Nora. I don't want you to get hurt."

"Thanks, Char." Nora was grateful for the non-judgment. Hanging up, she pulled out her compact and did a last check on her make-up. She applied her lipstick and brushed back her hair. She wasn't dressed in what she had planned for her first intimate encounter with him, but it was too late to worry about that now.

Hotel Provincial was a small, two story boutique hotel full of old world elegance. On the outside, it looked like a French Chateau. As Steve had advised, Nora entered the hotel and took the grand staircase up to the second floor. It had large crystal chandeliers and eighteenth century furnishings. The lobby was full of gorgeous mahogany antiques. He was waiting for her on the landing.

He reached out for her hand and brought it to his lips. Then, he escorted her down the hall to the *Suite Parisienne*. "I hope you like the room."

"I'm sure I will. You have excellent taste," she chirped. Nora was a bit uneasy. She was about to have sex with another man. There was no doubt about it.

The room was lovely. Perfect. There was a huge, hand-carved, wooden bed with an overhanging canopy. It was covered in a lush, blue and white floral comforter and matching swag draperies. As soon as he closed the door, his arms were around her.

"God, Nora. I've wanted this day to come since the first time I met you." He began to kiss her fervently. They stood on the side of the bed. He took his hands to her blouse and slowly began to unbutton it. Taking his fingers he ran the tips up and down her chest.

Nora took in a languorous breath. "Kiss me you fool."

"I am a fool. A love struck fool." He carefully lowered her shirt off her shoulders. He bent his head to her chest and began to kiss her along the rim of her black lace bra. Gentle, sweet, kisses. She unbuttoned her slacks, let them drop and delicately stepped out of them. He reached around her and unfastened her bra. It fell, exposing her large, full breasts and huge nipples.

His head descended to her right breast, taking her nipple into his mouth. He sucked it tenderly, driving her wild inside. He ran his tongue around it in circles ever so slowly, driving her crazy. Next, he moved to the other breast and did the same. Steve took his time moving his tongue slowly over her and tasting every bit of her flesh. Not wanting to be rough with her, he gently took her whole areola into his mouth again and began to flick it with his tongue.

"Sweet Jesus," she said. "What you do to me, the way that you suckle me, the way that you kiss me, it's orgasmic."

He whispered through his kisses, "You feel so wonderful, I want to make love to you, Nora." He picked her up and laid her down on the bed. Standing before her he disrobed, exposing his bare chest. She lay back propping herself up with on her elbows. She wanted to take him all in. Unzipping his flight suit, he let it fall to the floor. Then he lowered his boxers and stood naked before her.

Nora bit her lip, he was magnificent. Everything she had imagined. Large chest, cut waste. She drank in the site of his large, erect penis. He dropped to his knees and began to kiss the arches of her feet. Her head fell back in ecstasy. God he was good.

Slowly, he began kissing up her legs, higher and higher. He paused at the back of her knee and then again at her inner thigh. Reaching up, he unhurriedly removed her panties, exposing her. He took his fingers and parted her there, gently slipping in his finger tips. She was warm and wet. Next, he took his lips to her and began to tongue her, separating her folds. He darted it inside her, tasting her, suckling her.

Nora had never had a man's mouth on her flesh and it sent shockwaves of delight down her spine. She arched up her back as he continued. She reached down and clutched her fingers in his wavy hair. "Steve, oh gawd." He knew she was about to cum. Steve continued until he felt her spasm. Her body shook in delight. He looked up at her lovingly.

"Make love to me. Take me," she pleaded.

With that, he rose above her and parted her fully with his fingertips. She felt him enter her. At first just the head, probing in and out. She reached around and grabbed his buttocks towards her, pushing him further inside. He began to thrust deep within her. Slow, long, full strokes.

Nora, still reeling off her orgasm began to gyrate her hips against his thrusts.

She was tight and fit him like a glove. He made love to her this way for the longest time. Cradling her, suckling her neck. Running his hands over her nipples and flicking them with his fingers. When he could no longer hold back, he quickened his strokes.

"Oh, darling. Sweet Nora," he exclaimed as he exploded with her. She held his buttocks tight with her legs wrapped around his waist.

"Baby, yes," she cried out as she came again with him. Completely spent, they laid there together, him still inside her. She felt fulfilled, sated, and for the first time, fully loved.

Chapter 14

It was very late in the evening when the Ford Country Squire pulled into the garage. Nora was afraid that the sound of the automatic garage door opener would wake Frank. She prayed that he had spent another night out. Unfortunately, he had not. His car was parked in its usual spot. Lights inside the rooms were left on, but the house seemed quiet.

Nora tiptoed in through the kitchen, careful not to make a sound. It was then that she could hear his loud snoring. She noticed the opened bottle of Jim Beam on the counter. She could see his leg draped over the couch. He was passed out drunk.

She breathed a sigh of relief. No confrontation tonight. It bought her several more hours for her to think of an excuse for why she wasn't home last evening. Nora made her way to the dressing room of their master bedroom. She sat down at her vanity to take off her makeup and what little jewelry she had worn. She looked down at her wedding ring. Meaningless. The vows she had taken broken. But they had been broken long ago by the other party involved. She was saddened at the state to which her marriage had deteriorated. It had started out so hopeful.

But now, she had found love. Wonderful, exciting, intoxicating love. The thoughts of how she had just made love to Steve warmed and filled her heart. It was complicated, to be sure. But they would find a way, she thought, as she cleansed away her foundation with Witch Hazel.

They had to. What they shared was just too powerful not to be together.

It was a good thing the next morning that the kids were at Charlene's. The bedroom door was slammed open with a horrendous boom. "Where in the hell were you last night?" roared Frank.

Stunned, Nora arose out of her deep sleep. She ripped off her night shades to see her husband still dressed in the crumpled clothes he had slept in the night before. He was deranged with wrath. At first, Nora couldn't speak.

"Well?" he snarled.

"I spent the evening at my mother's. We were working on Kayce's dress for Bacchus." It sounded plausible. Nora often spent late nights sewing.

"You stupid lying bitch." He approached the bed. "Don't you think I'm smart enough to have checked that out?" Frank wrenched off the comforter of the bed, tearing it, and exposing Nora there in her nightgown. She was terrified. This rage was worse than usual. "Where in the fuck were you?"

"I don't have to answer to your beck and call, Frank," she stalled.

"Is that right? Miss fancy independence pants. Bull shit! You are my wife. I run this family. And I run you."

His statements enraged her. How dare he think that he ruled her as an adult. When she was younger, she was too naïve to take him on. But over the years, she came to understand him as a male, chauvinistic pig. It took every-thing she had not to scream back at him.

"Fine," she drew up her knees around herself. "I didn't want to tell you, but I was at the library. I'm thinking about taking a Cordon Bleu cooking class and I needed to get some materials. I got lost in the reading and lost all track of time." This story he might believe. He hated how much time she spent with her books.

"Show me the books you checked out," he com-manded.

"I don't have any. When I got to the counter, I had forgotten my library card." She came up quickly with another lie. Nora's pulse was racing, but she looked him straight in the eyes to challenge him back.

He got in her face, so close she could smell his rancid,

post-alcohol binge breath. "You listen to me, Mrs. Nora Greenwood," shaking his finger in her face. "You had better be telling me the truth," he yelled loudly. "I'd fucking kill you if you stepped out on me."

Nora sat in stone cold silence. His words struck a cord of fear deep inside her. She had no doubt he would do exactly that. What a hypocrite, she inwardly cringed. Lord knows how many harlots he had been with over the years. The many nights he spent away from home; yet wasn't travelling for business. It somehow gave her a credible edge of dignity.

He left her there, trembling in the bed and stalked off to the shower. Nora glanced over at her dresser. In his rage, he had knocked over one of her holy statues. Jesus as a small boy, wearing regal clothing and a crown. She crawled out of bed to put the statue back in its place. Standing before her dresser, she couldn't bear to look up at the framed picture of the sacred heart of Jesus above. His eyes would surely burn threw to the guilt of her soul, as she was now Nora, the adulteress. But she couldn't think about that now. God might know, but at least Frank didn't.

Nora heard Mabel come in the back door. Mabel. Thank God it was her day to come. Nora scrambled to put a robe on and headed to the kitchen.

"Howd' do, Missus Nora. How you dis mornin'?" Mabel's warm voice was comforting to hear.

"Oh, Mabel. Thank the good Lord you are here this morning." Nora wrapped her arms around Mabel's rotund waist and hugged her.

"O course, Missus Nora. But I can see, Mr. Frank's done been at it again, ain't he?" She noted the empty whiskey bottle. Nora sighed deeply and just hugged Mabel tighter.

"Worse than last time. He was passed out drunk when I came home late night. He accused me of having an affair."

"Sho' nuff? Silver spoon, spoiled, rat he is. Well he'da better not be hittin' my guhrl. You hear me, Missus Nora? Or Mabel'll sho' bring 'round Big Daddy to knock his brains out."

"No. He didn't hit me. You know I'd leave him in a

heartbeat if he ever did that."

"I hope so, Missus Nora. No woman's got to put up wid dat. No sirree."

Nora got out her coffee grinds and put them in the percolator. Mabel put on her apron and began to clean the kitchen.

"Anything special yous want me to do today?" she asked Nora.

"No, hon. Nothing special. Just you being here is a relief." She poured Mable a cup of coffee and made it like she liked it. Three sugars and heavy cream.

"Sit down, have a cup with me. And tell me about what Justine is up to," Nora encouraged. Mabel put down her broom and went into one of her stories. Nora still loved hearing them, and at the moment it was a comfort and welcome distraction.

By that time, Frank was dressed in one of his impeccable suits. He had his briefcase and was going out the garage door. He ignored Nora and Mabel. For that, Nora was glad.

The phone was ringing. Mabel answered it. "Good mornin' da Greenwood's residence."

Steve wasn't sure he should say anything.

"Hallo, any one dere?" Mabel inquired.

"Yes. May I speak with the lady of the house, please?"

"Yessir. Missus Greenwood right hera. I'll see if she will take a cawl."

Mabel looked over and Nora was nodding her head. "One moment pleasesuhr."

Nora figured it was some salesman. She was relieved to hear Steve's voice.

"Good morning darling," he said. "I just wanted to make sure you got home okay. And . . . that everything went alright."

"Frank was his usual tyrant self, but I'm fine," she said stretching the line into the laundry room. Mabel got the hint and gathered her things to start dusting the living room. "Thank you for asking. And you?"

"God. I can't stop thinking about you. Last night was amazing. You are an incredible woman, Nora."

She felt her cheeks grow hot just thinking about the previous night. "Mmmm, I'm glad you think so. I feel the same as you, Steve. I can't stop thinking about you either. You're pretty amazing too."

"I know it's dangerous, but when do you think I can see you again?"

Still shaken from this morning's battle, she wasn't sure. "I dunno. I will have to work something out. I may need to lay low for a bit. We can't be found out."

"I hear ya. In fact, that is why I'm calling. I've gotten sorta an odd invitation this morning."

"Oh?"

"Yeah, a bit too coincidental. It was from your husband." Nora felt her blood run cold. "He invited me to casino night. At the club, for this Friday."

"What?" Nora was dubious. "You've gotta be kidding me?"

"No. That's what I thought. I mean, my guess is he thinks it's some kind of good old boy thing. Getting in good with the instructor or something."

"I can't imagine."

"You don't think he knows, do you? Should I accept?"

Nora tried to process the situation clearly, from Frank's skewed point of view. If he suspected and Steve refused, it might draw conjecture. Metairie Country Club casino night was considered a posh evening. Most men wouldn't turn it down.

"I think you should accept," she suggested. "Frank usually doesn't take no for an answer."

"So, you're okay with it? By the way, he invited my wife."

Nora wondered if it could get any worse. His wife? After having sex with him, she would actually have to face his wife? She wondered if she could pull it off.

"Do you think we could pull it off?" he read her mind.

"Oh, Steve. I'm not sure. It would take an academy award winning performance."

Didn't Steve know either. He was so aroused by her any time she was near. He certainly didn't want his wife to pick up on it. "I know this has put you into an incredibly difficult position. Believe you me, I tried everything that I could get out of it. But your husband can be quite insistent."

Nora knew by now, Frank had probably already called

in the reservations. "Jesus. I can't imagine how it'll be, sitting across the table from one another. He'll see it on my face and yours."

"We'll just have to try like hell to be blasé."

"I guess so, darling." Nora shuddered at the thought of their secret being revealed.

"I'm sorry if this news has spoiled your day. It's regretful our paths have to cross like this. I don't want anything to happen to you."

"I know you don't Steve. Thanks."

"You should know me better than that. I'll always look after you and make sure you're okay. I would never be so stupid as to let us be found out. I realize what kind of impact it would have."

"So your wife, is she going to be there? I'll actually have to meet her?"

"Well yes, I would expect so. That is if she's feeling well enough. I dunno. I guess we'll just have to wait and see on the night."

"Is she ill?" Nora probed.

"I was going to tell you. My wife was diagnosed with multiple sclerosis. After our sixth child was born."

Six kids. Nora wasn't sure if it was the disease or the number of offspring, but she was taken aback. "You've had six children with her?"

"Yes. And it took its toll on her health. She's very weak and frail."

This information put a new twist on things. Nora felt immensely guilty. So that was why he seemed so hungry for affection. His wife was probably too sickly to care about sex. Her head was swimming with this knowledge.

Although Nora could only imagine how dreadful the casino night events would be, it was another chance to see Steve. Nora heard Charlene come in the back door. "Listen, darling. I have to run. I want you to know that I have no regrets. About last night."

"Me neither, Nora. I adore you."

"Take care, Steve. See you Friday night."

Nora turned her attentions now to Charlene. Her friend's eyebrows were raised. She had a devilish grin on her face.

"Was *that* who I think?" alluding to the phone. "Calling you this early in the morning? Eww wee, he must have the hots for you honey."

Nora gave her a smirk. "Yes. That was Steve."

"Well. Out with it. Details. Details. I couldn't sleep a wink all night waitin' to hear it. Heck, I almost got a ticket speeding over here through the school zone."

Nora laughed and poured another cup of coffee for them both. "Where do I start?"

"At the beginning and don't leave *anything* out."

"Please don't think I'm awful Charlene."

"Nora Jean. You know me better than that," she sympathetically smiled.

Sitting on a barstool at the counter, Nora began to relay the aspects of how her relationship with Steve had progressed. Charlene sat across from her engrossed in every facet of each chapter.

Chapter 15
∞ April, 1961 ∞

Friday nights at Metairie Country Club, under most circumstances, were fun events. They usually involved hard partying after the week's stresses. Almost everyone they knew came out. It was a babysitter's dream. The soiree's started with drinks and hors d'oeurves, followed by a four course dinner.

However, once a month was everyone's favorite Friday when after dinner they had casino night. During day events, everyone dressed in casual chicque, but at night, and especially on casino night, people put on their party best. The club became a mini Las Vegas. There was roulette and poker, usually five card draw. Lots of cigars, liquor, and levity. It was quite the evening.

Nora was having trouble selecting what to wear for a dinner at a table seated with Charlene and her husband, Steve and his wife, and Frank. She had been through ten outfits so far. But nothing looked right. Classy, yet a bit sexy was the look she was going for.

While she was getting dolled up, Frank chastised her, irritated that she wasn't ready. "What's the matter with you? You know what time this thing starts. Just put on anything and let's go. We're gonna be late."

"Keep your pants on Frank. I'm almost done. I just couldn't decide." Nora finally chose a maroon, damask, backless dress. It was a straight sheath and accentuated her slim, but voluptuous figure. She was pulling up her best sheer silk stockings and attaching them her garter belt.

"I don't get what your problem is."

"Nothing, Frank, I don't have a problem," she retorted.

"You've certainly got enough things in your closet to pick from. Hell, I need another bank account just to pay off your Maison Blanche card."

Nora gave him a snarky look.

"It doesn't matter, it's not about you anyway," he continued to rant. Classic Frank. It was about the networking he was achieving at the club. She was always the least on his agenda.

Nora was even more picky than usual about her appearance. Anxious, not so much about how she looked in front Steve, but his wife Marci. She didn't want to look like a courtesan, nor feel like one either. Yet she didn't want to be dressed too prim and proper. The maroon dress was perfect. Very simple, but elegant.

Standing at the mirror, she swept her hair up in a chignon, using a pearl and garnet comb to hold it together. She had carefully applied her makeup this evening for she wanted to look perfect. Next, she put on some moderately, dangly, garnet earrings and high heels that had been dyed to match the color of the dress.

She slipped into her dress and zipped it up. Her look was stylish, but not overdone. Carefully, she dabbed her Chanel Number Five behind her ears and on her neck. Lastly, she applied a coat of lacquer on her nails to match her dress. She was finally ready to go.

Finishing the last of his bourbon, Frank again yelled for her. "Damn it, Nora. If you're not out here in thirty seconds, I'm going without cha."

Mabel was silent but gave Frank a disapproving look. She hated the way he spoke to Nora. Mean sonofagun. Mabel had agreed to stay late this evening to make sure the kids were fed and bedded down.

Good old Mabel, her friend. She managed to keep Mabel in service all these years, having come to love her so. When they bought the home in Metairie, Mabel left the Greenwoods and came to help take care of Nora and her growing family. It was the one comfort Nora had during her young married life. She would never have survived Frank without her.

Arriving at the club, she greeted Charlene with her usual kisses and hugs. Charlene and Max had already selected a table. Nora scanned the room. Steve and his wife had evidently not yet arrived. Charlene took Nora to the bar to get some champagne with Chambord, their favorite.

"So what do you think, Nora? Will he bring his wife?"

"I have no idea," Nora was edgy as she lit up a cigarette in her long holder. Glad that during the sixties, it was quite fashionable for women to smoke.

"I can't imagine how uneasy you must be," Charlene chided.

"No kidding. I have absolutely no idea how I'm going to get through this evening. It's going to be absolute torture."

"At least we'll have great eye candy," Charlene joked to lighten the mood. Nora smirked. "You look ravishing by the way. Love the dress."

Nora saw him first. Sans Marci. Where was she?

"There he is," Charlene echoed the sentiment. "Lord have mercy. He is even dreamier than I remember," she exclaimed, clutching Nora's arm. "I can't believe you did it with him."

Nora shot her a glance. "Charlene! Watch yourself." She was afraid her friend's piercing voice was overheard. But the bartender appeared to be oblivious.

Steve looked incredible. So suave in his yellow turtle neck, dark blue double, breasted jacket and khaki pants. As he approached the girls, he was intercepted by her husband Frank.

"Steve. Glad you could make it." Frank extended his hand in a buddy shake. Watching them touch made Nora wince. Good old boy networking had staved off her having to meet his eyes. But Steve certainly noticed Nora. She looked stunning.

Frank brought him over to their table, which Max was reserving near the bar and ordered him a drink. Seven and Seven on the rocks, thought Nora. How well she knew. Charlene grabbed her friend's hand.

"It's now or never Nora. Come on girl, you can do this."

As the girls approached the table, Frank seemed already engrossed in his card game. Nora stood there for several seconds before Charlene's husband Max made the introductions.

"Steve, this is my wife, Charlene. Charlene. Steve."

"Nice to meet you," Charlene answered perfectly. Best supporting actress for sure. She extended her well manicured hand.

"Nice to meet you too," Steve continued the charade.

"And this is *Nora*," Charlene introduced, emphasizing her name just a little too heavily. Frank momentarily looked up from his cards, causing Nora to flinch.

"Right. Nora. Steve, from Lakefront. You know, the pilot instructor I was telling you about," Max continued. Frank returned his attention to his cards.

Nora had no choice but to extend her hand. Her palm was wet and felt heavy. Steve shook her hand gently. She almost couldn't look at him. Afraid that once she did, the whole room would know.

"Nice to meet you, Steve." She finally met his gaze. His eyes said everything. She bit her lip nervously.

"So where's your wife?" Frank asked. "She was invited you know."

"I'm terribly sorry. But Marci wasn't feeling well this evening. She won't be joining us."

Nora felt a bit let down, albeit a bit relieved. She was dying of curiosity, nevertheless dreaded meeting her in person. If Marci was the sweet woman Steve told her about, and they were as close as Steve said, she would know without a slightest doubt that something was amiss.

Charlene and Nora joined their husbands and Steve at the table. Nora took only small sips of her champagne, wanting to keep her wits about her.

"What's your pleasure?" Frank gestured towards Steve as he shuffled the cards expertly.

"Whatever's going. I'm game," Steve coyly replied.

"At the moment, it's five card draw." Frank began dealing the cards.

"Count me in," countered Steve.

Nora watched curiously as the men engaged in their poker posturing. She wondered how Steve could keep his mind on the game. After watching for what seemed the longest time, she was dying for a cigarette.

"Frank, have you got any smokes?"

"Nope. Just smoked my last one."

Steve then pulled a pack out of his pocket. They actually were the ones that Nora had left behind in the hotel room. She noticed the way the package was smudged with her shade of lipstick from where she had torn it open while she was driving. He pulled out a cigarette slightly and offered it to her. She caught his meaning, remembering their encounter and took it from him.

"Care for a light?" he leaned over towards her and flicked on his silver Naval Aviator lighter.

She carefully leaned into him. "Sure, thanks," she replied trying to remain ever so cool. All she could think about was how sated she felt in his arms, just days before, after they shared a smoke post making love.

Nora took a long, slow drag and watched as her husband played poker with her lover. Charlene had the most intent and fascinated expression on her face. They both speculated how all the men at the table, save one, could be oblivious to the obvious sexual tension between the pair of adulterers.

After Steve cleaned house with their husbands in two consecutive games, Frank had enough. Never a great loser he chortled, "Well, that's quite enough for me, thanks. Seems we have a shark in our midst."

"Aw, Frank. You are just sore. Not used to losing your shirt. Don't feel bad, Steve. I'm the one usually the one buying the next round of drinks as Frank counts his winnings," Max chided.

The game couldn't end fast enough as far as Nora was concerned. It was excruciating sitting across from Steve. She feared her noticeable loss of words would be transparent.

"It is getting late. I should be going," Steve was making his exit. He knew that Nora had been put through enough.

"Don't run off on my account, Steve. I will be happy to go round three with you, but only after I load you with a few more drinks." Frank tried to save face.

"No, no. I really do have to get home. I'll see you all on the weekend, when you come out for your lessons." It was Steve's way to confirm and relieve Nora's concern about their lessons over lapping.

Suddenly, Nora perked up. Next Saturday. Franks lessons would not be on Tuesday. Steve was brilliant. Now off the hook, she was able to gather herself. Standing, she offered her pleasantries. "It was lovely to meet you, Steve. Please offer your wife our condolences. I hope she feels better."

"Will do. Thank you so much," his warm voice responded like the gentleman he was.

"Here, Steve, we'll walk you out." Charlene rose, gestured to Nora and headed towards the door. Knowing Nora wanted to speak to him alone, she peeled off at the ladies room and gave her friend a wink.

When they were far out of eye and earshot, Nora and Steve spoke to each other more candidly. "I thought that night would never end," she sighed in relief.

"Me neither. And yet I couldn't take my eyes off you. It was driving me wild."

"Do you think anyone noticed?" Nora was fearful and shivered. He helped wrap her mink stole around her shoulders.

"No. Your performance and mine went unnoticed."

"That was tense."

They broke out in some nervous laughter. She walked with her arm briefly in his. It calmed her, having his support.

"I'm sorry about that close call. Your husband talked about it when he came for his first lesson. Then, when he telephoned again about the invite, I couldn't really say no."

"And so? What'd ya think of Frank?"

"Interesting. He's gruff enough to be sure."

"He's quite the networker. He kept his monstrous behavior carefully checked. He probably wants to make sure he passes your class," Nora rolled her eyes. "And your wife. Was she really ill?"

"Yes. That was the truth. She intended to come, but was stricken with some breathing difficulties earlier in the day. An upper respiratory thing and didn't want to get out in the night air."

"I see. Well, I have to admit it was a relief in a way that I didn't have to face her. I wasn't sure I could pull off seeing her in person."

He turned to face her. "I'm sorry that in our current situation we can't be more open. I hate it that being near you in public causes you any stress."

She appreciated his candor and understanding of the situation. It made her love him all the more. "Thank you for that." She gave his arm one last squeeze.

"When can I see you again? You know . . .?" he asked of her.

"Yes, I do know. I will see what I can arrange. I'll call you, okay?" He looked intently into her eyes. "I'm falling in love with you, Nora." With that, he reached for her hand and kissed it quickly. Thankfully, no one was on the front portico of the country club entrance. He darted beyond the tall pillars surrounding the circular drive and walked briskly toward the parking lot. The gas street lights that lit his way had hallows around them from the humidity.

Nora stood outside for the longest time. The moon peeking out from the antebellum oaks was full and cast shadows on her departing lover. Tragically, she longed to tell him, she was falling in love with him too.

Chapter 16
∞ May, 1961 ∞

A sweet smell of waffles was wafting through the house. It was Mother's Day, but Nora was at the kitchen counter serving them up to her brood. No breakfast in bed for her. Fresh strawberries and whipped cream were laid out. Getting the milk from the icebox, she called out to Leisel who was missing. "Come on now, hurry up. If you want to have a snack and not break your fast before mass, you only have ten minutes."

"I'm coming. I'm coming," Leisel called out. She was always the last one to reach the table for meals. Her nose was usually in a book, just like Nora's. When she arrived, she had a hand-made card for her mother.

"What's this?" said Nora, humbled.

"Happy Mother's Day!" joyously she cried out and threw her arms around Nora's waist.

"Happy Mother's Day," the others chimed in. Nora was in tears. At least her children loved her. They remembered her on Mother's Day.

"I don't understand why we can't take our time and just go to St. Francis," complained Kayce. "It's in our own neighborhood. St. Mathias is nearly to Claiborne, by *Memere* Greenwood's."

"That's the point, Kayce. I thought we would stop in to see your grandmothers for a visit. *Memere* Greenwood isn't your only grandmother," Nora explained rationally. It wasn't really the reason but sounded good. After not getting to see Marci at the club, Nora's curiosity that Sunday was in overdrive.

"Grandma Nellie is working," Cathy explained.

"Then we should bring her some presents to da hospital," said little Ignatius.

"That would be nice," Nora agreed.

"Is *Memere* havin' us for Sunday lunch? Did she 'vite us?" the ever pragmatic Cathy chimed in.

"We're always welcome at her table. We eat there once a month. But yes, she invited us for Mother's Day lunch. Even if Daddy is playing golf." Nora put the last of the dishes on the dish rack. "After all, today is a special day to honor all mothers. Plus, I don't have to cook lunch for you all," she wriggled Iggy's nose.

"I still think we could make 11:30 at St. Francis," Kayce argued.

"Look, we're going to St. Mathias and that's that." Nora wasn't taking 'no' for an answer from her children.

High mass services at noon were always crowded. With this being Mother's Day, the pews would be full. Nora wanted to make sure they got a seat. In the car on the way over, Kayce continued to carp. "Aren't you even going to apologize?"

"For missing your princess meeting?" of course Nora knew what she was really referring to. "Yes, Kayce. I was. I felt terrible about it, but something came up."

Kayce had never really known her mother to lie, however she wondered if this time her mother was telling her the truth. Would she take communion, since there was no time for confession before mass? Little did she know what other things her mother had to repent for; lies were the least of it.

Her daughter was peeved. Her mother wasn't herself. She was usually the organizer of everything. But now she was impossible and absent minded. To Kayce, her mother seemed out of it. To put salve on the situation, Nora tried to talk to her more about her princess meeting. Regarding that subject, Kayce lit up.

When she turned onto Broad Street, Nora visually searched the cars for Steve's Mustang. But it dawned on her, with the number of children he had; they would likely be driving a wagon or minibus.

The church was full, but there were a few open pews at the back. Nora sat her children there and knelt down as if to pray before mass started, but she was scoping the rows ahead for Steve. Sure enough, she found him. Center left, up near the front.

There they were, the Novaks. She recognized the wavy hair on the back of his head. Steve, Marci and four little stair-stepped heads walking down the aisle. Their oldest appeared to be about ten. He was holding another child; the smallest, a toddler son. There were three girls. At first, she recounted. Where was the other one? But then, she realized one child was serving as altar boy for mass. He had to be Steve's, he looked just like him.

Marci was indeed slight of frame, as Steve mentioned. She had short brown hair that was coiffed sort of like an Elizabeth Taylor Italian cut. Pretty basic. She was seated next to her husband. That was all Nora could see.

Being in church with them made it a bit too surreal. For a moment, Nora thought she would bail. However, she didn't want to have to explain to her own children why she changed her mind after insisting they go to St. Mathias. There were mothers everywhere, bedecked in corsages. Nora felt naked without one. It was going to be a long service, she sighed as she knelt before the processional.

When it was time for communion, she made her way up the aisle. When she got to the front, she briefly looked over at Steve. Startled at first, he recovered, giving her a faint upturned smile from his lips. Then, he quickly looked down as if in prayer. Nora approached the altar.

"Body of Christ," the priest said to her raising the communion wafer. Nora held out her tongue. Turning to head toward her seat, it was then that she noticed the cane, next to Marci in the pew. A cane. Nora felt a pit in her stomach. Suddenly, she was filled with anguish. When Steve mentioned Marci's illness, Nora had no idea it was so severe. Clearly his wife, in such a weakened condition, was unable to give her husband what Nora could. At that moment, Nora felt like a heel. A tear formed in her eye.

Taking a longer glimpse at her, Nora could see that Marci must have been attractive early on, but the illness had taken its toll on her body. She was ghastly thin and pale as a ghost. She had circles under her eyes and appeared tired. Her clothes, although fashionable, hung on her tiny frame. But there was her Mother's Day corsage, a pink orchid pinned to her suit. Nora accelerated her pace, head bent piously down. She could no longer look at them in this venue.

After mass, she quickly gathered her children, left the church, and hurried to the car. She wanted to make sure they were out of the parking lot before Steve and his family exited. What a mistake it was to come here. She choked back tears while directing her children quickly into their seats.

She made a right on Claiborne and gunned the station wagon towards downtown. Mass, Steve, Marci, it was all just too much to process.

To take her mind off what she had witnessed, she stopped at Gambino's for petit fours. Pure comfort food. Nellie loved them. They came in a variety of flavors. German chocolate cake. Angel food. Yellow with chocolate icing.

Next, she drove to Hotel Dieu to deliver them to her own mother. The clerk at the front desk paged her on the ward. Nora's children were underage and prohibited from visiting beyond the lobby. She apologized to the clerk for their rambunctious behavior as they waited for Nellie to come down.

Nellie was pleased to see her grandchildren. Dressed in her starched white uniform and cap, she hugged them all. But they could only stay a moment, as she was on duty in the ward.

"Happy Mother's Day, Mama," Nora said hugging her. "I am sorry you have to work."

"Did you all make mass?" Nellie queried.

"Of course, Mama. We always do."

"We went to St. Mathias," Cathy added.

"Off Fontainebleau? Why on earth did you go there?" Nellie asked in curiosity.

"To go to Gambino's on Claiborne, Mama. To get your favorites."

"Oh, silly me. Well, I love them and will share them with the nurses upstairs."

"It was good seeing you, Mama."

"Don't be stranger, Nora dear. I miss seeing you."

Driving home, Nora was quiet. Mother's Day had been

a downer. All she could think about was the picture of Steve's family. Her own husband was a jerk. But poor Steve. Even worse was pitiful Marci. And all those children. Nora wasn't sure she could be the other woman in this man's world.

Nora skipped lunch at the Greenwoods. She just couldn't stomach it today. When they got home, she fixed some fish sticks and macaroni and cheese for a late lunch with her children. While at Gambino's she bought a *doberge* cake for herself and the children to celebrate Mother's Day. If her husband wasn't going to treat her, she would treat herself. She made it a point to avoid spending time with her own hobbies and played board games with her children for the rest of the day. They loved Chutes and Ladders.

Frank arrived at around six that evening. Brushing by her, he noticed the card on the kitchen counter. "Crap, was it Mother's Day? Well, glad you kiddos remembered." He came around to Nora and made a kissing motion near her cheek. Clearly, after golf he had stayed at the club for drinks. She could smell it on him. "Well, Happy Mother's Day, Nora."

Later that evening, Frank's beer buzz had worn off. Nora was reading as he got into bed. He reached over and started rubbing her belly, descending slowly towards her pussy.

"Not now, Frank. I'm at a great place in my book," Nora tried to deflect him. Emotionally, she had decided to distance herself from Steve; but physically she could still remember each touch and embrace. Since she had slept with Steve, she couldn't bring herself to let Frank touch her.

He wasn't taking her hint. He slipped his hand down in her pajamas fondling her. "Come on baby. Let's celebrate Mother's Day."

She removed his hand. "Stop, Frank. Really. I'm just not in the mood."

He recoiled and became angry. "What the hell, Nora? Lately, there's always some excuse. I'm your husband and I wanna fuck."

Nora wasn't backing down this time. "Well too bad, Frank. I don't."

"You frigid little bitch. You goddamned frigid little bitch," his voice was rising.

She braced to protect herself. Her only weapon was her book. "That's enough, Frank. Stop it with the name calling. I've had a rough day, that's all."

"Look, Nora. I am sick of this shit. If you hate me so much, why don't you take your pretty little arse and just get out. Move back to where you came from. Believe me, there's plenty of women at the club who would be glad to take your place," he sneered.

That was it, it was a new low. Getting out of bed, she opened her night stand. "Like the little tart that left this behind?" She threw the Hermes scarf in his face.

"What the hell are you talking about?" he defended doubtfully.

"That scarf. It seems one of your little trollops left it behind from the dinner you had with her at the club," Nora yelled at him.

"Well what did you expect? When a wife doesn't put out, a husband's gonna find it elsewhere. Besides, you don't have proof that I laid her."

"Who needs proof? Everyone at the club knows you have screwed around on me for years. Your reputation precedes you," she quipped. "Take your scarf and shove it up your ass." She left slamming the bedroom door behind her.

As she stalked down the hall, she could hear him cursing her from behind the door. But she knew, with the kids in their beds, she was relatively safe. Frank wouldn't dare harm her in front of the children. Nora spent the remaining hours of Mother's Day trying to fall asleep on the den couch.

Chapter 17

The next day, Nora phoned Novak Aviation Services and made an appointment with Steve's secretary. She had made a decision that she was going to stick to; about Steve and about her lessons.

After the Mother's day debacle, Nora made up her mind that things between her and Steve needed to end. If she stayed in her marriage or not; it didn't matter. Now that she had seen the condition Marci was in, Nora knew she couldn't live with herself if they continued their relationship.

She was going to talk to Steve about assigning her to another pilot. They only thing she lacked was the in-seat flight time. Nora wasn't going to give up now. Especially since Frank had started lessons.

Although she had parent conferences in the afternoon, this morning she planned to sort things out. Her appointment was at 10:30 AM, but Nora arrived early at 10:00. She knew that Steve would be in class and wanted to wait in the lobby outside his office without him seeing her first. She was afraid if he did, she would chicken out.

Sure enough, at promptly 10:30 he came out of the classroom. He had a stack of papers in his hands and initially didn't notice her. But then, he saw her legs. Those legs only belonged to one woman.

"Hi, there," Nora greeted him first. Steve looked surprised to see her there on a Monday.

"Hey, what a nice treat. What brings you out?"

His secretary answered, "She is your 10:30." Steve

JEANETTE VAUGHAN

looked surprised. He wondered why Nora had made an appointment, dreading the answer. She didn't appear to be her happy self.

"Come on in," he gestured opening his office door for her. He closed it afterwards. "What' going on?"

She took a seat on the chair in front of his desk, like she had a few months before. She lifted her chin up and looked him in the eyes, clutching her purse. "I've made a couple of decisions, Steve."

"Is this about yesterday at mass?" he asked referring to St. Mathias.

"Yes and no," she began. "First, I want to talk about us. After seeing your family yesterday and your wife, I . . ." her lip began to quiver. She swallowed hard. "It's about Marci. Steve, I had no idea."

"I was going to tell you," he hung his head. "Or I was going to try to anyway. Marci has come to terms with her illness. In fact, sometimes, I think she purposely looks the other way because she knows she can't meet my needs as a wife. Although I have never before cheated on her. Until you."

"I just can't see you anymore. I can't be your mistress."

"Nora. Sweet, Nora. You were never my mistress," he rose to hug her. But she pushed him away with her gloved hands.

"I know that, Steve. That's not it. After seeing her, it was just too tragic. She is so frail. I just couldn't stomach hurting her by being with you," she began to cry. She reached for the handkerchief in her purse.

Steve at first was speechless. "Yeah, I know how you feel. I've been feeling pretty lousy about cheating on her myself," he admitted. "I adore my children and to be quite honest I adore my wife."

"Then, how . . . how could you have hooked up with me?"

He looked at her intently. "Nora you felt it too, the chemistry was too powerful. How could we not have ended up together?"

"I agree, but it has to be over now. It's got to be over. I just couldn't live with myself now having seen her. And knowing what I have been doing behind her back."

– 82 –

"Yeah. The guilt bug has been getting to me too. So what would you like to do?"

"We just can't anymore, Steve. No matter what we feel. That is why I am here."

"But that's just it, Nora. I have fallen in love with you. When I'm near you I can't think of anything else except holding you, kissing you, making love to you."

"All that has to stop," she shook her head.

"You're not dropping out of flight school are you?"

Nora collected herself. "Good golly, no. That's my dream. I would like to finish what I started. I came here determined to learn how to fly. I want to see it to completion."

"Yes, you did. Thank goodness for that."

"I won't give that up for anyone. Even you. I just don't know what to do about it. Whenever we are together; we end up in each other's arms."

"Let's see," he spun his lighter on his desk trying to come up with a solution.

"What would you suggest?"

"Well, it's almost summer. I usually put on some part timers. Retired military guys that still want to teach. You could hold off your in-seat check rides until then, I suppose."

"Really?" she sounded hopeful.

"It will only delay you finishing by a few weeks. Will that work?"

"My darling, Steve. Thank you," she rose to hug him; then reminded herself to tone it down and be as business like as she could.

He embraced her, keeping her body apart from his. Just the smell of her perfume and hair made him weak in the knees. He pushed her back gently. Taking her chin, he looked into her eyes. "You know, this will be hard as hell, being apart from you."

She held his stare. Her eyes were still glossy from the tears. "I know, but we don't have any choice."

"I guess that bastard husband of yours won out after all."

"Not really. I've made some decisions about that too."

Steve's expression changed to intrigue, "Oh?"

"Yes. I am going to ask for a divorce. Frank's treatment of me has reached a point of no return. I am going to see the priest soon."

"Don't look for any support from the Catholic Church, especially as a woman."

"I expect not. But while I'm there I am going to confession. I might as well talk about our sin too."

"Hey, gal. For what it's worth, you still rock my world you know?"

"I know," she smiled wryly.

"In another circumstance, we would've been great together. I'll miss you, Nora."

"You won't have time. I'll be out on that tarmac checking off my rides."

Nora rose to leave and extended her hand. Her long, lithe, lovely hand. For the briefest moment, he thought about grabbing it and bringing it up to his lips. In the most dignified gesture she could muster, she gave him a handshake. He squeezed her hand in return.

She gathered her things, put on her Jackie Kennedy sunglasses and turned for the door before he could see her tears welling up again. His gaze followed her from his window as she walked all the way out to her car. He knew he was watching the most captivating woman he ever met.

When Nora got into the station wagon, she burst into tears. Telling him goodbye killed a part of her soul. Emotionally and sexually. For she, too, knew she was madly in love with him. Damned Catholic guilt.

Chapter 18

From Lakefront, she went straight to Charlene's house. Her friend greeted her at the kitchen door.

"What up, toots?" and then she saw it written on her face. "My stars, Nora. Is it over?"

"Yes . . . it is over. I had no choice after what I saw at church the other day."

"Nora you are doing the right thing. You are both Catholic and he would never leave his wife in that condition."

"I realize you're right. It just hurts so badly. He was my soul mate. I just know it." Nora knelt down beside her friend and Charlene cradled her. After she had cried and cried, every possible ounce of sorrow out of her heart, she washed and dried her face.

"Here, you don't want the kids to see you looking like that." Charlene handed her a makeup bag. "Kayce would know something was up. Dry your eyes and put on some powder and lipstick. You are gonna get through this. And you know I'll be here for ya."

It was Nora who had carpool with the children that week and for that duty she was glad. Their distractions and the chaos of her daily existence kept her from thinking about the hole in her heart.

While they worked on their homework and beef stew simmered on the stove, Nora sat at her sewing machine. She sewed and sewed and sewed, finishing the yellow dress for Kayce's role as princess. She only lacked the beading now. As she sewed, she sang. Slow, sorrowful jazz tunes. Singing brought her comfort and she wanted to get Steve out of her mind. Sewing kept her busy. She was glad the dress was almost finished because now she could turn her attentions to anticipation of a happier time. Even though it was only spring, planning her children's Christmas outfits would be something to look forward to.

* * * * *

As summer arrived, Nora carried out her plan. When Mabel came on Mondays, Wednesdays and Fridays Nora went to the airport. She paid for her lessons with the funds that she stashed away from her grocery money and Greenwood birthday checks using almost every last dime she had. She wanted to make sure there was no trace of her aviation activities that Frank would find.

Since she ended the affair, the only thing he would be upset about was that she had signed up for a class. Yet another whim or stupid diversionary thing, it probably wouldn't have mattered. But the flying was her secret and she wanted to keep it that way.

Frank had progressed in his lessons as well. In fact, he took Nora to dinner at the club with Charlene and Max to celebrate his passing ground school. Frank was learning how to fly the Piper but he needed more consistency with his landings. Just as Steve had arranged, their paths never crossed.

It was all Nora could do to endure the evening, knowing that what he gloated about, she had already completed with flying colors. She and Charlene just drank, exchanging glances across the table.

It angered Nora so much that she seemed to be merely a doormat in Frank's life. Everything was always about him. *His* networking, *his* friends. Flying, sewing, and singing were the only enjoyments Nora had that were truly her own. For of course, even her children were Greenwoods shared with Frank.

Nora was ticking off her intermediate flight lessons and activities one by one. Taking off. Landing consistency. Stall recovery. She had mastered them all.

Her new instructor was an older gentleman retired

from the Air Force named Chet. Whatever he assigned Nora, she completed with exceptional vigor. He was impressed. Nora's solo, where she would takeoff, fly a short distance and land all by herself was quickly approaching.

She knew the decision she was about to make was made in spite. It was another mini form of revenge. But Nora had decided she was going to solo in the Piper. At her next lesson, she made the announcement to her instructor.

"Mrs. Greenwood, it's time to book your solo. When would you like that to be? Have you given that any thought?"

"Yes, I have. Quite a bit, in fact. I am going to solo in the Piper Aztec."

"The Greenwood's Piper Aztec?"

"Yes, that is the one."

"Well, that's not really possible, as all of your training has been in the Cessna."

Nora looked crestfallen, however she was unfazed. "Well, I'll learn the flight dynamics of the Piper," she countered.

"I apologize. Even though I'm rated as a multi-engine instructor I'm not checked out on the Piper. I will have to check with Mr. Novak."

"No, that is quite alright. I will handle it myself." Nora went straight to the office and knocked on Steve's door. Her hurried rap indicated the intensity of her agenda. She immediately made her request clear. "How much would it take for me to learn the flight dynamics of the Piper Aztec?"

"You want to fly the Greenwood's plane for your solo?"

"Yes, why not? It belongs to the family. Why shouldn't I learn how to fly it?"

"Well, for one thing, all your training has been in the Cessna, which is single engine. You're not 'qualled in multi-engine, that's a whole different ball game. Secondly, I can tell you that the only person that has permission to fly it, besides their personal pilot, is Frank. I don't even have that authorization. If I asked him, it would give your covert aviation scheme away."

Nora was fuming. Steve thought about it for a moment. "But there is another option, until you get permission."

"Oh?"

"There is another Twin Piper out here that you could lease for your flights. It isn't in use and it's almost the same as the Greenwood's plane, just not as nice."

"Lease? I can barely afford the lessons."

Steve knew how much she wanted to finish her training. He knew the owner well. "Nora, I can't promise anything, but I'll see what I can arrange. I know you won't take no for an answer."

Nora beamed. "You've got that right. Great! When do I start?"

He pulled the specs on the Twin Piper Aztec and handed her the papers to study. "It will be like starting all over. Study these and then we'll begin the check rides." As an afterthought he added, "The check rides will have to be with me, you realize that don't you? I mean . . . we were supposed to keep our distance, remember?"

"Steve. I can be professional. You'll see."

He could only hope so. Then he added wryly, "You've never told Frank about this have you?"

"Listen, these are my lessons. This is what I want to do. I'll work out what I am going to tell Frank about it." She took the stapled pages and shoved them into her purse.

Steve enjoyed seeing her streak of independence in full force. Teaching her would be better than arguing with her about it. Certainly, it would be the less of two evils. But the thought of being so close to her in a cockpit made him nervous. Before she left, she set up a time with Steve on Friday to do the first tests on the specs.

* * * * *

Several weeks later, Nora felt quite devious as she buckled herself into the seat for her first check ride. Once her pre-flight was complete, she readied the plane for takeoff under Steve's direction.

The Piper Aztec was twin engine and larger than the Cessna. It was probably just in her head, but there seemed like there were more controls. It certainly had more power. She radioed ground control under Steve's instructions. "Lakefront tower, twin Piper November, one, three, six, niner, tango ready for takeoff on runway two seven. It'll be due south."

Steve corrected her. "That's what you tell the tower. Right now, you are talking to ground. You need to tell them where you are taxiing. And although it's a right turn due south, ground doesn't care. That info is for the tower."

"Sorry. I'll try again." She did, and it was correct the second time. Nora had been perfect in her other rides, but today, being back with Steve, she was more uneasy. It was all still a new lingo. When she got to the edge of the runway, she radioed the tower. "Lakefront tower, twin Piper November, one, three, six, niner. Ready for takeoff on runway two seven. It'll be a right turn due south."

"Better," he complimented her. "They pretty much know this plane, so you really don't have to say November." She noted his coaching.

Nora felt ready. She began her takeoff roll. With two engines propelling her, it wasn't long before she was pulling back on the yoke. With a little more effort than the single engine Cessna, the Piper began to rotate and lift off the ground. Within a few moments she was off the ground and up gaining altitude. She was great at takeoff. It was only going to be a short flight, so she banked the plane to the right and they flew out briefly for a loop over the city. He was reviewing the approach and landing instructions.

Although she had some navigation skills and understood the instruments, Nora flew mostly by visuals. As a novice pilot, it was mostly visual cues that let her know where she was geographically. She landed without a hitch.

Steve could hardly keep his mind off of Nora as she taxied the plane back to the hangar. He was supervising her pilot skills, but he was also thinking about the time that they had spent together. He knew it had been painful when they decided to call things off. Not a day went past that he didn't recall making love to her.

As he was helping her out of the door, he paused for a moment in the hangar. "Nora, how have you been?"

"Devastated and you?" Nora answered with a straight face. She never minced her words.

"You know I feel awful about everything. The thing is, I can't get you off of my mind."

"I can understand those feelings Steve, but I plan on asking Frank for a divorce. It's just clear to me that you cannot do the same with Marci."

"You aren't divorcing him on my account are you?"

Nora thought that a bit vane. "Yes and no," she said. "You helped me to see that I deserve to be loved. Cherished. As long as I stay with Frank, that will never happen."

Her self-rule and sheer determination was what attracted Steve to her in the first place. A surge of feelings welled up within him. He wanted so badly to kiss her, but knew that it was just not their time. Walking back into the terminal, he was complimenting her, "You did a great job today."

"Thanks," she answered as though it was nothing.

Glad he could accommodate her, he wondered in the back of his mind what scheme she was up to. He was quite sure if Frank knew she was learning to fly the Piper, he would go ballistic. In all probability even knowing that she was learning to fly at all.

As they reached the terminal, she thanked him for his time and instruction. "I really appreciate you working with me on the Piper."

"Your check-ride was good, Nora. I think you are ready to go."

"Other than my taxi *faux pas*. Does that mean I am ready to solo?"

"Pretty much."

Before she left the terminal, she scheduled her solo on another day when Mabel was available to watch the kids. After she booked her flight, Nora couldn't help herself. She had to see what the Greenwood's Piper was all about.

Walking back out to the hangars where the planes were parked, she saw one of the workmen, "Excuse me, I'm Nora Greenwood. Can you tell me which hangar our Piper Aztec sits in?"

"Sure, hangar three," said the mechanic. "Just give a shout to Joey, the mechanic. He does the maintenance on it."

"Thank you very much." Sure enough, at hangar three Joey was working on some parts outside. "Hello, I'm Nora Greenwood."

Hearing the name Greenwood, he perked up. "Uh, how can I help you today, Mrs. Greenwood?"

"I would like to see the Piper. I understand it is quite a beauty."

"Yes, Ma'am, it sure is. I would be glad to show it to you." When he pulled back the hangar door, Nora was impressed with what she saw. It was in perfect condition. Gleaming white with blue stripes.

"It is really a beauty." Sleek and gorgeous, very similar to the one she had just flown in herself.

"Mr. Greenwood sure likes flying it," he said.

"Oh, does he?" Nora asked calmly.

"Yep, he wasn't out here at first. But now he's learning. I think he's fallen in love with this here plane."

"Is that so?" Nora smirked. "Maybe I will have to ask him to give me a ride in it."

"Yes, Ma'am," he said. Making a mental note to herself, Nora noted that inside the hangar, the plane was unlocked. As they left, she also watched as he took a key from his pocket and locked the hangar with a padlock.

"Thank you for showing me," she batted her eyes. "It really *is* a beautiful plane."

"No problem, Mrs. Greenwood. Any time." Joey placed the key to the padlock in his pocket.

As Nora drove home, she clenched the steering wheel tightly in anger. Here she was with a plane in the family and she was having pay rental time for her own training. It was all in keeping it a secret from Frank, but retraining in the Piper was so costly, she was almost broke.

Chapter 19

The day had finally come for Nora to solo in the Piper. In true Nora style, she purchased some light-weight, canvas fabric and made her own flight suit. She had it embroidered with her name on the front. The suit was camel and her name was in maroon. Although she didn't have any aviation or military patches, she wore it just as proudly. She put it on that morning with some military style boots purchased from the Army/Navy store. Around her neck she draped a brown and white scarf.

When she arrived at the terminal, Steve was pleased to see her. He booked and logged her solo flight destination. This was it. Her first takeoff, circle and landing on her own. When he saw her outfit he was bemused. Aviatrix Nora.

"Here, you will need these." He pulled his aviators off his head and handed them to her.

"Thanks" she said, "I will remember the gift."

"Gift?" he questioned half-serious. "I expect those back after your flight." He escorted her out to the Piper sitting ready out on the tarmac. "Ready?" he asked.

"Ready as ever," she replied, forthright and determined.

"Up, up and away," he gestured using an old military term. "You can do this, gal."

Nora walked around and did her preflight inspection of the plane. She took her time, being sure not to rush. Beginning with inspection on the outside of the plane, she checked the ailerons, elevators, and rudders. She made sure each of these pieces was not only fastened securely to the plane, but also able to move up and down freely. Steve was proud.

Next she looked at each wheel, to make certain there were no holes or items stuck in them. Also, she checked their air pressure. Next, she opened the engine and checked the oil level and sump checked the fuel tanks. After that, she opened up the fuel cap on the wing to verify her fuel level. Then she took a final walk around the entire plane, inspecting the body of the fuselage, including the wings and lights.

With all the fuel and oil levels verified, she climbed into the cockpit herself this time, without Steve's help. Checking all the switches and buttons on the interior instrument panel, one by one she went down her mental checklist. Wing flaps up, carburetor heat cool. Check. Throttle open, check. She was ready. Checking the wind she noted it was from the South. "Good to go," she announced with confidence. She fired up the left engine first, verified its function and then the right.

Nora made contact with ground. "Lakefront ground. Twin Piper one, three, six, niner, tango taxi runway one eight."

"Twin Piper one, three, six, niner taxi to runway one eight."

She guided the plane to the edge of runway eighteen. "Lakefront tower Twin Piper one, three, six, niner, tango ready for takeoff runway one eight." She checked the wind speed. "I'll be making a right turn to the west, over." she said proudly.

"Twin Piper one, three, six, niner, tango. Clear for takeoff runway one eight," the air traffic controller responded.

Nora sat at the edge of the runway. It looked like she would be flying out over her city today. Waves of exhilaration shot through her body. She was really going to do it. She pushed forward the throttle and started down the runway at thirty-five knots she then increased to seventy-five knots, then eighty-five. Pointing the nose in the air, she gained lift. She was up and going. "Oh, my goodness," she spoke out loud.

She lifted up off the runway, retracted the gear and

was in the air. Wings steady. No major prevailing winds. Nora was hundreds of feet above the ground and continued her ascent. She was going to level at three thousand feet for her cruising altitude. Nora was so proud of herself.

Using some basic navigation plots of where she was and the visuals of the Mississippi river, she crossed the city. Steve checked with the tower and knew that at this time, the air space would be relatively clear. Regardless, Nora checked her own visuals. It was magnificent. She felt self-actualized and independent. For the first time in her life, she felt free.

As she sailed upward, above the city that she loved, she realized all too quickly that it would soon be time to turn around. Passing over downtown and Metairie, she approached the swampy edge of the Bonne Carre' spillway. The tall forgotten cypress trees with their roots in the murky, green swamp loomed below her. This was her first taste of liberty and she wanted more. Making another right hand turn, she flew back over the lake seeing its dark swirling waters below, noting the pine forests of Mandeville and Slidell in the distance.

She wondered for a brief moment what Frank would think of her now? Forefront in her mind, however, was what her father would think if he could see his daughter. Nora Jean Broussard flying a plane by herself. She dropped her altitude steadily and progressively as she flew across the Ponchartrain. There was water, water everywhere and it made her a bit anxious. But she remembered that she did have her flotation device should something happen.

A few minutes later, she got a visual on Lakefront. Following Steve's exact instructions she lowered her speed and altitude for her approach. She was on a short final and approximately a quarter of a mile away from the runway. The plane was flying at a speed of eighty knots.

"Lakefront tower, this is Twin Piper, one, three, six, niner, tango requesting permission to land. I'm at a quarter mile to your east."

"Twin Piper, three, six, niner, clear to land runway one eight."

There was one edgy gentleman waiting on the tarmac

for her return. He was scanning the skies looking for her plane. And then, he saw it. "Well, I'll be damned." She had done it. Steve was immensely proud. He'd had many students in the past, but with this student, he was in love. As Nora's plane got closer, he could see that she was spot on in her landing. She was within hundreds of feet of bringing in the plane safely. "Flare, flare," he was calling out to her, as though she could hear him. But almost as if she could, the nose pulled up.

She reduced the power to approximately fifteen hundred rpms and extended the landing flaps ten degrees after spotting the numbers on the runway. She dropped her speed carefully, about five more knots as she descended. Nora extended the flaps another ten degrees, trying to keep the plane aligned by manipulating the rudder pedals.

"Steady, steady," he called out as the wings bobbled slightly.

Steady they became. One hundred feet, fifty, twenty-five and he could hear the wheel's rubber screech as they struck the tarmac gently. "Perfect. Stupendously perfect." She had done it. He couldn't believe it. Nora had done it! He was so excited, he ran out to the edge of the runway to greet her as she taxied in. Nora brought the plane to a stop, killed the engines and quickly climbed out of the cockpit.

"Oh my God, you are amazing. You were absolutely amazing," he shouted out, running towards her.

"I did it! I did it!" she cried out joyously. "Oh my God. The sense of freedom. It was fantastic. I really did it."

"I knew you could." In that moment both of them lost all sense of reality. He reached around and grabbed her around the waist and kissed her with zest out in the open. She, too, was so caught up in sheer joy that she kissed him back. It only took one spark for all their feelings to return. Just that one brief moment. When they both realized what was happening, they broke away.

"Nora. I'm so sorry," he apologized.

"No, it's okay. I was caught up too. I have missed you."

With that encouragement, he held her tight. Remembering her scent, the silkiness of her hair, the softness of her skin. "Please, Nora. If you can, I would really like to celebrate with you," he asked.

"Why not?" Nora said. "By golly, I deserve it." Leaving the terminal arm in arm, they took off in his Mustang, not giving a care who might see them. For today, in this moment, Nora was one of the boys. She felt she deserved all the accolades that Steve had to offer her.

"How would you like to celebrate?" he asked.

She replied, "I know exactly what I want. How about a huge plate of boiled shrimp and a beer?"

"You've got it sister," he said. "I know just the place." Steve drove her to Jaeger's and they sat down to a heaping plate of spicy, boiled shrimp and huge schooners of Falstaff. In characteristic Nora fashion, she ate them hungrily, pulling off their heads, squeezing the tails and popping them into her mouth. They shared exuberant conversation, asking about each other's children like best friends. Loosened up and feeling great about herself, Nora even asked about Marci. After stuffing themselves and downing a couple of beers, Steve got ready to walk her to the car.

"Say, did I tell you that I saw the Greenwood's Piper?" she ventured.

"No, but the mechanic mentioned to me that you did." Nora looked surprised. "General aviation is a grapevine," he laughed.

"It sure is a pretty plane."

"Yep. That it is."

"So, do the mechanics work for you?"

"Nope. They work for Lakefront FBO. They have a little office in our building. Why?"

"Just curious. That's all. The guy seemed nice when he showed me the plane."

"Yeah. Joey's an alright kind of guy. Think they'd ever let you fly it someday?"

"Please. They would stroke if they had an inkling I was even taking lessons."

He leaned into her, grasping her hands. "Hey, I am so proud of you and what you did today."

"Me too," she agreed. "You were a great instructor."

"Nah . . . you were a great student." He was lost in

her eyes.

"So," she said. "What's next?"

It dawned on him she was talking about flight instruction. He blinked and got back on track. "You only lack one thing, your cross country."

She knew what that meant. Flying across from one airport to another, all the while being in radio communication. Then landing at another airport a certain distance away. Some visuals; but mostly navigation points. "Alrighty," she replied energetically. "I'll be ready." Inside, the thought of flying such a long distance by herself and relying on aeronautical calculations scared the wits out of her. But there was no way she was giving up now, she had tasted freedom.

Chapter 20
∞ July, 1961 ∞

Cross country flight was a standard part of private pilot training. Nora had to accurately fly long distance routes between multiple airports. This required all of the skills needed to fly an airplane, including navigation, weather evaluation, and fuel management, all within the various types of controlled and uncontrolled airspace. She completed these check rides over the first weeks of summer with her instructor, Chet, after he checked out on the Piper. Nora and Steve thought it best she fly only with him from now on. He proudly signed off her log book with each accomplishment.

Steve started planning with them an agreed route for an appropriate trip. They poured over the VFR Sectional maps of the region and plotted out an exact route for locations of contact. The diagrams were detailed, visual flight rules, aeronautical maps published by the National Aeronautical Charting Office. Most flight routes were not straight lines, but instead a series of trackable way points. Nora chose to fly to Pensacola. They established her way points at Biloxi, Mobile, and then Pensacola Regional. Her visual target would be the beach along the coast line, which although curvy was a west to east course.

Although they planned the route a couple of weeks before the actual flight, Chet felt she would not be ready until the early July. Nora took several quizzes on reading the VFR maps. She studied the one that she was required to carry on-board.

One afternoon, as she crammed, she became overwhelmed. "Chet, these charts are getting so confusing.

The minute I think I understand them; I have to learn something else."

"Sorry, Nora. But you have no choice. Flying cross country requires that you know information about every airport in the area, the ground elevation at regular intervals, and the natural and man-made landmarks to help you verify your position. Plus for safety reasons, you've gotta be fully adept at delineating the different classes of airspace in the area."

"Okay, okay. I get how important it is. Just give me a few more hints on how to remember it all," she winked at him.

Nora met with Chet and Steve during the last few days of June to plan fuel consumption and weather predictions leading up to her flight. The weather appeared conducive and they plotted her cruising altitude based on wind forecasts.

The day finally arrived for Nora to complete her final test before getting a pilot's license. The cross country. It was another hot, muggy, mid-summer day in New Orleans. July 1st.

Nora decided on a morning flight, just in case she needed her visuals. She did a quick check on the weather before she left home. Today, she again pulled out her flight suit. For this occasion, she chose a blue and gold scarf to go with it. Navy colors, she thought.

She made a quick stop by church to say a rosary. Before getting out of her car, she checked the parking lot to make sure no one saw her in her aviation gear. Making her final sign of the cross, she put it in her pocket along with the pocket watch that her father had given her so long ago. The keepsake watch somehow denoted this remarkable time in her life.

Then, she drove to Lakefront. She had eaten a poached egg, toast and coffee to keep her blood sugar up. Everything had to be right to make the final moment of her dream happen. She arrived at the airport at about 10:00 AM.

When she was determined to do something, she was always early. Steve and Nora filed her flight plan with the flight service station at Pensacola, Florida. She figured by using the beaches as a visual, at least she'd have a nice view out her window along the coast as she flew east. The distance was short enough that she would manage to cross country qualify; that was all that mattered. Plus, she could make it back home in time before Frank got there.

As Steve had done before, he arranged for the alternate Piper Aztec to be booked for her journey. She went over the navigation charts one final time with her instructor Chet. This was truly her Amelia Earhart moment.

It was one thing to do a quick takeoff, a loop around the city and land. But this time, not only would she would be alone; she was responsible for controlling her whereabouts.

She and Chet had logged several cross countries and now she took all of his suggestions and put them into place. She perfected her lingo to contact the radio towers, giving them correct altitudes and locations. This was it.

As trained, Nora began with a visual inspection of the plane. She felt sure Steve would come out to wish her well, but he didn't seem to be anywhere around. She gave a wave to Joey, the mechanic. Nora's mental agenda was set on what she needed to do, but she was a bit disappointed that Steve wasn't there to see her off.

Luckily for Nora, the weather was cooperating. There were a few puffy clouds that had come in off the Gulf. Supposedly, there was a chance for an isolated shower or two near Mobile. But nothing widespread, allowing her to easily navigate around.

Chet came over, "Checkin' to see if you are ready girl."

"Yeppers. I think so," she said, hopping up into the cockpit to continue her pre-flight. She rechecked the wind sock and saw there was a mild wind from the southwest.

Nora pulled out the aviators that Steve had loaned her. She had forgotten to return them. Ready to go, she revved up the engines and gave ground a call. They cleared her taxi to runway one eight. When she reached that point, she radioed the tower. "Good morning tower, Twin Piper one, three, six, niner, tango preparing for takeoff on runway one eight. It'll be a left out with a turn to the east," she said.

"Piper one, three, six, niner. Hold short runway one

eight. There's a Piper on final. Over."

"Copy that, Lakefront." Nora nervously waited at the end of the tarmac. It was the longest thirty seconds of her life. She watched as the other plane slowly made its descent over her head. She couldn't believe her eyes. As luck would have it, it was the other Piper Aztec. The Greenwood's Piper Aztec. What were the chances Frank was at the controls? She couldn't see into the cockpit, as it flew overhead. She hoped it was the company pilot. She wondered who was on-board? What a sick and twisted coincidence. What would he think finding Nora behind the controls of a plane?

No time to waste on speculation now, she was cleared for takeoff from the tower. Countdown to zero hour had begun. She pushed forward on the throttle opening it up and began her takeoff roll down the runway. Forty knots, then sixty knots. Nose up. A little more speed and lift. She was up.

Runway one eight came right to the edge of the Ponchartrain and as she took off she was out over the water. Gaining more altitude, she could see water out in the Gulf for miles. Nora banked left and headed along the coastline. As she crossed over the swamp at Pearl River, she could visualize miles and miles of beaches stretching before her. The beaches made a jagged line that marked the coast lines of Mississippi, Alabama and then Florida.

The timing of her flight made it such that the sun was not in her eyes. But she wore her aviators anyway for it glistened and shone off the nose of the plane. There was an occasional oil tanker that she could see in the Gulf.

Nora was tense, but immensely proud of herself. She was a pilot. She felt the most incredible sense of autonomy and abandon. She climbed in altitude to five thousand five hundred feet. Months back, Steve asked her if she wanted to touch the face of an angel. Today, she felt she was.

In her pocket, she stroked her father's pocket watch. She brought it along with her as a good luck charm. That and the rosary. As she flew along the coast, she felt like the spirits were with her. Spirits of strong, independent women who had gone before. And of course the ever watchful eyes of her late father.

Nora radioed her first tower checking in, "Biloxi tower, this is Twin Piper November, one, three, six, niner, tango. Altitude, four thousand, three hundred fifty feet, VFR to Pensacola, over.

"Twin Piper one, three, six, niner. Altimeter three zero zero six, over," the tower controller answered her back.

"Roger that." Nora adjusted her altimeter as instructed and continued on her course. Two legs to go. The temperature was warm and muggy.

As she flew among the puffy, cotton ball clouds and viewed the coast line below, she was relaxed like she had never been. Although she had to focus, she was happy making this powerful journey by herself.

It was a life altering moment. Gone were the days when Nora would not stand up for herself against the verbal and physical abuse, exploitation, and harassment by her husband Frank. She made a mental note to talk to the priest soon.

As Nora completed her radio check with Mobile, there was some concern. It seemed that a small thunder head rolled in just east of Mobile, towards Pensacola. A bit of alarm set in. Her luck had precluded flying into bad weather before. Now, she was a bit scared. She radioed the tower to change her altitude in order to avoid the storm. Without an instrument rating, she was never to fly into clouds. Especially a storm. It could be disastrous.

"Twin Piper one, three, six, niner, tango. Climb and maintain six thousand five hundred feet," the tower advised her to avoid it. Nora pushed forward on the throttle and increased her altitude as directed. The storm wasn't giving up that easily.

She could hear the thunder and see small bolts of lightning. There was a mild drizzle on her windshield. Most of it was below her, but at her current altitude, she would have to fly through a small bit of cloud before she got her visual on Pensacola.

Nora said a small prayer to herself. "Little flower, in this hour, show you power, send a shower . . . of roses," referring to St. Theresa, Little Flower of Jesus. Her mother had taught her the prayer years ago. Nora hoped it worked. She gripped the yoke tightly and into the cloud she went.

Her visual references were completely obstructed; it was like flying while blind. She checked her altimeter and horizontal indicator to make sure she was level. Many small craft pilots, having been caught in a cloud ended up inverted from disorientation. Too close to the surface, they slammed into the ground. With this in mind, she scanned her gauges again and again. Things appeared to be okay. Raindrops were now dripping onto her windows. "Level, steady," she coached herself. Seconds seemed eternal.

Then, poof, she was out the other side. Sunlight. "Thank God. And St. Theresa." Now *those* thirty seconds had been the longest of her life. She could see again, and thought she had a visual on Pensacola. Or at least part of the city.

Nora could make out the Naval Air Station below. When Steve helped her plot her cross country, he had been careful to steer her clear of activity at the Naval Air Station. Steve cautioned her to stay her course and hold her altitude, as many a young Navy pilot flew faster and more agile machines as a part of their beginner aviation training. NAS Pensacola was one of their main training stations. For a moment she wondered what it would be like to fly combat aircraft. Just briefly, she reminisced about flying with Steve in the Corsair. Loops, barrel rolls, and chandelles.

But for now, she had to refocus on the task at hand. Pensacola was a busy air space. Having studied her nav charts, she knew she was close to Pensacola Regional. Three states. Nora Jean Broussard Greenwood had just flown across three states. She began her descent. Four thousand, three thousand. One thousand, she could see the airport and radioed the tower for her approach.

"Twin Piper, one, three, six, niner, clear for landing runway three six. The storm's changed course, over."

"Copy that, Pensacola." Nora banked right and out over the Gulf. She would be approaching to the north. Deftly, she maneuvered the plane into the correct position. She continued to drop her air speed and altitude. Nora could now see the numbers of her runway. The storm was far off to her left.

Two hundred, one hundred, her wings bobbled just slightly due to the intense crosswind off the Gulf. It was tipping them. "Steady, Nora girl." Fifty feet. She was over the runway and seconds away from landing.

She flared the nose and pointed it against the cross wind. Tail slightly down. Bounce, bounce, scrape . . . her wheels struck the runway. Nora could smell a bit of rubber as she hit ground. But she was down. She put on her brakes and slowed her speed. "Pensacola Regional Ground, Twin Piper, one, three, six, niner, tango taxi to general aviation." Once she confirmed where that was, she taxied right towards the tarmac and a tie down.

She completed her test. Cross country. The final hurdle. Nora was over the moon. She planned her route such that she had a small break before her return flight. What she didn't notice, at first, was the man watching her land.

As she approached, she couldn't get over whom she saw standing on the tarmac. She knew his shape anywhere. There he was, sandy hair flapping in the breeze. Steve.

"Oh my gosh," she guffawed. He was waiting with a dozen, long stem, red, roses. When the plane came to a stop, she leapt out of the cockpit. He had a look of immense gratification and was grinning from ear to ear. She ran to greet him. "Steve. I can't believe it. Holy moly!" she gushed. "I am now pilot Nora Jean Broussard."

"I can believe it. I am so proud." He gave her the biggest hug. "These are for you," he presented her with the roses. "And these," out of his pocket he pulled a pair of aviators.

Her own aviators. He had them engraved with the date and her name. She pulled off his and put on the new ones. "Guess I won't be needing these anymore," she handed his pair back. Nora tossed her head and laughed heartily, filled with glee. Crying out in joy, "They are beautiful, Steve."

"No. You are beautiful." Reaching down he grabbed her chin and lifted her glasses up to see her eyes. Gazing deeply into them, he planted a passionate kiss to her lips.

Although they had been stewards of their promise to stay away from each other all this time, the occasion was too powerful for them both. Grabbing her hand in his, he walked his valiant lover into the main terminal.

"Come on," he said. "This calls for another celebration." He placed his arm out for her to hold onto and steered her towards the bar. He ordered them glasses of champagne. "Only the best," he said to the bartender. "This lady's just finished her cross country. She's officially a pilot."

Several people clapped for her in the bar and shouted congrats. As the champagne was served, she related all the details of the flight and her manipulation through the storm. He admitted that he had been quite worried when tower control had briefed him about it. His anxiety hadn't lessened until he saw her coming into view with his binoculars. Only then did he go down onto the tarmac.

He was seeing her as he'd never seen her. More self-confidant and alive. Which made her even more charming than before. Again she was rocking his world. After a second round, he told her "I have another surprise. I'm taking you to lunch. But not just any lunch." Famished, it was not a suggestion that was difficult to refuse.

But even so, this was her day. It was about her decisions now. And she wanted one more moment in time with the man that she loved. "Let's go!" she replied emphatically.

Steve took her arm and escorted her out of the terminal. He had driven his Mustang over and took her to a secluded part of Pensacola Beach. It was a small cove surrounded by palm trees. The inlet had a intimate, vacant beach. They walked the twenty-five yards from the car on a trail through ferns and brush and came to the shore line. "It's incredible. Just perfect," Nora was pleased.

Steve packed a picnic lunch. There was a bottle of wine, her favorite chicken salad, some grapes, strawberries and Swiss cheese. He spread out a plaid blanket onto the beach. He had another gift for her inside the basket. A light, pink box was wrapped with a black satin ribbon.

She was getting a little warm on the beach in her flight suit. As he poured her a glass of wine, she undid her zipper to the waist allowing the cool breeze to enter her chest and cool her down. This exposed the outline of her breasts. Steve recognized the black lace bra. He couldn't take his eyes off her. Just that one visual was driving him crazy.

But he wanted to take his time. This was their moment today. "I brought you another present," he said.

"Steve, you shouldn't have done all this."

"We're at a beach with water. You can't expect to swim in your flight suit, can you?"

"Not unless I was in Naval Aviator training", she teased. He presented her the box. Undoing the ribbon, she found a blue and white polka dot bikini. Steve thought of everything.

"Do you like it?"

She was thrilled. "I love it. I've seen these at the shops and have wanted one. I wondered if I was skinny enough and brave enough to wear one."

"You just were brave enough to fly a plane over three states. I think you can manage a bikini," he endorsed.

"But where will I change?"

He motioned to the empty beach. "I don't see anyone around, do you?"

She threw caution to the wind and completely unzipped her flight suit. "Oh, what the heck." Stepping out of it, he noticed she was wearing black panties to match her brassiere. God she was sexy.

She undid the bra and let it fall, placing the bikini up around her supple breasts. "Can you help me fasten it?"

He came over to her, "Certainly." He went behind her and tied the back and neck strap as she moved her hair over. Being so close to her again drove him crazy. He bent down and kissed her neck softly. Feeling the touch of his lips again drove her wild.

Steve wrapped his arms around her from behind and gave her a hug. Then his hands reached out and cupped both of her breasts. "Sheer heaven. Baby, you feel amazing." She could feel him rock hard behind her.

Though they were hungry for each other and missing each other's touch, she let the rest of the flight suit down and shimmied into the bottoms. Dashing into the emerald water, she left him momentarily standing there on the beach. He quickly took off his clothes, leaving his trunks on the beach and ran into the water after her. They splashed and played like little kids. The cove made the waves gentle from the sea and they swam out a fair way. He grabbed her while they were in the water and kissed her all over.

Seeing her so different, with her hair wet and dripping, was a huge turn on to him. As he held her close, Nora could feel him against her. She wanted him so badly. They swam back to more shallow water. Kissing him more ardently, she wrapped her legs around his waist. He slid her bikini bottoms to the side. Steve touched the tip of his penis to her fold.

"Make love to me, Steve," she said gripping her arms around his head. He pushed himself smoothly inside her and she began to move with him in the surf. The emerald green, clear water surrounding them was sensual. The waves softly pushed them back and forth. She tossed her head back in rapture, feeling him within her once again. Then she stared into his eyes intensely and kissed him. She knew this was a moment that she would share with him for the rest of their lives. The day she became his equal, a pilot. The day she tested her personal strengths and won.

He stood with his feet in the white sand and continued to thrust inside of her. This position was incredibly stimulating. She gripped him tightly and when he could hold back no more, he burst within her. Once his orgasm was over, he hugged her tightly. "My dear Nora, I wish things were so different."

"I know you do, so do I." After he withdrew himself from her, they waded back to shore.

Both were both ravenous and feasted on the delightful food he brought for picnic. As cliché as it was, they fed each other grapes. Then devoured the strawberries and cheese. Steve downed a few glasses of wine. Nora, knowing she had to fly, had less than a glass. Instead, she enjoyed the chicken salad. When she was quite full, she lay back with her head on the blanket and looked up at the sky. "I just soared among those clouds." It was pretty phenomenal to think about. "Only a few hours before, I was up in the atmosphere."

"Yep, you did. It makes me love you all the more. You are a pretty dynamic woman, Nora Jean Broussard."

"I think it's pretty incredible what we share."

Steve was ready to make love to her again. He reclined down beside her and ran his fingers along her face. Along each eyebrow, he outlined and traced them. Down her nose. Across her high cheekbones. He couldn't help but wonder what his life would be like where she his wife.

When he kissed her, their lips and tongues joined in delight. Steve reached around and undid the top of her bikini, letting it fall. "Since you can't have any more wine, I'll let you enjoy it another way." He dipped his finger into the glass and made a line down her chest. Then, he kissed her down the line of the wine, driving her mad with desire.

With more wine on his fingertip, he traced a circle around her right nipple, lowered his head to it and suckled her. He did the same on the left. Steve's eroticism was stunning. He adored every ounce of her and she him. He dripped the wine down her belly and into her naval, kissing and suckling her there. "Geez, you are driving me wild," she groaned.

Lowering her bathing suit, he took two fingers with the wine and anointed her labia. Steve bent down between her knees and began to kiss her there. Slow, long, kisses, his tongue mingling with her flesh. She took her hands and parted her lips for him. He found her clit and began flicking and suckling it with his tongue. He could tell the way her hips were gyrating around that she was about to cum. Bringing her to the most intense orgasm, she cried out in deep, deep, pleasure.

"You drive me crazy." Taking her hand, she pushed his right shoulder to lie back. After the climax he brought to her, she wanted to provide the same sensation to him. She had never gratified a man orally, but she wanted to do so for Steve.

Totally naked, she straddled him. Anticipating her moves, he lowered the swim trunks he had put on. Nora bent over him and began to kiss his neck. She could still taste the salty water from the sea on his skin. Then, she slowly moved her mouth over his chest and to his nipples. With her right hand, she tweaked his nipple and with her mouth she sucked on his left. Flicking her tongue across him, she could hear his incredible moans of pleasure. It only drove her on. Next, she took her tongue and dragged it down his chest to his naval, making circles with it there.

Nora could see that he was erect and ready for her. Sitting across his legs, she then bent her head to the tip of his penis as she held it. She began to run her tongue around the head of it in circles. Then, she took the head into her mouth and sucked gently, cupping her lips around his rim. Next, she kissed down his shaft, around the base of him and up the other side. Long, luxurious, wet kisses. All the while, massaging his testicles in her hand.

Nora could feel him become even more firm and rigid. Moaning, he told her desperately, "I'm gonna cum."

"Wait for me," she pleaded. She was still wet from her own orgasm and raised up on her knees positioning herself over him. With her hand, she guided him to her pussy and slipped him inside.

"Oh, baby. You're amazing." He began to push himself deeper inside. Flexing her thighs she lowered herself onto him, moving his entire shaft fully within. She began to sway her hips, folding her arms back behind her head. She was glorious. He held her hips as she rocked against him back and forth. Back and forth. Writhing and twisting and turning her body. Her eyes were closed and her head was tilted towards the sky in ecstasy.

Her beautiful breasts, her narrow waist, and holding her hips against him brought about the most intense requisite for orgasm. When he was sure they were both ready to cum, he quickened his strokes and she matched his pace. Within seconds, they cataclysmically came together. For Steve, it was the sweetest orgasm of his life. She could feel how wet she was, filled with his semen.

Exhausted, she collapsed down on his chest and he cradled her there. "You realize we have given in . . . to what we held at bay. Nora, what we've done is so incredibly wrong," he began.

"On so many levels," she interjected.

"But to hell with rules. I love you. Damn it. I don't care. I love you more than anything in the world," he professed to her.

"I love you too, Steve. As complicated as it is, I love

you too." They fell asleep holding each other on the beach for a brief nap. When they awoke, they realized it was time to go.

Nora was a chasm of confused emotions, for she knew he might never make love to her this way again. Their love was star-crossed for sure. He realized the futility of it too. Catholics with children just did not divorce. The thought for both of them was arbitrary. He knew the church would not support Nora's reasons for divorce, despite her lousy marriage.

She slowly redressed in her flight suit and boots in silence. Words need not be spoken to communicate how they both felt. He walked with her, hand in hand, back to the Mustang and drove back to the airport. Both were reflective in the stolen moments they had just shared and were quiet.

Steve made sure the controllers knew her flight plan. He watched from the observation deck as she strode out alone out to the plane, completed her inspections and got into the cockpit.

Once clearance was verified, she prepared for takeoff. The emotions of the day came over her and as she lifted off, she burst into tears. In some bittersweet irony, the happiest day of her life was marred with pangs of sadness and foreboding. Nearly dusk, her flight back was quite uneventful. She made her well instructed communications and landed the leased Piper safely back at Lakefront. Nora knew she wouldn't see him there, as Pensacola was almost a four hour drive from New Orleans. Anticlimactically, she got into her station wagon and drove home.

Chapter 21
∞ September, 1961 ∞

The rest of the summer dragged on incessantly. The humidity was almost unbearable. When they weren't sewing, Charlene and Nora spent many afternoons sweating in the heat while watching their children swim at the country club pool. In their big floppy hats to protect their skin and sipping mint julep cocktails; they counted the days until school began.

When September finally came and the children started back, they made plans to work on the beading for Kayce's Mardi Gras ball dress. Nora walked around the block to Charlene's carrying the large dress box.

Greeting her friend at the door, Charlene helped her with the bulky parcel. Opening it, she took out the pale yellow gown. "Oh, it's lovely. Absolutely lovely. You did a splendid job, Nora. Kayce is going to look simply smashing."

"I appreciate you saying that," said Nora.

"It will be sublime when we finish the beadwork."

"That's where I need your help."

The elaborate beading, with mother of pearl and crystals in an intricate pattern was challenging. Charlene explained how to thread and track them through. As they beaded, she began to fill her in on the latest news. She blathered on about children, Max, business, and the juiciest gossip from the club. With all of Nora's flying, she hadn't seen her in weeks.

All of a sudden, Nora looked a little pale. "Are you okay?" Charlene asked. Nora figured her blood sugar was low, since that morning, she experienced another wave of morning sickness. Evidently, it had not gone away. She quickly dashed to the bathroom.

Charlene heard her vomit and gag with dry heaves, since there was nothing on her stomach. "Nora Jean, are you alright?"

"I am fine," Nora denied, head in the bowl.

"Do you think that you have a virus? Or food poisoning? It was no doubt from that Junior League luncheon a couple of weeks back and all that nasty crab salad. I think they let it get too warm. There wasn't even an R in the month." Nora retched again. "They should know better than to serve crustaceans in late August," Charlene prattled.

It was time that Charlene knew the truth. "No, that's not it," Nora professed.

"Well, here honey, let me help you." Charlene got a wet cloth for comfort. She rubbed the coolness on the back of Nora's neck and her forehead like she would do her own children.

Once the nausea stopped, Nora stood and faced her friend. "Let's sit down. I have something important to tell you."

Charlene followed her back into the sewing room. "Nora, what's going on?"

Nora began to explain. "I got a call from the doctor's office. I'm pregnant."

"My stars, Nora. Baby number five?" she lamented. "Is this cause for congratulations? I didn't think you and Frank were even still having sex. Mercy me."

"No, you don't understand. This baby isn't Frank's."

Charlene was rendered speechless and her hands flew up to cover her mouth. She just sat there blinking.

"Well?" said Nora.

"I . . . I don't know what to say. What a mess. Hells bells, whatever are you going to do?"

"I have no idea. I guess the writing is on the wall. I anticipated it would be."

"Whatever do you mean?"

"I've been dreading the confrontation with Frank about divorce. Now, I have no choice but to go through with it."

"You're gonna ask for a divorce, even with a baby on the way? Frank would stroke if he knew it wasn't his. Are you sure it isn't?"

"Quite sure. So I am certainly not going to stay with Frank now," Nora asserted.

"Does Steve know? About the baby?"

"No, not yet. You're the only one who I've told. But I fear Kayce knows too."

"Kayce? How does she know?"

"She was listening in on the other line when the doctor's office called." Nora was still extremely pale and weak.

"Oh, my goodness. Could this get any worse?" Charlene was shaking her head.

"Sure," Nora continued. "We already know that Steve won't leave his wife, so I will be a divorcee with five kids."

"Nora. I'd offer you a drink but I guess that's not an option."

"Not for nine months," scoffed Nora. She pulled out her cigarettes and got ready to light one up.

"Oh, no you don't Nora Jean Broussard. You hear what they're saying about women who smoke while they are pregnant. I've seen the ads on the TV." She took the cigarettes from Nora and put them in the garbage. "You have to promise me you're gonna give 'em up."

"Jesus, you can be difficult."

"This calls for a cup of tea, come on. Either that or a glass of warm milk."

"Please, no milk," Nora begged, feeling her stomach turn over.

Charlene put the kettle on. "We need to wrap our heads around this and formulate a plan."

"Let's hope Kayce doesn't tell Frank before I have a chance to."

"Well, toots, then you had better get on with it. Knowing the firestorm your relationship is with Kayce, all it will take is one spat and she'll spill the beans."

"Yeah, that's what I was afraid of."

"I tell you what, let's do this." Charlene was already forging ahead. "First, I want to make sure we look into getting you a lawyer. A damned good one. We wanna know exactly who that person is before this all goes down." Charlene put the tea bags into her china cups. "Next, we have to make sure the confrontation takes place when the children aren't at home. God knows, Frank is going to go ballistic. I wish you could hire yourself a body guard."

"I wish I had the money to. Unfortunately, I spent most of it on flying lessons."

"Hmph, I worried about that since you were keeping it a secret."

Charlene's cogs were turning. "I gotta ask ya. When you and Steve were together, did it dawn on you to use any kind of protection? I mean, Nora you're not a naïve little teeny bopper."

"No, that's just it. The first time, it happened so spontaneously, neither one of us thought of it. And I guess it was just the wrong time of the month to conceive." She took a sip of the peppermint tea. "I've only had actual intercourse with him twice. Well, on two separate occasions."

"Ohhh, Fertile Myrtle strikes again," Charlene wailed putting her hand fretfully over her brow. "I remember Nellie saying it. Ugh, Nellie. Whatever are you going to do about her?"

"I haven't gotten that far yet. But I really don't want her to know."

"How do you expect to keep it from her? She lives right here in the city."

Nora shook her head. This was more than a mess.

"Nursing's a pretty small community, not to mention the size you are going to be. You won't be able to write it off to just getting fat."

"I just can't bring myself to involve her."

"And what are you going to do? Just not see her for nine new moons?"

"That's just a whole 'nuther compendium of problems that I don't want to deal with. It'll be earth shattering enough finding out about the divorce."

"Oh, honey. I don't envy walking in your shoes for the next few weeks and months. But 'cha know I'll be there for you."

"Yeah, I know you will."

The wheels of Charlene's mind were still spinning rapid fire as she paced her kitchen. "I'll tell you what. If you're ready and up to it, I think I have an idea. Next month, they're showin' a special of the *Wizard of Oz*. I know about it from one of those *TV Guides*."

"A what?"

"That's some magazine about what's on TV." Charlene was up on all the latest fads. "Max picked it up when he bought us our new set."

Nora glanced over into the den, "Your new set is fabulous."

"Yes, it's the latest thing. Technicolor. Everything comes out in color. Most of the programs anyway. Some are still coming in black and white. But the kids adore it."

"The plan?" Nora tried to re-channel her.

"Right. How about I have a sleep over and they can watch the movie. That will leave you alone to lower the boom on Frank. We have to keep the kids out of it. What you do think? At least that gives us a few weeks to find a good attorney."

"It might work," said Nora. "Oh, Charlene what would I ever do without you?" Nora was thankful for her friend's cunning ingenuity. And her non-judgment.

"I don't know and I don't plan to find out. We'll get through it honey. One way or another."

Chapter 22
∞ October, 1961 ∞

Kayce so admired the big full skirt and beaded bodice of her princess gown, that she hung it proudly outside her closet. The dress required many hours of sewing on the part of her mother and Charlene. She planned to keep it on display even though it was only fall. Bacchus wasn't until March, another five months away. She placed her white patent leather shoes below it and hung the small princess tiara from the hangar. The pretty ensemble had become a shrine.

That afternoon Kayce was in the den listening to her brand new Shirelles LP. Nora purchased it to placate her. As she grooved to the tunes, she didn't notice that her little sister, Cathy snuck into her room. Kayce, as the oldest child, had her own bedroom. The two younger sisters, Cathy and Leisel had to share. Iggy, being the only boy, had the converted nursery to himself.

Standing up on a chair, Cathy strained and got the yellow ball gown down from the hangar to try it on. It swallowed her as she modeled in the mirror. She didn't see Kayce bop back into room.

When Kayce saw her in the gown, she was livid. "Stop it! Stop it," she screamed. "That's mine."

"I'm not doing anything, just trying on your stinking little dress."

"You leave it alone. I'm gonna be a Junior Princess and you're not."

Cathy stuck out her tongue at her, "Who'd wanna be some fairy princess?" Cathy was the tomboy, riding bikes and playing sports. She was the star player at basketball in fifth grade. Girl Scouts and going to camp each summer were her passion. She played all kinds of games with little brother Iggy, which Kayce abhorred.

Kayce stood watch as Cathy took off the dress. "Be careful. I don't want you to rip it." She carefully re-hung the dress and placed the shoes right below. Realizing how much she adored her dress, she suddenly felt guilty about how she had been treating her mother as of late. She went into kitchen where Nora was cooking red beans and rice and hugged her. "Mama, my dress is beautiful."

"I'm glad you like it doll face. I know you're just gonna be beautiful in it." Nora didn't have the heart to tell her that Mardi Gras, as they knew it, might not happen that year; once she asked for a divorce.

"I just wanted to thank you. And I'm sorry I've been so mean to you lately."

Nora couldn't believe that Kayce was apologizing to her. Recently, Kayce had been a monster, making daily coexistence with her hell. "I'm glad you like it darling. I think you will be a beautiful princess." It felt good to have Kayce's hugs again.

"I'm sorry I got so angry at you about the baby. Daddy will sure be excited."

Nora's happiness faded. She had to think fast. "Let's not say anything to Daddy. He is under a lot of stress with work. We'll save it as a surprise for now. Can you keep Mommy's little secret?"

"Sure," said Kayce.

It was now only a few weeks before Halloween. Besides making Kayce's dress, Nora was frantically trying to finish the kid's Halloween costumes. She had put the Christmas outfits on the back burner. This year they were going as characters from the Wizard of Oz. Charlene's initial plot failed. The kids saw the movie at Charlene's house, but Nora had yet to get up the courage to ask Frank for the divorce. She stalled for more time.

Nora had become an excellent seamstress. She adored sewing for them. When she was stressed or needed time to think she would sew, finding solace at her machine.

Preparing ahead, Nora was in the process of making several a-line dresses and tops for herself. She was two and a half months pregnant and not really showing yet, but she wanted to hide it as long as possible. The cuts would afford just enough room to hide her future pregnancy pooch. It was advantageous that she was long-wasted.

The clock was ticking to revise a plan of what to do. At this point only three people knew, herself, Kayce and Charlene.

Having put it off for months, Nora made it a point to speak with the priest today. He was holding penance services. Being a Mabel day, she could get away for a bit by herself. Uncharacteristically, Mabel was running late.

She entered the kitchen hurriedly, "Mornin' Missus Nora. How you be? Sorry, I's late. I missed da first bus."

"It's alright Mabel, relax. I'm good. How's Big Daddy treating you?"

"Just fine, Miss Nora. He gots a new job in da Quarter. Working maintenance at some clubs."

"That is wonderful news. Listen, Mabel, the kids are off from school today and playing. There's some egg salad in the fridge. I'm gonna run a few errands. I should be back right after lunch. Okay?" Nora said getting her keys to the wagon.

"Okey doke, Missus Nora. We be awright."

Nora summoned up courage to talk to Father Timothy today about the divorce and what it would mean for herself and her children. St. Francis Xavier was a couple of blocks away on Metairie Road. She waited with other parishioners in the creaky old pews until it was her turn for the confessional. She was wearing a big scarf around her hair and large sunglasses to not be recognized. She was glad the church was dark.

Stepping into confessional, she knelt down on the kneeler and finally removed her glasses. "Bless me father for I have sinned. It has been several months . . . um . . . since my last confession." She started to stammer.

"It's okay my child, whatever you have to tell me you can," the priest offered.

She began to weep. "Oh, Father . . . you don't understand. It is the worst thing I have ever done."

"Open your heart and feel free to share with me," her priest encouraged.

"It's dreadful," whispered Nora. She began to tell her story. About the fights with her husband. How hard she had tried to make the marriage work. Frank's drinking. The women. His pushing, shoving and obscenities.

Then she told him about how she met Steve. The affair and adultery. She waited for a sound of shock or disbelief.

The priest took a big breath and began to speak, "What you have done is against God's holy law and the ten commandments. You know which ones you have broken. But God is a forgiving God and will absolve you from your sins. However, my dear, you must promise to end this relationship and hold tight to your marriage. For you have made vows before God. You cannot break that covenant."

Nora wasn't surprised at the expected response. Forgiveness, okay. But no matter what a bastard you were married to, stay wed.

"For these sins, I request the following penance of you . . ."

Before he began, Nora interrupted, "Wait. You don't understand. I can't end it."

"You must," ordered Father Timothy.

"No. No. It's not that . . . I am . . ." she couldn't bring herself to say pregnant, so she paused. "I am going to ask for a divorce. My husband is cruel to me."

There was a long silence and a change in the priest's demeanor. "I would caution you against this decision. My dear, divorce is not supported by the Catholic Church. When you took your vows, they were for life."

"Yes, father."

"Should you choose to go against the church's wishes, you will be excommunicated and fall out of favor with your faith. It is not a step that the church recommends. And it is certainly not a step I am recommending. You need to tread carefully here and understand your place as a wife and mother. I think you should put that idea out of your head."

Nora was shattered. "I see, Father," was all she could manage. She didn't know what she had expected. Acceptance? Understanding? Forgiveness? Evidently, forgiveness for the church came with strings attached. At this point she certainly wasn't going to say anything about the baby she was carrying.

After the priest gave her penance, she exited the confessional. Nora knelt in adjacent pew and stared up at the stained glass rose window above the altar. She didn't bother to finish the prayers. Taking out her rosary and prayer book, she was tempted to leave them in pew. She knew what she had done was wrong, but believed that she was not an evil person.

Leaving St. Xavier, Nora was distraught. She drove to the French Quarter and went for a long walk to sort out her thoughts. Climbing the steps to the levy, she turned around and looked at St. Louis cathedral. So many years, she had knelt in those historic, dark oak pews. So many rosaries. So many masses. Such hopes. Such faith.

Nora made a profound decision. Some God, maybe not this Catholic one, was forgiving. Taking her rosary from her pocket, she hurled it into the turbulent waters of the Mississippi below. In that moment, she vowed never to return to the Catholic Church again.

Chapter 23
∞ November, 1961 ∞

Halloween came and went. Her children looked adorable in their Wizard of Oz outfits. Preparations were underway for the huge Thanksgiving celebration at the Greenwoods. Nellie was elated to receive her invitation. Nora dreaded it, knowing that her mother would take one look and know she was pregnant.

After her meeting at the church had gone so poorly, Nora reviewed what few options remained. She went over and over the dismal choices. As promised, Charlene had come up with a fantastic, powerful divorce attorney. However, Nora couldn't afford the retainer to get started. Despite that fact, time was accelerating. At four month's pregnant, she decided that tonight was the night she would demand a divorce.

She arranged with Charlene for her kids to sleep over. As they had previously discussed, what she had to tell Frank was explosive. She didn't want them anywhere near. The kids were happy to go see Saturday night's *Gunsmoke* though still in black and white.

Nora was on edge as she waited for Frank to come home from his golf afternoon. As usual, he stayed at the club into early evening, having drinks. There was now a soft rain falling.

Despite the doctor recommending not to smoke, Nora couldn't help herself. She lit up her second Benson and Hedges and paced the living room until she heard Frank's car drive up. When he came in the door, he threw down his golf bag. "So where are the kids?" he asked.

"Over at Charlene's watching something on color TV."

"Good. Great," he exclaimed, much relieved of their absence. Frank poured himself another drink. "I need a break."

"Did your game not go well?" she asked rhetorically.

"Yeah, you could say that." He began to describe what holes he had parred and bogied. As he rambled on, Nora summoned up her courage.

"Frank, the reason the kids are at Charlene's is because there's something I need to talk to you about".

"There's always a reason. Some God damned reason. And what would that be tonight Nora? Overdrawn on your charge accounts again? Just call my office; I am sure they'll cover it."

"No, Frank. I think you need to sit down."

He gave her a dubious look. She'd drawn up some notes and had them on the dining room table. Nora was so afraid, she was visibly shaking. At this point, Frank could tell by looking at her that something was up.

"What have you botched this time?"

"Frank, I . . ." she was having trouble getting started. She took a deep swallow and decided to just blurt it out. "Frank, I'm not happy and I want a divorce."

He cleared his throat, and grunted. "A divorce?" he looked stupefied. "You want a divorce from me? Have you lost your mind?" he derided. "What the hell, Nora?" he began to explode, chugging the rest of his drink whole.

"Yes, Frank. That is what I am telling you. You know you haven't been happy with me for quite some time."

"Let me get this right. You want to divorce me, Frank Greenwood? Are you fucking kidding me Nora?"

"No," she said resolutely.

"You've been watching too many soap operas. We're Catholics. Divorce? No."

"Well, I have already made up my mind. I think it would be best."

"And exactly how would you support yourself? Crocheting booties and selling them at the French Market?" he hollered.

"I haven't thought that far ahead yet, Frank. But you have to admit, you know I don't make you happy."

"That's par for the course. But so what? This is a

bunch of bullshit, Nora."

"The only time you want me sexually is when you need to get your rocks off. You don't care about me or my feelings as a person. I am just your brood mare."

"You are so full of crap."

"No, I'm not. You don't give a darn about what I think. Or what I feel."

"Feelings? I have given you everything," he waved his arms around the room. "I've put up with all your crazy ideas. And trips. And shopping. Hell, my Mother got you into the damned Junior League so that you'd be accepted as a part our social strata."

"You just don't get it, Frank."

"Well then what *is* it then?"

She was on a roll. "For one thing? It's your excessive drinking. You are nothing but a belligerent, alcoholic, abusive, jerk."

With that, Frank exploded. He lunged at Nora, but she dodged him. Or so she thought.

Shoving her, he began to rant. "You little Cajun bitch. How dare you ask for a divorce from me? After everything my family has done for you."

Nora knew he had some valid points, but remained undeterred. "For everything they have done for me Frank, I have given back tenfold." She was regaining her stand from the shove, nearly losing her balance.

"You're ridiculous, Nora." Frank gulped down his drink and went for more liquor on the sideboard.

"What about what I have done for you? I've put with your drunken, raging fits. Your verbal abuse. Your shoving. All of your controlling. With everything that you've prevented me from doing for years," she continued to rant. "When you prevented me from going to school. When you prevented me from having a career. When you held me back from anything," she continued to spew forth her requiem. "I have produced four children for you. Including a son. Hell, I was a baby making machine until you got what you wanted and all the while never complained," she screamed. "Frank, you are nothing but an asshole."

With that comment, she incited him. Before realizing what happened, she felt a walloping whack to the side of her cheek. This time, he had gone too far. In his drunken rage, this time Frank actually hit her.

The sound of the thud resonated in her head. He struck Nora so hard, she completely lost her balance. She felt an intense amount of pain and a cracking sound as she hit the ground. Touching the side of her lip, she felt blood there.

"You bastard," she wailed. "You absolute hideous bastard."

For a moment he looked horrified at what he had done, but then his expression turned to rage. Frank went to the fireplace and grabbed a poker. He swung it at her and missed, as she rolled and cowered on the floor. He hit the coffee table glass and smashed it into bits.

"Get out you stinking guttersnipe. Just get out." Swinging it again in her direction, he hit the fireplace. "You want a divorce? Then get your ass out," he screamed.

He stomped off toward their bedroom, poker in hand, and whacked a hole in the hallway wall. Entering, he stalked toward the closet. Frank began to drag out her clothes. He ripped them off their hangers and threw them into a pile. Then, he gathered it up and trudged to the front door. Flinging it open, he threw her things into the yard. Shoes, purses, handbags, suits. Anything and everything.

"Stop it. Stop it," she pleaded.

"You want out, Nora?" he raged. "Well this is how you're gonna get out. This is how it's gonna be. You're gonna be nothin' but a guttersnipe in the street. Take what crap I've thrown out and get the fuck out of my life!"

Nora was anxious to get away from his path, fearful he might strike her again. While Frank made another trip to the closet, she scrambled up and eloped to the door. All she had on was a sweater and a pair of trousers. She grabbed her purse from the front lawn.

It was a two block walk to Charlene's and the rain continued to pour, soaking her to the bone. Her head was beginning to throb with intense pain that extended from her jaw to her cheek. She wondered if the fall had hurt the baby. What she hadn't noticed was the purple swelling of her left eye which was turning black and blue.

Frightened she would pass out and fall, she made her way down the street as quickly as she could. It was now dark and the only light was from the gas street lamps flickering in the finely manicured yards of her neighborhood. But she was glad, for she didn't wish any of her neighbors to see the beat up, unkempt state she was in.

When Nora rang Charlene's doorbell, she was thankful it was her best friend who answered. Charlene cried out in horror as she saw Nora's face. "Oh my God, bejeezus, what has he done to you? Look at your face!" She had no doubt how Nora had ended up in this state. She was sure it was at the hands of Frank. "Come in, come in," she said wrapping her arms around Nora's shoulders.

Charlene accompanied her into the house. At the site of Charlene, Nora was reduced to tears. However, she tried to be quiet, not wanting her children to realize she was there.

"Christ have mercy! What in tarnation happened?" Charlene asked.

"Sshhh . . . I don't want the kids to know."

"Okay," whispered Charlene. "Let's go up the back way." She snuck through her dining room and to the back stairs of the kitchen. The children were glued to the TV set in the den. She helped Nora up the stairs and into her bedroom, assisting her to sit on the bed. Nora looked weak and in a state of shock.

"What on earth happened?"

"I tried to ask him for a divorce. That was all it took."

"That ogre, I can't believe he hit you. But I'm not surprised. I've always thought that was the way things were headed. And even when you're pregnant?" She had her hand over her mouth as she saw the extent of the damage to Nora's face.

"No, no. Frank doesn't know about that."

"You didn't tell him about the baby? Oh, Nora you look dreadful. Here," she handed her friend a wet washcloth. "Let me go downstairs and get an icepack for your face."

It was then Nora stepped into the bathroom and saw in the mirror how horrendous her face looked. Still stunned and in a state of shock, she licked her lip and noticed the salty taste from the blood dripping. He had really lost it this time. Thank God. Thank God it's over, she thought. Finally she'd confronted him about the divorce. "At least I'm on the road to getting away from him," she murmured looking in the mirror at the damage. But she had paid a high price in return.

Charlene returned with the ice pack. Her dear, sweet, sister-like Charlene was caring for her. "When you asked him for the divorce, what did he say?"

"You can see the result," she said touching to her face. "That's when he flew into a rage."

"What are the terms?"

"Terms? He kicked me out. The terms are that he threw my things out into the rain in the front yard."

"Do you get to keep your house?"

"Doubtful. Hell, I don't even have a car? Clearly, we never got that far."

"Right. I'm sorry. I am just not thinking right," Charlene apologized realizing how stupid her questions were.

"After he hit me, I wanted to get away before he struck me again. All he could threaten me with was 'how dare I?' How dare I divorce one of the almighty Green-woods."

Nora dabbed the icepack to her eye. "He thought I was daft. I don't think he really took me seriously."

"Well, you are going through with it aren't you? You can't stay with him now."

"God yes. Do I have any choice at this point?" She motioned to her stomach.

"I guess not. My stars, Nora . . . what a nightmare. But I want to make sure that physically you are okay.

"Yes, I'm alright. I hope the baby's okay. I fell pretty hard." Charlene just now thought about the baby. Nora hid her pregnancy well.

"This was a long time coming. Long before the com-plications with Steve. I've hated the way Frank treated me since our honeymoon."

"Agreed. We just have to figure out how to pay for that lawyer," Charlene was telling her. She almost didn't hear the doorbell. Max was downstairs and answered the front door. As Charlene descended the stairs, she could hear shouting in the foyer.

"Where is she? Where is that little cunt Nora Green-wood?" Frank bellowed. He had the poker waving wildly above his head.

Before Max had a chance to answer, Charlene bounded down the stairs and intervened, "I don't know what you are talking about. Nora's not here. But your kids are. They are spending the night after watching our color TV."

Max adeptly stepped in front of him. "Frank. Put down the poker. Now," he commanded.

"Or we'll call the police," Charlene chimed in.

Frank dropped it clanking onto the tile floor. Then, he barged past them both and strode into the den. "Come kids, let's go."

"What? Why Daddy?" their confused voices asked.

"Because I said so. Get your stuff. We are going home."

"But the show is still on," Cathy stated.

"Yeah, we can't go . . . it's just where the bad guys get rounded up," chimed in little Iggy.

"I don't give a crap. I am taking you home now. I'm your father and what I say goes," he boomed.

"Frank, just calm down. It's not only your kids that are hearing your yelling." She put her arm around her own, who looked horrified at his behavior. "You just need to settle down. I know you and Nora have had another fight. She called me on the phone." Max gave her a look, knowing Nora was still upstairs. Charlene lied to cover her friend's tracks.

"I think it would be better to have the kids stay here for the night, until you've gotten control of yourself. Besides, you're drunk. It's likely not a good idea to take them in the car with you." Charlene knew she was playing with fire when she made that statement.

"Max, tell your wife to mind her own God damned business and back off. They're my kids and I can do with them whatever I like."

"Now, Frank. Don't be talking to my wife like that." Max defended.

Charlene knew the predicament. Once the kids were back with him at the house on Woodvine, Nora would have no access to them. Yet, she felt caught in a Catch-

22. She was desperate to protect Nora who was still hiding upstairs. She feared that if Frank detected she was there, he would kill her.

Determined that the children were not going to see their mother attacked with further violence, she made the only choice possible. The kids had to go with Frank. Temporarily.

Kayce looked embarrassed. Cathryn confused. Leisel and Iggy upset because the show was still on. In spite of that, she gathered their things and did as Frank asked. Charlene hated that they were getting into the car with a drunk driver. At least it was only two blocks.

"What the heck was that all about?" a startled Max asked her as they left. Sweet Max, thought Charlene, she didn't have the heart to burst his deluded bubble regarding their best friends. At least not now. He had absolutely no idea the true extent and turmoil of the Greenwood's marriage. For up until now, they kept it well hidden.

"I think it is only the tip of the iceberg. There are stormy waters yet to come," she offered.

After Charlene was sure Frank's car had pulled out of the driveway, she returned upstairs to check on Nora. Nora was distraught and nearly hysterical. She had heard it all. "My kids, my kids. Christ, he has my kids. What am I going to do?" she cried in agony.

"I don't know," said Charlene. "We had to make a decision. To let him take the children or let him find you here. Nora, he was armed. He would have utterly come unglued had he caught on. The children were a buffer."

"He was in such a rage. I know you're right, but I have to get them back. I have to find some way."

"You will," Charlene comforted her. "We'll help you. After what I've seen tonight, I'm gonna ask Max to help you pay for that lawyer. Because taking on the Greenwoods, you're gonna need one. They're just so darned powerful. I'm sure that first thing tomorrow, Frank will be on the phone to the best divorce lawyers in town. With all his connections and endless money, they will crucify you."

"That's what scares me," trembled Nora.

"He can't find you here. What about Nellie? Can you stay with her?"

"Stay with Nellie and destroy her dreams of me being married to the Greenwoods of New Orleans? Geez, no. I can't. She would have a coronary. Not only that, but she would take one look at me and know there something up."

"Yep, you are right."

"She's going to find out soon enough. God forbid she discovers I'm pregnant from an affair. It would be the scandalous."

"With Frank hittin' you, I almost forgot," Charlene exclaimed. "What on earth are you going to do about that?" she pointed to Nora's tummy. "Have you even told Steve?"

"No, he still has no idea." Then it suddenly struck her. The other person that knew besides herself and Charlene. Kayce. "I just remembered, Kayce knows too."

"Well, shit," Charlene cursed. A shocker Nora had never heard before.

Nora was desperate to keep the secret intact. Now that Kayce was with her father and would hear about the divorce, there was no guarantee. She really wasn't sure if her daughter might be swayed to take sides. Nora knew that Kayce would be furious. All of her hopes, plans and dreams would be dashed. There would be no Bacchus ball. No Junior princess. No big family Christmas at the Greenwoods. Her country club lifestyle would be over. In one single moment, Kayce's life as she knew it had gone up in smoke.

Nora naively hoped Kayce would recover. Hopefully in time, even forgive her for ruining their lives with this tumultuous sequence of events. Little did she know just a few blocks over, hell was breaking loose.

By some miracle, Frank managed to negotiate the turns up the road with Nora's station wagon. He unloaded the kids and tripped over the front step into the house, managing to catch himself.

Kayce knew he had been drinking heavily. She could smell the alcohol. "What's wrong Daddy? What is going on?" In his drunken state, she wasn't sure she would get the right answer but asked him anyway.

"What's wrong," he slurred, "is that your mother is a selfish bitch and has asked for a divorce."

"A divorce?" Kayce was dumbstruck. "But you can't

divorce, we're Catholic."

"Tell your mother that," her father belched.

"Oh, no. What is mother thinking? It must be her hormones. Or maybe she's just upset that she's having another baby."

Frank was momentarily aroused out of his drunken stupor. "A what?" he questioned her.

It never dawned on young Kayce that her mother had never told her father about the pregnancy. In Kayce's mind, her father had paternity to that child. In that instant, she had created a firestorm.

Frank's wrath boiled over. He staggered into the master bedroom and stood at Nora's vanity. "You fucking little whore," he said. Picking up her perfume, he threw it and smashed it into the mirror. He knew they had not been intimate in months.

Taking his arm, he swiped all of her religious statues and items from her dresser onto the floor. Next, he ripped open her jewelry box throwing it all onto the carpet. "You stupid, slutty cunt." He raged on. The pocket watch that Nora's father had given her fell onto the floor and he smashed it to bits with his foot. That act was all he could manage. Frank suddenly broke down in tears and wept. Slinking next to their bed, he eventually passed out from his intoxication.

Kayce had no idea why her father was so enraged. Nora had managed to keep the clandestine meetings with Steve a total secret. It was only Charlene who knew the full story. Walking into the master bedroom, she noted her father unconscious on the floor. At first, she ran over in concern. But then, she heard his snoring and realized he was just drunk. Getting a blanket from the closet she put it over him. He never stirred.

Next, she went into the living room, gathered up her younger siblings and readied them for bed. She made them put on their pajamas and brush their teeth. She closed the master bedroom door, so that they didn't see the state of their father.

Finally, she went back into her room. Still hanging on the closet door was the beautiful gown her mother had made. Kayce wasn't crying for she had no idea the depth of what was really going on. She was clueless that in a few short weeks, everything would be turned totally upside down. As far as she was concerned, her parents had only gotten into another cat fight. This time, Kayce assumed, it had been so severe her mother spent the night somewhere else. Perchance at Nellie's. For Kayce, it was just another Saturday evening. For Nora it was the devastating start of a nightmare to come, the eye of the hurricane.

Chapter 24

The next morning, Frank woke with a massive headache and hangover. He was still reeling from the news of the previous night. As he recalled the information, he began seething with anger. Nora pregnant? Was that what Kayce said? He couldn't remember all of the details from the previous night. It was sketchy at best.

He was trying to do the math in his head, which was impossible. Not only from his hangover. Frank had no idea how far along she was in conception. She certainly hadn't told anyone. He was trying to think of the last time that he had fucked her. But he couldn't wrap his head around an exact time frame. Pregnant. Divorce. He kept trying to remember.

Maybe he could talk some sense into her and call it off. Divorce was simply not an option in his family. The hitch was he had no idea where she could be. He speculated that after she left, she might have gone to Charlene's. But the station wagon was still in the driveway, parked where he had used it to pick up the kids the night before. It wasn't impossible that she walked to the club and caught a taxi, taking it across town to her mother Nellie's.

At this point, Frank decided not to call Nora's mother. He just didn't want to hear her histrionics. He certainly wasn't going to be telling the Greenwoods either. He would nurse his hangover and try to take care of some business he had taken home. He needed time to mulch it all over.

Kayce was suddenly at the doorway. "Daddy what are we having for breakfast?" Frank had not given it a second thought. "Uggh, the kids," he remembered rubbing his aching head. It was Nora who always provided their meals and managed their daily needs. Cooking, cleaning, and taking care of the house were not his concern. "I don't know," he blubbered. "Go walk to the market or just have cereal."

So by default, Kayce picked up her mother's duties and got four cereal bowls from the cabinet. Her siblings were unmindful to what was going on. For all they knew, their mother was away at some charity function or mass. Sunday cartoons were on. They sat in front of the set eating their cereal on TV trays in the den. By lunch time, they still had not heard from Nora. Frank was beginning to question if she was going to return.

Impatient, he decided to find out for himself. Her clothes were still in the front lawn. What must the neighbors think? "Kayce, get your brother and sisters out front and pick up your mother's crap out there."

Kayce looked out the front window at the mess of clothes that were now soaking wet. She hadn't seen them in the dark the night before. Humiliated, they now looked like trailer trash. "But, Daddy, it's raining." Kayce didn't want to go do such an embarrassing task.

"It's only a drizzle. Do what I said, Kayce." His voice was getting louder.

"Oh, alright. Alright." She corralled up her siblings and they went outside with paper bags. "Ugh, this is niggers work."

"Kayce, that's the N word. I'm gonna tell Mama and you're gonna get it." Cathy threatened.

"Oh, really smarty pants. Well, where in the heck do you even think she is? Do you see her around? I'm soooo worried."

Cathy hadn't really thought about why her mother wasn't home. She certainly had no idea why her mother's clothes and shoes were all over the yard. Nonetheless, she continued to pick up the sopping items and put them in the bags.

After they were finished, they sat the bags in the

foyer. "What would you like us to do with it all?"

"I don't really give a damn. Put it in the garbage," her father said coldly.

Things must be worse than Kayce thought. She just couldn't throw her mother's things away, so she shoved all the bags in the laundry room.

Frank gave Charlene a call. The phone rang and rang and rang, but no one answered. He reckoned Max was predictably out on the golf course. There would be no answers about her whereabouts for now.

But Charlene had heard the phone ringing and so had Nora. They assumed correctly it was Frank. Sitting in her kitchen, Charlene fretted as Nora tried to figure out what she was going to do. Charlene had fixed her a poached egg and toast, but Nora could eat nothing. "Honey, you really should eat something, you're gonna need your strength."

"I just can't. I have too much on my mind. Gosh, Charlene, those look awful." In her hands, Charlene had the Polaroids that she had taken the night before of Nora's injuries. Nora was thankful she now had evidence of his abuse. She would need some grounds for the divorce and resulting custody battle that she anticipated Frank would wage out of pride.

Pragmatism in full force, Charlene was thinking about where Nora might go. With no legal safeguards in place, her home was too close in proximity for Nora to be safe lodging there. She dreaded telling her friend. "Look Nora, you know I would have you stay here in any other circumstance."

"I get that," said Nora. "Frank would figure it out."

"And I am hating it. Just hating it that you are my best friend and I can't offer you refuge."

"It's okay," said Nora. "I understand. I'll figure it out. But if I could ask you one favor. Can you take me out to the airfield? I really need to talk to Steve."

"Sure Nora, anything. Anything you want."

The first thing Nora had to do was tell Steve. It was high time he knew about the baby. She just had not contrived a way to do it. Nora's clothes were a shambles from the night before. There were blood stains and her blouse was ripped. Charlene went to her closet and pulled out some things to loan her. They were about the same size, as Nora was only just beginning to show. She pulled out some loose fitting tops and pants with elastic waist lines. A couple of pairs of shoes and a purse.

She also opened her vanity drawer and removed a large pair of sunglasses. "Here, darling, a must," she said. Nora's eye had become a fully gloried, black and blue shiner of three inches width. The lid was drooping. The bottom of her left lip was split and swollen, but other than that, her face was intact. By some miracle, she avoided getting stitches. Charlene had applied a butterfly strip to hold the laceration together.

Getting out an overnight bag, Charlene packed the clothes. "Where do you think you are going to stay?"

"I don't know." said, Nora. "I still just can't think. At the moment, I just have to get through today. One task at a time. I'm trying to decide what to tell Steve."

"Oh dear, and all those children he has. And they are so Catholic. Do you think it's possible he might ask his wife for a divorce too?"

"I doubt it," said Nora. "I'm not sure I would ever ask him to do that. She is so sickly; I doubt he could bring himself to leave her." Nora had told Charlene all about the sites she witnessed at the Mother's Day mass.

"I'll just have to think about all that tomorrow. All I know is that I love him. And he loves me and now we are having this baby. There has to be some way. We'll figure it out."

Nora had hardly eaten anything all day. She was afraid that she couldn't keep anything down. She took another two sips from her coffee. Then, she rallied herself to make the phone call. She knew he would be at mass until noon. Luckily, it was only Steve in the office on Sundays and she wouldn't have to deal with any secretaries. She dialed the phone number. Her hands were trembling as he answered.

"Novak Aviation Services." She was comforted at the sound of his voice.

"Steve, is that you?" she asked rhetorically.

"Of course it's me. Nora what's up? You sound upset."

"Steve." She began to sob. "I have to see you. I have

to see you today."

"Are you okay"

"No," she answered softly.

"Well, I have check rides until three. Your husband's scheduled for a flight in the Piper. But he hasn't turned up. I could meet you around then. Let's go have a drink."

"No, that's not possible. I don't have a way to get there."

Charlene piped in, "Don't worry, hon. I can take you then. Okay?"

Nora turned back to the phone, "Alright Steve. Three it is. I will see you then."

Step one in the right direction, Nora was relieved as she hung up the phone. But Steve was concerned on the other end. He heard the pain in her voice. He could hardly keep his mind on the flight logs on which he was working. He was worried that something was drastically wrong.

At five minutes to three, he heard the door of his office open. He dismissed the students early knowing that Nora was on her way. As had been the pattern, Frank never showed up.

She walked in with her head covered in a scarf and some very large sunglasses. Once inside, she removed the glasses and he looked at her in disbelief. Steve was aghast noting the swelling on her left lip. "Oh my God, what has that asshole done to you?"

"I'm okay," she said.

"No you're not. That sonofabitch hit you."

"It's not that bad. Frank got angry when I told him I wanted a divorce."

"That's no excuse, Nora." He was startled. "You asked him for a divorce?"

"Yes," she said. "I am desperately in love with you. I can't stay with Frank. Besides, I am through with how he treats me. This," she motioned to her face, "is the last straw."

He came around from his desk and wrapped his arms around to hug her. "Nora. My darling, Nora." He took her snuggly into his arms and embraced her protectively. "I am so sorry this has happened to you."

"Thanks. And I am okay. I've done it. It's over. I have

broken free of the almighty Greenwoods."

"What are you going to do? Where are you and the kids going to go?" he asked.

"That's just it. I'm not sure. And what's worse, he has the kids. I have to find some way to get them back."

He sat her down on the couch in his office and cradled her. She was a pitiful site. Not like the strong, robust woman that had flown a plane cross country. It appeared that Frank had shattered more than her face.

He got her a glass of ice water and they continued to talk. He asked about her children and if they were alright. Their wellbeing was his main concern besides her. But she didn't know. She assumed they were at the house and hoped that they had gotten there safely.

"I'm scared that he won't let me back to get the children. I'm pretty certain he'll sue me for custody out of sheer pride, not because he really wants them."

Some of Steve's friends had gone through divorce and he knew the process and custody battles could get nasty. Lawyers sought out any flaw in the defendant spouse and took them to the cleaners, ruining their reputations. He could only imagine what a field day Frank would have if he found out about the affair. With the wealth of the Greenwoods, there was no doubt they would hire the best lawyers in town; discrediting Nora royally and casting her out of New Orleans society. The aftershocks might even affect his own business.

As these thoughts went through his head, Nora suddenly grabbed his hand. "Steve, there is something else I've got to tell you." Her lips began to tremble.

He reached up and touched her face. "It's okay. You know you can tell me anything."

She kissed his palm. "Please just promise, that you won't be upset with me."

"No, Nora. You know I won't. I love you."

His words brought her comfort, strength and courage. She took a deep breath and looked into his eyes. "I got a call a while back. From the doctor's office."

His mind began to jump to conclusions and he wondered if she, too, might be ill in some way. "Yes?"

"My dear, Steve. It makes things more complicated." She started to weep. He reached up and with his thumbs wiped away her tears.

"Nora, whatever it is. We'll handle it. We will get through it together."

"I hope you mean that," she said. "I'm pregnant. I am pregnant with your child."

He looked stunned for a moment, but didn't want to let on. "Nora. I can imagine that was shocking news to you. A baby? Are you sure?"

"I am pretty sure." she smirked. "In fact, I am about four and a half months along," she raised up her shirt for him to see her belly.

"Four months?" he repeated. "What are we going to do?"

She was glad she had used the term 'we.' But Nora suspected that his next phrase wasn't going to be, 'Of course I'll get a divorce and marry you.'

"I'm going to have to figure out what to tell Marci."

"So you are going to tell her about us?" she was surprised.

"I dunno. I guess. Considering the circumstances of the child, I have no choice."

Steve had no earthly idea how. It would devastate her. It was a disastrous dilemma. What shocking revelations. There was so much to think about; they couldn't come up with any strategies that day.

Time stood still while they just sat. Planes took off and landed overhead. After a bit, Steve reached for her hand and kissed it; asking if he could drop her off somewhere.

Although Nora had no place to go, she asked him to take her to The Quarter. It was the one place in which she could lose herself. For now, she just wanted to walk and walk and walk.

Chapter 25

Dusk was falling on Decatur St. as Nora walked alone, wrapping her coat tightly around her. There was a crisp November wind blowing through the narrow alleys. She tried to remember what bar Big Daddy was working for, but was at a loss.

It was hard to comprehend the confounded turns that her life had taken. Moments of sheer bliss and devastating lows. Her extreme pride in her flying. Now the dilemma of her pregnancy. She was not unlike her father, Jack. She wished she had him now. He would not judge her and inherently, would know what to do.

She became angry when she glanced up at the spires of St. Louis Cathedral in the square. So much devotion to a religion that turned its back on her. All the time with the nuns at Ursuline. Rigors and education that now meant nothing.

Walking gave her time to think. Without her children, she now had way too much time on hands. She continued northward through narrow alleys of The Quarter. Jazz trumpets and accordions. Vendor carts and street performers. Odd knick-knack shops. In a strange way it made her feel at home.

Nora contemplated what type of job she could obtain. She had never worked a day in her life. Her typing skills were rudimentary at best. There wasn't any money for training. She had to eat and find a place to stay. The baby was kicking and moving inside her. She touched her tummy and wondered if it was a girl or boy. She almost hoped it was boy, so that he would never have to live within the limited confines of being a woman.

Taking her last quarter from her pocket, she entered one of the beatnik coffee houses that had become popular. A poet was reading out verses as a lone harmonica player blew a soulful tune.

"What can I get for you, Miss?" Nora looked up and thought she recognized the face of the person speaking. Her coloring was dark and exotic. Then, she saw her eyes and knew. Despite having aged, it was the mysterious woman Nora had seen so long ago at Jack's burial. She stared at her a bit too long.

"Are you havin' a drink den?" her strong Jamaican accent repeated. "Please, take your eyes away from me."

"I'm sorry," said Nora. "I just feel I have seen you somewhere."

"If you've spent anytime time in da bowels of society down here, maybe you have."

"I'll have a strong coffee. Thanks."

"Very well," and then she moved away. Nora debated if she should mention her father. Floods of childhood memories came over her. The poet began another verse.

In a few minutes, the beauty returned with the hot coffee. "Just black?"

"Just black, thank you," Nora continued to gaze at her.

"Why you keep lookin' at me?"

"Did you ever know a Jack Broussard?" Nora blurted out.

The woman appeared to have seen a ghost. Then, her face softened. "Yes. I knew Jack Broussard, long ago. But he is long since dead."

"I know. I am his daughter."

The lady then took Nora in visually. She could see the resemblance in Nora's cheekbones, dark skin, and eyes. "You look very much like him," she said painfully. "But I don't wish to speak of Jack."

"No, please go on."

"It is too painful."

"I'm sorry. I didn't mean to hurt your feelings. I miss him too. Greatly. I just remember seeing you, very long ago, at the cemetery."

"How could dat be? You must have been only a child. Confused wid grief."

"Yes. That is true. But I never forgot your eyes."

The woman paused for a moment and then told her, "Yes. It was me dat was. I took his death very hard. I knew him well from the riverboats."

"So you were the *belle catin*?" Nora had heard her mother tell stories.

"Is dat what dey called me?" she huffed. "I was more dan dat. Sorry if dat bother you."

"No, it doesn't."

The woman continued as she carefully sized up Nora. "Twas a crazy time, on da boats. Lots of highs. Lots of lows to dat life."

"Lately I have more of an understanding of what that must be like. Life's roller coaster."

"You seem sad."

"Yes, well it's difficult to love someone that you cannot have," it felt safe to unload her sorrows on a stranger.

"It is almost da worst pain in da world. Save dat of losing a child." the woman offered. Then she looked away. "I have said too much. Enjoy your coffee." She slowly moved back into the darkness of the coffee house.

Nora was struck by what she meant. Feeling the baby inside her, she feared having to make a similar decision. She would not allow herself to think that. She wanted to find out more about her father's lover, but it was getting late in the day. Right now, she had more pressing issues. A place to go before it got dark.

As she was leaving, she spied a notice on the wall. A club nearby was looking for a torch singer. She pulled down the notice and put it away in her purse. Leaving her quarter on the table, she abruptly left.

The Blue Room of the Roosevelt Hotel was on Dauphine St. just a few blocks away. Having no other prospects, Nora hurried there, hoping she had not missed the opportunity. The venue was an upscale jazz club with a low key atmosphere. There was a large grand piano on the small stage. The walls were decorated with pictures of the jazz greats, Herb Albert, Louis Armstrong and the like.

Nora approached the bartender and asked for the

manager. "I'm the manager. Mr. Weiss, the proprietor. The help's got the afternoon off. How can I help you Miss?"

"I'm here about the singing job."

The owner gave her a once-over look. Nora's belly was hidden in front of the bar. "Question is, can ya sing?"

"Yes. What would you like to hear?" she forthrightly answered.

"That's up to you doll. I just gotta be impressed. Hey Ted," he motioned to the piano player. "Play a few bars of something will ya?"

Ted began to play a torch song that Nora knew well, *Oh, you crazy moon* by Peggy Lee. The bartender listened. "Your voice ain't half bad, kid. What else do you know?"

Nora began to sing one of the spirituals that Justine had taught her a capella. The bartender and the piano player exchanged looks.

"Look, it don't pay much. But you get to keep your tips." The manager then looked at her stomach. "What up with that?" he queried her.

"It won't be an issue. I'll dress to cover it. Even sexy."

The manager looked suspect, but he was past his deadline. "Oh, jiminy crickets. As long as you can sing and bring in tips, who the hell cares."

Nora had an income. Thank the Lord for that. Next, was finding somewhere to lay her head. Fatigue was hitting her hard. As she left the Roosevelt, she thought of Mabel. When Mabel missed the bus, Nora had taken her home. But she didn't have her address. She thought it was somewhere just past the *Vieux Carre*. But where?

It was getting dark as Nora made her way through the enigmatic alleys and streets. Tourist revelers were already drunk and making lurid comments her way, as though she was a woman for hire. She was tired and felt weak. Almost twenty four hours had passed without eating anything.

She stopped to take off her shoes and rub her feet. Carrying her overnight bag had given her shoulder a workout. What in the heck was she doing? Her children were miles away at her home in Metairie. Here was their mother, scouring the streets of The Quarter for her next meal. Flustered, she was about to give up, when she heard a familiar voice.

"Missus Greenwood. What chou doin' down here at dis time o night?"

It was Big Daddy. Nora perked up to see his friendly, round, black face. "Praise God. Big Daddy. Aren't you a sight for sore eyes?"

"Come on, Missus Greenwood. You don't needa be out in da cold. Les go to da house." He took her hand and placed it in his strong arm. He was just getting off work from the one of the clubs at which he worked.

"Where are we going?" she asked willing to follow him anywhere.

"To my Mabel's house. It's not but a few blocks from here."

Nora felt like her guardian angel must have been watching over her. She picked up her pace to keep up with his longs strides. She didn't care that she was the only white woman heading for this neighborhood. Big Daddy was a saint. And she was happy to oblige his kindness.

After a few blocks, they reached the house Nora remembered. It was a quaint, small shotgun on Marias, just past Esplanade. Mabel was waiting for Big Daddy on the porch and came out to greet them.

"Missus Nora. How you be?" She reached out her arms and took her in for the biggest hug. Mabel didn't care about the details. Her girl, Nora, obviously needed her help. Enough said.

They went into the snug house and Mabel set out some supper for them both, happy to see Nora eat. The gumbo was so good, Nora asked for seconds.

After the meal, they sat in the kitchen and Nora told Mabel what had happened. Mabel listened intently as Nora poured out her troubles. Miss Nora could sure get herself into some messes. They agreed that Mabel would keep her secret about her whereabouts. Mabel invited Nora to stay with her and Big Daddy. That way, she was close to the club making it possible to walk there. Mabel would continue to work at the Metairie house as though nothing had happened so Nora could get updates on her children.

Chapter 26
∞ December, 1961 ∞

At Frank's request, Mabel began working at the Greenwood's daily. She had to in order get the children off to school. Arriving at the crack of dawn, she made sure they were fed for breakfast and had on their school uniforms. The children were physically okay, but emotionally despondent. The absence of their mother was very confusing.

Once the children were away, Mabel would telephone Charlene daily to update her on their condition and Nora. Charlene brought over some cocktail dresses and evening wear for Nora's use at her singing job. Mabel became their confident and go-between.

Nora started singing nights at the Blue Room. As she had been warned, her wages were paltry. But she brought in scads of tips from eager tourists living out their fantasies in the French Quarter. Even five months pregnant, Nora knew how to vamp.

Mable kept her well fed. Sweet potato pie. Grits with bacon. Red beans and rice. Mabel's cooking rivaled Nora's for sure. In the wee hours of the morning, it was comforting that Big Daddy was always there when Nora completed her sets to walk her home to Marias. The edge of The Quarter was rough at night.

After a few weeks, Nora had saved quite a large sum of cash. It was early December and there were plenty of tourists. People were generous in the Christmas spirit. She was almost ready to make her move.

Steve had no way to contact her and he was worried

sick. Nora had literally dropped out of sight. He phoned Charlene, but she would not divulge an ounce of information.

The guilt had begun to show on his face. He looked haggard and drawn. Marci had noted it too. His worry over the whole situation made him feel miserable. For the first time in his life, he felt helpless. It was time to come clean. One Sunday afternoon, after mass, he asked to speak to her alone.

"Marci, you know that I love you. We have been together since we were young." Marci braced herself, for she knew this wasn't going to be good news. "There's something that I feel I must confide in you."

"Go on. I am listening." She took a seat on the brocade chair of their parlor.

"I have wronged you, my dear." Steve looked like a forlorn dog. "Things between us; we haven't been intimate for so long . . ."

Marci dreaded what she knew she would hear next. She realized she had not been able to fulfill her wifely duties for years. However, it did not lessen the sting of what was to come. "Let me guess. You have been seeing another woman?"

"Yes. And I am so sorry, Marci," Steve began in regret.

"Who is she? What is the extent of the relationship? Is it just sex?"

For a moment, he was surprised to hear her openly use that term. "It started out that way. But I fell in love with her."

Marci thought she was going to faint. She gripped the chair with her hands turning her thin knuckles white. "What are you saying, Steve? Are you leaving me?"

"God, no. I could never do that. I made vows to you and I do love you. The thing is, I love her too. Even though I know it is impossible."

Screwing a concubine and loving her were two different things. Marci was devastated beyond belief. "You have broken your vows. So what are you wanting from me? Forgiveness? My blessing? What?"

"There's a complication. It seems . . ." there was no good way to say it. "She's pregnant. And the baby is mine."

Marci felt her extremities grow numb. She had done everything in her life right. Catholic schools. Marrying her sweetheart in the church. Giving birth to his six children. Battling an unforgiving illness. And now this? "What do you want me to say, Steve?"

"I'm not sure. But I don't want a divorce. I made a vow to care for you and our children. My selfish needs have wreaked havoc on our lives."

"Well, your righteousness is humbling. What would our children think? Their father, the bastard maker?" Marci knew she would already be going to confession for the words she chose and wicked thoughts that were swirling around in her head. She was hurt. She was angry. But strangely, she felt sorry for the woman carrying her husband's child. For she knew, he would not ever leave their marriage.

"I cannot tell you how sorry I am. Ultimately, I never meant to hurt you."

Marci stared coldly at him in silence. "So who is this woman?" she bravely asked.

"Her name is Nora. She was a student in my flight school. I taught her how to fly." Steve suddenly felt tremendous guilt as he related their story.

"Go on. I might as well hear all of it."

He continued to explain about Nora, her disastrous marriage to her husband. Her Catholicism. Her four other children. The more he told, the sadder the tale became. Marci was appalled at the indiscretions of them both; choking down the bile that threatened to erupt from her throat. And yet, her heart went out to the four children whose mother thoughtlessly ruined their lives. How, as payback for her sins, she was now powerless; pathetically on the streets and without them.

Marci sat primly in her chair, her arms neatly folded in her lap. She held tight to the rosary beads always kept by her side. Marci didn't speak for the longest time. She sought solace in prayer to help her get through this excruciating moment.

"If you plan to stay in our marriage, then what do you feel are your responsibilities for this child?" she demanded to know, her voice trembling.

"I don't know. I can't see taking it on with our six."

"And what does this Nora want to do?"

Steve was unsure how to answer. For he knew that in some delusion of reality, Nora wished he would divorce Marci and take her as his wife. "I don't think she has thought that far. Right now, she is just trying to survive financially and get her own children back."

"Well," Marci said rising with difficulty. "This is a stunning turn of events. I need to pray about it. I will process everything you have said and let you know what I think in the morning." Marci's body had reached its limit for the day. Taking her cane in her hand, she made her way arduously up the stairs to their bedroom. Steve moved to help her. "Please don't touch me," she motioned. "And Steve, sleep in the den tonight. I wish to be alone."

Her stoic dignity and demeanor astounded and endeared her to him. She never once raised her voice or shouted. He knew she must be in tortured anguish. He prayed for forgiveness.

Chapter 27

It was now advent, Nora realized. Although she was staying true to her vow not to return to church. Advent in the Catholic Church consisted of the four weeks leading up to Christmas. This year, Nora was not fasting, almsgiving, or preparing for the coming of the baby Jesus. She had not been attending mass. On Thanksgiving Day, she was singing at the club. Not feeling very thankful, knowing that she would not see her children as they were at the Greenwood's. Nora had never been away from them on a holiday. She felt pretty blue.

Singing at the club was her only salvation and it continued to go well. She had now been working there for several weeks making great tips and pocketing them all. Her bank account was growing day by day. As was her outline in her after-five wear.

Mabel and she had been in cahoots about what to do next. She was desperate to get her children back. Through her maid, Nora knew exactly what her children's schedules were. Where they would be at any given moment. In desperation, Frank had increased Mabel's hours again.

They believed they had come up with a strategy for the return of her children. On one of Mabel's days during the week, Nora would show up, just after the children were out of school. She would time her arrival to coincide with Mabel having the children play in the front yard before supper.

Mabel knew where Frank kept the keys to the station wagon. Charlene was now driving the carpool daily. After the children were at school, Mabel would drive the station wagon around to Charlene's house and park it. Thus, Nora could pick it up and drive around to her home on Woodvine. She would make it appear to be a celebration and reunion with her children and take them for ice creams and sodas.

It was daring, as it involved a theft of sorts. But it was the only way Nora knew to get her children back and away from Frank.

On the appointed Friday, Nora and Mabel went over the details in excruciating fashion. It was a moment of desperation and had to go off without a hitch. Nora was filled with trepidation and sadness. For once she had her children, she would be a fugitive. Contact with Mabel and those she loved would be gone until the custody battle and divorce was final.

She and Mabel hugged and said their prayers that morning. Like clockwork, Mabel took the bus and went to her regular shift. She made the coffee, packed the children off to school and continued to clean the house until two thirty in the afternoon.

When the clock struck that hour, she took the keys for the station wagon and carefully backed it out of the driveway. Not the best driver, she slowly inched it down the road. Mabel memorized Charlene's address. Left hand turn onto Geranium and then a right on Iona. She carefully pulled the station wagon into the driveway and got out to see Nora.

Nora had been at Charlene's since early morning, arriving just after Charlene had taken all of the children to school. She had her bags packed with more clothes Charlene loaned for her and the children. It was time to go.

"God speed, Nora. Isn't that what they say to pilots? Do what you have to do to get your children." Misty eyed Charlene hugged her best friend.

"I love you, Charlene. You've always been a sister to me. This is part one. Let's hope I make it to part two. I promise you, when this is all over, we'll be back to normal."

"I hope sure hope so." Charlene held onto her with a death grip. Mabel too, joined in the hug.

"I could never have done any of this without your help," Nora assured.

"Missus Nora, I is da help." Mabel laughed deeply and they all followed suite. Bittersweet as the sarcasm was in the midst of the South. "T'ain't nothing I wouldn't do for you. Be safe now, y'here?"

They hugged one last time. Charlene departed to pick up the carpool. On her way, she dropped the Mabel back by the Woodvine house. When the children got home they would not notice that anything was up. Mabel closed the garage door.

Nora stayed hidden in Charlene's sewing room. When she heard Charlene return from carpool, it was time to deploy her scheme into action. She exited out their back door like a stealth agent. She put her keys into the ignition of the station wagon and backed it out onto Iona.

Just like they had plotted, Mabel had the children out playing in the yard. She was just about to serve them afternoon snacks from a tray. Kayce had on her earphones and her portable transistor radio. Cathy, Leisel and Iggy were playing hide and seek. As the station wagon pulled into the driveway, Nora shouted out to them. "Howdy doody kiddoes. Guess who's home?"

They all looked up from their games. It was Ignatius who saw her first. "Mommy, Mommy, you're home." He ran and greeted her as she exited the wagon in the driveway. They all came over and joined the hugs. Nora wrapped her arms around them, crying and kissing them. It felt wonderful to hold them all in her arms again.

"Well, lawdy mercy. How you be, Missus Nora?" Mable came to hug her. Boy Mabel was good.

Even Kayce came over for a hug. "Where have you been?" she asked indignantly.

"Staying with family. Working things out." Nora left it at that.

"So are you home? For good?"

"Maybe so. We'll see," Nora lied and felt guilty about deceiving her daughter, but there was no other choice. There were three younger ones who needed their mother.

"Mommy, you cut your hair off," Leisel said, putting her fingers through Nora's short, curly new do.

"Yes. I did. I needed a change. Hey, I have a great

idea, let's go to Brocato's for gelato," Nora taunted. She knew it was one of their favorites.

"Yay. Let's go." Cathy was ring leader and game. The other's echoed her sentiment. Leisel and Iggy got into their regular seats in the wagon. Kayce was still skeptical.

"Does Daddy know you are here?"

"Sure, of course." Nora forged another lie. "Come on, let's go. I hear a tutti-frutti calling our name."

Kayce was used to her mother's sudden, spontaneous adventures. She hated to admit it, but she was happy to see her too. Kiddie duty was over. Taking off her headset and radio she got into the car with her siblings.

Without wasting another moment, Nora drove off. Mabel sighed in relief and then made plans for her exit as well. Big Daddy came to be at the house. He waited in the back yard for the afternoon, close by pretending to garden. In the mean time, she carried on with her work; not to arouse any suspicion. Although she was going to take the early bus home, Big Daddy was backup in case Mr. Greenwood got home early and all hell broke loose.

Nora drove down the Causeway and made her way to North Carrollton off of Canal. Brocato's was just blocks away from Frank's office. Knowing that gave her shivers up her spine. She bustled the kids into the ice cream shop and they ordered their delights. It felt wonderful to be around them again.

Kayce kept staring at the bulge under her mother's large top. While the other kids dug into their ice cream, she interrogated her mother. "So, when do you plan on telling Daddy about the baby?"

"In time, Kayce. Let's not talk about it now. I'll give you all the details later. Tell me about school and what music you are listening to. Have your heard the new Elvis?" Nora tried to distract her.

"Yes. But when are you going to tell Daddy?"

"Soon, Kayce. I promise. So how are everybody's treats?"

Their voices erupted in glee. When they were finished, she hurried them into the station wagon. "Come on now guys. Let's roll." They scrambled back into their seats. It was Kayce who noticed that Nora didn't head towards Metairie. Nora turned the station wagon onto Airline

Highway, U.S. 61 towards Baton Rouge.

"Mama, why didn't you turn right on Canal to Metairie Road?" she sounded alarmed.

"Just relax, Kayce. We are going on a little road trip."

"But we have Girl Scouts tomorrow," piped up Cathy.

"I'm sure your leader will excuse you, just one time. Come on, we are going to have fun. You've always wanted to see the LSU tiger. We're going to Baton Rouge to see him for real." Nora thought of anything that would keep the kids enticed. They had been on many road trips before. She hoped they believed this was just another one. At least for a short while.

On the edge of town, Nora met Justine at the A and P on Airline, just as Mabel had arranged. Although she hadn't seen her in years, Justine looked exactly the same. Mabel and she had kept in touch. Justine was retired from domestic service, but she was happy to take the job of watching Nora's children when Mabel told her the tale of Frank Greenwood's recent exploits. Mabel would therefore be able to deny her involvement. It added another layer of mystery and secrecy to Nora's plan.

Plus, Justine was someone that her children remembered from the Greenwood's mansion. She was horrified when she realized the extent of the domestic violence existing in the Greenwood household. She gladly became Nora's liege.

Nora exited the city and began the journey over the bridges across the swamps. New Orleans was but a reflection in her rear view mirror. It was getting late and becoming dark. Nora prayed that the car held up and she didn't get a flat on the long stretch of road ahead. The bridges crossing the swamps were long with no exits.

It was about a ninety minute journey. She was glad to finally see the lights of Baton Rouge come into view. She parked at a Travel Lodge and rented a room under Justine's name. No one would recognize that. Nora made sure she paid cash for everything, so as to leave no traces.

It was almost nine. Even Kayce's eyes were drooping. They hadn't eaten dinner, but no matter, for her children were exhausted and ready to drop into bed. Nora asked for a cot to be brought to the room. With the double beds and the cot, they would all have a place to rest their

AgeView Press

Thank you for purchasing a first edition printing of Flying Solo. Congratulations, your personalized, signed copy is destined to be a collector's item. After the first print, the author noticed a few typos and wanted them corrected. The next mass printing will reflect those minor changes. As a holder of a signed first edition, your purchase will become collectable. Remember that proceeds from the sale of this book go to support Harrison, the author's son, who suffers from Duchenne's muscular dystrophy.

heads. Iggy and Justine bedded down in the cot. Nora put Kayce and Leisel together in one of the beds. She would sleep with Cathy in the other.

Before Nora climbed into bed, she thanked Justine in advance. She could only imagine how enraged Frank would be returning home to an empty house. He would go ape. Nora looked over at all her sleeping children. At last, she had them back.

Day one, escape complete.

Chapter 28

Marci appeared more pale and wan than usual. She was dressed in a basic blue sweater and matching skirt. Day clothes, albeit a little too formal for home. She was waiting for Steve in the living room of their large three story home, which sat off Napoleon on Galvez. It wasn't a fancy home, but large enough to accommodate their big family.

The formal living room and dining room were actually on the second floor, as well as the kitchen and master bedroom. The bottom floor consisted of a den, two bedrooms, storage and a small converted garage apartment which they rented out. The third story had more bedrooms for their girls.

Her cane made noise on the hardwood floors as she paced back and forth laboriously, anticipating Steve's arrival. She had promised to discuss her thoughts of his debacle. As such, she saw only one possible way of the mess that Steve had created with his affair. Thoughts of how she would miss this house, if they chose to act on it, were forebodingly painful.

She saw him drive up in his Mustang. He normally parked outside on the street under the large sycamore tree, as there was no garage. Steve bounded up the two flights of palazzo tile stairs that lead to the big front porch of their abode.

"Hi, Marci, I'm home," he greeted her like always.

"I've been waiting for you, Steve. Sit down, we need to talk." Exhausted from anxiety, she made her way towards their dining room table. She hoped she could get through this discussion while their children were downstairs in the den watching television. She wanted no distractions.

"What's the matter?"

"Nothing. Everything. But I have thought long and hard about this, and I have come up with a possible solution for your . . . problem."

She commanded Steve's full attention. Marci had the most determined look on her face. Her voice was icy and direct, but without malice.

"Okay. What is it?"

"Remember the job offer you had, not long ago, to fly for Humble Oil?" Steve did remember. "I think you should take it."

"But Marci, that's in Tyler, Texas. We'd have to move."

"That's the idea. It would be a temporary move, to get us out of this city and away from this scandal. I won't be able to face any of our friends or family when this all comes out. And I know it will."

"What about Novak Aviation? It's my business. The kids? Our house?"

"I've thought about all that. Chet could run your business for a year or so. We could rent out the house, or have our tenant's rent reduced by keeping maintenance on it. I'm not giving up my home."

"And the children? Their schooling?"

"I have already found a Catholic school in Tyler. St. Gregory's. We are almost at Christmas break, so they could start in January."

Steve was running his hands through his hair. She had really done her homework. It was so much change. So much uprooting. "But why do we have to move? Isn't the issue with Nora? She's the one having the baby."

"That's just it. I feel sorry for the woman. According to you, she's out on the streets somewhere. Away from her children. The Greenwoods are a powerful family in New Orleans. Even I know that. They will take her to the cleaners and she most likely will lose custody of her children. Steve, she is carrying your child. As much as I hate it, that is a fact."

"But I still don't see what that all has to do with us."

"Everything." She sat down in one of the dining room chairs. Calmly and quietly, she laid out her rationale. Marci believed so strongly in her faith, their marriage and their life; that the only solutions to this dilemma were humility, forgiveness, and charity. Here vows to her husband, for better or for worse were sacred. She could not tolerate having one of Steve's offspring come into this world without care. In her view, that baby was the victim in this situation. The child had a soul and deserved a decent start at life.

Marci explained that she planned to allow Nora to work for them, as a caregiver. Her strength had been slipping lately. She knew from talking to Steve that Nora could cook and sew. A move to Tyler would distance them away from this scandal. She would delay hiring any maids at first, therefore allowing Nora to fill in as help until she had the baby. When Nora, delivered, she could give the baby up for adoption. Whatever she did after that did not matter. At least she and her husband could rest assured that they had given this mistake, this baby, every possible chance.

"That is one crazy plan," Steve said shaking his head.

"I don't think so. It sounds like a viable alternative to me. Humble offered you a huge salary. By flying their corporate executives around the oil fields of Texas, you'd be making only short commuter flights. You'd be home most days of the week. I think you should give them a call today and see if they are still interested."

Steve was still working it out all in his head. A temporary move. Until the baby was born. Adoption. Then, it would be over. "What if she won't agree to it? She was born and raised here."

"At this point, does she have any choice?"

"No. Not really. I found out she's working as a singer in one of the hotel clubs. The Roosevelt."

"Well, how long do you think that is going to last? No one is going to want to see a greatly pregnant night club singer in a spangled dress." Marci felt her blood pressure rising. She took a deep breath to calm down. "Poor me a drink, Steve."

It was rare that Marci partook in hard alcohol. But he obliged, giving her a gin and tonic on the rocks. She felt her throat burn slightly as she swallowed the bitter liquid. In an instant, it warmed her to her toes and gave her resolve to continue this discussion.

"After you have talked to Humble, and accepted the job, you need to set up a meeting between us all."

"You want Nora, to come here?"

"Well. Yes. If she is going to be helping me and caring for our children, I think they should meet her." Marci pondered what kind of woman would risk everything, just to learn how to fly a plane.

"You know, she has four children of her own."

"I'm aware. I guess you had better rent us a big house in Tyler. We're going to need it."

With that, Marci rose to go lie down in their bedroom. The stress of this exchange had completely depleted her energy. It would take her several hours to recover and in all likelihood render her bedfast for the evening. Great duress precipitated massive fatigue.

Steve was still in awe of Marci's attitude about the whole affair and resulting pregnancy. He knew she was devastated and disgusted at what he had done. The guilt related to how it all impacted her illness made him feel like a worm. He knew he didn't deserve her forgiveness, but was very thankful for her kind heart. Despite adoring and loving Nora, he knew he could never leave the mother of his six children. He was married until death. They would have to make this work.

Knowing that Nora was so far advanced in her pregnancy, he didn't want to wait another moment. He telephoned the Blue Room bar at the Roosevelt to set up a time that Nora could meet with them.

The bartender answered the phone, "Roosevelt Blue Room, would you like to reserve a table?"

"No," Steve replied. "I would like to speak with your singer, Nora Broussard." Steve guessed she would have used her maiden name.

"There's no one that works here by that name, sir."

"What about Jean Broussard."

"Oh, yeah. Jean. She was here, but she isn't anymore."

"What do you mean?"

"Exactly what I said. She was singing here, but now she's gone. Never showed up for her gig a couple of nights back."

Steve didn't know what to make of that news. He couldn't imagine that Nora would walk off a job. What about her children? Had she run away and left them? It was unfathomable. "I see, well thanks anyway."

"Yeah, if you see her, she's got a few bucks in pay she never collected."

"Okay, I'll tell her. If I see her."

Hanging up the phone, Steve was in a quandary. What now? Good God, Nora. Where could you possibly be?

Chapter 29

Hurricane force emotions were erupting at the mansion on St. Charles. From the moment Frank had arrived home to find the children and the station wagon missing, he had not slept. The house was vacant and he suspected Nora was somehow involved.

Taking off a couple of hours early, he found only Mabel there, finishing the washing. He interrogated her regarding Nora's whereabouts. She played dumb and wouldn't answer him. Frank knew her relationship with Nora to be close. He was sure that Mabel had some inkling of what was going on. She was just too calm. Frank would have beaten it out of her, but her common law husband was there out back of the house. Big Daddy stood six foot five.

When Frank raised his voice to Mabel, he took a few steps and leered at him. Frank just didn't want to take that on. If Mabel didn't cooperate soon, he would just fire her. For now, he let it drop.

The interrogation of Mabel a failure, he thought about phoning the police. But he knew if he did, they would file a report, which would become public record. With the words Greenwood, divorce, and child abduction; his family's name would immediately be on the front page of the *Times Picayune*. He would never drag them into scandal unless absolutely necessary.

As a last resort, he phoned his father and mother. His father agreed the salacious information was cause for scandal. As such, he called a family meeting at the mansion. They contacted the legal firm that handled their business and were referred to a family lawyer who was known about town for being a shark. The Greenwoods were going to pull out all the stops. The soonest Frank could get an appointment with him was on Monday morning, as it was the weekend. For now, his family was going over all of the details of what had happened.

"She asked for a divorce about three weeks ago," Frank explained.

"Did you try to reason with her or talk to her, Frank?" Mother Greenwood asked.

"She fucked around on me, Mother. Or it appears that she did."

Mother Greenwood put her hands over her ears. "Please, Frank. Don't use that kind of language around me."

"Sorry, Mother. I am just so angry."

"Well, Frank, your slate isn't exactly clean," his father said referring to his numerous affairs. He didn't know the details, but plenty of people around the Greenwood Oil offices had speculated on his dalliances. Unfortunately, his son didn't have the best reputation. "This all happened three weeks ago?" his father bellowed.

"Her demanding a divorce? Yes. The kids have only been missing since sometime today," Frank sheepishly answered.

"You simply screwed up in not telling us earlier. The minute you kicked her out, you should have called us. Now you've given her the upper hand." It irked the elder Greenwood that at times Frank was not the sharpest tool in the shed.

Frank's older brother, George Jr. was there too. Along with George Jr.'s wife. She had known Nora as a sister-in-law and superficially through the Junior League. But they had never been close. George Jr. also worked in oil and gas for the family firm.

In addition, they asked Nora's mother, Nellie, to be present. Mainly to scrutinize what she knew about the situation. She was still dressed in her nurse's uniform. "I still just can't believe it. She stole your car?" Nellie was worried sick. "That's not like my Nora Jean." She wiped tears from her eyes.

"Hell, she stole my kids," Frank yelled.

"Please, Frank. We have guests, try to lower your voice," his mother cautioned. She called for their new maid. "Minnie, dear, could you please make us all some tea."

"Make it a bourbon for me," Frank commanded.

"Frank, it is ideally best if you don't drink," his father suggested. "If we have to call the authorities, I don't want that in the report."

Frank acquiesced to his father's dominion. It was clear who was in charge here. "Now, let's all agree. If anyone here receives any type of communication from her, a phone call, anything. You are to call my private office or our home phone immediately." They all nodded their heads. "In the meantime, Frank will meet with the lawyers. We will get the best advice possible on how to handle this situation." He turned to Nellie. "I am sorry it has come to this. But considering the circumstances, when the divorce is filed, we will sue for full custody of the four children. I don't want anything to do with the bastard she is carrying."

"George Sr. please don't call an innocent, unborn baby a bastard," Mother Greenwood was horrified. "If there is one. Frank was drunk that night. He may not have heard things correctly."

"Well, that's what it is. It certainly is not a Greenwood," George Sr. pointed out.

Nellie could only look down, carefully wiping away silent tears. "Are you certain she is pregnant?" She was still not convinced. "I feel sure she would have told me by now."

"That's what Kayce says," Frank retorted.

"But she's just a teen. Who knows what the truth is," Mother Greenwood offered.

Nellie hoped that they were all wrong. A divorce was bad enough, but an illegitimate baby? From another man? It was unthinkable. Nora would have told her.

New Orleans was known for its colorful characters. Vixens, vamps, and voodoo witches were legendary inhabitants of The Quarter. An iconoclastic array of artists, musicians and other less than desirable members of society also called it home. Most of them lived in and around the neighborhoods of the *Vieux Carre*. However, the rest of the city was a microcosm of mish-mashed cultures. Italians, Greeks, Polish and French all contributed a strong cultural influence on its various neighborhoods. Not to mention the large Blacks population, many of whom were descendents of slaves which had worked along the River Road Plantations before the Civil war. Plenty of their ancestors inhabited the city today.

The Greenwoods had lived in New Orleans since the mid 1800s making their fortunes initially from sugarcane and rice. Later, their riches increased via the oil and gas that was discovered in the 1930s. They were proud of the lineage that had produced doctors, lawyers, and millionaire businessmen well known in society. They believed they were righteous, upstanding Catholics.

George Greenwood Sr. was not going to let some Cajun tramp that his son married sully the Greenwood name with her escapades. It just wasn't going to happen. "I think she should go to jail. For stealing the car and stealing the children."

"Now, darling. Let's not act too quickly. We are going to let the lawyers handle things, to make sure there are no loopholes," offered Mother Greenwood.

"Jail? Surely, you are not serious. She is the mother to four other children." Nellie was horrified. "I am sure that we will hear from her." Nellie tried to sound hopeful. "I just know it. Nora would never do anything to harm her children or a child she was carrying. That I can bank on."

"Well, that is a comfort, Mrs. Broussard. Thank you. I can imagine you are taking this very hard," Mrs. Greenwood handed her another tissue.

"Yes." Nellie dabbed her eyes and blew her nose. "Any mother would."

"It's just unfathomable. NASA can send a chimp up in space, but we can't find a renegade Cajun, housewife with four kids in a station wagon," George Sr. raged. He took another swig of his bourbon.

They called for a taxi to take Nellie home. As she waited, Nellie went over and over in her mind the memories of her daughter. She thought of her husband Jack and wished he were here. His tenacity would have prevented any of this from happening. He would have found a way to somehow prevent the Greenwoods from their railroading.

Nellie felt remorseful about her encouragement of Nora to marry Frank. After today's display, she now understood what Nora had been trying to tell her for so long. Frank was an impossible chauvinist. Maybe she had been too hard on Nora, too strict. As her mother, she just attempted to do the right thing and raise a nice Catholic girl. Some of Nora's outlandish ideas scared her. Often, Nora didn't think of the outcomes and this was no exception. One thing was for sure, she was not going to let these people harm her daughter or her grandchildren. Nellie reached for her rosary and began a special novena to pray for the safe return of her only child.

Chapter 30

Nora knew the clock was ticking. She didn't have much time to make part two of her plan work. Stealing Frank's plane was a huge risk, but she had to take it. She knew by now that Frank would have contacted his parents and gotten their powerful legal firms in place. If she was going to make a move, it was now or never. By Monday morning, a lawyer would be onboard and the court systems back open. If they were ugly about it, they could post a warrant for her arrest. Luckily, nothing could be done legally, in terms of filing protective orders, until then.

Her children were restless in the hotel. They were going to be there at least over the weekend. Kayce knew something was amiss. Tomorrow, on Sunday, her mother planned to skip mass. Even when they traveled, her mother always made arrangements to find a mass. She tried to get information out of her, "But why are we here?"

"Kayce, just to see the sites. There's LSU and the LSU tiger. There are museums and lots of Christmas decorations. You all can go see Santa Claus at Holmes. I just thought it was a nice little mini-vacation. That's all. I have missed you guys."

Today was Saturday morning, however, and the younger children were engrossed in the cartoons on the color television of the motel room. Nora used the car to get some basic groceries at the Piggly Wiggly. Milk and cereal. Cold cuts for the kid's meals. She made sure there were snacks and things for the kids to eat a picnic lunch. She even found a large, wicker, picnic basket, just like the one they had at home. When she returned, she went over the day's plans with Justine. Although Justine didn't have a driver's license, she knew how to drive. Nora reviewed some basic traffic rules. She wanted no mistakes. It would ruin everything if Justine got pulled over by some bigoted Baton Rouge policeman. Her children would be ID'd almost immediately.

Nora planned to have Justine take the children to the museum complex at LSU. There were park grounds on campus with ducks and swans to feed. An endless array of activities to occupy their day. If Nora was not back by the end of that activity, Justine was to take the children to a movie. She had Justine bring along her formal maid's uniform from when she worked at the Greenwoods. Even in the racial South of the sixties, no one would question a nanny on a day trip with a clutch of children.

But first, Justine would drop Nora at the train station. She arranged to take the *Amtrak City of New Orleans* from Baton Rouge back to the crescent city. Charlene was going to pick her up at the train station and take her out to Lakefront Airport.

Nora planned to fly Frank's plane to another state. Then, Charlene was going to drive approximately one hundred and twenty miles to meet Nora at Pine Belt Regional Airport in Hattiesburg, Mississippi. It would take her about almost three hours to get there across Lake Ponchartrain on Highway 11. From there, once the plane was locked up, Charlene would drive Nora back to the Baton Rouge. Another hundred and thirty some odd miles to get back to the children. It was doable in a day, as long as traffic permitted. One wreck on the Lake Ponchartrain Bridge or the elevated highways over the swamps and the strategy was kaput.

Prior to heading to Baton Rouge, unbeknownst to Steve, Nora had filed a flight plan. She was flying the Greenwood's Piper Aztec to Pine Belt Regional where she had already rented a hangar. The plane was the leverage she planned to use to get her children back from Frank. It simply had to work. It was her last trump.

Since it was Saturday, Charlene explained her excursion to Max as an all day shopping spree, followed by some volunteer work for the League in the evening. He was happy to watch their children while getting in some putting practice in the yard. It was a mild, sunny December day.

Nora loaded her group in the car. She was having trouble deciding how to explain why she was taking a train somewhere. It wouldn't make sense to them. Instead, she told them that she was meeting with a priest to talk about how to handle the divorce. It was the only excuse that sounded rational, as they knew how pious she was previously. She certainly didn't want them to know that she would be out of town and even out of the state of Louisiana for the day. Another lie, but it was just unavoidable.

Justine dropped her off at a street corner of buildings near the train station. She waved goodbye to them. "See you all in a bit. Have a fun time in tiger town." Then Nora said her St. Theresa prayer again. Hypocritical, since she was refuting the Catholic Church. However, it worked before and she hoped it worked now.

The silver Amtrak pulled into the station right on time. It was a commuter rail that ran four times a day. Nora bought the cheapest fair she could. She was tightly crammed in coach, but it didn't matter. She was wearing khaki slacks, which actually belonged to Max, black loafers, and a large matching A-line top. Inconspicuously dressed in some of Charlene's loaner clothes, she put a baseball cap in her purse for later. She intended to fly today without her flight suit, so as not to attract attention to herself at the Lakefront hangars.

She settled back into her seat, closed her eyes and went over the game plan again in her head. Then, she pulled out her VFR map and plotted route to make sure she knew her points of contact. There would be no coast line visuals, so she had to get the landmarks right. Mississippi's topography was dense piney woods north of Lake Ponchartrain and they all looked alike.

It was a short, two hour train trip to Union Passenger Station. Charlene was waiting for Nora in the lobby. As soon as she saw her, she ran to hug her. "Honey, you are a sight for sore eyes. Golly I have worried about you."

She embraced her for a hug and then linked arms as they walked. Charlene didn't really want to turn her best friend loose.

"Charlene, you saw me yesterday," Nora scoffed at her melodrama.

"Yes, but now you are on the run."

Nora and she quickly hopped into the blue Cadillac. Charlene had already stopped by Esso and gotten a full tank of gasoline. Merging into traffic, they drove towards Lakefront. They talked about what all Nora had been through in the last few weeks. Living at Mabel's. Having Big Daddy walk her home from the club. The mysterious woman in the bar. Her recent escape with the children. Even about the baby.

"How have you been feeling? I worry that you haven't been seeing a doctor."

"Don't. I've done this five times now. I pretty much know how it goes."

"Are you taking your vitamins?" Charlene worried.

"Until they ran out. I can't afford them right now."

"Well, we could stop by the Katz and Besthoff's and get you some."

"Charlene, there's no time for that today. We have to stay completely on schedule. Okay?" Nora knew Charlene was frantic with worry. You could hear it in the shrill of her voice. "I promise I will get back on them. But first, I have to get through today without getting thrown in jail."

"I know honey. I am just worried. About it all."

When they arrived at the airport, Charlene parked out of the line of sight of Steve's office. Nora hoped that he was busy teaching a class and didn't notice her. They figured it would be less obvious if Charlene just dropped Nora off. Hugging one another, they wished each other well on their journeys.

Nora put on her large sunglasses and a scarf and entered the FBO. She scanned the lobby for Steve and it was clear. Then, she headed for the mechanics office. It was unlocked and no one was there. Her timing was perfect; they were clearly on break. She looked on the peg board for the keys to the hangars. There were lots of them. Thankfully, she found the one she wanted hanging on a peg marked *Hangar Three*. Taking the key, she exited the FBO and made her way to the tarmac. Hangar three. The coast was clear; there was no site of Joey anywhere. So far so good. Nora unlocked the hangar and rolled back the door.

She removed her scarf and large sunglasses. Walking around the plane, she rapidly completed her pre-flight inspection. Once she finished, she donned her baseball cap and aviators. Time to start the engines. Steve was up in the tower, discussing some flight plans for his students. He was filling time until Frank Greenwood came for his late afternoon lesson.

The air traffic controller questioned him about today's flights. "Say, I thought you'd be down with Frank Greenwood. Has he soloed yet? The Aztec is logged for a flight about noon."

"Noon? That's gotta be an error," Steve checked his log books. "Mr. Greenwood isn't scheduled to fly with me until later this afternoon."

"Well according to this plan he is." The controller showed Steve the flight plan that had been filed by an F. Greenwood. It showed a takeoff schedule for 11:45 AM, with a cross country routed to Pine Belt Regional in Hattiesburg.

"What's this? When did it get filed?"

"A couple of days ago. I didn't think to mention it because I assumed you were planning his cross country."

"Well, this can't be right. Maybe Greenwood Oil is flying someone out and they listed Frank's name." Steve rationalized.

"Could be."

"Geez, I hope they get back in time for our lesson. Frank will be pissed if he can't fly his own plane." Steve looked at his watch. It was 11:42 AM. Right on schedule, he saw the Greenwood's blue and white Piper Aztec slowly moving across the tarmac. The sun was shining overhead and causing such a glare, that even with binoculars; he couldn't see who was in the cockpit.

"I'll ask him about it when I see him later at his lesson. Could be some snafu." Steve scampered down the stairs of the tower to go meet his next student. What he didn't hear was the female voice that called the tower.

Chapter 31

As instructed by ground control, the Piper Aztec was positioned at the end of the tarmac. "Lakefront tower, this is November, Twin Piper six, niner, one, five, foxtrot requesting permission for takeoff." Nervously, Nora awaited clearance. If she got it, she would be on her way. If they stopped her, she might be arrested and lose her children forever.

There was a brief pause. "Sorry about that, Twin Piper six, niner, one, five, foxtrot. Clear for takeoff on runway two seven."

With a huge sigh of relief, Nora taxied the plane to the end of runway twenty seven. Good to go. She pushed forward the throttle and began to increase her speed for takeoff. Within seconds she was aloft. The Greenwood's Piper, in immaculate condition, flew just like the other Piper that she had flown with Steve. The controls were basically the same. But of course, the Greenwoods had equipped theirs with the latest avionics. Avionics Nora had no idea to operate.

Nora's short hair was tucked up in her cap. She was wearing aviators; trying to appear as much like the Greenwood's pilot as possible. Seventy-five knots, eighty-five knots. Lift, she was off the ground heading west.

Flying out, she could see downtown New Orleans on her left. But as planned, she banked right and made a turn north crossing back over Lakefront and Lake Ponchar-train. Previously, she had only flown over the mouth of the lake, which in and of itself was over five miles. Flying over the diameter of the lake was nerve wracking. Once she got over the middle, there was water as far as she could see. As the second largest salt water lake, it was huge. Forty miles east to west and twenty four miles from its southern shore northward. Exactly the direction Nora was flying. She was relieved when she could see shoreline coming into view near Mandeville. She increased her altitude and leveled off at her cruise.

Now, it was just a matter of identifying her landmarks along the way, making sure she followed her course. She had studied the maps more intently than any previous flight. It was going to be tremendously difficult to differentiate where she was over the acres and acres of pine forests. Once she hit land at Mandeville, she knew that she was about to cross the border to Mississippi. Then, the plane would be safely in another state.

The state of Louisiana operated under Napoleonic law. Baton Rouge was where her children temporarily were. Therefore, had she chosen to fly there, it might have been considered theft. At this point, everything she had just left was still considered community property. With the Greenwood's power, Nora suspected they would find some loophole and have her arrested. At the moment, no legal papers had been filed; technically, she was still a Greenwood. By flying to another state that recognized community property, Nora avoided the Napoleonic law implications.

Hattiesburg, Mississippi was an ideal location. A small to medium sized city, close enough in geographical proximity to Baton Rouge and New Orleans to make her plan work. Plus, Pine Belt was a general aviation airport large enough to have hangars for rent. As Nora continued to fly over the immense pine forests she realized how harrowing finding her visuals was going to be. There were acres upon acres of them. Tall, lush, and stately under most circumstances unless you were attempting to find a landmark. Pinpointing her point of reference was like trying to find a needle in a haystack.

Nora plotted her journey along the parallel route that Charlene was driving on Highway 11. Nora knew that construction had commenced for the future Interstate 59.

With both roadways running together in jagged patterns they made a decent north south vantage point for her to follow.

Nora made contact with the first tower. "Poplarville tower. Twin Piper, November, six, niner, one, five, foxtrot. VFR, four thousand five hundred feet landing Hattiesburg. Over."

"Twin piper six, niner, one, five, foxtrot copy over."

First check point done. There weren't going to be as many checks to towers this time. There was no need. Generally, as long as she could follow her landmarks she would be okay. She sustained her altitude of four thousand five hundred feet. The gods were looking down upon her, for the weather today was absolutely gorgeous. There were only some ribbon-like, cirrus clouds in the sky. Otherwise, it was baby blue.

As she flew, Nora thought more about what she was actually doing. She was playing the poker card game of her life. Her outcome was to regain custody of her children and her freedom. She would absolutely have to hook Frank into her bluff.

Her normal exhilaration when flying was marked with fear today. She thought about the Naval ideals that Steve had taught. Honor, courage, and commitment. Her courage and commitment to her children were driving her actions. Well, at least she had two out of three. For there was certainly no honor in her first totally independent act as a pilot; which was now stealing a plane.

Nora started to see dwellings increasing in numbers and proximity. She realized she was on the outskirts of Hattiesburg and would be flying over the city's western edge. Pinebelt Regional was north of the city. Almost there. Just a few more moments and she would be home free.

She made contact with Pinebelt tower when she was ten miles out. "Pinebelt tower. Twin Piper, November six, niner, one, five, foxtrot. Three miles southwest, requesting permission to land."

"Twin piper six, niner, one, five, foxtrot clear to land runway three six."

Nora recognized from studying her maps that runway three six required her to bank left when in proximity of the airport. She received another radio communication from the tower, "Twin Piper, niner, one. Winds are currently zero four five, at twenty-five knots, gusting to thirty-five. Clear to land runway three six." Nora knew that meant she would be getting quite a bit of crosswind as she attempted to land the plane.

It suddenly began to dawn on her the risks of this mission. If she somehow failed her landing, and crashed the plane killing herself; her children would not only be motherless, but stranded in Baton Rouge. Although these thoughts began to cross her mind in flashes, she tried to put them out of her head.

"Come on Jack. Help me out here," calling on her father's spirit. He was either in heaven or hell, she really wasn't sure. She took a deep breath, put her head on straight and mentally focused on the task at hand. When she saw the airport come into view several miles out, she pulled back on the throttles and began a gentle descent. A few minutes later she could visually see the numbers of runway three six.

Nora was also starting to feel the wind. It was difficult to hold her course and her wings were rocking like a boat on rough seas. To maintain her heading required lots of rudder input to compensate. Unfortunately, she was sometimes over compensating causing her to overshoot her course in the other direction. She was struggling to keep the nose up. It was going to be the landing from hell.

In fact, it was so bad, she radioed the tower. She was dropping too much speed and couldn't pull the nose of the plane up to stabilize. "Pinebelt tower, Piper one, five, foxtrot, going around." She had to bail the landing.

"Piper one, five, foxtrot, clear for the go around. You're the only one in the area; clear to land at your discretion."

She pushed the throttles forward and leveled off flying just above the runway. Once she started gaining airspeed, she pulled back on the yoke and began her climb into the sky.

Sweat was pouring from her brow. This time it was going to take more skill and concentration. She made a climbing bank to the west, leveling off at one thousand five hundred feet. She was now re-established in the traffic pattern ready to attempt another approach. "Come on Nora, you can do this. You have to do this," she coached herself.

Making a sign of the cross, she approached the runway again. This time she was much more aggressive in her rudder control to compensate for the gusting crosswind. She pointed the nose in the direction of the gusts as Steve had taught her. Keeping her hands steady, she kept the nose up and lowered her speed to begin her descent. "Steady, steady," she said. One hundred fifty, one hundred, fifty, twenty five feet. She was at the end of the runway and boom. Nora was down. Smoothly. A huge sigh of relief came over her as she lowered her speed and applied her brakes. She was here. Thank God she was here.

Nora taxied the plane towards the hangars for general aviation. She had rented a temporary space from Grayson Aviation. The mechanic planned to meet her. Pulling the plane safely into the hangar, Nora ticked off yet another step of her strategy. Once she parked, she closed up the Piper and applied the pad lock to the outside door of the building.

"Would you like us to hold the key for you here, Mrs. Greenwood?" the mechanic asked her.

"No, thank you. I will hold onto them. I appreciate the offer, but I know the co-owner will be anxious to get them." Nora then took off her glasses and baseball cap. It felt good to shake out her hair. Despite it being December, it was drenched with sweat. She walked from the FBO over to the general terminal. It would be another hour or so before Charlene arrived, so Nora ordered a Coca-cola mixed with Orange Crush and took a seat in the bar to relax.

She couldn't help but watch the clock, wondering how Charlene was making it up Highway 11. Her friend had quite a lead foot; she hoped she wouldn't be pulled over by the Mississippi Highway Patrol. Nora had given a detailed map to Charlene on how to find the airport.

It was almost three o'clock and Charlene's Caddy was nowhere to be found. Nora got up and walked outside the terminal to look for her. She didn't want to appear like a loiterer in the terminal and she couldn't drink too many sodas due to the baby. The caffeine and sugar was already making the baby kick incessantly.

Nora rubbed her tummy. "I wonder if you will be born with the spirit of Jack Broussard?" she questioned the life inside. Nora felt that although her recent actions were unlawful and bit dodgy, her father would be proud that she was a fighter.

A flash of baby blue rounded the corner, tires screeching. Charlene! The Cadillac pulled up to the curb. "Good golly miss molly! I thought you would never get here," a relieved Nora exclaimed.

"Well, heck sister. I had my eyes so glued on that detailed map that I missed a damned turn with all the construction. Then, I was worried about rain, so I stopped to put the top up. God, I need a drink."

"No time for that, we have to get back on the road and back to Baton Rouge. Especially before we hit rush hour traffic." At this point, it looked like they might just make it.

"Nora Jean, I'm at least going through the Dairy Mart drive-thru to get a coke float. This girl's gotta have some sugar. I'm plum nearly wore out."

"Here, move over. I'll drive then. And yes, I'll stop at Dairy Mart."

"So, how was it?" Charlene had to get all the details.

"Nerve wracking. I almost couldn't land. But I made it. The plane is safely locked in the hangar."

They hugged and gave a big "yee-haw" out the windows of the Cadillac. Nora could breathe a sigh of relief. Now all that was left was to get back to her kids and call Frank. Devilish delight danced in her eyes as she imagined his face realizing his plane was gone.

Chapter 32

After having missed several weeks of flight instruction, Frank turned up for his lesson at Lakefront. A perfectionist when it came to clothes and appearance, first he took time for a shoe shine in the general aviation terminal. It was there he ran into Steve.

"Frank. Good to see that you showed up for your lesson today."

"Yeah well, I've had a little bit of trouble at home. Some complications on the domestic front. That's why I haven't been able to come," his normally cavalier attitude was definitely awry.

"I see," Steve eyed him over. Frank looked horrible with bags under his eyes and slightly unkempt. Certainly not his normal standard. "I assume you will be flying your Piper today."

"Yep. You got that right. I've come to love that damned plane. It's magic."

"Yeah, smooth ride. You're pretty lucky. It's a really a nice aircraft," Steve looked at his watch. "Whenever you are done, let me know. I am going to stop by the mechanic's office. Then I'll meet ya at the hangar."

Frank finished up his shoeshine and took a last couple of puffs on his cigar. Looking down at his shoes he grumbled, "A hell of a lot better than what Mabel does." He then gave the shoeshine boy a far too skimpy tip.

Frank was thinking about his flight today. It would be his last check-ride before his solo. When he reached the hangar, Joey and Steve were already there. As he approached, he noticed the stunned look on their faces. "What's up guys? Is there some problem with the plane?"

"Yeah, you could say that," the mechanic blurted.

"Mr. Greenwood, I dunno what to tell ya," Steve said as he rolled back the door of Hangar three. "The Piper's gone."

"What the hell?" Frank spit out his cigar onto the tarmac. "You gotta be kidding me. Where the fuck is it?" he screamed.

"We were hoping you could answer that question. The Piper was scheduled for a flight earlier this afternoon. We figured that it'd be back by now if Greenwood Oil had taken it out."

"Greenwood Oil wasn't scheduled to take anything out today," Frank claimed. "There isn't any company business planned for the whole weekend. In fact, our pilot is out of town."

Both of Steve and Joey looked ashen as they realized that the plane had been stolen. "Well Mr. Greenwood, I hope you have insurance," said the mechanic.

"Insurance! Is that all you can think about? You people need to report this to the police," Frank was livid. He strode back into the FBO to get on the first phone he could find. Phoning his father, he reported the latest developments of the missing plane and confirmed that his information was correct. There were no company trips planned that weekend. The Piper Aztec was really gone.

Frank returned to the aviation office where he found Steve and Joey. "I'd like to file a formal complaint of theft. What kind of operation are you running? Don't you all have security folk?" It was then they noted the key for hangar three missing.

Although Joey looked perplexed, in the back of his mind, Steve knew that Nora must have had something to do with it. "Here, Mr. Greenwood," Steve said getting out some paperwork, "I will prepare the documents for you. We'll go ahead and file the complaint. No need for you to worry about that."

"You have all the info," Frank grunted in disgust. "Call the police. And get in touch with me as soon as you find out something."

"Will do, Mr. Greenwood. On behalf of Lakefront, I

apologize about what happened today. Would you like to fly one of the other Pipers?"

"Hell no. Not after all this," roared Frank. "I have bigger fish to fry." Much to Steve's relief, off he took.

With the cancellation of the lesson, Steve immediately called the police. They arrived quite late in the afternoon. After Joey and he carefully answered their questions, they reported the plane as stolen. Steve decided to stay late and work on the books. He also planned to call Chet Monday morning to discuss the possibility of managing the business should he take the position at Humble Oil. It was weighing heavily on his mind. He was knee deep into figures when the phone rang. "Novak Aviation Services. It's a great day to fly. How can I help you today?" he said half-heartedly.

"Steve." He recognized the voice instantly. "It's Nora."

"Jeepers, where in the heck are you? You've turned the entire Greenwood family and the city of New Orleans upside down looking for you. I called over to the club and you weren't there."

"I'm sorry, it's complicated. Look, I just wanted you to know that I was okay," she explained.

"And there's another thing, the Greenwood's Piper was stolen. You wouldn't know anything about that now would you?" Steve asked, already dreading the answer.

"Let's say that at this point it isn't stolen."

"Christ almighty, Nora. What have you done?"

"What I had to for leverage. I had to have some kind of bargaining chip. Don't worry. I know what I am doing."

"The stakes are high here, Nora."

"Don't I know it. But whatever you do, you have to promise me you won't call Frank."

"No. I wouldn't ever rat you out. But the police were already here. Frank wanted me to file a report for theft. Nora you could go to jail."

"Not if I play my cards right with Frank. This is my only shot at getting full custody of my children. Please Steve, trust me. Let me finish it my way."

"Holy smokes, Nora," he shook his head. "You have some crazy ass ideas."

"Yes, I know. I hooked up with you didn't I?"

He smiled wryly. "Yeah, you did. I have lots to talk to you about, too. By the way, where are you? When can I see you?" he spun his lighter around nervously.

"I'll get in touch with you very soon. There's is a lot we need to discuss, but I need to take care of this first."

"Sure I get it. I'm just glad to know that you're safe. What about the kids? Are they okay?"

"Yeah, just not happy about where I have carted them off. But they are safe."

Still concerned about her whereabouts he asked, "Do you need any money?"

"Not right now, but I'll know more after I make this phone call to Frank."

"Please take care of yourself. And the kids."

"You know that I have their best interests at heart. Alrighty then, talk to you soon."

As Steve hung up the phone, he could only imagine what she must be feeling. Taking on one of the most powerful families in New Orleans was auspiciously dangerous. She was playing with fire. He certainly didn't envy being in her shoes. Hearing her voice and knowing she was in one piece, brought him immense relief. He put his head down in his hands and rubbed his brows. Nora was something else. Courageous, but reckless.

Chapter 33

Nora and Charlene arrived safely back at the Travel Lodge. To their relief, the station wagon was parked there too. It was about 5:30 PM and her kids were ready to see her.

"Mom."

"Mommy, we've missed you."

"You've been gone all day," Kayce complained and rolled her eyes. Charlene was happy to how gleefully they greeted their mother. Save one.

One look at Kayce's face gave away what she thought. It was clear that her museum outing and picnic had not been entertaining. She stood in the room with her arms folded defensively.

Nora re-introduced Justine to Charlene. "Good to see you again, Justine."

"Mrs. Hebert, what are you doing here?" Cathy asked.

Now Charlene was on the spot with more white fibs. Bless me father, she thought in reference to the church confession she was going to have to make. "Oh I came up to shop and ran into an old friend. Hey y'all. I don't know about you, but I'm starving."

Nora agreed. "You guys hungry? Let's all go out and have a Baton Rouge food-fest!" The kids were excited to get out of the motel. They dashed around to find their shoes and jackets.

"Justine, you've just been a miracle worker!" Nora thanked her profusely for what she had accomplished.

"There is just no way I could have gotten this done without you," she hugged her tight.

"No problem, Missus Nora. I would do anything for ya. Mr. Frank's never been kind to me and it's somethin' that I always remembered."

"I apologize for his behavior to you."

"No need Missus Nora, I just glad to help out. He'll get whatsa comin' to 'im."

Nora smiled just a little.

"If'n you remember my stories, I was in a *simular* situation myself."

"Yes I do remember, and that is why I so appreciate your kindness."

They all got into the wagon. Nora paid Justine generously and dropped her off at the train station. She planned to take the *Southern Belle* back to New Orleans. Then Charlene and Nora took the kids out for a nice meal. Big Boy burgers and fries.

The street lamps and shop windows were bedecked with twinkling Christmas lights. It was odd for Nora. Christmas coming was the last thing on her radar screen. While the kids occupied themselves with shakes, burgers and Big Boy hats, Charlene inquired about their next step.

"I think I have a phone call to make. To the best of my guestimation, Frank has surely gone ballistic realizing the plane is missing. So now it's time for me to play my final hand."

"Golly, I hope it works, Nora. For everyone's sake."

"Me too. I'm really ready for the game of espionage to be over." They both laughed.

"Hey we weren't half bad for double-O sevens," Charlene teased.

"Half bad?" Nora quipped. "I just stole a plane and you drove the get-a-way car. I'd say were pretty close."

Once back to the motel, Nora stepped out to the lobby payphone and put in her quarters to phone Frank. New Orleans was long distance. Charlene was going to watch the kids until she was back. She knew she needed to catch Frank before he was drunk. Expecting him to answer, she jumped a little when he did.

"Frank Greenwood," he answered sober.

"Frank, this is Nora," she said as calmly as possible.

"Well, well you don't say. Just exactly where in the God's green earth are you? And where in the hell are my kids?" the shouting-fest began.

"Settle down, Frank or we're not going to have this conversation."

"No siree. The minute we find out where your little ass is we're gonna have you thrown in jail for stealing my car and my kids."

"That's what I wanna talk to you about. Is that the only thing you're missing?"

There was dead silence on the phone. "The plane. You know about the plane?" Frank was stunned.

"Yes, Frank, I do. In fact, your plane isn't stolen. Well, let me correct that. It's missing."

"From the hangar. How do you explain that?"

Then victoriously, Nora played her trump card. "I'll tell you exactly how I know Frank. I flew it."

"How is that even frickin' possible?"

"Because. Unbeknownst to you, I've been taking flying lessons too. In fact, I already soloed and cross-countried quite some time ago. Interestingly enough, in a Piper."

"What?" he bellowed.

"The very one that is now sitting in a locked, rented hangar."

"What is going on? God damn you, Nora. And why have you taken the plane?"

"Because, Frank. Because it's a prize you treasure. And right now, until any court documents are filed, it's community property.

"Not in the state of Louisiana it isn't," he shouted into the receiver.

"That's exactly why it isn't in the state of Louisiana." Nora was enjoying this.

"What the fuck, Nora? Just what do you think you are up to?"

"I will lay it out for you, Frank. It's going to work like this. I have the kids and I have the plane. And I don't plan to keep both. If you'd like your plane back, here is what you're going to agree to," she paused to let him catch up. "By the way," she fibbed on this one, "I have you on tape. So be careful what you say. I know that you probably have an appointment set up with a lawyer."

"You bet we do."

"But here is what you are going to say. You will give me full custody of the kids."

"Oh, no I won't. The kids are mine too," he argued.

"Not in this agreement they're not. I want full custody and I want the children's belongings. Clothes and toys. Other than that, I want absolutely nothing from the Greenwoods. You will sign the divorce papers citing irreconcilable differences with me as primary custodian of the children."

He could no longer stand holding his tongue, "The hell I will, Nora. How dare you think you can steal a plane and threaten me with it."

"I would be careful about using those terms. They are not technically correct. And let me tell you another thing. If you so much as contradict, change or don't sign those papers on Monday; not only will you never see your plane again, but I will make it a point to contact the media. I'll let them know exactly what kind of abusive marriage I was in with Frank Greenwood. I will paint you as a womanizing, alcoholic tyrant who beats his wife."

"Nora, what a bunch of crap. You don't have any proof."

"Oh, but I do. That, dear Frank, is where you are wrong. How would you like a picture of how you beat me up on the front page of the *Times Picayune* and every other Associated Press newspaper that would pick up the story?"

"You wouldn't dare."

"Oh yes, Frank. I would. I have nothing to lose and everything to gain."

"You bitch," was all he could come up with.

"And this time, for once in your life; you're not gonna win this hand of poker. I'll be in touch." She hung up the phone and sighed with relief. Nora had just won that round.

Frank nearly ripped the phone out of the wall he was so outraged. He couldn't believe her audacity making those demands. Yet, as he mulled them over in his head, he couldn't imagine having charges filed against him for spousal abuse. Not to mention going to jail. That would be the scandal of all scandals. Recalling his father's words to him, he knew he had no choice.

Furious, he got in his car and drove to see his parents on St. Charles. Once he laid out the terms, his father agreed there really was no other option. Due to Frank's indiscretions, violence and overall unsavory behavior, he would sign over full custody of the children. Everyone at the club knew he was an ass.

Nora would receive no money from the Greenwoods. Any potential scandal would be avoided. They would quickly and quietly divorce in closed courts, signing through the lawyers. The predicament Frank had gotten himself into would be avoided. As the CEO and founder of Greenwood Oil, he had to consider the ramifications. If charges were filed against his son, as the leading attorney for the company, it would make headlines across Louisiana. Way beyond the boundaries of New Orleans. That was a situation George Greenwood, Sr. desperately wanted to circumvent.

With reluctant trepidation, Frank agreed. On Monday morning, he would meet with the divorce attorney and spell out the terms to which they agreed.

The signed divorce papers would be delivered by courier to Nora's attorney. Nora Jean Broussard Greenwood, petitioner, would then be sole custodian. They would be rid of her.

Chapter 34

By Sunday evening, Kayce's growing concern about why they were not returning to New Orleans was about to boil over. She was moody and on edge during their morning *beignet* run and ferry trip across the Mississippi River. The sun was now going down and her mother not making moves to return to New Orleans. It was confrontation time. "Look mother, you may think that I'm naive but I'm not. I know something is going on. You just aren't telling me what it is. Why are we not going back home? It's Sunday night and we have school tomorrow."

Nora tried to stall. "I don't understand why you can't relax and watch TV with your brothers and sisters. *Walt Disney* is a brand new one and it's on color. Just settle down and enjoy the show."

"Mother, I don't give a darn about some show. I know that we're not going back. Are we?"

"Kayce let's go in another room to talk about this."

"What other room? This rinky-dink motel room only has beds and a bathroom. There isn't even a kitchen. So exactly where would you like to go?"

"Let's step outside, then."

"Fine," she flounced. They stepped out onto the second story balcony of the Travel Lodge. "Look, everyone else in there doesn't realize that you are pregnant, but I do. I'm not retarded. Plus, I heard you over the phone."

"Yes, I remember the eavesdropping."

Kayce ignored the jab. "I don't understand why you want to wreck everything by getting a divorce. And I sure don't get why you won't tell Daddy about the baby. Doesn't he have a right to know?"

"In time."

"You are just going to ruin our goddamn lives."

"Kayce Lee don't you dare use that kind of language with me."

"Well somebody needs to. You're messing up everything. What about school?"

"What about what, Kayce? Metairie Country Club? Is it about losing that little silver spoon in your mouth?" Nora had struck a nerve.

"I hate you mother, I just hate you," Kayce screamed.

"Kayce you listen to me," Nora grabbed her by the shoulders. "I know you're upset. And you think you know all the answers, but you're wrong. I can't and won't go into the details right now, but very soon I will be able to. There are a couple of other things that have to happen first." Nora wished her daughter could wait a mere twenty-four hours.

"Get your hands of me, Mother." Kayce yanked her shoulders away and began to stomp off down the balcony.

"Kayce you come back here right now."

"Oh yeah? Make me." Kayce was defiant. "If you won't take us back to New Orleans than I'll take myself." She was bound toward the external stairs of the motel that led to the parking lot.

Nora hurried to the edge of the balcony. "Kayce Lee Greenwood, get your butt back up here to this motel room or I'm going to come and get you."

"Like to see you try. Let's see you run in your condition." With that, Kayce dashed down both flights of metal stairs. Once out in the parking lot, she broke into a sprint.

"Kayce . . ." Nora screamed. Highway 61 was out in front and that is where she was headed. "Get back here."

But that only made Kayce run faster. She ran past the Dairy Mart, the Esso station and the Waffle House. It was twilight and getting dark fast. There was Kayce running on the side of the highway in traffic. Nora was beside herself.

JEANETTE VAUGHAN

She went back into the motel room where the kids were. Not having Justine any more, there was no one to watch them. "Hey kiddos, you all keep watching *Disney*. I'm going to get us some Poptarts for tomorrow's breakfast. Okay?"

"Sure Mom. I'll be in charge of everyone. I can do it," brave Cathy volunteered.

"Okay, hon. Great. But don't open the door for anyone, unless you hear my voice. Understand? Lock the door behind me and promise you won't open it, okay? I mean it." Nora grabbed her keys and purse and as quickly as she could, without tripping, went down stairs to the parking lot. She had seen Kayce take off towards the right down 61. Hopefully she was still going in that same direction. Ugh, Kayce was impossible.

Nora started up the wagon and proceeded down the highway scanning the streets frantically for Kayce. But to no avail. She was nowhere to be seen. Nora was looking and looking, left and right. She stopped into the Esso station and asked the attendant if had seen anyone.

"Not that I know of," he said. She drove a little further down the street. Kayce had no ID, no purse, nor money. Nora broke out in a cold sweat imagining what could possibly happen to her young daughter. Highway 61 was as truck route into New Orleans. It was packed with eighteen wheelers housing lonely truckers coming and going. Relatively, this was a safe part of the country, but roadside abductions had occurred. Although Kayce dressed rather juvenile, she was very well developed for her age. Still, she was merely a twelve year old, defenseless girl.

With her windows down, Nora continued to call for her daughter. "Kayce. Kayce, I love you. Please come out if you are hiding. Please." But there was no response. Nora was veritably sick with worry. She drove around for at least what was close to an hour with no results. She realized she had to get back to the other three that she had left alone in the motel room. Disparaged, she thought about what to do. Christ, Kayce's stunt could just sabotage everything. Nora was filled with dismay.

The other kids were safe and nonplussed when she got back to the room. "I thought you were getting us some

Poptarts?" Cathy inquired.

"Everything was closed, Cathy. Plus, I forgot we don't have a toaster. Perhaps we'll go to the Waffle House in the morning."

"Where's Kayce?"

"I don't know.

"We know you had a big fight. A really big one," prodded Cathy.

"Did Kayce run away?" Leisel asked.

"It appears that's the case," answered Nora.

Cathy started crying. "Where's Kayce? When is she coming back?" she sobbed.

"I dunno," Nora regretted having told them. "Let's just wait and see. I am sure she will come back."

"Yeah. She doesn't know anyone here," said Leisel.

Nora's nerves were absolutely frazzled. She wished she had a cigarette. She was completely spent and exhausted. So were the kids. Their eyes were getting droopy. It had been a big couple of days.

Running some bath water, Nora got them all into the tub together, much to Iggy's chagrin. She only had a limited amount of energy left, but they needed a bath and to get to bed. Cathy helped the others put their jammies on. They said prayers for Kayce's safe return. Nora told them not to worry, that by the time they woke up, Kayce would be there. Then kissed them goodnight. Although she was giving them hope, she worried that may not be the case.

When the children were asleep, Nora used her last bit of change to call Charlene. Surely she would have gotten home by now. Nora feared if Kayce called anyone first, it would be her father Frank. Nora just needed someone else to know what was happening to give her some advice. She was afraid to call the police, as then her gig would be up. There was too much at risk. And yet, she was terrified for the safety of her daughter. She prayed that Kayce came to her senses and returned.

Charlene almost didn't answer the phone because it was after 9:00 PM. No decent Southerner would ring at this hour. But then she realized it could be Nora. When she picked it up, she could tell Nora was frantic.

"Charlene, oh God. You won't believe what has

happened."

"What? I thought everything was fine. I just got home. What's going on?"

"It's Kayce."

"My stars. Is she causing a ruckus? I worried about that."

"No, you don't understand. She's run away Char."

"She's what? To where?"

"That's just it. She left the motel and I chased after her. As soon as I got the other kids settled, I drove around forever looking. But she had a head start. I couldn't find her anywhere."

"She's nowhere to be found?"

"No," Nora sobbed.

"Nora. Kayce'll come back. She has no one and nowhere to go."

"I know. She doesn't have any money or even any change. All she has are the clothes on her back. She's twelve for gosh sakes."

"Nora . . . I know you are worried. Try to calm down and we'll just pray she comes back."

"I'm trying, but it's impossible. This is atrocious."

"What do you want to do about everything else? Should we continue as planned?"

"Absolutely," said Nora. "I think. I mean, normally I would say yes, but now this Kayce mess."

"It's already all set into motion. You work on getting Kayce back. I'll take care of the rest with the lawyers."

"Yes, I think Frank is going to sign over full custody to me. He was furious, of course, but the plan worked so far. He was speechless."

"I think you've got him by the balls. The lawyer has the courier scheduled to go present the papers for signature tomorrow. She's finding out from his family who their attorney is. It will all be handled through them. You won't have to speak to anyone. I think that is best."

"I do too. You're a goddess, Charlene."

After witnessing what Frank did to Nora's face and how he threatened her life, Charlene and Max put down the retainer for Nora's lawyer from their savings. The street savvy, prizewinning attorney already had papers drawn up for full custody. They were to be delivered to

Frank's attorney's office first thing Monday morning for signature. Nora had given Frank the deadline of end of business day and planned on sticking to it.

"I'll keep you posted."

"And if you hear anything about Kayce . . ."

"You know I'll call you straight away."

"I am just worried sick. She's such a little girl."

"Honey, I know you are crazy with worry. But you have to look out for yourself, the baby you are carrying, and the others too."

"Do you think I should call the police?"

"If she doesn't return soon, then yes. You don't have much choice. At least they would be out looking for her."

"Good point, I agree." Nora could do nothing but pace the room as she thought and thought about where her daughter might be. She knew in some ways that Kayce had the same independent streaks as she did. That's what worried her. She knew how heartbroken Kayce was about everything. Out of all of her children, Kayce was closest to her father. And was the most influenced about his affluent lifestyle. When Kayce had still not returned two hours later, Nora picked up the phone and called the police.

"Baton Rouge Police. Is this an emergency?" droned the dispatcher.

"Well, yes and no."

"It either is or isn't. What is your emergency, Ma'am?"

"My daughter is missing."

"Yes Ma'am. How can we help you?"

"I think she's run away."

"Ma'am you can't file a missing persons report for twenty-four hours. That's our policy."

"But she's only twelve."

"Ma'am we have teenagers that run away all the time. And return safely. We can't file a report on everyone who is just missing for a couple of hours. That's the policy."

"So you are going to do nothing?" Nora was outraged.

"Can you give me a description Ma'am?"

"Yes, of course. She is about five feet tall, medium build. About a hundred pounds. She has shoulder length, strawberry blonde . . ." and then Nora broke into tears as she began to describe her eldest.

"Ma'am, I'm sure you must be upset."

"I am. Dear heavens. We are visiting Baton Rouge. We don't even live here."

"Where are you from Ma'am?" he queried.

"New Orleans," Nora gave away.

"And her name?"

"Kayce Greenwood."

"Date of birth."

"April 4, 1949," Nora sobbed softly.

"Alright, Ma'am. We'll see what we can do."

"Thank you, officer."

In sheer exhaustion, Nora fell asleep in her clothes. But she woke up at 3:00 AM with a cold shiver down her spine realizing that Kayce was not back at the motel. Her necked ached from sleeping in the chair. The baby was kicking and in an uncomfortable position too. She went outside to the balcony and looked up at the stars. There was a full moon. At least it was a clear night. "Kayce, my baby girl, where in the world are you?"

Chapter 35

When Kayce took off from her mother, she had no idea where she would go. She ran past the Esso and Waffle House and kept going. When she heard her mother call for her, she ran faster down the side of the highway until she got to the Texaco station about a half mile down the road. Tuckered out, she stopped. Crying and distraught, she was not sure what direction she was travelling on the highway. Up or down? Towards New Orleans or further into the city.

While she was weeping at the Texaco, a truck driver approached her. "Can I help you Miss?"

Kayce looked up. He was an average, nice enough looking, middle-aged man. She hesitated, having always been taught not to talk to strangers. But then she realized she had no choice. "I've run away and I'm trying to get home to New Orleans," Kayce explained what was partly true.

"You've run away? And how'd you get here?" Kayce turned her head and looked the other way. "I see. You don't want to tell anybody. Well, how do you expect to get back?"

"I dunno," said Kayce. "I don't even know what direction it is I am supposed to be going."

"New Orleans is about an hour and a half south," he pointed, "across the swamps."

Kayce shivered as she thought about having to cross the long, lonely bridges of the swamps in the dark. There were alligators in there.

"Highway 61 runs into Airline highway on the western side of the city, near Kenner. Have you got any money?"

"No sir."

"I see. So you can't even make a phone call home?"

"No sir".

"Well it's your lucky day, 'cuz I happen to be headed to New Orleans."

Kayce recalled the horror stories; her mother had warned her about hitch hikers. But, she wanted to get as far away from her mother as possible. Home to her Daddy. She wasn't sure what she should do. She knew she had no money and no way to call. With no other alternatives she could see, Kayce did the unthinkable and hitched a ride.

"You can ride in the side of the cab there," he pointed. She nodded and climbed up the steep stairs to the cab, just hoping he wasn't some vile ax murderer. The truck rolled out and started down the highway. It was pretty late in the evening, about 10:00 PM. As the truck rumbled along, Kayce fell asleep in the cab. Luckily for her, the truck driver had a family and children. Some of which were teenagers. He knew what kind of trouble teens could get in. Out of the kindness of his heart, he was happy to return a wayward one back home.

He continued his journey through the swamps and arrived in New Orleans at about midnight. Gently, he woke up Kayce, "Hey little lady, we're on the outskirts. Where do you want me to drop ya?"

Kayce didn't want to give away where she lived, so she sleepily told him to leave her at the K and B on Canal Street. It was the only thing she could think of. Plus, it was open twenty-four hours a day. "I'll call my father from there."

"Sure thing," he said. The K and B wasn't far. Its huge sign was lit up in bright neon with a big K & B in purple and white. He pulled the large rig to a stop and helped her down. "How you gonna make a phone call without any money?"

She looked sheepish. He pulled out a five dollar bill and handed it to her. "Here, make your call. If you can't get in touch with him, take a taxi home. But go home."

"Thank you so much. I appreciate it. I'm going home

to my Daddy," she assured. As she got down from the truck, she looked up at him. "That was a very nice thing you did."

"Nah. I got kids. Now you get on with it little lady. This here's a very dangerous place to be alone at night. I want to make sure wherever you are gettin' you get there safe."

Kayce walked inside the drug store and got change from the clerk. She walked over to the pay phone outside Katz and Bestoff. Putting in a dime, she called her father. He didn't answer on the first few rings.

"Frank Greenwood. Who the heck is calling at this time of night?"

"Daddy. Daddy, it's Kayce."

"Kayce where in tarnation are you?"

"I've run away. I'm somewhere downtown near Canal Street."

"And where in the hell is your mother?"

She could tell by her father's slurred speech he had been drinking. "Mother's with the rest of the kids."

"And what is it you want with me?"

"Daddy I want to come home and live with you."

Frank tried to get some clarity in his head to think about what he was going to say. He had already agreed with his father to sign the custody papers tomorrow. And for now, was advised not to see the children. He hesitated for a long time. Then, he dropped a bombshell on her. "Your mother's made her own bed and she's gonna have to lie in it. As far as you all are concerned, you're no longer my responsibility." He hung up the phone.

Kayce couldn't believe her ears. "No . . . Daddy. No," she screamed into the receiver. She began to cry hysterically. She couldn't believe that her own father was rejecting her. She was all by herself in downtown New Orleans and her father would not come pick her up. Going home had been her only thought. As she looked around the dark streets, she suddenly felt very frightened and alone. Kayce had no idea what to do now.

She became despondent. "Why are you doing this Daddy?" she balled. Kayce was at a total loss. It was cold and she had no coat. So, she began to walk down the block toward what lights she saw.

As she got closer, it became brighter. The Quarter never slept. Crossing Canal, she entered its edge near Rampart St. Kayce could hear zydeco music and revelers from inside the bars and nightclubs. She passed a voodoo shop. She had never been in this part of town at night. It was lurid and scary.

The dank, putrid odors from the back alleys made her nauseous, so she continued to walk along the main streets. She passed by some peculiar, multi-colored painted individuals from a tattoo shop. Strange. There were prostitutes on the street corner. Some lewd men up in the balconies were making jeers at them. The Quarter at night was a dichotomy of music and mystery. There were some boys, tap dancing with metal tacked to their leather shoes. They were younger than her.

Kayce walked for what must have been four blocks and stopped in front of a building that did not appear to be a bar. The sign read, *The Ryder Coffeehouse*. She thought about calling her mother's friend Charlene, if she could find a phone. But decided against it; as Charlene would only take her back to her mother. She wasn't even sure if she knew the number. She hoped that if her father saw her in person, he would change his mind. She was his Kayce girl. That is what she believed, anyway.

As she crouched outside the coffee shop, a tall, dark, grey-haired women came outside for a smoke. She had the most haunting eyes. As she was about to light up, she turned and looked at Kayce. "Girl. What yer doin in a place like dis at night?" Her accent was very strong. Kayce almost didn't understand it.

"I ran away," Kayce said. "And I've called my father and he won't come pick me up."

"Girl you are cold. Come in side and sit down. I'll get you a warm drink. Some tea to get da chill out. We'll figure out what to do." The exotic woman was the same one that Nora had met in the coffee shop a few months before. Jack Broussard's lover.

She brought Kayce inside the dark, moody club and sat her down. There was a ring of smoke that circled overhead. There was some kind of mandolin music playing along with a harmonica. People were dressed in Bohemian clothing of dark colors. There were young women with heavy eye makeup. A heavy odor of incense pervaded. Just about everyone inside was smoking while drinking coffee or wine.

While Kayce was sitting at a table, the woman returned carrying warm tea with milk and some chocolate cookies. She wasn't quite sure what to do with a twelve year old who was clearly out of place.

"Thank you."

"Tis nothing, a lil' *lagniappe*."

"Lagniappe?"

"Tis a Cajun word. It means a lil' something extra. So you are a runaway?" Kayce nodded. "And where is your mother den?"

Kayce wasn't sure if she should answer or not. All of these people were so odd and she was frightened. "My mother is in another city with my brothers and sisters."

"And how did you get here child?"

"I hitched," Kayce held her chin up high.

"My child dat is so dangerous for you. Being out at sucha time at night. Dere are men out dere who would happily take advantage of you."

Kayce looked down and shuddered. She held on tight to her hot, steaming tea. It smelled of cardamom and soothing cinnamon.

"And where are you to go now?"

Kayce's pride evaporated. She held back tears. "I don't know. My father won't let me come home."

The woman could empathize with her situation being somewhat of a gypsy herself. "We will sort it out. Maybe dere is some way dat you will get back in touch wid your mama. You will find, my dear, dat it is your mama who will watch over you and take care of you." Kayce was listening. "It is our mudders dat we hold dear."

Kayce wondered how she could make such statements not knowing anything about her mother. She slowly sipped her tea. It made her warm inside. The woman brought out her tarot cards. "Have you ever seen into da future?" she said spreading out the cards.

Innocently, Kayce shook her head. "No. I don't believe in that kind of stuff." She had heard about voo-doo and black magic in The Quarter.

"Well how can you doubt it if you never tried it? Here

let me read your cards." She deftly began to shuffle the cards several times. Then one by one she turned over four separate cards. "Ahh . . . dis card shows here dat you are troubled."

Kayce gave her smirk, "Well that's kind of obvious isn't it? I mean, I've run away and I'm alone in The Quarter with nowhere to go."

"A sharp tongue in someone so young."

Then Kayce looked down and realized how rude she must have sounded. The woman was silent. "I'm sorry, that was so ugly of me. I apologize. I'm just scared."

"Understandable," said the woman. Kayce was fascinated when the woman pulled over another card. "You have loss in your family and dis is what has caused you such grief." The third card was turned over, "Ah. Dis grief will last for quite some time for dere are stormy waters ahead."

Kayce again was dazzled. It wasn't unlike her own situation for she knew there would be trouble ahead with her parents getting a divorce. She was quite intrigued with the woman and the tarot cards. "How long will it last?"

"Dat I cannot say yet. But let's look to da future to find out." With the last card she turned over, "Some time ahead in your life dere will be peace. For da conflict you feel. At last when you have put it right, all will be well."

Kayce wondered if she was making all this up or if she really saw the future in the cards. The whole phenomenon was bewitching to her. All of a sudden she heard a deep voice.

"Is dat Kayce Greenwood?" the deep voice beckoned.

Looking up she wasn't sure who it was. A large, very tall Negro man was standing over them. "How do you know my name?"

"Because I know your mama very well and she sho' would be worried about you."

For Kayce, things were getting more and more bizarre. In fear, she got up from the table to leave. All this mystery was spooky. Totally freaked out, she moved for the door.

The man softly touched her arm, "I don't think so. You won't be going out into da night again by yoself."

"You can't stop me."

He laughed deeply, "I think I can. It's time for you to listen. I'm gonna help you."

Kayce didn't realize what he was talking about until he started explaining the situation. He motioned to the woman, Gia. "Thank you for taking your time and making dis child safe. I do know her mama. She is Missus Nora. Broussard."

"Greenwood." Kayce gave him a look. "My mother's name is Nora Greenwood," she said emphatically.

He turned back to Gia, "Her maiden name was Broussard."

It was Gia that looked like she had seen a ghost this time. "Broussard . . . was her father? Jack Broussard?"

"That I wouldn't know," said Big Daddy. "But I's know someone who would. I'll ask my wife when I get home. She know Missus Nora very well."

Kayce looked at the woman. "Jack Broussard was my grandfather. But he was dead long before I was born."

The woman looked carefully at Kayce. She looked nothing like Jack. Gia remained silent. She was not going to reveal anything further to Kayce. Turning to Big Daddy, "Tell your wife, Miss Mabel dat I do know of dis woman. Should she ever come back down dis way I would like to visit wid her."

"I'll be happy to repay you and do as you wish, Gia. You's been a kind soul to dis wayward child."

"I do what I see must be."

"Come on, honeychile, *les go*. You's don't need to be in dis place." Big Daddy took Kayce's hand and walked her to Mabel's house. Mabel was surprised to see her with Big Daddy. Kayce was a little weirded out to be there, in an all colored neighborhood. It was certainly a part of New Orleans that she had never seen. But then, she recognized a face.

"Mabel," Kayce cried out running to her.

"Goodness gracious child. Where you've been and how on earth did you get here?" Mabel extended her arms from her large body.

"I ran away."

"Oh my geezus. Your mother must be sick wid worry."

Kayce could hold back no longer and burst into tears. For the last couple of hours she had been terrified. "Oh

Mabel, it's terrible," she sniveled. "Mother took us and they are getting a divorce and now Daddy says I can't come home. And that he doesn't want me," she said between sobs.

"I am so sorry chile. I knew dat split would be very tough on you all."

"Take me home Mabel, I want to go home."

"I can't do dat child. Your Daddy done lemme go. He fired me. I have no job wid da Greenwoods no mo'."

Kayce felt her world was falling apart. "What am I going to do?" she cried harder.

"Look chile. We need to talk. Your mama loves you. Very much. And you need to be wid her right now. Your Daddy. He has dese situations he need to work out. When it's better, maybe you will see a change. He might be a daddy to you den."

Kayce wasn't sure she fully understood, but she didn't argue with Mabel. It felt good to be in her warm, comforting arms.

Chapter 36

Mabel could see, as late evening wore on, how uncomfortable Kayce was out of her own environment. The poor girl had been put through the ringer. She was horrified when Kayce began to tell her about how she had hitchhiked away from Baton Rouge. She was lucky not to have been attacked. After serving up some comfort food, she had Kayce lay down on a cot. It was close to four in the morning and way too early to call anyone now. She would wait a few more hours and give Nora a call at the motel. Justine had told her they'd be at the Travel Lodge in Baton Rouge.

Before the crack of dawn, even though still in the wee hours, Mabel crept out and made her way to the corner phone box to call Kayce's mother. Mabel had no telephone at home. She knew Nora would be desperate to know that her daughter was okay. She had enough change to call and get operator assisted long distance to Baton Rouge. When the receptionist answered, Mabel asked to speak to Justine Marcelle knowing Nora had registered under her name.

The operator connected Mabel to the room. "Hello," said Nora groggily.

"Oh, Missus Nora, yous never gonna believe, but I gots Kayce here wid me."

"Praise the lord for that. But how is that possible? Where has she been?"

"All I knows Missus Nora is dat she here wid me and she safe. I just wanted you to know."

"Oh, thank goodness," Nora exclaimed.

"She done hitched a ride wid one a dem truckers. And dey dropped her off near Canal Street."

"Is she okay?" Nora was flabbergasted.

"Yeah, she awright. She done called her daddy and her daddy wouldn't take her in."

"What? Frank wouldn't let her come home?" the cogs in Nora's brain began to spin. "Oh, she must be crushed. Tell her that I love her and that I will come into town this morning to get her."

"Awright, Missus Nora. Sho nuff, will do."

"I know you have to work Mabel, so if need be Charlene can come get her."

"Naw, she awright for now. Yous come when you can. I gots a day off today."

While the children still slept, Nora went back to the pay phone and rang Charlene. She knew she would be anxious to hear the update. "So sorry to ring so early."

"Did you hear anything about Kayce?"

"Yes. She's alright. Evidently she hitched a ride with some trucker back to New Orleans. It's a long story, but Mabel's got her."

"That child is one lucky duck. But I am glad she is safe, Nora."

"Me too. It's Mabel's day off. So for now, I'm covered. I hadn't planned to come back to New Orleans so soon, but I guess I don't have any choice."

"Well, she most likely is a bit out of sorts being down in Marigny, but I'm sure Mabel will watch over her. That's a good thing. It'll keep her in one place. And away from Frank, bless her heart."

"I hope you're right," said Nora relieved. Crisis averted. Now she just had to wait and see how things played out with the legal papers.

After the kids got up, she had them pack and took them to the Waffle House for breakfast. Full of carbs and maple syrup, she loaded them up into the station wagon and traversed back to New Orleans. The gators along the bridge had sure seen plenty of the Greenwoods, lately.

Their journey took them back across the long stretches of swamp towards the crescent city. Now, it was a waiting game. Sweating out the hours until the end of the business day to see if her elaborate plan had worked. Not knowing was excruciating. It was mid-morning and the car trip back to New Orleans would require another two hours. Nora reached Airline Highway at about 11:00 AM. She turned towards downtown. She now knew her way well toward Marias St.

Kayce was rather quiet when Nora arrived and initially wouldn't look at her. Mabel greeted Nora with big hugs. "Tell Big Daddy thank you for coming to the aid of my family, yet again."

"No problem, Missus Nora."

Nora looked down empathetically at Kayce, "I understand you've had quite an adventure last night."

Kayce turned her gaze away. "Come on Kayce. Cheer up. You're not the first teenager to run away and you won't be the last. I just hope after this experience, that you realize how much you were missed. We were worried sick."

Her daughter looked up at her mother in tears. "So you're not going to punish me?"

"I think your adventure and terror has been punishment enough, don't you?"

"Oh, Mama," she ran to Nora and hugged her. It was a temporary reprieve to the discord that had been occurring. For that, both of them were relieved.

"Come on, we've got things to do."

When Nora was about to leave, Mabel gave her another message from Big Daddy. "You know da coffee shop, where Big Daddy works?"

"Yeah, I know the one."

"Dere is dis woman. A tall, dark-skinned woman."

"The one with the mysterious eyes," Nora said.

"She says she might know you."

"I've only met her once. But you are right." Nora was surprised the connection had made its way back to Mabel.

"Some kind of connection to your father."

Nora was piqued at the mention of his name. "Yes. I believe she knew Jack?"

"Dats what she say. She knew da name Jack Broussard. She wants to see you."

Worried about her legal dramas, she really didn't give much heed to what Mabel was saying. There were so many tasks to complete. She had to put that request on a back burner until her legal and domestic issues were sorted out.

* * * * *

Early Monday morning Frank was already in the lawyer's office waiting. Just like she and Charlene arranged, the courier delivered the papers to Frank's divorce attorney. Although he didn't want to, under the pressure of his father, he signed them whilst the courier waited. The courier then returned them to Nora's lawyer.

Meanwhile, once Nora had Kayce back safely in the car, she stopped for coffee and gave Charlene a call. "All is well. We're back in the city. I've gotten Kayce. Now it's just a matter of time to see what happens."

"Nora, I have good news on that. Frank was at his attorney's office at 09:00 AM this morning. So they sent the courier over early."

"You've got to be kidding? Is it done? Is it over?"

"Thankfully, Nora, yes. Your scheme worked better than you thought. From what I understand, the Greenwoods weren't happy. But they felt they had no other options. The attorney filed the papers with the courts this morning."

"Oh, my God. I can't believe it's really over. I'm free. Thank you so much Charlene. I really, really appreciate it. You're the absolute best friend ever!" Nora was elated and hated to impose further. "I do have one more small favor to ask."

"Am I surprised?"

Nora didn't wish to speak to Nellie. She asked Charlene to phone and let her mother know that they all were okay. She just couldn't cope with Nellie's drama right now. Nora had her fill of stress for one day, but wanted Nellie's worries to be over. Charlene volunteered.

"I'm going to the attorney's office to drop off the keys to the plane," Nora explained.

"Sure thing, toots. Nora Jean, I am so proud of you," Charlene said with relief in her voice.

When Nora hung up, she drove straight to the office on Carondelet. As promised, she planned to deliver the keys to the hangar, the address of which hangar the plane was located and a map. It would be Frank's worry to figure out how to get it back to Lakefront.

She also wanted to get a copy of the signed papers in her hands for protection, just in case Frank tried to pull a fast one. The bigshot lawyer that Charlene and Max hired was on the twelfth floor of one of the high rises in downtown. Nora took her children up the elevator with her.

When she stepped into the office, the secretary buzzed and gave her name, "Nora Broussard Greenwood to see you."

The fancy beveled glass office door opened. "So this is the infamous, plane stealing Nora Greenwood?" a short, sassy Jewish looking woman with spectacles spoke.

"That's Nora Broussard now," she smirked. "I am not sure I want to own that title."

"I wouldn't expect that you would," the attorney laughed. "I have to say in all my years, this has been my shortest retainer. And I expect that I won't have any other plaintiffs capable of pulling quite such a stunt to finalize their case."

"Should I take that as a compliment?" Nora beamed.

"But of course."

"As promised, here are the keys to the hangar and a map," she handed over the envelope.

"Excellent. Frank did make some stipulations regarding the children's belongings, toys and various other minor things."

"Oh?" Nora worried.

"Due to the violence involved with the case, I took the liberty of establishing protective orders. You are each under a protective order not to see each other, nor come within two hundred yards of each other, if at all possible, unless at a public function regarding the children. Yadee, yadee."

"No problem there."

"He also spoke to how he would get the children's and your things to you. He will be dropping them by the Hebert's sometime today."

"Excellent. Then it appears we're done."

"So you can really fly?" the female attorney looked

impressed.

"You better believe it."

"Where'd you take that thing, anyway?"

"Just a hop, skip and a jump away. To another state."

"Clever. I'll have to remember that if I ever need a hijack for leverage."

Nora liked this attorney. Charlene had done well. She put one of her cards in her purse, just in case. Nora had no plans to tell Frank about the plane's location herself. She was glad the attorney would handle it. That was worth gold. The last conversation that she ever had to have with Frank Greenwood happened with her triumphant phone-call.

The next errand she planned was to Lakefront Airport; where a very worried Steve still waited to hear news of her whereabouts. She parked the car and helped the children get out. Airports were always bustling with activity, and today was no different. It dawned on her as they walked into the FBO, that this was the very first time Steve would be seeing her children.

Since they had been so good during the road trips, she bought them all the candy of their choice from the vending machines. Plopping them down on the couch in the office of Novak Aviation, she inquired from the secretary if Steve was available.

"He's in a meeting, but I will let him know that you are here, Miss?"

"Broussard."

"He should be done in a moment."

"Fine, I'll wait," she felt she had to see him.

In about ten minutes, the door to Steve's office opened. Noting the children were there, he tried to muffle his euphoria at seeing her. "Ah, so these must be the Greenwoods."

The children all raised their heads and stared up at him. "How do you know our name?" asked Leisel.

"Well, your father and your mother have taken flying lessons here. "

"Mommy can fly a plane?" asked Ignatius.

"Yeppers. And she can fly it pretty good," answered Steve. "She knows how to fly several," he looked over and winked at Nora. "You have a good looking bunch of kids here, Nora."

"Yes, I think so too."

"Kiddos. Do you think you can be good if I let you play with some models?"

"Yessir." Iggy piped up first.

"Yeah," the rest exclaimed. Kayce thumbed through a magazine. He got down a couple of planes off the shelf for them to play. As soon as he closed his door and Nora was inside his office he threw his arms around her.

"You had me worried sick woman. I still can't believe you stole the Greenwood's plane. By the way, I like the hair."

"I had to do what I had to do," Nora defended. She was glad that he noticed her physical appearance. She put her hands up to her short do and twisted a curl in her fingertips. "Nothing and no one was going to come in between me and my children."

"You are one heck of a lady," he said. Nora wasn't sure, but she thought she saw a tear in the corner of his eye. He wished he could hug her and hold her forever. Her scent was intoxicating. He was disinclined to pull away, but did.

"Thanks, Steve."

"Nora, there are a lot of things we need to talk about."

"Yeah, ya think?"

"I've told my wife," Steve blurted out.

"You told Marci about us? About the baby?" Nora was astounded. "Why? What did she say?"

"She was quite devastated, as would be expected."

In the back of her mind, she hoped that his next words were that he too, had asked for a divorce. Seeing her as a dynamic, aviatrix. Wanting to be with her forever. But somehow, noting the expression on his face, she knew that wasn't going to be the case.

"So who all knows about the baby now?" he continued.

"Besides you, me and your wife? No one. Well, save Charlene and Kayce.

"Kayce knows?"

"Unfortunately, yes. And I have no idea if she has told Frank."

"How does she know?"

"She's twelve. It's not like she can't see my shape changing and figure out why. That and she eavesdropped on the telephone. The other ones are clueless at the moment."

"The only other person is Charlene, right? The Greenwoods don't know?"

"Heck no, not that I'm aware. There's no way I want them knowing."

"And what about your mother?"

"Nellie? Nah, not in a million years. It would just crush her." Little did Nora realize, but it already had.

"I see," Steve was deep in thought.

"I've won part one of the battle, but there's another piece. And the solution to that remains to be seen. I'm not sure how long I will be able to support myself. My job at the night club is understandably toast since I walked off it. I'm not sure I can get it back. My name is mud there."

"Yeah, they weren't happy to say the least."

"You've spoken to them?" she questioned.

"Yeah, when I was looking frantically for you."

It pleased her that he had been worried. She was looking for every sign that he cared. "So maybe I could work for you as a pilot," she chided.

"Despite your heroics, you don't have enough hours under your belt. But, there is something that I do have in mind."

She had only been kidding. "What's that?"

"I've had a job offer. Flying oil execs around for Humble. Out of Tyler."

"Tyler, Texas? What would you do about your business?"

"I'm not going to leave it, Chet's going to run it for a while," Steve began to pace his office. "But there's more. It involves you."

For just an inkling, Nora's heart leapt for joy. Was he going to marry her? Were they going to run off into the sunset? Was she going to work at Novak Aviation?

"Marci and I feel it would be best that you consider working for us."

Nora's spirits torpedoed. "As what? Her maid?" she

asked sarcastically.

"No, more like a personal assistant or caregiver. As you know, she's rather sickly. We felt it would meet everyone's needs."

She started to anger. "You want me to work for you and your wife? Have you lost your mind?"

"Now, Nora, don't get upset. Just listen. It makes sense. You don't have a job or income. You don't even have anywhere to stay. Besides, since you don't want your mother to know about the baby, it may not be a bad idea.

"And what about all the kids? You've got six. Me four. What is this? *Yours, mine and ours*?" she said referring to the Helen Beardsley story.

"Yes, it would be quite a houseful. But that's just it; you're a great cook and a great seamstress."

"But I'm not a nurse or a maid. And I just can't fathom working for your wife."

"Nope . . . no one would expect that of you. You basically would just be a help to Marcy. In a few months, the baby will be born anyway."

"And what about my kids? How do they factor in?"

"Marci has already checked into it. We'd be willing to cover the tuition for all the kids to attend Catholic school."

"Hmph," Nora fumed. It was arrogant of him to think that she would go along. Who would have ever dreamed up this plan? What was he thinking? She doubted whether she could have even come up with it herself.

"You have to admit, it has possibilities."

"And negatives. I don't know. I'll have to think about it. I can't give you an answer about it right now."

"That's understandable. Marci had another request," Steve continued. Nora rolled her eyes. "She'd like to meet with you. In person."

Steve had really lost it. "Meet with me?" Nora was abashed.

"Well, yes. If you are going to be living in our home, she would at least like to get to know you better first."

"I certainly hope that you don't expect us become friends," Nora imparted, her hands on her hips.

"Of course not, I am sure it will be difficult."

"That's an understatement."

"Just do the best you can, gal."

Nora was quite taken aback by this turn of events. What kind of woman had the gumption to take in her husband's mistress until their love child was born? Marci certainly had more humility than Nora. It was just too much to wrap her head around today.

Chapter 37

The next thing on Nora's agenda was finding a temporary place for them to stay. She took Charlene up on her offer to stay in Metairie; although she wouldn't be driving anywhere near Woodvine to stay compliant with the protective orders. When Nora's Ford pulled into her driveway, Charlene rushed out to see her, "Girl, you're a sight for sore eyes. Is it time for a celebration? Do you know anything?"

"Yes, we've done it. I'm free. Frank signed the papers," Nora boasted waving them in the air.

"I declare, Nora. That is fantastic. I sure wish you could drink."

"As hard as I've worked for this, I don't think one would hurt do you?"

"No. Just think moderation. Come on, let's go inside," she said putting her arm around her daring friend. The kids were happy to play with the school chums they had known for ages. Nora sat at the kitchen table. She wondered if she would ever see this kitchen again. The champagne popped as Charlene cracked it open and poured her a glass in a tall crystal flute. "Mimosas?"

"Definitely."

"I got this bottle for my birthday and I have been saving it for something special. And boy is this special. I'm stunned everything worked. That was such a huge risk you took."

"Yeah, but you gotta remember. I've been married to Frank for over ten years. I know how his brain works."

"You sure did, girl. But I still can't believe it. I would never have the moxie to do something like you did."

"Charlene, you never know what you're capable of when it comes to your children."

"I guess that's right. So what's next?"

"Not sure. At this point, I suppose I need to find a place to live and get a job."

"Honey, it's gonna be so hard supporting four children by yourself."

"I'm not going to be living the Metairie Country Club lifestyle, that's for sure." Nora perused over the boxes stacked in Charlene's foyer. "It looks like Frank has already made good on his end of the bargain."

"Yep. These are all the suitcases and toys he brought over. Do you think it will all fit in the wagon?"

"We'll just take what we can when the time comes. Once I find out where we will be staying."

Charlene took a long sip from her champagne flute, "Now that there is a protective order in place, and everything is settled, you can stay here as long as you like."

"Yes, thank goodness your home is just outside the protective order zone. Thank you Charlene. I just don't know how I will ever repay you for everything you have done for me. You're a sister for sure."

"Honey you don't have to repay me. Just making sure that you are safe and your pretty little face is not getting beat on, is all the thanks I need."

Nora looked over their belongings. She recognized most everything, but on the top, there was one big, white box tied with a bow. The tag on the box said *Kayce*. "What's this?"

"Sugar, I dunno. When Frank brought it all over, he just left everything on the doorstep. I didn't have a chance to ask him. It looks like it's some kinda present."

The large dress box was tied with a gold, green, and purple satin bow. Mardi Gras colors. The kids were elated to see their toys and belongings again.

Kayce came over, hearing her name. "Is this for me?"

"Your father left it for you."

She looked at the huge box and could only imagine what was inside. The tag hanging from the bow had only her name on it. She carefully untied the ribbon and took the lid off the box. Taking in a large gasp, "Oh Daddy, oh Daddy." She reached in and pulled out her beautiful junior princess dress. "It's my Bacchus dress. I know he still loves me. I know he does."

Nora and Charlene exchanged looks. Also inside the box were Kayce's patent leather shoes and her tiara. The sight of it made Nora cringe. One more capricious stunt by Frank to manipulate her child. It was cruel of Frank to use the dress that Nora had made as a weapon. At this point, she was pretty sure that the Bacchus festivities would not be including her children. However she sure wasn't going to let Kayce in on that information yet.

"Oh, my dress. My dress." Kayce wrapped her arms around the gown and held it close to her, dancing around Charlene's living room. At the bottom of the box was a card.

"You forgot the card inside, honey," Charlene handed it to Kayce.

She opened it and it read, *You'll always be my princess especially at Bacchus.*

"Oh, Mama," Kayce exclaimed. "Isn't Daddy wonderful?"

Charlene and Nora thought they would choke on their champagne. But Nora, not wanting to spoil the first happiness seen in her daughter for weeks said, "I am sure you will look beautiful in it."

With Kayce out of earshot Charlene griped, "Can you believe he sent her that?"

"It's Frank. Of course." Nora followed Charlene back into the kitchen. "There's something else I forgot to tell you. Get this, Steve has told his wife about everything." She looked down at her belly.

"You're pulling my leg?" Charlene almost spit out her drink.

"Evidently while all this drama with the plane and the Baton Rouge escapade was going down," Nora continued.

"And what'd she have to say?"

"Who knows? But Marci has requested a meeting to discuss what kind of alternatives we have."

"What does she mean by that?" Charlene said taking another sip of champagne.

"Some kind of working arrangement."

"For who? You?"

"Yeah. That's what Steve said. I was so shocked that he had told her, I'm not sure of the details. I don't know if I will even go."

"I don't blame you. Meeting with Steve's wife? Now that would take some balls."

"I know. I am really uncomfortable with it."

"Honey, this tale has taken so many twists and turns, it's worse than the Mississippi. God only knows. When are you supposed to go?"

"Tomorrow."

Charlene started doing the napkin dance around the kitchen singing "M, I, crooked letter, crooked letter, I . . . as the bucket swirls. I tell you what Nora Jean. Your life is a damned soap opera. Heck, it's a movie of the week," Charlene said biting into a strawberry. They both hooted. "Come on Amelia Earhart, let's finish our champers."

* * * * *

Later that night, Nora and her children were safe in Charlene's guest rooms. Despite the champagne, Nora had a very restless night thinking about her meeting with Steve and his wife. What she couldn't understand was why they wanted her children to come too? If Marci was going to humiliate her, she didn't want it to happen in front of her children. Nora wracked her brain trying to think of all the possibilities of what this meeting was about. Marci's motivations seemed odd.

Nora was fretting about many things, making sleep impossible. She got up and walked around quietly downstairs. Charlene's Christmas decorations were flawless. The large, fifteen foot, blue spruce was decorated in silver and blue. Its fresh pine scent made Nora wistful. It was so kind of Charlene to take them in, but she missed her own home. Her own Christmas trinkets that she had left behind.

Since it was nearly Christmas break, Nora wasn't going to bother to resend the children to school. At this point, they would just be having an extended holiday until Nora could sort everything out. She didn't want to re-introduce them to their old lives, in order that they would be ready to handle more change. Now that the clean break had been made, they needed to stick to it. Christmas, Nora lamented, and she hadn't even finished their outfits. Nor bought a single present. Who knew where they would even be on Christmas day?

By 6:00 AM, Nora was up brewing the coffee for her and Charlene. She was trying to select her outfit. Pulling out her one suitcase, she noted Frank had literally dumped all her make up from her vanity drawers. She began to sort through the mess. Today, she finally would be able to put on her face. And what a face it was going to have to be.

Nora had taken a bath, washed her hair the night before and set it, putting it up in sponge rollers. She was ready to back comb it out. By some miracle, Frank included some of the A-line tops she had made. She must have left them out on her chaise lounge at home. At least she would have something fresh to wear. By now, she was getting pretty large in the belly. She put on some stretch pants and a pullover top with a long sleeve blouse. She wanted to look as attractive as was humanly possible at almost five and a half months pregnant.

Charlene started a load of wash for the clothes that they had worn for several days straight during their escapade. Taking out the address Steve had written down, Nora asked Charlene about it. "Do you know where Galvez Street is?"

"Galvez. Galvez. I think so."

"Isn't it off Napoleon, not too far from the Tulane Loyola complex?"

"I think you're right. Here honey, let's look it up on a map." They pulled one out. Nora would take the Causeway over to Claiborne and then to Fontainebleau.

She could see that their house address was only a few blocks from where she had seen Marci the first time at St. Mathias. Nora got the kids dressed and told them that they were going to meet some friends of hers. Kayce didn't cause her too much kafuffle about going. She was still riding some kind of high from getting her gown, as Bacchus was only a few months away.

Nora drove through the familiar streets with a bit of anxiety. She parked the car at 4449 S. Galvez. A very frail, apprehensive woman watched from behind the curtains as Nora and her children got out.

"Wow, look. It's a three story," boasted Leisel bounding up the tile stairs in the front.

Nora was careful to take her steps up the two short flights onto the portico. She let out a big sigh as she rang the bell. Steve answered the door.

"Hello, Nora. Welcome you all. Come on in."

Nora entered the front door with her children with apprehension. It was then she noted Marci seated in the formal living room. "Don't get up," she implored, as she saw Marci struggling to rise. Marci again took her place and folded her hands neatly in her lap.

"How do you do, Mrs. Greenwood?" Her tone was stiff and formal.

"Quite nicely," Nora said. Not wanting to go into the crazy details of the past forty eight hours. She looked Marci in the face and Marci stared back.

"Well, Nora . . . " Steve cleared his throat. "I suppose we should introduce your children."

"Um, okey dokey? This is Kayce, age twelve. Cathryn, ten."

"That's Cathy," her daughter offered. Nora gave her a look.

"Leisel is eight. And Ignatius, four."

"I see," Marci said wanly. "Ignatius. What an important Saint's name for a small boy," Marci tried to smile. "What a lovely family you have." All she could think about was her husband's body molded into this sultry woman's arms. Marci winced slightly and bit her lip.

"Yes, my children are beautiful and I adore them."

"Hey kiddos. We have a whole mess of kids to play with," Steve offered. "I am not sure where all six of them are right now, but I'm sure we can find out."

"Six kids," exclaimed Cathy. "Wow! You have a big family." Kayce looked horrified and rolled her eyes.

Marci smiled slightly. Steve led Nora's children downstairs into the playroom leaving Nora and Marci alone. Nora looked around the room, noting the prim, faux Louis XIV looking furnishings. Carefully chosen, she was sure by Marci; they were simply hideous. The floors were hardwood and there was a floral rug in the center of the room.

Downstairs, Steve made brief introductions to his kids. "These are the Greenwoods and their mother is visiting with us for a while. Why don't you all play some games?"

"Sure Daddy. We have lots of games," one of his daughters displayed opening a cabinet full of various board games. Iggy began to play cars with one of Steve's sons. Leisel sat down to watch TV. Kayce and Cathy tried to choose between Scrabble and Yahtzee.

"I'll be back in a little while with snacks for you guys." He quickly returned back upstairs to help smooth over what was going to be an uncomfortable meeting.

When he returned, Marci addressed him. "Nora and I have just been talking about the benefits of Catholic schooling."

Nora speculated, with how frail Marci was, if they ever even kissed. She tongued her bottom lip inside her mouth remembering Steve's lips on hers.

"Right," said Steve.

It was Nora who cut to the chase. "Look this must be difficult for everyone. I know I've been filled with anxiety wondering what this meeting was all about. Can you help me to understand?"

"Would you like some tea, Mrs. Greenwood? I just had the maid make a fresh pot." Marci seemed to need to emphasize her status as matron of this home.

"Yes, that would be nice," Nora accepted.

"Sugar?" Marci's voice was becoming acrid.

"No, thank you. Just milk or cream."

Steve thought Nora looked so lovely. Despite her anxiety, she almost glowed. Pregnancy became her. He remembered how she looked asking for milk in her coffee long ago. The maid served Nora the tea.

Deciding that he would be the spokesperson, in order that Marci was not put in that position, Steve began to explain. He sat down next to his wife, reached for her hand and placed it in his as a sign of his loyalty. "As you know, I have told Marci about our situation."

Nora was silent and just stared at him. She basically was hanging on his every word. What he said or didn't say would have a huge impact on her future. As Steve spoke, it was evident that he had not let on to Marci he'd already told Nora of their idea. Marci clearly existed in a state of protected reality on many levels.

"There's been a recent development related to my job that I'd like to discuss with you." Nora still said nothing but looked on inquisitively. "I've gotten a job offer to fly for Humble Oil in Tyler, Texas."

"So, you'll be moving then?" she asked, already knowing the answer.

"Yes. We will temporarily relocate once I have taken the position. In light of the scandal that might occur with you and the baby, we thought it might be best to take a brief out of town assignment. Especially considering the possible fallout of a divorce and custody battle."

"You were afraid that you might be subpoenaed?

"Possibly."

Nora was suddenly enjoying Steve's charade. Making an offer to her on behalf of his wife. She continued to pretend to listen intently. The man that she loved more than anything else in the world was about to ask her, his lover, to move in with him and his wife. Soap opera indeed.

"I am not sure how this all concerns me?" she played along.

Steve gave a look to Marci. "To get to the bottom line of the situation, this move will put a great deal of stress on Marci's health. Any stress renders her bedfast for days. We know that your separation from the Greenwoods will put you in a financial bind, making it difficult to provide for your children's well being. Therefore, we would like to propose having you and your children move with us to Tyler. At least until the baby is born."

"You would be employed by us, as a domestic." Marci couldn't resist the dig.

What a performance. They were completely avoiding the pink elephant in the room. Her affair with Steve. Nora was not quite sure how to respond. But she couldn't resist. "You want me to move in with your large family to be a maid?"

"No," said Steve perturbed at her crass sense of humor. She was really giving him the business. "Marci requires a lot of assistance. With your cooking and seam-stress skills we would like to have you assist our family as a caretaker of sorts," Steve suggested.

"Uh, huh," Nora nodded.

"It would be easier on you than a real job. Plus, it would give you somewhere to stay."

"What about my children?"

"They are welcome to move with us. I have been looking at some large homes that are for lease in a lovely neighborhood in Tyler."

"And of course we would enroll all the children in Catholic school there," Marci added. "They have quite a good reputation," Marci pointed out smugly.

As if her children needed to be reformed from their mother's indiscretions. Blessed for her sins. That bit irked Nora. She was still reeling at the thought of living with her lover and his wife. Not to mention all the children. Nora mulled it over in her head. On the one hand, it was a huge relief; they'd have a roof over their heads. Some time for the dust to settle after the monstrous chaos that had been recently occurring. It would give her time to think and get her out of the city of New Orleans. Away from Nellie, thus avoiding her finding out about the baby. In addition, she would be living with Steve. Seeing him nearly every day.

The more she thought about it, the more realistic it became. She looked Marci in the eyes. "This is a tremen-dous act of charity towards me."

Marci raised her eyes up and looked at Nora. "I pray you understand, I am not doing this for you. What you've done in carrying on this affair with my husband has broken my heart. It is something that will burn for the rest of my days. However, besides my marriage to Steve, my faith is the number one thing. My relationship with God and his son, Jesus Christ," she paused coughing slightly. All that was missing was her rosary and a choir of angels singing, thought Nora.

She was quite out of breath. "I had to search my soul for the strength to handle all of this. I wish I could say I was a better person. But for now, my only concern is for the unborn life that you carry. Nothing more. Is that quite clear?" Marci looked like she was about to faint.

Nora completely understood. The charity was for the baby. It would take forever for Marci to forgive her. "Well, then. When is this move supposed to take place?"

"As soon as we can get legal arrangements made for the house, hopefully at the end of this week," Steve explained. He handed Marci a glass of ice water.

"This Friday? Before Christmas?" Nora asked. It was happening so fast.

"Yes, we felt it would be best. It would give the children time to settle into their new home before the school semester started. Plus, the kids would be on holiday and be able to get to know one another."

"I see," said Nora.

"We would be willing to give you a small stipend so that you would have spending money. That way, working for us would be a paid endeavor." It was clear that Marci intended this to be a business relationship.

"Well then," Nora said making an instant decision. "I guess in a week or so we will be living in Texas."

"Do you have belongings and things for the children?" Steve asked her.

"Yes, we just got them delivered. Currently, they're at my friend's home in Metairie."

"Could you get your things here by next Friday when the movers are here? Can that be arranged?"

He was being so business like about this, it was driving Nora nuts. "Sure, I'll bring them over in the station wagon. That shouldn't be a problem."

"So it's settled then. I guess the last thing to do is to let the children know."

Diplomatic to a tee. Yet, now that it was becoming real, Nora was barely coping. She couldn't imagine what her children would think. But, she thought it was best that Kayce hear it in front of strangers. In front of the Novaks, her reaction would be less severe. Steve rounded the children up and brought them all into the living room. There were ten of them and not enough chairs, so a few of the older ones stood.

Nora was doing the math in her head as she looked at all of their faces. How many packages of spaghetti? How many hot dogs? Boxes of macaroni and cheese? How many pounds of ground beef for tacos? Good, God. She had never cooked for an army. Their ages ranged from twelve to three. Kayce was the oldest of the group.

Steve began his announcement. "I hope you've had a good time playing downstairs. We have something that we would like to share with you." They all looked on curiously. "Mrs. Greenwood here, has agreed to . . ."

"By the way, that will be Broussard in a few weeks," Nora interrupted.

"Er, Ms. Broussard has graciously accepted our offer of employment to be your mother's assistant." Kayce's interest was spurred, as she saw the woman's cane. Her mother had never worked as a personal assistant and never as a nurse.

"In doing so she will be joining us on our move to Tyler."

"Tyler?" Kayce blurted out. "Where is that?"

"Texas," one of the older boys said. "East Texas."

Kayce's cheeks turned red and Nora figured she must be steaming. But at the moment, she was biting her tongue.

"We're moving to Texas?" Cathy asked.

"Yes, I have decided to accept this position. So for a while, we will be trying it out," Nora explained.

"Yeah," shouted Iggy. "Cowboys and Indians. Can I get some guns?"

"We'll have to see about that Iggy," Nora assured her son.

"I just can't believe that we're moving. It'll be an adventure," Cathy sounded excited. "We're going to Texas."

Kayce was incensed. Nora knew by the look in her eyes that she was going to get an earful when they got in the car. Her daughter feigned politeness to the Novaks.

"Mrs. Novak," Nora turned to Marci graciously and extended her hand. "I certainly appreciate the opportunity that you have given me."

Marci gently shook her hand and looked down. "I am sure", pulling her hand out of Nora's quickly, "it will all work out in the end."

"Ms. Broussard," Steve extended his hand.

"Yes, thank you, too, Mr. Novak." Nora shook it.

"I will be in touch," he said. The formality felt weird.

Nora gathered her children and made her way to the door. She carefully navigated her way down the stairs, got into their car, and prepared for the passive-aggressive on-slaught from Kayce.

Chapter 38

The door to their station wagon had barely closed when Kayce lit into her mother. "Tyler, Texas. Are you off your rocker? There is no way I'm moving anywhere. I'm supposed to go to Ursuline next year," Kayce ranted. "And what about Mardi Gras and Bacchus?" Nora just kept driving. "I am betting there's no Mardi Gras in Texas. And no way do they have a Bacchus parade. Daddy just sent me my dress for the ball."

Nora wasn't sure which one of these difficult postulations to answer first. "There will be other years."

"But this was *my* year, Mother. I knew I should have never trusted you. I forgave you. And now it's just all screwed again."

"Kayce, you are over reacting at this point."

"No I'm not. Now I hate you even more. I hate you for doing this to me." Kayce could only simper and cry.

"It's okay Mom. I will go to Texas with you. Do they have Girl Scouts there?" Cathy tried to help.

"What about Christmas?" Leisel asked.

"Yes, of course. I am sure they have Girl Scouts and Christmas." Nora continued to navigate the lanes onto Claiborne without getting hit by a streetcar.

"Yeah! See Kayce. I won't suck like you said. I'll sell plenty of Girl Scout cookies in Texas and go to Texas camp." She looked at Kayce and stuck out her tongue.

Nora couldn't wait to share this latest development with Charlene. Listening to the girls argue in rush hour traffic was pushing her over the edge. When they got back to Metairie, Kayce exited the car and slammed the door. She was giving everyone the silent treatment. Nora was fearful about having Kayce so close to the Woodvine house, as she might run away again. Especially after today. She was going to keep her on a short leash.

Nora found Charlene in the sewing room. "How did it go? What did they want?"

"You're never gonna believe it. Brace yourself for this one. It seems that Steve and his wife feel that my best opportunity to salvage my *situation*, is for them to look after me. They offered me the job as Marci's personal caretaker."

"What? As some kind of nurse?"

"Not exactly." Nora laid out the proposition. The temporary move to Tyler to avoid scandal about Steve's involvement with the baby. Flack from the Greenwoods. How it was some act of charity on Marci's part for the baby's sake, not for Nora's benefit. Humble Oil. And how Nora would not only be moving, but living with them until the baby was born.

"Surely, you're not considering it. Are you?" She looked at Nora's face. "Oh, no you didn't."

"Yes, you are looking at Marci Novak's new personal assistant."

"Nora, how are you possibly going to live under the same roof as your lover?"

"Ex lover."

At that, Marci snorted out loud. "I know you too well. You are still in love with this man. There is no way you will get any closure on this and be able to move on with your life as long as you are in proximity to him. Much less living in under his roof. I think you answered too soon. This is a mistake."

"I've thought about all that, but what choice do I have? They are offering me a place to stay, a stipend and schooling for my children. And all I have to do is basically what I did for ten years. Cook and take care of the children's needs. Without the verbal and physical abuse of Frank. How hard could running errands for Marci be?"

"Just the stress of being under her thumb would be enough to drive you crazy, Nora."

"I don't have to clean, they are going to hire a maid. Or at least they better."

"Hmph," grunted Charlene.

"I know it sounds crazy, but stop and think about it. It's a way to get out the city and have this baby without anyone knowing."

"And what are you going to do after the baby?"

"Who knows? Right now I am only thinking about the pragmatism of survival."

For the first time, Charlene knew that Nora was right about that. She was getting through only one day at a time. "When is this supposed to take place? You only have three months left."

"The end of the week. The moving van comes Friday."

"Friday? So quick?" Charlene thought about how she was going to miss her best friend. Pangs of melancholy made her insides churn. "How is Kayce taking all this?"

"You can see for yourself," she gestured as they walked down the hall towards the living room.

Kayce was sulking and angry. She went over to her dress and held it sobbing into the chiffon yellow layers. "Mother if you make me move to Tyler and take everything away from me, I will hate you for the rest of my life."

"Kayce, I have made a decision. We are all moving to Tyler and that is that. You simply are going to have to make the best of the situation."

Suddenly her daughter began ripping and shredding the dress. Screaming, "I hate you. I hate you. I hate what you have done to my life. I'll never forgive you." She tore it into shreds.

Charlene was horrified to see the hours of beadwork that they had done strewn all over the floor. Kayce threw down the dress and stomped on it. It landed in heap with beads running all over the braided rug. Abandoning the dress, she ran to one of the bedrooms of Charlene's home and slammed the door.

"Here we go. Round two," Nora exclaimed.

"She's ripped it into shreds. All the work we did," Charlene held the ruined ball gown in her hands.

"I'm sorry, Charlene."

"Nora, you had better tread lightly with that girl. So

much has been taken away from her. It's obvious she isn't handling things."

"Well, at least she's not suicidal. I'm thankful for that." Nora stooped down and began to pick up all the little beads on the floor.

"It will be a cold day in Hades before she ever forgives you," Charlene began to Hoover up the hundreds of beads.

"She'll have to learn to cope with life's disappointments. When it throws ya lemons, you make lemonade. Besides, I can't take on Kayce's issues at the moment. Her recent runaway fiasco scared the living daylights out of her. I don't think there is a risk of her repeating that."

"No, but that girl definitely needs counseling," Charlene pointed out.

"I guess I'll have to look up what to do about it in Texas." Nora sadly put the shredded dress in a paper bag.

Charlene shook her head and went back to sewing. She pressed on the foot pedal and the Singer began to whir. Neither of them heard the phone ringing.

"Hebert residence," Cathy proudly answered using the Girl Scout etiquette she had learned earning her badge for manners.

"Good afternoon, I would like to speak to Mrs. Nora Greenwood," a proper voice said on the line.

"Grandma Nellie, is that you?" she recognized the voice. "It's Cathy."

"Why yes, Cathryn. Where have y'all been? I have been worried sick."

"Baton Rouge. The airport. We've been gallivanting all over.

"Baton Rouge. Whatever were you all doing there?"

"Staying at the Travel Lodge. Until Kayce ran away. Are you working at Hotel Dieu today?" Cathy adored the fact that her grandmother worked as a nurse and got to see such cool stuff. She thought of her as Florence Nightingale.

"Yes, dear, I just got home from my shift. Is your mother there?"

"Yep. She's talking to Mrs. Hebert. Want me to get

her?"

"Please, darling." Nellie was relieved it was Cathy that answered the phone, as she could generally be counted on to spill the beans. She couldn't imagine what Nora was doing in Baton Rouge. And Kayce had run away? Nellie was now more worried than ever. She wondered if Nora would even take the call.

Nora didn't hear Cathy calling for her at first. "Mama. Maaammaaa. Grandma Nellie's on the telephone." Nora looked up from her bead gathering down the hall.

"Grandma Nellie?" Nora didn't want to speak to her, but couldn't think of an excuse fast enough.

"I told her I would get ya."

"Thank you darling," she rose from the floor. "I'll take it in Charlene's bedroom." She didn't want the kids to hear what might occur in this dreaded conversation. Nora picked up Charlene's pink princess phone.

"Hello, Mama." Nora waited to hear it.

"Nora Jean. What on earth is going on?" the drill began.

"What do you mean, Mama?"

"Don't play dumb with me, Nora. I already know from the Greenwoods that you and Frank are splitting up. And there's talk about a baby."

"Mama. I don't want to go into details, but yes, we are getting a divorce." Nora knew that would crush Nellie deeply.

"Catholics don't divorce, Nora Jean."

"Well, this Catholic just did. I am not willing to be beat up, Mama."

"What on earth did you do to make him hit you?"

It was a typical Nellie response. Not the fact that a man hit her, but what Nora did to cause it. Nora sighed deeply and tried to count to three before answering her. An earlier response would have included profanity.

"That's not how spousal abuse occurs, Mama. Look, I'm just not in the frame of mind, nor place to have this discussion. Just know that for now, we are well. I am making plans for our future."

"And what does that entail?"

"We shall see, Mama. Say a rosary for us and a special novena. Merry Christmas, Mama. I will talk to you soon, okay?" Nora quickly hung up before Nellie could respond. She hated cutting her off so abruptly, but was glad that was over for the moment.

Chapter 39

Friday was fast approaching. The lists Nora were making to get everything ready for their move kept increasing. She had no idea what the future held; so she was wrapping things up in New Orleans as though she might not return. Much to Charlene's dismay.

To thank Charlene for everything she had done, Nora took her out for a lunch she could afford, a fried oyster po-boy from Matassa's Grocery. Once they had their sandwiches, they took a stroll to Jackson Square. They picked a wrought iron bench that overlooked the Mississippi and the bridge.

"I can't believe that in a few days, you are going to be way over in Tyler. My long distance bills will be atrocious."

"Me neither. Pretty crazy huh?" Nora took a bit out of her sourdough, deep fried delight. "Mmm, I'm sure gonna miss these."

"You betcha. I'm sure no one in Tyler has heard the word po-boy. Much less made one." Charlene reached for Nora's left hand. "Nora Jean, where for goshsakes is your wedding ring?"

"Hocked. I wanted nothing to do with it, so I pawned it for some cash."

"Nora. It was so beautiful."

"Ah, well. Maybe someday, I'll get another one. It was part of my old life which is now over. Besides, I needed the money, Charlene. There are some people I need to thank before I go. In fact, come on, I wanna show you this funky little coffee house."

They tossed what they didn't eat and walked down Dauphine St. You could hear the loud honking horns of the steam boats on the Mississippi. The bells of Jackson Square cathedral were chiming. As they passed by all the street artists, cart vendors, and *avant garde* paintings Charlene remarked, "Aren't you gonna miss all this?"

"Yes. Tremendously. But I always have my Charlene that I can come and visit. Or heck, get in that Caddy and come out Texas way."

They reached the coffee house that had been the scene of so many enigmas lately. Walking inside, Charlene felt she was transported to another world. "So this is where the beatniks hang out?"

"Supposedly so." Nora looked around for Big Daddy. He was just coming from the kitchen.

"Missus Nora. How you be?"

"Well, thank you. And you and Mabel?"

"Fine. Jus' fine. Why you ladies down here?"

"I came to see you, Big Daddy. There's something that I want you and Mabel to have. Just a little something to thank you for all you have done for me and the children."

"Aw, Missus Nora. You didn't have to do dat. My Mabel, she adores you. Ever since yous at the St. Charles mansion."

Nora looked down. It had been so long ago. Lots of good times and good eating in that kitchen. So much had changed. "I feel terrible about Frank letting Mabel go. Especially since it was because of me. So, here. Take this. For the both of you and Justine." She handed him an envelope. It was full of cash, from where she had hocked the ring.

"Naw, Missus Nora. Dat too much. We can't take dat from you. You's gonna need it."

She held his arm. "I'll be fine. Please. I want you to have it. Split it between all three of you," she reached up and kissed him on his cheek. "You've saved my life and my daughter's. Y'all mean the world to me." Big Daddy looked like he was going to get emotional. With the racial uprisings in New Orleans being what they were, a white woman like Nora Broussard was a rare breed.

From the dark recesses behind the counter, Gia eyed

the small group. Noting her presence, Big Daddy introduced her. "Missus Nora, dis is da woman I was telling yous about."

Nora stared at Gia with her pale blue eyes. "Hello again. I remember you. From the night I was here."

"Yes. And I have also met your daughter. But she looks nothing like you."

"No. She takes after her father."

"Please, can we sit?" Gia led them to a small table. Charlene was still mesmerized by the incense smell and unique people. There was a whole other side of Nora she was getting to know.

Big Daddy excused himself to get them some coffee. Gia looked at Nora carefully as though she had something she wanted to tell her. "Remember when you saw me at your father's burial?"

Nora would never forget it. "Yes, of course."

"Jack and I knew each other very well. In fact, we were lovers."

"I had guessed as much."

"I recall seeing you dere. Crying so hard. My heart was breaking for you losing your father so young."

Nora was catapulted back in time to that painful event. Thankfully, Big Daddy brought the coffee. It would ward off the chills surging through her body.

Gia continued, "It was da first time I had seen you in years. Such a sad time. I so wanted to speak to you. But you were wid Nellie, da mudder dat raised you." Nora thought her choice of words unusual. "I wondered if I would ever see you again. And den here you came into da club."

"I wanted to thank you for you kindness to my daughter, Kayce."

Gia ignored her and continued with her story. "Dis happen for a reason. You being here. I turned to da cards to know why. Den your daughter came."

"What are you trying to get at?" Nora looked confused.

"Please, what I have to say. Don't let it upset you," Gia touched Nora's arm.

Charlene wished she had popcorn. This was better than the Saturday matinee. She sat quietly, but intently, waiting for what was going to come next.

"When Jack and I were togedder, we were very much in love. It was not to be, for he marry Nellie. He wanted a good life wid her. Twas hard to see him go, but I knew I was best. My life was on da river. But life for Jack and Nellies was not as happy as dey wished. She was sad dat she could not give him a child." Nora was riveted at what Gia was saying. "Jack could only see me when we rode da riverboats. Den, twas magic. And I come to be wid child. I was young and could not provide a home. My home was da river. Nellie wanted a baby. And so. Dere you be."

"What are you saying?"

"Dat, you are mine. I gave you life. And gave my most precious gift to Jack."

Nora sat very still. She was rendered completely speechless; trying desperately to make sense of what she just had been told. Gia's appearance. Her skin tone. Jack's. It was no wonder Nora looked the way she did. "I am quite stunned. To say the least."

"I tell you now, because I know you carry a baby. One who's future is uncertain." Nora wondered how she knew that. Had Big Daddy told her? Could she read the future? Kayce had told her mother about the tarot cards. Nora began to tremble slightly.

"Giving up a child. It will be da hardest ting you ever do. Tink about it carefully. From your heart. What is best for all. Not just what you want. You see?"

Nora touched her belly and rubbed it slightly. So much had been going on; she had taken her state of pregnancy almost for granted. A life was growing inside her. One which had far different circumstances than her other children. Maybe Gia was giving her a message. Things to consider. "I am touched by your candor," Nora began. "What you have told me is a lot to take in."

"I do not wish to disrupt your life as you know it. But wid da happenings lately, it was time to tell you. Dat is all." Gia rose from the table and went back into the darker areas of the club. What she had shared must have been gut-wrenchingly hard on her. Nora was deeply moved and captivated by this mysterious woman.

"Nora? Are you okay?" Charlene worried.

"Yes. Strangely so. It's bizarre, but somehow I am not

surprised by what she just told me. Like, in some way I knew all along."

"Could your life just slow down in the drama department? I am having trouble keeping up." Charlene took a gulp of her coffee shaking her head. She too, was floored at what had just occurred. The French Quarter certainly lived up to its reputation.

Nora finished her coffee and gazed in the direction of Gia. "Come on. *Les go*. I have had enough melodrama for one day." As they walked back to the car, Nora felt the baby kicking. Life, in its uncanny way, was repeating itself.

Chapter 40

Moving day. The sun was just starting to peek out between the oak tree branches after sunrise. Charlene shared the last cup of Community coffee that they would for quite a while. For almost a decade they had been almost inseparable. It was killing Charlene to pack up her best friend in the world and send her to Texas, of all places. Looking at the maps, they figured it was at least a full day's trip to Tyler. Roads through every small town in Louisiana all the way to Shreveport before turning west another hundred miles or so to Tyler. All in all, over four hundred miles. Every time Charlene thought about it, she had to grab for her Kleenex.

All of the children helped load the suitcases and boxes into the station wagon. Charlene didn't want Nora to overdo it by lifting. Driving that horrendous distance would be stress enough. The roads in many places were two lanes up through the swamps and into the backwoods of Louisiana. Nora planned to follow the moving van. At least she would have her own car. Riding in a vehicle with Marci would just be too close for comfort. Living in the house with them would be bad enough.

"What am I gonna do without you?" Charlene broke down again.

"Write me lots and lots of letters. You can practice your typing skills," Nora tried to lighten things up. "Heavens knows they need it."

"Oh, you. Stop it. Who's gonna make me laugh? Who's gonna lead me on crazy adventures to the bowels of The

Quarter; much less steal a plane?"

"Charlene. I hate it too. Hopefully we will be back before you know it," she half heartedly justified. They hugged for the longest time. Theirs was the rarest of friendships. Genuine. Closer than most sisters. They adored one another.

"God speed, Nora." Charlene turned and went in the house, just not able to look. Her children were in the yard waving.

The wood paneled wagon pulled out of the driveway on Iola and headed uptown to Steve's. Nora pulled her shoulders back and held her head high. "Okay, kiddos. Who's ready for adventure in Texas? Tyler, Texas here we come!"

They yippeed. Iggy started singing the Lone Ranger theme. Only to be shoved by Kayce, "Shut up will you?" He looked disappointed.

"Kayce, that's quite enough. Don't rain on their parade."

It only took about fifteen minutes or so to get to Galvez. A huge moving van was parked in front of the house and there was a flurry of activity. Beds, chairs, tables, and toys. It was all going in. Steve and Marci were leaving only a skeletal amount of furniture for the rental of their home. They had easily found tenants.

Seeing so much of Steve on a domestic front was interesting. He was wonderful with his children, disciplined, yet firm. Patient and kind with a wry sense of humor. Marci was resting in her bedroom until the last moment. The trip would be arduous and taxing on her.

Steve perked up when he saw Nora arrive. Even pregnant and hiding it, she was radiant, a big smile on her face.

"Hey there. Let's get this show on the road. We're ready to roll," Nora exclaimed.

"Good morning, Nora. You're fully of energy this morning."

"Charlene's strong coffee," she joked.

Normally, Steve would have taken her in his arms about now. This was going to be so difficult, their new arrangement. Way too many eyes around. Plus, he believed they both planned to move on after getting through the baby's arrival.

It was hard for Nora, too. Although she had placed a protective shield of armor around her heart to keep it from getting broken, she felt there might be a chink in it. Self control and keeping her emotions in check around him was difficult.

As the last things were loaded, Marci appeared on the steps. Steve vaulted up to assist her down. He gave the keys to the landlord and it was time to go. Slowly, he guided Marci down the stairs. In her frail state, a fall would be severe. Reaching the bottom, she looked up to see Nora.

"Morning, Mrs. Novak," Nora said politely.

"Nora. You may as well get used to calling me by my first name."

"If that is what you prefer. Sure." Nora approached her to assist and got her purse. She opened their station wagon front passenger door. Once she was loaded, they were off.

A caravan, not like any other, with a brigade of children. They made good time to Baton Rouge. Then they took Louisiana 1 up through the Morganza spillway. Who would have ever dreamed that so many towns could be settled in flood zones? They passed house boats and bayous. Nora thought about the life Gia might have had living on one. The kids were always on the look for alligators and turtles. To pass the time, Nora listened to AM radio. Elvis Presley, Chubby Checker, Bobby Vee. And of course The Shirelles. Kayce was happy for that.

They stopped for lunch in Alexandria at the Holiday Inn. It required some doing for the wait staff to put together tables to hold thirteen. Once bowls of gumbo, red beans and rice, and plenty of hamburgers and fries were eaten, they were back on the road. Marci seemed to be holding up well. After Steve loaded her in the car, he came over to Nora.

"How ya holding up, gal?"

"Great. I love to drive. And travel."

"You're a trooper, Nora Jean. Thanks for being so good about all this."

"Sure," she managed. She wanted to tell him she would do anything for the man she loved, but held her tongue. Charlene was right. Being around him only made her fantasize about a life with him. As his wife. For the moment, she let herself hope.

By evening, they passed through Shreveport and crossed the Red River. At nightfall, the roads became hilly and there were pine trees everywhere. Nora was sure she could smell the odor of natural gas. She was correct. Natural gas wells abounded in these forests. They arrived in Tyler at 8:00 PM. Being December, it was already dark. The kids were cranky, having been cooped up in a car for hours. They drove up to a sprawling, two story home on a hill. It was grand.

Steve had somehow found a five bedroom home. The moving van had arrived before them. Less stops for the bathroom. Steve helped an exhausted Marci out of the car and into the house. She walked around it briefly and seemed pleased. "Steve, please get me a folding chair, so that I can sit." He pulled one out from the back of their station wagon. Marci had bags under her eyes. She was very quiet. This was hard on her too. Harder than she had imagined; seeing Nora's beaming, exuberant, and overtly attractive persona.

The movers were instructed to unload the beds first. That way, Nora could begin putting on some sheets that they had packed separately. The kids helped unload the station wagons and put the boxes and suitcases in their respective bedrooms. Steve had made up a flow chart showing who was sleeping where.

The kids would be divided into three bedrooms. Three, three, and four. For tonight, they would be sleeping in sleeping bags until the bunk beds could be assembled. Steve and she worked on getting the kids to bed, and assisted Marcie to lie down. It was going to be long night. The movers were going unload the rest of the truck in the morning.

Baths were scrubbed for the evening. After everyone was bedded, it was only Steve and Nora that remained up in the den. There were a couple of folding chairs. Nora pulled out a percolator from one of the kitchen boxes and made them some coffee. She had packed a couple of mugs. Steve headed out to the back porch. Nora followed with two cups of coffee. The steam from their breath and the coffee rose into the dark, starry night. "We made it, gal."

"Yep. We sure did. Like some coffee?"

He took a cup and turned to face her. "You're really something."

"Why do you say that?" she lowered her eyes.

He reached up and touched her chin. "Because. All of this. You seem to manage to get through it completely unfazed."

"I logistically relocated. Big deal. It's not like I'm Jackie Cochran."

"Breaking the speed barrier in a T-38 jet trainer. Wasn't that something?"

"That's what I mean. As a woman, to me, that is something."

"Still, you're tougher than most."

Little did he know, Nora thought. "I'm just doing what I have to, Steve. Don't think it doesn't affect me."

"You miss flying don't you?"

"Heck, yes. I loved it. I hope someday, I'll actually get to do it again."

"Do you think we're crazy? Hatching this scheme?"

"Without a doubt. It will make for some great gossip later," Nora giggled. It jostled the baby. "Hey, give me your hand." She reached out for Steve's hand. He gave it to her and she put it on her belly. "Feel that?" The baby kicked.

"Yep. You never get over it. Feeling a life inside there." When he felt the kick, and touched her, all of his feelings for her surfaced.

"I know. Today, it's really been active."

"Nora, you really should see a doctor," he encouraged returning to restraint. He withdrew his hand and put it in his pocket. "Don't worry. I'll cover all the expenses for the baby."

"Thank you, Steve. For doing all this. Helping us out."

"It's my obligation."

That was her Steve. A good man. Bound by honor. Not perfect, as his flaw in not being able to resist her, belied. In that moment, Nora wondered if she would ever have him for herself. Would he be a father to this baby?

Chapter 41

Even though Nora had now been sleeping in other locations other than her own home for weeks, it was weird to be in a house in which she felt like a total outsider. Her bedroom was separated from the others, off the den. She guessed it had been added on by the previous owners. It was no coincidence that Marci had placed Nora at the other end of the house. Steve was installing an intercom system, such that when Nora was in the back of the house, she could hear Marci call if she needed something. In the mean time, Marci also had a little silver bell.

As Nora awoke, she wrapped herself up tightly in the one thing that she had from her previous life, the brightly colored duvet that her father Jack had given her. Somehow, it made her feel grounded and gave her a sense of belonging.

Although it was early, she could already hear the thunder of twenty feet. The children. First task? Breakfast. Nothing had been unloaded, so in response to their demands to be fed, Nora offered to go get some groceries. She took her pocketbook and traversed off into her new city.

Now that is was daylight, she could see more of her surroundings. The house was located in an upscale older neighborhood, on the corner of Second Street and S. College Avenue, very near Bergfeld Park. Nora backed her car out of the driveway onto Second Street. She began down College, which was made of brick and then towards a large cross street. Surely there would be a grocery store near the highway. She spotted a Brookshire's. It wasn't A and P, but it would do.

She returned with milk, cereal, eggs, sandwich fixings, fruit, chips, paper picnic wear, and some Hostess Twinkies. That would get them through breakfast and lunch, until Marci could make out a full shopping list. As Nora returned to the house, she noted some of the shopping center businesses. There was a fabric store. A Frostie Rootbeer stand. Kress' 5 and 10. Tyler wasn't looking so bad. Remotely like Mississippi with all the pine trees around.

Having already shown up, the movers were beginning to unload the furniture. After serving up some scrambled eggs, toast and cereal, Nora started to unpack the labeled boxes. Many of the furnishings were Early American. Yuck, Nora thought. But she had to remind herself, this wasn't her taste, or her home. When they unpacked the couch, Leisel spoke out, "Look Mama, it's fuzzy," referring to the velour covering. Then, Nora heard a call from the master bedroom.

"Nora. Could you come in here please?" Marci was ringing her bell. She was still in bed in her nightgown. "I'm still quite fatigued from yesterday's journey. Would you mind bringing me a cup of tea?"

"Certainly, Mrs. Novak." Even though Marci wanted her to call her by her first name, it was just too early for Nora to be chummy. So this is how her life would be, waiting on this woman. Nora gritted her teeth, but she was determined to make it work.

After she brought Marci the tea, Nora began to receive instructions. "Do the best you can in unpacking. Just make everything functional for now. I will reorganize it with your assistance when I feel better. I am sure I will be in bed for the next few days." Oh, boy, Nora thought, can't wait. However, the plus side to Marci's need to recuperate would be that Steve and she could actually talk and be near each other.

He was supervising the movers. The kids were unpacking their clothes and toys and putting them away. Kayce had kitchen detail, helping Nora unpack dishes, pots and pans. It was strange unpacking someone else's home. Nora directed Kayce to put things where they made sense for how she cooked. She put on another pot of coffee.

Nora brought Steve a cup. She made it liked he preferred; with milk and one sugar. "Thanks for that. How'd you sleep last night?"

"Alright. But it will be nice to get all of our things unloaded," she responded pragmatically.

"It should take most of the day. Then, tomorrow, we can take the kids to mass and finish up."

Nora remembered how her vow about refusing to go to Catholic mass. "I may not go with you."

"Oh? Why not?"

"As a divorcee, I've been ex-communicated."

"That's not really how it works, Nora. Besides, no one knows that here. I think it would be good if you could help me manage all the kids."

"Hmm." So much for resolutions, thought Nora.

"It will be good for the kids to see where they will be going to school."

"That's a thought. Maybe afterward, we could see a little of the city. I've heard about the Rose Gardens."

"Maybe. But it's winter. Nothing will be in bloom."

"Just making suggestions. I guess we have a lot of work to get done with it almost being Christmas. What about getting a Christmas tree? I saw signs for a Christmas tree farm, we could cut our own."

"No need. Marci has one."

"A Christmas tree?" Nora wondered what he was talking about.

"Yeah, it's aluminum. And has a colored light."

Oh Lord, one of those tin ones. Nora had seen them and thought they were hideous. "Nice," she lied. She would get her own Christmas tree when things settled.

"She got that one because she's allergic to fir trees."

"Mmm, hmm." There went that idea. Steve's life with Marci was so different then Nora imagined. So constrained. To Nora, it seemed plastic and fake, like their Christmas tree. No wonder he was more fun when he was with Nora.

"I wanted to let you know that Monday morning, I

report to Humble Oil. I'll be going out to the airfield to orient on their planes. This job will require me being gone sort of at their beck and call." Nora wondered if that meant he would be out of town. He answered that question. "It will mean that sometimes, I will be out of town for a couple of days."

"And I will be here with Marci?"

"Yes. Are you alright with that?"

"I suppose."

"Look, I know it is uncomfortable for you both right now. Give it time, it will get better. She is just hurt."

Nora hoped so. Ninety days, the approximate time she was due, was a long time to be miserable. She went back into the house to work on more boxes. It was almost time to get lunch on for the kids. Cooking, chauffeuring, and running this family was going to require organization. In order to make it work, Nora decided that she would make a chores chart. The older children would have assigned tasks, which if they completed, would result in some allowance.

She brought Marci a tray with a sandwich, some fruit, and another cup of tea. "Just place it on the end table for now. I may eat a bit later." Nora didn't know much about multiple sclerosis, but it sure wiped Marci out. Steve had told her there would be good days and bad. On the worst days, Marci even used some oxygen delivery with prongs up her nose. Poor Steve. If riding in a car wore her out, she couldn't imagine when the last time must have been that they had actually had sex.

Steve got the TV working. It was cold outside, so the kids were all indoors. *Sky King* and *Mr. Wizard* were on. All of their chatter was about astronauts and the chimp that was sent into space. Next would be John Glenn's launch. They all planned to watch it on TV in the new year. She was giving them a break before assigning them more chores.

If Nora played her cards right, Steve would see that she was a wife extraordinaire. Not only capable of taking care of her kids, but his. How she could manage it all, even while pregnant. She was convinced, he would fall more in love with her. That somehow, someway, he'd break away from Marci and get a divorce. Maybe Marci would die young? As a widower, he would be free to marry. She was lost in these delusions when she heard the little bell ringing again. Steve still didn't have the intercom installed. Priority one, as far as Nora was concerned.

"Nora, dear. I'd like some warm milk for my tea. Would you mind?"

"Sure. You didn't eat any lunch." Nora noted the full tray.

"No, I am afraid I just can't keep anything down. My stomach is a bit queasy from my medicine. Maybe I'll have some broth and crackers later. How is the unpacking going?"

"Fine. I hope to have the kitchen, bathrooms, and den functional before the end of the day."

"My, you certainly work fast."

"Thank you, Mrs. Novak." She turned to leave.

"Nora?"

She turned around. "I appreciate you trying to make this work."

"Yes," was all Nora could manage to answer, feeling guilty about her subterfuge notions.

Chapter 42

It was Christmas week. Nora had worked like a Trojan getting the Novak house unpacked and arranged. She had completed all the rooms, even managing to get Marci's Christmas decorations up. The kids set up the nativity scene under the aluminum Christmas tree that was spray-painted white. Cathy, Leisel, and Iggy loved watching the white tree turn colors with the lights. Kayce and Nora thought it was the tackiest thing they had ever seen.

Nora also set up her sewing machine. She was putting the finishing touches on her children's outfits. Marci remarked how lovely they were. Her children had matching outfits too, that had been purchased and shipped from Macy's.

One Saturday, Nora and Steve took the children to see the Christmas parade and Santa Claus in Old Town Square. Marci wasn't feeling up to it. It was the way many outings went. Marci only attended a rare event out. If the temperature was too cold, she stayed inside. Nora wondered if the neighbors assumed that Nora was Steve's wife and that Marci was some invalid live-in relative. They had already been mistaken as such at mass when they were buying the advent wreath. When Marci did not feel up to attending, Nora, despite her vow not to, attended mass with Steve. She was not going to miss one opportunity to be with him, even if it meant reneging on her promise. She refused to go to communion, however. At least for now.

Steve had made several overnight trips. On those

nights, Nora didn't get much sleep. Marci got up at least once. Although she was able to maintain her own hygiene, she often called for Nora to bring her water or tea. Other than that, Nora cooked, ran errands, and managed the children. Thankfully, Marci had hired a maid.

Nora planned on making the best of Christmas. She finished the outfits and was planning a huge meal. Turkey, dressing, and homemade cranberry sauce. She had discovered Village Bakery in Bergfeld Center and ordered some rolls, pies, and a Black Forest cake. They had never heard of *doberge*.

She still hadn't booked an OB appointment. She was too busy with things for the holidays. With all the trauma in her children's lives from the divorce and upheaval, she wanted to make sure Christmas was wonderful. Nora decorated the home to the hilt. There were scented candles, mulling spices in an incense vessel, since Marci couldn't tolerate live spruce; she had even completed sending Christmas cards. The house was beginning to look like a home. So what, if it wasn't hers.

On one of Marci's good days, she and Nora registered the children at St. Gregory's Catholic school. The head nun, who served as principal didn't ask many questions and assumed that Nora and her children were some type of extended family. With the baby inside Nora, that was partially true. Nora organized purchase of all the uniforms and had the children fitted with saddle oxford school shoes from Thom McAn.

When they returned home, Nora got a Christmas postcard from Charlene. It was the first thing she had received from her in the post. With a Santa on the front, it simply read:

> *Missing you. The club Christmas dance was a bore*
> *without you. BTW, call your mother. She is frantic*
> *to know your whereabouts. Hugs, Charlene*

On Christmas Eve, Steve and Marci took the children to evening mass, with Nora in tow. Another compromise to please her children. The children's choir was singing carols. The black velvet dresses with the fluffy, pink chiffon skirts were lovely on Kayce, Cathy, and Leisel. With the service in candle light, they were luminous. Many women gave compliments to Nora, which pleased her. Nora looked beautiful in her Christmas best, even six months pregnant. Her skin glowed in the subdued ambiance. All Nora could think about during mass was being with Steve. The magic of the season somehow eliminated Marci's presence, if only in Nora's realm. Following the service, they bedded the kids down in wait for Santa Claus. Marci, worn out, retired early to bed.

Nora and Steve put out the Santa Claus presents for all the children, arranging them under the hideous metal tree. The NASA space race was in full swing and the therefore the theme of many of the gifts were rocket related.

Then, Nora poured them a glass of egg nog spiked with a little brandy. She made hers with slightly less. Both tired from the day, they sat in the living room with a roaring fire. It had been a lovely evening; what she imagined it would be like if they were married. Damned Marci.

"Nora, you did an fantastic job with Christmas. I loved the tamales," Steve complimented.

"Someone said it was a Texas tradition. I got them from a Mexican restaurant, El Charros."

"You think of everything."

"I'll admit, I love the holidays. Sometimes, I go overboard. But I hope they enjoy their Santa presents." Nora put some Christmas music on the stand alone stereo record player.

"No, it's great. The children adored it all. I have something for you." He pulled out a small velvet box from his pocket.

"Steve. You shouldn't have," but she was glad he did.

"I hope you like it. You deserve it with as much work as you have done in the last few weeks."

Opening the box, Nora pulled out a lovely cameo broach. It was beautifully made and quite expensive.

"I got it especially for you. Here, let me put it on." He reached into the box and began to pin the broach onto her the lapel of her maternity topcoat. She looked down at the lovely broach and then up at him. It was closer than they had been in months. He took her hand and began to slow dance with her to the music.

The brandy had lowered their resolve. As he danced

with her, he rubbed his hands up and down her spine which sent shockwaves of pleasure through her body. When *Silverbells* ended, he paused and looked into her eyes. He couldn't help himself and kissed her lips softly. Starved for physical affection, she returned the kiss. All of their desire for one another returned. He kissed her more ardently. And again, she responded. "Oh, Steve," she moaned.

Suddenly, Steve pulled away. "Damn it," he whispered. "It's happening again."

"It's okay Steve. I feel it too."

He hung his head in shame, "But it can't be, Nora. I was an idiot to think that I could live under the same roof as you and not want to hold you, kiss you. Hell, even make love to you."

"I want you too."

"It's impossible. Please, excuse me." He quickly took leave of her, exited, and went to the master bedroom; softly opening and then closing the door so as not to wake Marci.

"No. It's not impossible if you love me," Nora whispered. Running her tongue over her bottom lip, she instantly recalled his lips on her. She sat alone in the living room until the record was over. Gazing out the window, she noted it was snowing lightly. She ran her fingers over the broach and recalled his hands on her. Their kiss had been the same. Soft, sensual and full. Nora rubbed on the baby inside her. Steve's baby. She took the last sip of her egg nog and retired to bed happy. She knew by the moments they had just shared, Steve was still in love with her.

Chapter 43
∞ January, 1962 ∞

New Year's Eve and the beginning of the new year passed without much drama. Steve was required to fly the Humble execs to various parties. Nora and Marci celebrated quietly at home with black eyed peas and cornbread on New Year's day. Nora's energy was holding. She was now seven months along.

The first week of the new year, all of the children, except for Steve's toddler, began school. That son remained home with Nora and Marci. Nora developed a system for lunches on Sunday night. She would purchase cold cuts and cheese at Brookshire's and bread rolls at Village bakery. Then, as the kids watched *Disney* on Sunday evening, Nora completed an assembly line of sandwich making. That way, she had them done for the week. She insisted Steve purchase a deep freeze to store her army-sized purchases of bargain commodities.

After the Christmas Eve incident, Steve was maintaining his distance. Nora put the Christmas card she received from Nellie via Charlene and first letters Charlene had sent by her bedside table. Whenever she missed her old life, she would get them out to read. Conversations with Marci usually involved the children or domestic issues and remained cordial, but superficial. Nora craved the irreverent gossip sessions she used to share with her friend.

There were certain things that Nora adored. Strong coffee, sewing sessions, her record albums and singing. None of which fit into the lifestyle of Mrs. Novak. Marci's days involved slow starts to any given morning.

Nora would make breakfast for her, of which she would leave more than half on the plate. Nora would drive her to the beauty parlor, doctor's appointments and of course mass. Marci always made her mass. Small interactions with all her children would completely drain her.

It was the most boring existence Nora had ever experienced. She was thankful for the moments when she had an excuse to run her own errands and get away from the house. In those moments, the radio got cranked. Nora sang her heart out in the car. She relished her own beauty appointments. She didn't even mind going to see the OB doctor about the baby.

Nora finally made the appointment that Steve requested. She was evasive about the questions on the initial visit form. Where she planned to have the baby. What hospital she preferred. The paternal information. Nora and Steve had not initiated those discussions. As expected, Nora was found to be in perfect health with this pregnancy. Luckily, she never had any reproductive issues. Through all her previous pregnancies, her blood pressure, circulation, and overall health were vigorous.

This baby, however, was very large. It was getting more and more difficult to hide her bulge. This evening was no exception. At the dinner table, there was some clandestine, whispered conversation and giggling among the children. Finally Nora demanded, "Okay. What is up? Out with it."

It was Cathy who revealed all. "The Novaks and Leisel think you look fat. That you have a pot belly." At that, they all began to giggle. Kayce just gave Nora a glare. To date, she had kept Nora's secret. It was just too humiliating to acknowledge the truth. At twelve, it was most embarrassing to have a mother who was pregnant. It meant she had sex.

Marci sat quietly at the table. She certainly wasn't going to offer an explanation to her children. None of them had received the sex talk. The oldest Novaks being boys, needed to hear it from their father.

"Yes. Well, there is a reason for that," Nora began. "It's the Texas food. It is so tasty and I am such a good cook, I can't stop eating it." They all laughed. Crisis averted. Marci had to admire her tenacious parenting skills. Besides being her husband's ex-lover; she had to admit Nora was a wonderful mother.

Steve was due home that evening from a flight to Beaumont. Nora was anxious to see him, for this time he had been gone for five days. Also, Valentine's Day was nearing. She hoped he had her on his mind.

After clearing the dishes, Nora prepared to sit down and put her feet up with a cup of Chamomile tea. She knew she would have to make one for Marci and looked forward to one herself. Suddenly, there was a loud bang.

"What on earth?" Nora put down the pot she was scrubbing and rushed to the bedroom hallway. Iggy was in tears. Steve's kids were skedaddling to their rooms. There was blood coming from Iggy's ankle. A hurricane-style lamp was on the floor broken into pieces from the girl's room. "Okay, what happened?" Nora inquired of them all. They stood with their mouths hanging open.

"Those boys we live with did it. We were having a pillow fight and they knocked it over."

Nora bent down and applied pressure to the wound. It was bleeding more than a Band-aid could manage. "My stars, it's gonna require stitches."

With that, Iggy began to ball louder. "No. No, I not getting stitches. They hurt." He knew well, as he had experienced them several times. Leisel was so upset; she began having one of her asthma attacks.

"Cathy, go tell Marci, she will have to watch the kids. And go get Leisel's inhaler." Cathy, true scout, took off on her emergency mission. "Come on, darling." Nora picked him up. She shouldn't be lifting, but had no choice in order to get him in the car.

Kayce came out of her room hearing all the commotion. She grabbed Iggy's arms and Nora carried his legs awkwardly to the wagon. "Get a move on. Let's go. We have to get Iggy to emergency. You too, Leisel. I'm sure you are gonna need a breathing treatment." She hurried them into the Ford. "Cathy, you and Kayce stay here." The less drama at the ER the better.

Nora backed out of the driveway so fast, that she failed to notice that one of the kids forgot to shut the rear passenger door well. Her speed caused it to swing open and hit the fence of the neighbor's yard on her way out. Bang. It dinged her door pretty badly, but it still would close.

"Crap," she let out. The kids both exchanged stares.

The nearest hospital was Mother Frances a couple of miles away. Nora hurried to the ER. She had been through this many times with her daredevil son who was always getting into this or that. The same for Leisel. Her asthma had worsened from the East Texas cedar and pine.

Nora entered the triage driveway and put the car into park. "Can I get a wheelchair?" she asked the orderly, who was standing outside smoking. Soon, they had Iggy inside with Leisel in cue. Nora initially started to go park the car. But the triage nurse already had both children inside and was taking their vital signs.

"Is there anyone that can answer questions?" she asked Nora.

"I can. They're both mine. I am their mother." Nora began to answer the triage nurse's questions about what happened. The triage drill was second nature. So even though it was urgent, she wasn't in a panic. The car would have to be handled later.

Luckily the ER wasn't full that evening. After a short interim in the waiting room, they were called back and began treatment. Nora cuddled Iggy as he whimpered. In between puffs from her breathing treatment, Leisel was taunting him, "I hope they don't have to cut it off." This only made Iggy wail louder. Nora gave her the warning look.

The ER physician was putting the lidocaine into Iggy's ankle. The kids had done a job on it, requiring at least eight stitches. Iggy squirmed in Nora's arms. "Oowwww."

"I'm sorry darling. Come on now. Be tough. G.I. Joe." Nora did her best to encourage him. Within about an hour, the crisis was averted. As she stood at the desk, completing the papers for billing, Steve entered the ER door.

"Nora. Is everything okay? Marci told me what happened."

"Yes. Thank goodness. I think one of your boys knocked over a lamp on his ankle. No big deal."

"I'm so sorry. Were they fighting?"

"No. Just rough housing." She was so calm and collected. Nothing seemed to faze her.

"Well, I got here as soon as I heard. Those boys may get the belt for this one. Is that your Ford still parked in the ER bay?" He picked up Iggy to carry him to the car for her. Nora just laughed. Thank goodness there had been no additional ambulance calls. The motor was still running and the lights were on. When they had the children loaded, Nora let out a big sigh.

"I'm glad you are home. It has been a long week without you."

"Sorry about that, I had multiple flights to make. Marci said you really went above and beyond this week, helping her and the kids out."

"Hmmm. Did she?" Nora had wondered what she told Steve behind their closed bedroom door. She was glad that neither Marci nor Steve could read what feelings were going on in her head most of the time. Some weren't the most pleasant about his wife.

"I am really proud of you, Nora. For all that you do. Especially, so far along with the baby." He looked down at her stomach which appeared to be growing week by week.

"At some point, Steve, we need to talk. We need to make plans."

"You're right. I promise. I will put some time in for us."

"And without Marci," Nora sounded protective.

Steve understood. "Without Marci." He wasn't sure how he was going to arrange it, but he was going to try. It was a difficult situation for them all. He knew Marci's wishes. Steve felt that he could convey them to Nora better when he left the tension of her presence out.

"This baby is ours and we need to make the decisions on our own." They didn't recognize it in each other, but both were existing on two separate planes of reality. Nora believed that in time, Steve would be true to himself about his feelings for her. Somehow, he would find a way for them to be together. Steve, however, was postulating around some way to convince Nora that the best thing for all was to give the baby up for adoption. She needed to care for her other four children, sans Steve. He had no intention of leaving Marci in her condition.

Chapter 44
∞ February, 1962 ∞

One afternoon, when Nora returned home from picking the children up from school, she found Marci in her room. Nora had been gone longer than usual, stopping at Kress' to let all the kids pick out their school Valentine cards. "What are you doing in here?" Nora was startled.

Marci was holding the broach that Steve had given Nora for Christmas. On the bed, there was a picture of Nora in her flight suit with Steve's arm around her standing in front of the Piper. Steve had inscribed the photo marking the date of her solo. "This is a lovely broach. Is it an antique?"

"No," was all Nora answered her. Even though Steve rented and paid for running the household, Nora felt violated having his wife in her room. How dare she go through Nora's things?

"Where did you get it from?" she asked, twisting it in her hand.

"It was a gift," was all Nora would give her.

"From my husband, I suspect." Marci grabbed her cane and went to the bed. "And this picture that you keep. With my husband. I am sure it is dear to you."

Nora knew where this was going and said nothing. She wasn't going to get into petty jealousies with Marci.

"Are you still in love with him?" Marci looked at Nora directly. Nora gazed away and then looked down. "No need to answer," Marci continued. "I know you are. I see it." She picked up the picture. "Hold onto this, because it's the last time he will ever have his arms around you like that again. He's not going to leave me, you see. Ever. He would never break our covenant and sacrament of marriage."

Nora was damned if she was going to let Marci see her cry. She stood her ground and returned Marci's gaze. Inside, her heart had been pierced by the spear of reality. Marci's reality. It stung with a vengeance.

Knowing she had deprecated Nora with her words, Marci made her way out. "Don't bother getting me tea tonight. My husband is home. He'll be bringing it to our bed." This nervy demonstration wiped out Marci's reserves. She had been fuming over the picture and broach all afternoon. She swayed slightly hitting the wall on her way out. Nora moved to help her.

"Please, don't touch me right now," Marci advised. "I will make it on my own." She continued her slow hobble into the den and down the long hallway to her and Steve's bedroom.

Once she was gone, Nora let out her feelings. She picked up the picture and put it behind the broach on her dresser. She grabbed a tissue to blot the tears in her eyes. Marci had inflicted a wound, but it wasn't fatal. Although the pressure of living all in one household was escalating to a boiling point, Nora loved Steve too much to give up now. Collecting herself, she washed her face. She was dying for a cigarette or a drink, but could have neither.

A chronic eavesdropper had overheard the conversation between Marci and Nora. Kayce came from around the corner ready for battle, "It's his? The man we are living with? Oh my God, Mother. How could you?" Kayce was disgusted. She turned around and stomped to her room.

"Well, crap. Could the day get any worse?" Nora miffed, going to follow her. She knocked on Kayce's door. "Hey, open up, please. We need to talk."

"Go away mother. I don't want to hear a harlot's explanation."

"Kayce, please. Let me just talk with you."

"Why? I hate you Mother. The more I know. The more I learn. I just despise you." She opened the door so that only her face showed. "Now I know the real reason for the divorce. You screwed around on Daddy."

Nora was so exhausted, she really wasn't thinking clearly. "I am not the one who did all the screwing around Kayce. It was your father who could never keep his pants zipped, drunk or not."

"You witch. Don't you ever talk about my father like that again. I vow to hate this baby for the rest of its life." She quickly shut the door in Nora's face. Her mother had really hit below the belt. Nora felt horrible about what she had just said, knowing how much it hurt her daughter. But she was emotionally spent. Her words could never be taken back. She could hear Kayce sobbing. Damage control would have to take place later. It was time to feed the army.

It was a busy day. TV trays were set up and they were all gathered around the set to watch the launch of the Friendship 7 rocket. John Glenn was to become the first person to orbit the earth in a space capsule.

Steve was home for supper and to watch the launch. Nora made his favorite home meal, goulash with penne pasta and bolognaise. All of them ate heartily, and Marci gleefully chattered about her day and the children's progress reports from school. She never let on about the discourse instigated with Nora earlier in the day. The nerve of this woman grated on Nora's regained composure. Nora hoped that she would retire early, so that Steve and she could finally have their talk.

It was Kayce and Cathy's turn to do the dishes. But Cathy had to do them alone, as Kayce chose to skip dinner and stay in her room. Nora supervised, sitting at the table; too tired to get up. She pulled out the letter that she had received from Charlene earlier in the day.

Dearest Nora:

It is hard to believe that it's been two months since you've left. Feels like two years. I miss the heck out of my coffee drinking, gossip girl. The club is an absolute drudge without you. Didn't take long for the rumor of you and Frank splitting to hit the grapevines. There are young floozies lined up at the bar and card tables on casino night like vultures, just waiting to make their kill.

That Greenwood money is just too tempting. Although I've seen Frank flirting, I don't think he's hooked up with anyone yet.

I'll keep you posted.

Enough talk about his trashy self. I have wonderful news. I have been working on Max lately. He sees what a mess I am without you. He's just about to break and let me come and see you. There's no way I could make that drive, so I am gonna pull a Nora and fly there.

That's right. Charlene Herbert is gonna take to the sky's (as a passenger of course) on Continental! TWA doesn't fly to Tyler. But have no fear, I am coming to bring you a little Mardi Gras. I've already talked to the travel agent, I am gonna book us a girls weekend at the Blackstone Hotel.

Keep your head high toots! I want you in full gossip glory when I get there. I'm dying to hear all the juicy details about living with the wan barracuda.

Love ya, Charlene

Nora read and re-read the letter. Contact with Charlene was the only thing keeping her spirits up. In just a few weeks, a part of Nora's normalcy would be here in person. Hopefully, with some gently used maternity wear. Nora was tired of wearing one of the three outfits she had made. She wouldn't buy anything new for herself, however. Every penny from the stipend that she was paid was judiciously saved. Once this all was over, she needed some operating funds. No matter how it all turned out.

After the tuck and tail bath routine was complete, the children were bedded down. Steve served Marci her tea, just like Marci predicted. When he came out into the kitchen, Nora was still sitting at the table. Finally, her feet were propped up.

"Hey, gal. You look exhausted. How about a Bailey's coffee?"

"Heaven. I'd love one."

"It's okay right, with the baby?"

"A rare drink of alcohol, once in a blue moon, won't hurt. Right now, after the day I've had? *'Frankly my dear I don't give a damn.'* So there." she mocked.

"Rebellious to the core. I love hearing you laugh," Steve chuckled.

"It's cold outside and it will warm my toes. That's a good thing for the baby."

Steve made her one, just like she liked it. He put a dollop of whipped cream on the top. Nora happily took a sip. It felt nice for someone to take care of her for a change. When she lifted her lip from the cup, she had a cream mustache.

"I know you fly like a man, but now you look like one." Steve teased. He reached up and wiped the cream from her lip. Electric. Nora was hormonally horny. She licked her lip where he had touched it. Even as tired as she was, she would have laid him in a heartbeat.

Steve sat at the table and noted her swollen feet propped up in the chair. "So, about that talk."

"Yeah," Nora started. "This has been harder than I thought."

He reached down, took off her shoes and began to rub her arches. It felt so good; therapeutically and sensually. She almost couldn't remember what the talk was supposed to be about. "Oh, that feels divine," she moaned.

"The talk, Nora," he gently reminded as he continued to rub.

"Right. I am trying to do the best I can. Caring for Marci. But sometimes, being around her. It's just so painful. Damned painful."

"I know. I'm gone a lot and it's still hard for me."

"Not the care. Just knowing that she is your wife," Nora clarified.

"Oh. I get it," he paused. His lips pursed into thought mode.

Nora wasn't going to waste this opportunity to advance her cause. "Today, I found her in my room, going through my things. She wasn't happy about the broach you gave me."

"No, I expect she wasn't," he smirked.

"Steve, I've been thinking about what is going to happen, especially after the baby is born. About us."

Steve was afraid of that. No matter how hard he tried to suppress them, he experienced the powerful chemistry, desire, and amorous feelings between them too. There was just no way, conscientiously, he could act on them. His loyalty to Marci was too deep. However, he didn't want to break Nora's heart either. "Nora, we've talked about this."

"But how can you deny it, Steve? You know as well as I do that when we are alone . . . near one another . . . the chemistry between us is cataclysmic."

"I'm not saying I can. But it's more complicated than that. I'm torn. You know how I feel about my obligations."

"Obligations. And so we are just to cast off the love we feel for one another? Because of some vow? Some Catholic rule?" She knew this would irk him, for Nora had come to detest the binding restraint inflicted upon her by the church. Now, when she attended mass, she was not allowed to share in the holy Eucharist. According to the Pope, she was a divorcee sinner.

"We need to be realistic. I have six children."

She corrected him. "You have seven."

"Yes. That is what we need to talk about. Realistically, I feel that we should think about putting the baby up for adoption."

Nora withdrew her feet from his hands. "What?" She couldn't imagine giving away the life that she was carrying in her womb; that she felt kick. The baby was part of them both. "That isn't an option," she was adamant.

"I know it is painful to think about."

"Stop it. Stop talking about the baby as an *it*. We conceived a child. It is moving around inside me." She began to cry softly.

"Nora." He rose to comfort her. "I didn't mean to hurt you. But we have to talk about our options." He knew now was not the time. Although he had planted the seed, she needed time to think. He held her. As he did, he could feel the baby move. Nora rested her head on his shoulder and continued to sob.

More than anything, he wanted to rub her back. Reach down and lift her chin to kiss him. Instead, he cradled her head and brushed her hair away from her face. She was right, what they shared between them was very difficult to control. He knew even holding her; it fueled desire between them both. But, he forced himself to resist. If only they had met in another circumstance.

Once she had stopped crying, he released her. She sniffed, "I'll . . . I will be alright." He handed her another tissue.

"Try to be strong. I believe in you, Nora. You actually motivate me with your strength."

"It's all an act. Can't you see?" she laughed acerbically through her tears.

Steve noted the Valentines cards on the kitchen counter. "Gosh, time has flown. I didn't realize it was almost Valentine's Day. Guess I better get on the ball."

Without a doubt, Nora knew he was referring to his wife. Forlornly, she wished he was thinking about her.

"Do you think you could watch the children? So, I might take Marci to dinner?"

Taken aback, Nora looked at him with disbelief. Had the last moments not meant anything to him? She was wounded. "Sure. Of course. I'd be happy to," she sarcastically answered. With that, she burst into tears and hurried to her bedroom shutting the door. Nora opened her bedside table and pulled out the Valentine that she had purchased and spent hours deciding what to write. Her hopes. Her love for him. Their future. She ripped it into bits and put it into the waste basket.

Chapter 45
∞ March, 1962 ∞

No one in East Texas paid much attention to Mardi Gras or the significance of what the celebration meant. Now March, Mardi Gras Day was just around the corner. So Nora made her own King's cake with the baby inside. She painstakingly rolled out the cinnamon-laced, yeasted dough and twisted it into a braid. Then, she iced it with the customary yellow, green, and purple sparkly glaze, which represented riches, good luck and royalty respectively.

In New Orleans catholic tradition, Epiphany is the point at which the magi arrived to see the Lord in the stable of Bethlehem. Mardi Gras season occurs after Epiphany during the weeks which lead up to Lent. Each week, Nora was used to a Mardi Gras party being held, usually sponsored by one of the themed krewes. At each party, there was a king's cake. A small baby representing Jesus was placed inside one piece. Whomever got that piece was bestowed with luck and also hosted the next party.

All of the kids were happy to select a piece and see who got the baby king inside for good fortune. She purchased plastic beads from Kress' and colored paper hats. To heck with Texas, they were going to celebrate Fat Tuesday regardless.

It was only weeks before the baby was due. Nora was huge and had begun to waddle, ever so slightly. Steve, Marci and she had discussed how and where she would have the baby. Not in Tyler, that was for sure. With the city's small town grapevine and all the children in Catholic school, they all preferred more privacy. Steve was scheduled to take a business trip requiring several flights out of Love Field in Dallas. He was to train on and pick up Humble Oil's new plane. It was decided that Nora would travel there with him by car. He would rent her a hotel room as close to the due date as possible. Periodically, Steve would check in on her for the last week or two of the pregnancy.

What happened after that, remained up in the air. According to Steve and Marci, Nora was going to give up the baby for adoption to Catholic Charities. In Nora's mind, she was still not convinced.

Thank heavens for the distraction that drove up in the driveway. Hearing commotion, Nora looked up from the pansies she was potting. Charlene was here. "Hey honey pie," she called out from the taxi as loud as she could. God, Nora had missed that shrill.

As soon as the taxi came to a halt, Charlene bounded out in fully glory. Brightly colored spring dress, matching purse and pumps. She was a vision straight out of the Maison Blanche spring catalog. Nora waddled down the porch steps to greet her.

"Well, my stars, woman. You are big as a barn!" Charlene cackled seeing Nora's thirty-six week bump. "No Oscar de la Renta; the Oscar the Tent maker couture suits you well."

"Stop it you, or I am gonna whack you with my garden tool," Nora joked. She dropped the trowel and hugged her friend dearly. Just seeing Charlene reduced her into a pregnant mush of blubbering.

"Aw, honey. If I had known you missed me that much, I woulda come earlier. Dry those eyes darlin' or your eyeliner will run." Nora was already laughing. They walked arm and arm into the large home of the Novaks. "You done well, toots. Very well," Charlene referred to the huge home.

"I've done most of the decorating myself. With their things, of course."

"It's sorta like *Better Home and Gardens*. Not bad. Not bad at all," she remarked walking through the living room. But then she got to the den, "Oh dear. It's fuzzy," referring to the Early American couch. "Ick."

"That was my reaction, too." Nora snickered. "And Leisel's."

Charlene put down her pink, circular makeup case and matching luggage. "Where should I put these?"

"Ssshhhh. Marci is down for her morning rest. My room is just through the den. Put them in there and then let's have a cup of coffee on the porch out back."

"Sure thing, toots." Charlene entered the bedroom and noted the colorful spread on the bed. She was glad to see that Nora had some of herself there. One room was at least something. She took off her gloves and sat her cases next to the bed noticing a book on the end table, *Thank you, Dr. Lamaze*. Picking it up and reading the jacket inside cover, she noted it was a book about a new form of childbirth. Breathing techniques and relaxation instead of drugs. No drugs? How horrific.

Nora made their coffee strong and served it in *demi-tasse* cups. They absconded out to the back porch for some girl talk. "It is so wonderful to have you here. I can't believe you came all the way to Tyler. I was really tanking."

"I could tell. Plus, I haven't spent a Mardi Gras without you in years."

"But you are going to miss all the big parades, especially the Bacchus ball."

"Honey, what's Bacchus without you?" she smiled endearingly at Nora. "So come on, spill. Let's hear how this is working out."

Nora told her about her duties, her daily routine. Marci's demands. Marci's remarks. Marci's looks. The battles with Kayce. Charlene was the good listening ear that she needed.

She validated all of her concerns. "I'm glad that despite everything, you are not smoking," Charlene nodded.

"No. I am not smoking. But I want to. I can't wait for this baby to be born, just to take a long slow drag."

"Toots, you are coping amazingly well. Besides your shape, you look beautiful. Glowing even. So, what are the plans once the baby is born?"

"I'm still not sure."

"Nora, you better be sure. It's due in a few weeks."

"I know," Nora said, repositioning herself in the chair for comfort.

"Tell me about that book. The Lamaze thing on the table in your room."

"Yeah. I got it at the library. Great stuff. It is talking about how when you have a baby, you don't have to be totally snowed."

"No pain medication?" Charlene appeared appalled. "It sounds perfectly barbaric to me."

"No. No. You use relaxation and breathing techniques and it controls everything. It's so much better for the baby. You're awake and everything. You actually get to see your baby being born."

"Why on earth would you ever want to see that? A twat expanding to the size of a grapefruit? Don't think I would ever have sex again after that. Ya know Nora, maybe since there is so much *involved* with this baby, you should just do it the regular way."

"I've done my homework. I have a choice. If this is the last baby I ever have, I want to see it actually born."

"Then more power to ya. But for me? Give me heavy drugs," Charlene kissed the air. "I wanna be out." Charlene could tell that something was on Nora's mind the way that she was stirring her coffee. "So what else are you cogitating on?"

"Steve still wants me to give the baby up for adoption."

"And how you do you feel about that?"

"Torn. I have carried this baby for nine months. He or she was conceived with the man that I love. It would be like giving away a part of us."

Charlene reached over and put her hand on Nora's. "But honey, as hard as this is to hear, you have to face the fact that Steve may never consider you and him an *us*."

"I know he's still in love with me, Charlene. It's obvious."

"Have you all . . . you know?"

"Here? God no. I barely get five minutes with him

when the baggage is around. But the sexual tension when we are near each other is orgasmic. No telling what would happen if his wife wasn't here."

"That may be, but it doesn't guarantee that he will leave her."

On cue, Nora heard Marci's cane approaching. "Speak of the devil."

Marci poked her head out the back door. "Who is this?"

"This is my best friend in the whole world, Charlene Hebert. She is like a sister to me."

"How lovely to meet you," Marci nodded her head.

"Same to you, Mrs. Novak. Thank you for letting Nora have the weekend off."

"She has worked for it. She needs time before . . . things change." Marci couldn't bring herself to refer to her husband's baby.

"Well, I sure appreciate that. I have missed the day-lights outta her," Charlene wrapped her arm around her, and then managed then put in her societal dig. "We were inseparable at Bacchus and Metairie Country Club." She knew Steve and Marci, with all their children, could never afford such extravagance. Below the table, Nora reached over and smushed Charlene's toe to squelch her comments. Marci put on a pleasant face and excused herself.

"You are just down right wicked, Charlene Hebert."

"Well. I can tell just from looking at her, what you must have endured all these months. Nora, you are a saint."

"Tell that to the Pope," she sneered and they both laughed.

Steve was due home for the weekend, and as soon as he arrived, Charlene planned to take Nora to the Black-stone Hotel. Then, she would stay on for two more days, helping Nora out at the Novak's before returning home on Ash Wednesday. After services and ashes of course.

As soon as Steve drove up, they were ready to go. The station wagon was packed with Nora's overnight bag. "Hey, Steve," Charlene, waving gregariously, gave a shout out.

"Hello, again, Charlene. Thanks for coming. I know Nora appreciates having you. Things . . . well let's just say things have been hard on her."

"Nothing that a good ole' girl's weekend out won't cure," Charlene winked.

He turned to Nora. "Have a good time, okay? All the kids will be fine. You weren't the only person who was a scout leader you know," he referred to himself.

"Thanks, Steve. I do appreciate this," she said sincerely. Plopping down into the passenger seat of the wagon, she called out from the window, "Charlene means the world to me," Nora couldn't wait to get away. Charlene was going to drive.

The Blackstone was everything they had read about on the brochure. Opulent. Luxurious. Perfect. Charlene was blessed for booking them. They had a suite rented for the weekend, complete with a huge Jacuzzi tub. As Nora walked around in awe, Charlene unpacked her makeup bag. "Manicures. Pedicures. The works for my girl." All of her potions, lotions, and lacquers were out on the bed.

Nora came over and hugged her again. "You are just the absolute best."

"Yeah, don't you forget it. What do you want from room service?"

"Oh, Charlene, I can't afford that."

"This weekend is on me. Order up," she handed her the menu and phone. That set the tone for their whole time away. Charlene intended for Nora to be pampered. She did her hair and her nails. It was bliss. In addition, there was plenty of uninterrupted time for girl talk.

The recurring themes of conversation were Nora's plans for after the baby. Charlene knew how hard it was going to be contemplating adoption, but tried to reason with her regarding her other children. Especially, Kayce.

Charlene and Nora put on the thick, white terry cloth Robes provided by the hotel. "Here put this cap on your head," Charlene directed Nora. She was squeezing out some green goo and rubbing in into her palms. "She is at that age, Nora. Practically a teen." Charlene began to apply a facial mask on Nora. "She needs your full attention now. There are only a few years left."

"That's a valid point. Although I have no idea how to repair the huge crevasse in our relationship. Mmm. That smells like the tropics."

"Apricot and lime it says on the box. It's about time and love, honey. That's what it is going to take. She may not forgive you for years, but you stick to your guns. Be there for her." Charlene smeared gobs of the green cream over Nora's cheekbones.

"She just hates me so."

"She hates the situation. Her silver spoon was ripped right out of her mouth at a difficult period of transition. Being a teenager is rife with drama. Oh, I am gonna try this blue coconut one," she grabbed a tube and began to apply thick blue cream to her own face. "Think about it. Just learning about the birds and the bees and then getting slammed with them in her face. Not to mention the Bacchus debacle."

"You're right. But I am the one responsible for adding all that drama. I just wonder if she can ever forgive me."

"I hate to say it, but with that baby as a constant reminder, I am not so sure. As much as that hurts to hear." Charlene and Nora returned to the living area of the room. Nora stretched out on a chaise lounge. Charlene poured herself another glass of champagne.

"How long does this have to stay on? My face is getting tight," Nora queried touching her face.

"That means it's working. I dunno. Guess I outta read the box."

Nora knew Charlene was right about how the baby was affecting her oldest daughter. Despite how much she believed Steve loved her, his code of honor would never let him leave his wife. And it didn't appear that Marci was dying anytime soon. "I am such a fool. I even bought the baby a layette set."

"Oh, honey. Don't rub salt in your war wounds. Don't you dare take that to the hospital." Charlene knew her friend so well. Nora already had it in her stack of items to pack.

"You have four other children, Nora. Including a pre-teen daughter that desperately needs your validation. You are so blessed. Think about it. Somewhere out there is a couple who can't have a baby, no matter what they try. It would be like a gift, you know?" she wrapped her arms around Nora and held her.

"It is just so hard." Nora thought about Gia. "I can

feel the baby move. It's a part of what I dreamed of having. Of mutual respect and love. With Steve," her bottom lip quivered. Tears were eminent.

"Darlin' let's not wallow in it. That just won't be good for anyone involved. You are not a bad person, Nora. It's just sometimes, you think like a man."

"What's that supposed to mean?"

"Don't get yourself all worked up. I just mean that men can go out there. Take on the world. Make whatever decisions they want and not have to always think of the consequences."

"Go on," Nora couldn't wait to hear the rest.

"I admire you for your guts. I don't know many women who can fly a plane. But honey, you just need to learn to work it better. Once we rinse this stuff off, I say let's get in that Jacuzzi!" Charlene tossed her a maternity swimsuit and they made the best of a painful situation.

"Work it better, you mean with men."

"Yeah, honey. Working the feminine mystique. Getting to do some of those audacious things, but keeping things status quo. Avoiding choices that have dire consequences. Ya know? Your choices haven't actually been stellar."

Steam was rising from the bubbles and swirls of the jets from the indoor oval tub. Charlene helped her friend over the steps and down into the basin. "Now *this*, is almost heaven," Nora sighed lowering her own body into the water.

Charlene sipped out of her champagne flute. "I just adore a hot tub."

"Worth every penny," Nora poured some ginger ale into hers. Charlene had thought of everything.

"Nora, I have known you a long time."

"Yes. You were a life saver when I married into the Greenwood family. Before you, I thought I was suffocating."

"I have a question. Please don't get mad, okay?"

Nora knew her best friend never held back. "Go on, you know I'll answer it truthfully."

"When you were with Steve. Another man. What was it like?"

That brought a gleam to Nora's face. "Amazing. He was everything that Frank wasn't. Frank took me brutally.

Sex was like some kind of domination. I was young and didn't know different. But with Steve, he truly made love to me."

"I never realized how awful it must have been for you. All those years with Frank."

"That's okay. There were lots of diversions, like you, thank goodness."

"With Max, I wouldn't know if he was a good lover or not. I mean, we were both virgins. He seems to enjoy me. Even this baby battle-scarred version. Every once in a while, I get a tickle or twinge of something."

"Have you ever climaxed?" Nora took a sip of ginger ale.

"Like orgasmed?" Charlene pondered. "I don't really know."

"Believe me. You would know. I'm convinced that so many wives have sex for years and never know what that even feels like. They just submissively go through the motions. What positions do you all do?"

"Positions?" Charlene looked baffled.

"Dear me, don't tell me all you've ever done is missionary style? All these years?"

"Lordy me, what does that even mean?" Charlene took another drink from her flute.

"You on bottom. Him on top."

"Is there any other way?"

"Heavens, yes. Sex with Steve was unbelievable. We pleasured each other."

"How did you even know what to do?"

"I dunno. It just happened. The chemistry was intense and we just did what came naturally to us. Girl, as soon as I get through this, we are gonna have to go to The Quarter and get you some books. It's time you knew all about an orgasm."

Charlene turned flush red, and then laughed. "Yah. Perhaps you're right. Can you imagine that at the next straw poll of the Junior League? So ladies, when was your last orgasm?" Charlene guffawed.

"And was it with your husband?" Nora sniggered. "Good golly, I have missed you, Charlene."

"Hmmm. I know. Why do you think Max agreed to pay for this little trip? I was going nuts without you. Thank goodness it's only a few weeks until you pop that baby out and can come back home."

Nora rubbed her belly covered in bubbles from the tub. "Just a few weeks." It was hard for her to imagine how she would relinquish what was inside her. But stoically, she smiled at her friend.

Sunday evening, they unenthusiastically packed their bags and returned to the Novak's. Nora gave Charlene a letter to give to Nellie. She didn't want to mail it and have her snail mail address in Tyler showing. It would be posted from Metairie. Charlene helped Nora with the assembly line to ready the school lunches for the next week.

Unlike New Orleans, Texas schools did not give any time off for Mardi Gras. In a way, that was nice, as Nora and Charlene got to spend another day together. Charlene was a godsend helping Nora with her chores and tasks related to the care of the children and Marci. With Charlene present, it was a quiet and non-eventful week. For that, Nora was thankful.

On Fat Tuesday, Charlene helped Nora cook a New Orleans feast. Shrimp Creole. Jumbalaya. Gumbo. Loaves of French bread. Brioche. It was heaven. Charlene brought real Mardi Gras beads and doubloons from parades held earlier in the month. Noise makers. Even petit fours from Gambino's. Anything Marci Gras related that she could fit into her suitcase. The kids were thrilled to stand in the den and holler, "Throw me something, Mister. Throw me something," like they had at so many Mardi Gras parades back home.

Steve was pleasantly surprised at how much effort Charlene put into bringing a little bit of New Orleans to her homesick friend. Nora's smile and characteristic laugh were infectious. He put some Dixieland jazz on the record player. Even Marci joined in when they began singing *When the Saints go Marching*. Using Marci's fine linen for the napkin dance, the kids pranced in circles around the living room. It was glorious. Nora didn't want the night to end. For she knew when it did, she would be saying goodbye to her emotional lifeline. Letters and the telephone were just no substitute for Charlene Hebert.

Chapter 46

Nora took Charlene to Ash Wednesday mass. They attended the early morning service at St. Gregory's with the children and the rest of the school's students. Steve and Marci were there, as well. Although she received ashes, Nora again did not receive communion. Steve and Marci, however, most certainly partook. The somber service, with the crosses of ash marking their foreheads did nothing to brighten Nora's affect.

At the conclusion of the mass, Nora knew she had to say goodbye to Charlene and took her to Tyler Pounds Regional Airport. Her Continental Airlines flight was to depart just before 10:00 AM. The timelines for the next instance they would see one another were in limbo. All of that relied upon the decision that Nora made regarding the baby.

"Nora, I know our conversations have been tough."

"What gives you that impression?" Nora said sardonically; drying her sniffles from already crying.

"This may be the hardest thing you ever do in your life, but it's got to be the right one. Remember that, Nora Jean Broussard. You are Jack Broussard's daughter. You're a strong woman. I know you can get through this."

"If you say so, dear one," Nora sniffled.

"No matter what, I swear on my life," Charlene put her hand on her heart, "I will be your friend forever."

"Even when I am the waitress at Metairie Country Club, not your lunch mate?"

"Even then. By the way, don't expect me to tip you

big." Charlene tossed back her blond head of Marilyn Monroe, platinum curls and chuckled.

"I wouldn't dream of it," Nora managed a smile.

"Nora Jean you don't have to be Joan of Arc you know? Always off on some adventure. Sometimes, quiet and still are good. The simple life." Charlene wondered if Nora got her meaning. Who knows, maybe she thought it was all horse hockey. "Be good to yourself, okay? And by the way, please call your mother so she will quit hounding me."

"Okay. I promise," Nora assured. The overhead call came for Charlene's flight. It was time for her to leave. "Hurry now. Don't miss your flight. I'll be watching from the end of the field."

"Love you, honey." Charlene picked up her pink luggage case and hurried down the corridor. Nora couldn't bear to go to the gate. Once outside, she drove to the end of the runway; planning to watch as the plane took off. As she sat there, behind the chain link fence, she was grateful for Charlene taking the time to support her despite the mess in which she was involved. It had all started with flying.

Nora wondered how long it would be before she ever got to fly again? Considering the cost, no doubt when hell froze over. She remembered the sensation she experienced when the plane lifted. How her hands felt controlling the throttle. The absolute sheer exhilaration and freedom she felt when aloft.

The Continental aircraft was making its taxi. She reckoned Charlene was waving out the tiny window, even though she couldn't see her. A few weeks. Just a few short weeks and then Nora's life would take yet another turn. The baby inside her began to kick ferociously, almost in protest. It was going to be the longest fortnight or so of Nora's life.

Nora remained at the end of the airfield for several hours. It was a time for contemplation and reflection. She wasn't expected back at the Novak's for a while.

Knowing that Nora's pregnancy was in its advanced stages, Marci had lessened her demands. Nora could get through helping Marci, but by the time she reached carpool duty with the children and making the evening meal, she was getting tired. With Nora's previous preg-nancies, she had always gone into labor by week thirty nine at the latest. The due date of this infant was a mere twenty days away. Nora was into the last countdown of time that she would spend at the Novak's. Ninety sleeps had gone by quickly.

The plane that Steve was to pick up for Humble Oil was being re-outfitted in Dallas. It was a short two and a half hour trip west. Nora would wait out the pregnancy in its final days there.

Since she had done this four times before, Nora felt pretty sure she could pinpoint her approximate labor day with a fair amount of accuracy. When she felt the baby drop and increased pressure in her pelvis; she knew she was close. Steve intended to keep in contact with her by phone. He had only one overnight flight scheduled in which he would be away. Other than that, the training runs would be short day trips. Plus, he had business at the Dallas office for Humble Oil.

It all sounded good. What hadn't been worked out were the details regarding which hospital and the Catholic Charities adoption. Due to the logistics of the trip, Nora intended to wait until she was actually in the city to make those arrangements. Also, it bought her more time to make a final decision about the baby. An eternal optimist, she saw a different outcome. In the recesses of her brain, she harbored an inkling of hope. Steve, her children, and the infant they created riding off into the sunset.

Putting her pipedreams aside, Nora realized it was getting close to 3:00 in the afternoon. Time to drive back and complete her final carpool run at St. Gregory's.

* * * * *

Kayce got into the front passenger seat; it was her self- imposed privilege. No riding with her younger brothers and sisters, or the riff-raff, which is what she considered the strangers with whom she was living. Nora was hoping to thaw their existing permafrost, now that the sting of Mardi Gras and Bacchus were over.

"How was your day?" Nora attempted first.

"It was school. And not Ursuline. How do you think?"

Nora was not giving up that easily. "Well, Ursuline may not be as improbable as you imagine."

"How's that? Since we now live in Tyler."

"There will be more changes soon."

"If you are referring to that," Kayce pointed at her gigantic bulge, "having it will only make things worse."

"Look, I can't really converse with you while everyone else around," Nora whispered. "But we need to have a talk. Maybe tonight after supper, okay?"

For once, Kayce looked interested. "Okay."

"Help me with the dishes tonight. Then, after everyone gets their bath, come to my room and we will have a chat. Okay?"

Kayce appeared skeptical, but relished anytime away from the brood. "Alright."

At this point, Nora had no idea exactly what all she was going to tell Kayce. But it was one more step to repairing the emotional damage. She wanted to give her hope.

Steve was away on an overnight. After Nora served supper and the table was cleared, she and Kayce worked on the dishes. Kayce still couldn't fathom that all of the other children were still so clueless about her mother's obvious condition. To them, their mother just wore big, unshapely tops. It never dawned on her siblings what the expanded top was intended to hide. She almost envied their naivety and spared humiliation.

Once the others had been put to bed and Marci's needs met; Nora quietly knocked on Kayce's door. She shared a room with Cathy and another of Steve's girls who were fast asleep. "Ready for our convo?"

Kayce put down her book and followed her mother to her room on the other side of the house. "What's this all about?"

"I want to talk to you, about everything that has been going on."

"There's nothing you can do about it now. Life as we knew it is gone. Forever." Kayce plopped down on Nora's double bed.

"That may be, Kayce. But there's a whole big world out there that starts every day when we wake up. We have our future."

"I'm not interested if it involves living in Tyler with these people. Or taking care of a half brother or sister."

Nora moved to the bed and put her arm around her. "That's just it. What I wanted to talk about. What happens after I have the baby?"

"I already told you I would hate it."

"Yes. And although that is a hurtful thing to say about an innocent life inside a womb, I have heard you. I've tried very hard to understand your feelings. I am asking that you try to understand mine."

"So this is all about you? That's a shocker," she said sarcastically.

"Please. Kayce. Just try to hear me out."

Kayce sat with her arms crossed and lips pouted tight.

"There are only a few days until this baby is born. I plan to accompany Mr. Novak to Dallas. He has to go there to work. I am going to deliver the baby at a hospital there."

"Okay. So what does that have to do with me?"

"While I am gone, you will stay with your brothers and sisters here. They are going to hire a temporary nanny to handle all the domestic things for you all. Once I deliver the baby, I will ride here on the train, meet you all and we'll drive back to New Orleans."

Nora finally had her attention. "We're going home? To New Orleans?"

"Yes. But we will be living with Nellie. At her apartment until I can find one of our own."

"Who cares? At least we will be with our own family. Not living with your boyfriend and his kids." Kayce's eyes had a glint of happiness that Nora had not seen in months.

"I figured you would be pleased. Don't say anything to the others right now. Okay? I plan to talk to Leisel, Cathy and Ignatius before I leave for Dallas."

"How long will you be gone?" Kayce looked concerned. It would leave her and her brothers and sisters with Marci and yet another stranger, a nanny. Dreadful.

"I think it will be at least a week. The baby is due at the end of March."

"When we go back, will it be just us? Or are you bringing *it*?"

Nora was silent. It was just too painful to answer.

Kayce could see the look on her mother's face. "Never mind. What about school?"

"Obviously, that is a concern. You all will have to finish out the year back in New Orleans. I am not sure where at the moment."

"Can we go to our old school in Metairie?"

"I don't think so. It would be . . . I don't know at the moment. We will work that part out. But it does mean Ursuline is possible for high school." Nora thought for a brief moment, Kayce looked hopeful. "For now, I need you to be as helpful as you can. I know I have hurt you Kayce. But as your mother, I do love you."

Kayce did not make a move to hug her, but at least she was not giving her vile looks. Nora wrapped her arms around her on the bed and gave her a squeeze.

"I just want this nightmare to be over. I just want to go home." Kayce rose to leave.

"I know. In a way, I do too."

Kayce looked at her mother trying to gauge her authenticity. She hoped that was true.

When she left, Nora went to her chest of drawers. She pulled out the baby layette set running her fingers along the embroidered pale, yellow bodice. She imagined what the face of the tiny infant might look like in the warming hat. The thought of never seeing her baby was just too agonizing.

She got the book from her nightstand about Lamaze and was determined to finish its contents. This was her baby. Her delivery. She planned to do it her way.

Chapter 47

The night before Steve and Nora were to leave, they sat at the kitchen table and had a meeting with Marci. All of the final plans were discussed. Nora had the children's bags packed, except for the school uniforms and underwear they would need for the next week or so. She left out a set of play clothes for each of them.

Marci wrote out Nora her final paycheck. "I appreciate your decency in getting through this. I hope everything goes well with the birth of the baby." Her voice was quiet and subdued, lacking warmth.

"I know it hasn't been easy with me being here," Nora offered. "But I do appreciate your kindness and generosity to my children. And to me."

"Very well, then. All the best, Nora."

Nora rose to shake her hand, which Marci did not offer. Marci simply turned her back and began down the hall using her cane. Nora gave Steve an insightful glance.

"What did you expect? This has been very difficult for her having you here in our home," he reminded.

"I'm sure. Guess it's just really time for it all to be over. We've overstayed our welcome. I managed the best I could." Nora began to put on a pot of coffee for them both.

"You did great. We all did. It was a bizarre situation. Did you find a hotel?"

"Yes. I am going to be staying at the Melrose." Nora handed him the brochure she got from the travel agent.

"It's right near the hospital, on Cedar Springs, down the road from Inwood."

"Looks a bit pricey."

"It is. But it is the last expense you will be paying on my account. I'm not spending a week in a cheap motel. This way, I can get out and walk."

"Oh, alright. Don't get upset."

"I'm not. Just defending my choice. This is hard on me, too, you know?"

Gazing at her with sincere understanding, he reached for her hand on the table. "I know it is. You've been a trooper through this whole process. I am really proud of you."

That made Nora immensely satisfied to hear. She reached around with her hand and gripped his. This time, he didn't pull away. "In another couple of weeks, I am delivering our baby."

Steve let out a big sigh. "I hope Catholic Charities can find a nice couple. Someone who will give it the love and support it needs."

In her heart, Nora knew she and Steve could have been the parents doing exactly that were the situation different. "I never told you, but I found something out about my own birth."

"Oh?"

"It appears that history is repeating itself."

"I don't understand."

Nora looked down. "My father, Jack. He had a lover. An exotic beauty from the riverboats."

"While he was married to your mother?"

"Yes. Evidently."

"Go on." Steve was anxious to hear the story.

Nora reluctantly took her hand out of his and got up to pour them both a cup of Folgers. The Community coffee they had brought with them had long since run out. Piggly Wiggly did not stock New Orleans coffee with chicory. "I never knew this, but Nellie had trouble conceiving. I don't know all the details. She certainly has never spoken of it to me. But Jack had an affair and this woman had a child. And that child was me."

"So, you were adopted?"

"I never knew I was. I'm quite sure it was not official.

The woman was unable to care for me. When Nellie miscarried yet again, she gave the baby to Jack and her to raise as their own."

"Stunning. When did you find all this out?" Steve ran his hands through his hair.

"One night when I stopped for coffee in The Quarter. I saw this woman there. Her eyes, they are very unusual. She's dark in complexion, maybe mulatto, but her eyes are crystal blue. Later, when Kayce ran away she somehow ended up there too. And Big Daddy works there, as well. It's all such a fluke. When I went back to thank Big Daddy, Gia, that's her name, approached me and told me the story."

Then it dawned on Steve, why the thought of adoption was so difficult for Nora. He knew she cared for Nellie, but had never felt they were cut from the same cloth. "Nora, I don't know what to say." He again touched her; this time cupping her shoulder. He wanted to wrap his arms around her and hug her, but knew where that would lead.

"There's nothing to say. Nellie raised me. Loved me. Gia says she gave the ultimate gift to Jack. His child. At least I didn't grow up a bastard."

"True." Steve was astonished at this news.

"But it does explain a lot. I was never anything like Nellie."

"That's why we have to do what we have to, Nora. You have four children who adore you. Kayce, who desperately needs you. If you kept our baby, it would be starting out a life without its father. And with an older sister who, whether or not she does, vows to hate it."

Nora was considering his every word.

"The odds would already be stacked against this innocent's life. Not to mention how hard it would be economically for you to start over."

"But this is never what I wanted. You know that. I wanted us to be together."

He got up and began to pace the kitchen. "That was never possible."

She rose to face him. "Can't you admit that you at least thought about it? Wanted it? Did you ever truly love me?"

Steve turned to face her. "You know I did and still do. My feelings for you are genuine," he said putting his arms on her shoulders. He took her face in his hands. "Damn it. I've loved being with you more than any other woman in my life. Don't you know that?"

"Yes. I do." She stretched up to try and kiss him, but he gently pushed her shoulders away.

"Please, Nora. Try to understand. We can't. Ever."

She bit her lip. "I won't ever stop. I won't ever stop loving you. You will have to live with that."

"Yeah, I will. But I won't ruin any more lives. It is hard enough knowing that I will never be a father to my own flesh and blood you carry inside you. It's killing me." He looked away and Nora was sure it was due to the surge of emotion within him. Bittersweet love tinged with extreme sadness.

"I'm sorry, Steve. I promised myself I wouldn't go here. It's just that when we are close, I fall in love with you all over again. I know I should be stronger and resist it, like you. But my heart just overrules that."

"That's why, no matter how much it hurts, it is better that you return to New Orleans and start a new life. In time, you will forget about me."

"No, I won't!" she was defiant.

He stared into her eyes intently, their azure blue searing into her soul. "Yes. You will. In time you will. What we shared may always be special to you, but time is a great healer."

It was tortuous to wrap her head around that at the moment. Those were thoughts that, for now, she shoved to the far reaches of her heart. Steve took leave of her. Having had her under his roof for three months took all the self control he could muster. Although he would miss her tremendously, he was almost relieved the torture would be ending tonight.

Determined, Nora forced herself to focus on the final preparations for tomorrow's trip. It would be another night of restless sleep, but her last under these circumstances.

The next morning, Nora was up early. She helped her children get ready for school, but made sure she had a few minutes extra to say goodbye to each one of them. "I will see you guys in a couple of weeks, okay? Try to be good and get along. When I see you again, we'll be going on a long road trip."

Anticipating a fun excursion, Nora hoped, would lessen the strain of her being away. Marci watched from the window, as Steve loaded all of the children, his luggage, and Nora into the one of Humble Oil's company vans. In addition to picking up a new plane, Steve was delivering some equipment. Humble loaned them a large passenger van to ferry to Dallas for their trip. They planned to drop the children off at school and then set out on their journey.

As they approached St. Gregory's, at first it seemed like any other school day. But after dropping them off, Nora suddenly felt very alone. She would miss them over the fortnight. Now it was just her and Steve in the van. She contemplated asking Steve to circumvent driving through downtown Tyler. She was more than glad it was the last time she would see the city. For Nora, it would always remain tragically poignant.

Due to her short stay, she would miss what Tyler was famous for, the Rose festival. Driving amidst the out-skirts, they passed acres and acres of rose bushes and road side stands selling them. Nora made a mental note to banish roses from future floral arrangements. In the past, she found their fragrance romantic. Now, however, they would only bring back painful memories of this time.

After about twenty-five miles, the red, sandy dirt and pine forests changed to rolling pastures and small scrub oaks. The hills became smaller and the landscape more flat. The distance was nearly a hundred miles. With the emotional roller coaster of last evening, both of them were quiet and resolute. There was nothing more to say. It was difficult for Nora to accept that the next few days with Steve were her last.

Going west on Highway 80, the prairie grass hills became progressively more undulated. Trees, more sparse. Grey shapes outlined the high rises of Dallas in the distance. It was a large and commercial city. They entered heaps of construction on Interstate 20, just east of the heart of downtown. Following Nora's navigation on the *Humble Oil Happy Motoring Map of Dallas-Fort Worth*, they passed by Fair Park and the Cotton Bowl. Nora saw the biggest Ferris wheel she had ever seen in her life.

"Steve look, it's huge!" she exclaimed.

"That's part of the fairgrounds for the State Fair of Texas. It is a real big deal." As they progressed on Commerce, Steve exited right onto Pearl. Steve pointed out the Humble Oil high rise off of Bryan St. Taking Pearl north to Ross, they snaked their way around to Cedar Springs. The Melrose was on the corner of Maple and Oak Lawn. Dallas was gleaming and cosmopolitan. There were lush green parks filled with tulips and huge skyscrapers. Noted for its fashion, Nora was interested in going to Neiman Marcus downtown.

The Melrose was lovely. They pulled up its circular drive for valet service. At the front desk, Nora registered under her own name. Steve had a room of his own which was paid for by Humble. After they checked in, Nora went up to her room. Gracious and oversized, it was impeccably appointed with European marble floors at the entry. She collapsed down on the huge bed. Unfortunately, she couldn't sit back up.

Steve, who had been helping unload her bags with the bellman, came to her rescue. Pulling her up by her arms, "Careful old girl. You're a bit top-heavy."

"Not for long. I figure about another five days or so."

"You think it's gonna come that soon?"

"Yep. I can already tell. I'm having to take a whiz constantly. The baby has dropped down into my pelvis. See at the space I now have under my ribs?" she measured with her hands. Nora was pleased with her surroundings. "Look at the tub. Isn't that divine?"

"I am a bit worried about you getting in and out of that."

"Well I have to bathe. I'll be careful. I am sure there is some attendant who would come to my rescue."

"That's what makes me nervous. Now that we're here, I am really a wreck at thinking about leaving you alone."

"Steve. I can fly a plane. I've had four babies before. I know the routine. I'll be fine."

He smiled and smirked, "You're probably right. What are you going to do during the day while I'm gone?"

"Shop till I drop. This is Big D. Neiman Marcus is

here. Not to mention Sanger-Harris and Titche's. Believe me, I won't be bored. Did you see all the shops on Oak Lawn?" She opened the curtain to reveal a dramatic view of the city.

"Glad you will have something to do."

"I may not have much money, but there is a lot to look at. Plus, I am finally about finished with my book." She pulled out the Lamaze guide.

"What's that?"

"A new way to give birth. You control the pain with breathing and relaxation. You're awake and actually get to see your baby be born."

"Nora, considering . . ."

"Considering what? I am going to be awake for this birth. And that's that."

"It might make it harder."

"What. Giving my baby away? You better believe it is going to be hard, but I am going to see it born. It may be the only time I ever get to see our child," her voice rising.

He decided to avoid any further arguments. "Okay. Okay. Your turf there. Not mine. I have to go out to Love Field. You take a rest and I will meet you for dinner, okay?"

"Alright. What are you in the mood for? Dallas has hundreds of great places to eat according to the travel agent."

"Surprise me."

"Always," she winked. Once he was gone, she returned to the window and looked out. Dallas was fabulous. She was glad to be away from Tyler and Marci. This was more her element. Energized, she grabbed her purse and set out for a walk.

Dallas's Oak Lawn district had wonderful shops. Stationery. Florals. Clothing boutiques. If only she had more money. Steve had given her a twenty. For now, window shopping would have to do. Nora walked for what must have been blocks. Tyler was a hick town compared to this. When her feet were swollen and painful, she turned around to head back. She popped into the Woolco lunch counter for a quick soda. Nora saw the cutest head bands and bought herself three for a dollar. She put the red one on right in the store.

By the time she got back to the Melrose, she was pooped. When she entered, the doorman greeted her by name. Off the elegant lobby, she could hear a piano playing. Lovely. Arriving at her room, she ran a hot bath and planned to take a long soak in the Egyptian tub. She placed the thick, luxurious, complimentary robe on the vanity chair and carefully stepped down into the warm water. Relaxation at its best.

After a long soak, Nora took her time at the vanity applying her makeup. It had been months since she was out to dinner with Steve other than to Captain Spaceburger or the Frostie Rootbeer stand with the kids. Tonight they were going to Kirby's Steakhouse on Greenville. Texas was known for its beef and Nora wanted to check out the Dallas legend recommended by the concierge.

She selected an A-line evening dress, another loan from Charlene, and some comfortable shoes. No high heels tonight. Her feet were at thirty-nine weeks gestation and her ankles were huge. From the breasts up, she didn't look half bad. Steve knocked on her door to see if she was ready.

"You look lovely, Nora," he declared as she opened it. "Did you have fun shopping?"

"Window shopping. My grand purchase for today was three head bands from the Woolco."

Steve broke out into a laugh. "My nifty, thrifty, Nora."

"Tomorrow, I plan to take a taxi to Neiman's. They have a lunch place there called The Zodiac Room."

"Do tell," he exclaimed in mock Charlene.

"Hey, go easy on me. Once I have this baby and get back to New Orleans, it will be work, work and more work to support myself and my brood."

"You could always stay in Tyler."

She gave him one of her looks as she grabbed her purse.

"I will miss you and your wit."

"I'll miss you too."

"Until your divorce is final and you meet someone else."

"There won't be anyone else for a very, very long time. With me, love is illusive; for the man that I love is taken."

He knew what she meant. And decided it was better to not to say anything else about the future. They took the van up Central Expressway to Mockingbird and then to Greenville Avenue. Nora loved the vibe of the "M" street neighborhoods of Dallas. There were unique steeped roofed houses with lots of stained glass. Very quaint and English with immaculate lawns and gardens full of flowers.

Kirby's was splendid. You could smell the aroma of beef cooking on an open flame. She ordered a large T-bone steak and loaded baked potato. Steve ordered the same. Nora did her share of people watching. Tall Texans promenading their dates. The women were decked out to the max. She longed to wear attractive clothing again. The food was delicious, but even with the baby dropping; Nora was only able to eat half of her meal. This baby was huge and pressing up against her ribs making her full.

"I looked up the Catholic hospital in the Yellowpages."

"And," he said mouth full of succulent Angus beef.

"It's St. Paul Hospital. Run by the Daughters of Charity. Near the large Parkland hospital complex on Inwood and Harry Hines. I'm glad it's not the county hospital." Nora thought of Nellie and Hotel Dieu.

"Great. Maybe we can swing by there so you can see the outside and be able to tell the taxi driver, if I am out on a flight," he said chewing. "Damn this is good."

"The concierge recommended it. How was the plane?"

"A beauty. A Beechcraft Twin Bonanza. It can do a hundred ninety eight knots."

"Nice," Nora treated herself to a tiny glass of burgundy.

"I imagine they'll fly that until the testing is done and production begins on the Lear jets. Have you heard about them?"

"No. Been a little busy."

"They're just stellar. From a company out of Wichita. But it'll require some major retraining and check-rides. Not to mention logging lots of hours. They fly totally different." Steve loved talking aviation with Nora. Despite being a woman, she got it.

"It's pretty stunning that flying Mach is just not a big

deal anymore. You hear sonic booms all the time."

"Yeah. Oh, to be Chuck Yeager. I'd love to go back to flying jets."

"Sounds like you are going to stay with Humble."
Nora was surprised that he wasn't going to return to New Orleans any time soon.

"Maybe for another year or so."

"Oh. I was hoping you'd be returning to Lakefront."

"Chet's doing a great job running the business. So for now, the Humble job is extra income. God knows I need that. When do you think you'll be flying again?"

"Considering my economic situation, I would say when pigs fly."

"I hope it's sooner than that. You're really great on the yoke."

She basked in his compliments.

"By the way, Frank finally finished. He had to rent a plane. According to Chet, he screwed his first three solo attempts."

Nora laughed so hard she almost spit out her wine. "Serves the bastard right."

The candlelight made Nora's skin glow. It warmed Steve's heart to see her so happy. Dynamic and stylish, eating out in a restaurant and enjoying the nightlife, Nora was again in her element. He hoped her future life would bring her joy. He hated that it wouldn't involve him. There was just something about her; she brought out his zeal. There would never be another woman like her.

When Steve walked her back to her room at the Melrose, she asked if he wanted to come inside. The wine had mellowed them both. He could hardly take his eyes off the outline of her pregnancy enhanced breasts. Despite her expectant situation, it had been a magical evening.

"I had better say goodnight here. I don't trust myself."

"Steve, I am big as a barn. I don't think I'm very fuckable."

"You," he held her close, "are dangerously fuckable." He lowered his head to hers and gave her a soft kiss on the lips. She melted. Then, he pulled away. "Good night, Nora. Stay out of trouble tomorrow."

"Will do, over." She giggled. "Don't forget to leave your telephone numbers. So that I can somehow reach you."

"Roger that."

She watched him walk down the hall. He knew better than to look back. God, he adored her.

Chapter 48

After her date, that wasn't a date with Steve; Nora felt great. She knew the situation was futile, but somehow it made her feel good inside, more self actualized to know that he still loved her. And she was sure that he did.

Nora had a big breakfast of eggs Benedict, strong coffee and orange juice. She was already dressed and eager to start the day. Neiman's. Ready, set, go. The brochures given to her by the hotel concierge described how you could get an entire facial including makeup for free. Nora planned to spend the entire day there.

She arranged for a taxi to pick her up at 9:45 AM sharp, anxious to arrive when the store opened. There was an urban legend which claimed that when upper class Dallas women died, they specifically requested their caskets face the direction of Neiman's. Surely it wasn't true, but the sheer obnoxiousness of it made her laugh. She had to experience this place herself.

From the moment she entered the store, Nora was enraptured. The affluent surroundings. Fabulous displays. Sales attendants at your beck and call. The store concierge had a white gloved attendant accompany her to one of the makeup counters. Her facial was scheduled for 10:05 AM.

The make-up associate and her two assistants were dressed in smart-looking matching smocks, embroidered with the Neiman-Marcus logo. They began with a facial cleanser and progressed with five different types of moisturizers. Lancôme, Elizabeth Arden, Helena Rubenstein. The whole process took about two and a half hours. By the time they were finished, Nora looked like a Grecian goddess. It was far more cosmetics than she was used to wearing. Huge false eye lashes and lots of liner. More like night time makeup. But she didn't care, it was Neiman's. It was time for her lunch at the Zodiac Room.

The Maître' D escorted Nora into the luscious dining room. White linens, china and crystal adorned each table. Another little bit of paradise. The leather bound menus contained delicious selections for a woman's taste. The waiter appeared and spoke to her in a posh accent. She ordered a sparkling mineral water and shrimp cocktail to start. They brought her a little bowl with lemon water for her to cleanse her hands, complete with a warm towel to dry.

The shrimp rivaled Brennan's. She enjoyed every morsel. A complimentary bread basket with signature Neiman's pop-overs appeared. Taking out a warm pop-over, she spread it with strawberry butter inside. Succulent. Then, it was time to order her entrée. Carefully perusing her selections, she discriminately ordered the poached salmon with a vegetable sauté on the side. For desert, she planned to taste the famous Neiman's chocolate chip cookies *a la mode*.

While she waited for her food, Nora again began to people watch. She questioned if she would ever again aspire to be a part of upper echelon society. Doubtful. Middle class would suit her just fine. Working at the jazz club, was an eye opener. She had a new appreciation for how hard Nellie had to work for her money. As he waiter brought her salmon, she envisaged what type of job she might find back in New Orleans.

The entrée was every bit as good as her shrimp appetizer. She unabashedly finished every bite. As she swallowed the last morsel, she suddenly felt a cramp. Down low. "Oh. No, no!" she quietly exclaimed out loud. She was in labor.

Nora motioned for the waiter. "Can you please bring my check?"

"*Madame*, is the lunch not of your liking?" he asked in his heavy French tinged English.

"No. I mean, yes. It was lovely. But," she was mortified to say anything more, "I may be in labor."

He appeared shocked at first and then stared at her belly. "*Madame*, please. Right this way." She took his hand as he escorted her discreetly towards the door.

"What about the check?" Nora reached for money in her purse. She handed the Maître' D a twenty. "Keep the change."

"Should we telephone someone for you?"

"No. No. Just get me a taxi. Quick." With this being Nora's fifth baby, she knew she didn't have long. A few pushes and bam, she would be having a baby at Neiman's.

A security guard for the store arrived at the entrance to The Zodiac Room. "Here *Madame*, let me help you." People were beginning to stare. Nora waddled as quickly as she could towards the entrance. Just as she passed the designs of Marchesa, she felt her water break. It spewed across the shiny marble floor.

"Oh dear. Oh my. Ugh, how embarrassing."

The security guard held tightly to her arm, such that she didn't fall in the slippery mess. Just a few more steps to the exit. Taxis were waiting in the que. "Taxi. Taxi," he motioned.

"Thank you so much," Nora managed getting into the Yellow Cab, wet dress and all.

"Take care, Ma'am. Best wishes."

The taxi driver sped off down Main Street and into traffic. Nora's contractions were coming at five minutes apart. She held her legs tightly together and tried to deep breathe.

"St. Paul Hospital, please. And hurry."

"Yes'm," the black taxi cab driver sped into gear.

A classic. Labor at the Zodiac Room of Neiman's. She hadn't even finished her salmon. Amniotic fluid all over the fine marble floors. Nora should have been mortified. But when she thought about it she broke out in a fit of laughter. Charlene would love this story. The driver gave her a strange look.

"Please, Ma'am. Whatever you do, don't be having no baby in my cab."

"Well drive fast then, because it is on its way."

Six minutes later, the driver was pulling into the ER

entrance of St. Paul. The attendants, seeing her enlarged pregnant state, quickly put her into a wheelchair and rushed to the maternity ward. It dawned on Nora that she didn't have her Lamaze book.

A nun in a long, ceil blue dress with a large white coronet was at the desk of obstetrics to check her in. "Don't panic dear, it is an act of holiness you are about to receive. The gift of life."

Nora shot her a look. "I've done this four times already, Sister. I know exactly what is in store." She could tell her contractions were now quickening. Not long now. She let her legs un-squeeze to help her dilated cervix now expand and relax. "My contractions are three minutes apart."

"Well then, let's get you back to delivery post haste. But first, I will need some basic information. Can you fill out these forms?"

Nora scrunched her face in light of another oncoming contraction. "Not at the moment," she gritted her teeth. Then, remembered her breathing. She started her Lamaze patterns of "He, he, he, ho, ho, ho."

"What on earth are you doing?" the flustered nun questioned.

"Lamaze."

"Um, we don't do that here." She turned to the orderly. "Page anesthesia, stat. She's going to need her injections quickly."

Nora cried out. "No. No injections. I am going to give birth naturally. With Lamaze."

The nun just ignored her lamentations and began asking her basic questions. "What is your name dear? And your husband's name?"

"I am divorced. I have to call the father. But my name is Nora Jean Broussard."

The nun gave her a stern look, "I see. Who is your OB?"

"I'm not from here. He, he, he, ho, ho, ho," Nora grunted.

"I beg your pardon. But you are planning on having a baby here? Have you even had any pre-natal care?"

"Some. In Tyler."

"Is that your address then, in Tyler?"

"Not exactly. But you can put that down." Nora squeaked out the address in between her breathing. "Look, you need to hurry. The baby is crowning."

"The doctor will be the judge of that," the nun shook her finger at Nora. "Take her back to delivery room two. And re-page that anesthesiologist."

As they were wheeling back, Nora called out to the nun. "By the way, this may be an adoption case."

"Bless me father," the nun made the sign of the cross. She semi-jogged towards Nora, her rosary jingling from her belt. "Did you say you were giving the baby up?"

"I think so."

"Well, dear. You need to be sure. That changes everything," the nun rolled her judgmental eyes as she tore up the forms and garnered a different set. As they passed the labor and delivery receiving desk, the nun motioned to a nurse and another nun. They were whispering, "adoption," as if Nora could not hear them.

Nora could tell this was not going to go as planned. "Please. Nurse. Can you have someone call my . . . the father?"

"Sure, hon. What's the number?" a nurse in regular nurse's uniform asked.

"It's in my purse. Here," Nora said thrusting forward her bag.

"Right away doll," she unfolded the crumpled paper with *The Melrose* embossed on top. The nurse looked surprised as she knew the Melrose was quite posh.

"He's a pilot. For Humble Oil. That number is the . . . ahhhhhhhh. Uggghhh." Another contraction took hold of her as she was wheeled into the delivery room. Green gowned and masked men seemed to surround her. She was lifted onto a hard delivery table and her legs put up into stirrups. Her arms were strapped down. They raised her dress up and cut it off up the front. Then dressed her in a grey hospital gown. Off came her panties. Snip, snip. She had on no panty hose.

She felt a sharp poke in her arm. An IV was being started.

"No drugs. Fluids only. No drugs," she demanded.

"Please, Mrs.?"

"Ms. Broussard. And I am telling you. No drugs. I

want to see my baby born. Gaahhhhhh . . ." a contraction gripped her to the core. She could feel the baby's head.

An OR nurse attempted to argue on Nora's behalf. "She said no drugs. She wanted to try Lamaze. What about the patient's rights?"

Her efforts were ignored. One of the gowned men, the obstetrician, griped at the anesthesiologist. "Get on with it, this baby's crowning. It'll be out before she is."

"Alright. Alright," he injected Nora's IV with something. She felt cold go up her arm and her head became hazy. Psychedelic colors appeared on their gowns. She could smell something sweet. A rubber cone was placed on her nose. They were giving her gas. Muffled by the mask, she called out, "No. No." Then the room faded black.

"Twilight sleep. Induced."

"Thank Christ for Scopolamine and Morphine."

"Don't forget the Nitrous," the anesthesiologist pointed to her face.

"Son of a gun this baby is huge. Get the vacuum forceps," he directed a nurse who was scrubbed in.

The spoons of the vacuum forceps were placed on the baby's head. The machine began to whir. Within seconds, it was out. A nine pound, ten ounce baby girl. All ten fingers. All ten toes. The physician turned it upside down holding it by the feet and slapped its behind. It began to wail loudly. "This one's gonna Apgar high. Holy shit."

"Time, 2:45 PM. Wednesday, the twenty-eighth of March," the nurse called out to verify what to put on the birth certificate.

The baby was rubbed dry with warmed towels by a nurse nun and then placed in the baby warmer. It had a beautifully round, large face, and almost no hair. Just tufts of dark brown fuzz surrounded her olive complexion. Huge eyes. "What a beautiful baby girl you are. Such a shame your mother isn't going to keep you." As the doctor predicted, the baby Apgar'd at nine and ten. It was perfectly healthy and wailing up a storm. "A feisty one you are," the nun said swaddling her and placing her in a bassinet. Nora was still out. "Take the baby to the *special* nursery," the nurse directed the orderly. "Not the general nursery. The one in the back, okay? Her mother is not to see her. It is an adoption."

"Right," the orderly answered. It was done. The baby that Nora carried for nine months was wheeled anonymously away.

The obstetrician was finishing up. Nora's placenta was delivered intact. "No tears. No episiotomy. Fit as a whistle. And tight I might add. How many babies has this woman had?"

"Five," the nun answered. "She's Catholic. Or was. She's divorced."

"I see," said the OB. Addressing the gasser he remarked, "Give her another round of twilight. She needs to be out for a while, no need to remember the birth, okay?"

"You're the boss," the anesthesiologist complied. He re-dosed Nora with another round of Morphine and Scopolamine. Luckily, she had no cardiovascular issues as the medication dropped her blood pressure significantly. The anesthesiologist bolused her with another liter of IV fluid. Nora, completely unconscious, was lifted onto a gurney and transferred to a ward off the obstetric unit in the women's gynecology area. Away from obstetric mothers, newborns, and anything related to having a baby.

By the time Steve was notified and flew back to Love Field, it was late in the evening. He dashed into the hospital front door. Once he found out Nora's room number, he climbed the stairs instead of waiting for the elevator. "Gynecology?" he questioned reading the sign on the wall.

Another blue-dressed nun in a huge, starched, white coronet approached him. Their hats curiously reminded Steve of wings, like they could takeoff. The ward was dark and the only lights on were at the nurse's station. "Excuse me sir. Visiting times are over. You can return tomorrow."

"My . . . my girl. She's had a baby."

"You are on the wrong floor then, the waiting room for fathers is on two." Another nurse approached the nun. She whispered something and they both gave him searing looks, realizing he was the biological father of the adopted baby.

"I don't care what you say. I am going to see her," Steve demanded. "She doesn't have anyone else here."

As they were about to rebuke him, he heard Nora call out from one of the rooms near. "Steve. Steve," she moaned. He peered in the nearest door to him and there she was. Like he had never seen her. Her cosmetics were smeared all over her face. Nora's heavy eye make-up had dripped down her cheek bones from her tears. She still had the remnants of lipstick on her lips. Her hair was a fright. Disheveled and miserable, she was horrific looking.

When she saw him, she burst into tears. "Steve," she began to sob heavily, waterfalls of black mascara streaming down her cheek.

"I'm here, darling. I am here," he rushed to the bed, lowered the side rails and took her in his arms. Heavy, deep, cathartic sobs wracked her body. She cried and cried and cried. He held her tight. Cradling her head against his shoulder, "I know, sweetheart. I know. Let it out. I am here."

She sniffled hard, wiping her nose on the sheets she raised to her face. "It was horrible. Just horrible. They drugged me."

"What?" he wasn't sure he understood. "What do you mean, for the pain?"

"No. They didn't listen to me. I wanted to do Lamaze. To see the baby. And they drugged me without my consent," she sobbed heavily again.

"Nora. I am so sorry. Damn it, I should have been here."

"They took the baby away. To some secret nursery. I want to see my baby. Oh, God," her cries were hard and painful to hear.

The nurse came in with some sedation on a silver tray. She was preparing to give Nora another injection.

"Get that syringe away from her, now. Do you hear me?" Steve's voice was raised and intimidating.

"Sir, the doctor ordered that we keep her sedated. She is hysterical."

"Of course she is. She just had her baby taken away from her and was drugged against her will. You come one step closer with that and I'll shove it into you. Do you hear me?"

The nurse took the tray away quickly. Steve wondered if he had just bought himself a visit with hospital security. He turned his attentions back to Nora. He held here there long into the night as she wept. Eventually, he laid her back onto the bed and climbed in next to her, just to hold her. When she was finally asleep, he slept next to her in a chair, never letting go of her hand.

When he awoke, she was awake and more alert. The sun was just coming up and she was sitting up in the bed. "The nurses hate you, you know."

"Well, after the way they treated you, they deserve it. Damned control freaks," he yawned, stretching his cramped neck and arms. He wiped his fatigued eyes. "What time is it?"

"Seven. AM."

"Oh, geesh. What a night. How are you feeling?"

"Empty. Hung over."

He noticed that her face was free of makeup. The nurse had given her some hot towels to wash the garish stuff off. As usual, even in her current state, she was luminous.

"They were pretty rough on you. What happened? When did you go into labor? At the hotel?"

"No. The Zodiac room at Neiman's. My water broke in the Marchesa designer racks."

He giggled slightly, "I am sure you are now one of Stanley Marcus' more memorable customers."

"Shut up, Steve," she looked at him sheepishly. But it was kind of funny.

"Typical, Nora."

"Yep, that's me."

He took her hand in his and kissed it. "I am proud of you. You brought that baby safely into the world and gave someone the gift of a lifetime."

"Not yet I haven't. I have not signed final adoption papers."

"Well, there is that."

"That's not what I mean. I have not completely made up my mind."

"Nora," he looked at her skeptically. "Now I know you have been through a lot, but we have been through this a million times. Think of your kids. Of Kayce."

"I am. But they took that baby from me. They drugged me against my will. *If* I give this baby up, it is going to be on my terms this time."

Steve knew that look in her eyes. He dreaded what was to come next.

Chapter 49

A young, thin, attractive woman was hanging out her Monday laundry in a small yard on Tumbleweed Trail in Fort Worth. The early morning gusts of wind were blowing her short, thick, brown, wavy hair into her eyes. As she tried to put up the last shirt, she struggled. Several pegs dropped to the ground. Bending down to scoop them up, she placed the stray pegs into the hamper and decided at that moment to ask her husband for a clothes dryer. She could hear her phone ringing.

The laundry had to wait. She hurried up the back steps of her small, conventional, two bedroom brick home reaching the phone on its last ring. "Hello, hello?" a New Orleans accent answered.

"Mrs. Charbonnet? Am I speaking to Odile Charbonnet?" The person on the line gave it a hard "t" at the end. As in char bonnet.

It was grossly mispronounced, as usual. "Yes, this is Mrs. Charbonnet," Odile corrected politely. Her voice was sweet and delicate.

"Mrs. Charbonnet. Is your husband at home? This is Catholic Charities."

Odile's pulse quickened. Was it a formality? Another form they needed? Was this the call she had waited for? After four years? "No, my husband Stew is at work. At General Dynamics. How can I help you?"

"Mrs. Charbonnet, you will want to contact him right away. We have wonderful news. We have a baby girl for you if you want her. She was born a couple of days ago."

"A baby? You have a baby for us? Good heavens." Odile began to cry tears of joy. "Oh, thank you. Thank you so much."

"Mrs. Charbonnet. Are you okay?"

"I'm just . . . we have tried for so long," the tears were running now. She brushed them off her lovely, porcelain complexion.

"Now you go call your husband. Right away. You can pick her up from St. Paul Hospital in Dallas. You all will need to be here at promptly 11:00 AM. I will meet you in the lobby at St. Paul's okay?"

"Alright. I understand."

"Mrs. Charbonnet, do you have everything you need to care for her? Bottles, that sort of thing? She'll need some Similac formula. We'll give you the first bit."

"I think so. If not, I will call my neighbors to help me get what I need today."

"Fine. Just fine. And bring a baby outfit. See you at eleven. Sharp."

Odile hung up the phone. She nervously dialed her engineer husband, Stew. "Pick up, pick up," she twirled the cord nervously.

He did on the fourth ring. "Stewart Charbonnet."

"Stew. They have our baby. We have to pick her up at eleven today. They have our baby," her voiced quickened.

"What? A baby?"

"Yes. A girl. Our baby girl. Catholic Charities just called. Oh, Stew. My prayers have been answered. We have a baby."

"What do we need to do?"

"Get everything ready, I guess. I have a few things. I have to call Greta, down the street. She will know what to do. And my mother. Stew, darling. I am so happy. They have our baby."

"When was she born?"

"Only a couple of days, ago. In Dallas."

"Dallas? Are they sure it's okay to get her that early?" It was so hard to believe it was happening after all of the forms, interviews, home visit and waiting. Not to mention Odile's rosaries, novenas and special masses.

"At St. Paul's, the Catholic hospital. Yes, I am sure it

is fine. They are going to meet us there," she began to cry joyfully.

"Hold yourself together, Odile. I'm going to take off early. I will be home in twenty minutes. We have to make sure we're ready."

He hung up the phone. Odile ran to the bedroom they had prepared months ago. The crib had all sorts of odds and ends stacked in it. It had become a dumping ground for clutter. She boxed up the items and changed the crib sheets. Straightening the lamp and checking to see how many diapers she had, she thought about the time that had passed. Their initial high hopes of getting a baby through adoption were dashed as the waiting drug on month, after month, after month. At one point, she had almost given up hope that they would ever get called at all.

Odile and Stew had been married for nine years. They never used contraception, both being Catholic. Yet, Odile had never conceived. Three exploratory surgeries and a multitude of tests later, it was determined that Odile's tubes had scarred. At age nine, she had suffered a bout of peritonitis, secondary to a ruptured appendix. Stew was fertile, but in 1962, they had exhausted all fertility options. Alternatives were few. Adoption was their only answer.

The Charbonnet family originated in northern Louisiana. Stew met Odile when he was completing a summer internship for Louisiana State University, LSU. As a petroleum engineer he was designing some parts for the offshore drilling rigs near New Orleans. He was a tall, good looking gentleman with wavy dark, brunette hair and soft, kind brown eyes.

Odile was raised in uptown New Orleans, near the Carrollton street car line. She was one of six children. Her French-German mother had grown up on a sugarcane plantation near Donaldsonville. Odile and Stew now lived in Fort Worth. Due to the cold war, a career in the expanding market of defense aviation replaced his petroleum background. Stew was working on the design for the F-111 fighter plane for General Dynamics.

It was strange. Neither Nora, nor the adoptive parents could imagine the similarities, indeed parallels, of their separate lives. The South. New Orleans. The French culture. Catholicism. The aviation industry. In an instant, indeed a last minute decision, the life circumstances to which the baby would belong were forever altered.

Odile still couldn't believe it. She lit a candle under St. Theresa, little flower of Jesus and another one under her statue of the infant Jesus of Prague. She knelt at her *pre du* and said a rosary of thanksgiving. Her prayers were answered. God had blessed them, finally, with a baby.

Chapter 50

A cluster of activity was making a racket on the gynecological floor of St. Paul's. The Mother Superior of the Daughters of Charity, in full regalia and coronet, was clambering down the hall, clipboard in hand, rosary beads clanging. She was followed by an entourage. A man in a business suit and a gaggle of four other nuns dressed in their long blue habits, also with starched coronets, were trying to keep up with her strides as she marched forth.

"Which room is she in?" the nun demanded, directing her question to the charge nurse on duty at the desk.

"Room 302. Just there," she pointed across the hall from the nurse's station.

The Mother Superior entered Nora's room without knocking. The other members of her party filled the rest of the room. "Miss Broussard, I understand you are causing quite a ruckus with my nurses."

"I beg your pardon?" Nora wanted her to clarify, setting her up.

"With your impossible demands. Let me be perfectly clear. You have given your baby up for adoption. It is against all policy and procedure to let you see that baby. It just isn't done. Not here, not anywhere."

Nora's nostrils flared and she tried to control her anger. Self-control was the only way she was going to win. She pulled out her Lamaze book. "Well let me tell you something, Sister."

"That's Mother Superior," the haughty nun corrected.

"Whatever your title is. It is becoming common practice to change the way labor is done. Women don't have to be subjected to mind altering drugs and sedated out of their gourd." Nora held up her book. "I'll have you know, I repeatedly refused sedation and medication of any kind. Yet, it was given against my will."

"That is common practice for delivery, Miss Broussard."

"That's Ms. Broussard. And I believe that is against my patient rights. This isn't a sanitarium of the 1930s. Or is it?" Nora was losing her temper.

"We are simply following hospital policy."

"Well maybe your antiquated policy needs revision? And," Nora was on an impassioned roll. "If you are following policy, then you should know that I have rights. To my baby. And to my care at this facility. I am telling you right here and now, that if you don't start listening to me; I am not going to sign those adoption papers."

The man in the suit began to speak, "Now, now. Ms. Broussard. There's no need to threaten anything."

Steve was in the corner loving this performance. That was his Nora. He rose and stood next to her bed.

The Mother Superior glared at him. "And who is this?"

"I am the baby's father. I would start listening to her. You're not going to change her mind."

"And if you don't, I will be happy to call my lawyers," Nora bluffed.

The staunch nun glared at them both. Pausing for the longest minute, she took a deep breath and huffed. "What exactly is it that you want, *Ms.* Broussard?"

"I want to see my baby. I refuse to sign the final papers until I do so."

"Ms. Broussard, are you aware that the adoptive couple has already been called? They are on their way now, as we speak. You are putting us in an impossible situation."

"Not impossible. Just difficult. And those are my demands. Bring the baby to me, or get no signature." Nora crossed her arms over her large and swollen breasts. Her milk had come in. But even in her nightgown, she was determined to look as indignant as possible.

Mother Superior was rapping her fingers on the bedside table. She was absolutely livid. The gaggle cowered behind her. They knew this stare well. She let out another big breath and began her response in a slow, deliberate, and unnerving tone. "Very well. I would hate to crush the parents who are already on their way. They would be broken hearted with your selfish reversal of decision." She turned to one of her underlings. "Go get the baby quickly. Take it up the back elevators and get it in here without anyone seeing you. Chop, chop," she commanded. The young nun quickly darted out of the room and scurried down the hall to the elevator. She nervously pressed the button ten times until it came.

"As for you," the disdainful nun addressed Nora, "I will give you five minutes exactly on the clock. And you will be supervised by one of my staff."

"I will have ten. And it will be me and Mr. Novak. Alone. Your staff can wait outside the door and guard it if you wish," Nora replied tempestuously.

"Fine. Unconscionable. Your irreverence and insubordination. Just unconscionable," she roared, her face screwed into a heinous contortion. In a swirl and swish of starched fabric, petticoats, and rosary beads, she turned to leave. The gaggle and the suit man followed.

"Bravo. Bravo." Steve clapped for her. "That was quite a performance."

"I was a real bitch wasn't I?"

"Yes, you were. But you got what you wanted."

Nora tossed her head back, "I should try that more often." The gleam in her eyes was back. She scrambled out of bed in her nightgown and reached for her overnight bag. "Hurry. We don't have much time." Out of her bag, she pulled a layette set and one of the new Polaroid cameras.

Steve looked confused, "What's all this?"

She hid them under her pillow and got back into the bed. "When they bring me the baby, I am going to dress it up in these clothes, nurse it, and then you are going to take a picture, okay?"

"Don't involve me in your little scheme. I think you may be breaking some kind of law."

"That's ridiculous. They aren't going to send me to jail

for taking a picture of my own baby. I still haven't signed those papers."

"Nora, are you sure? I mean. It will be hard to hold it and then . . ." he couldn't bring himself to say it. There were tears in his eyes.

"Now don't go all to mush on me. They'll know something is up. Please, Steve. Do this last thing for me, okay? Please."

She looked at him with those beautiful chocolate eyes. He was putty in her hands.

"Okay. But just one. Alright? I don't want you to get caught."

In another few minutes, they heard the door open. A nun pushed in the bassinet. "I will be starting the timer now. I will be just outside. Mother Superior is at the desk."

"I understand," Nora replied. Steve wheeled the bassinet close to the bed. Nora reached out and picked up her precious baby. She unfolded the swaddled blankets. "It's a girl, Steve. Look we had a baby girl. Lord, she is a big one too."

Nora looked into the sleeping baby's peaceful face and began to recite the poem Steve had given her. "Oh, I have slipped the surly bonds of earth . . . and danced the skies on laughter-silvered wings." She touched the baby's cheek and by response the baby turned and began to suck on her finger. "Aw, Steve, she's sucking."

Steve was almost afraid to look, but he was glad he did. He gazed down upon his daughter, his seventh child. She was beautiful and so innocent sleeping there. The face of a cherub. "I wonder who is feeding her?"

"The nurses, I imagine. Bottles."

Nora undid her nightgown and unsnapped her support bra. Steve was aghast. "Nora, I don't think you should."

"Ssshhh. They will hear you. This is my baby and I am going to give her part of myself. Besides, I want to give the best start possible. It's healthy for her to have that colostrum."

"Good God they will stroke if they catch you."

"That is why they won't." Nora took her breast and stroked the nipple on the baby's cheek. The baby opened its mouth and began to suckle. Tears formed in Nora's eyes and she blinked them away, not wanting to miss a moment with her tiny daughter. She let her suck for a few minutes, knowing time was ticking away. Steve sat mesmerized, yet very sad. After a few magical moments, Nora reached up to the corner of baby's mouth and broke the seal.

"Hurry, get out the camera. Make sure it's ready. I am going to put on the clothes." She reached under the pillow and pulled out the special pale, yellow smocked gown. She took off the nursery t-shirt and placed on the gown, cap and booties. She wrapped the baby in the white and yellow blanket she had crocheted. "Okay. I'm ready."

Nora held the baby in her arms. Steve quickly snapped a photo. They were both afraid the flash would make a loud noise. Then, Nora changed the position of the baby on the bed, so Steve could take a full body shot. "There, like this." Nora held the baby up slightly. Snap, snap the camera shot the photos. Steve wanted to make sure that they got a clear one.

"Okay, done." Nora quickly took off the baby outfit and re-dressed the baby in its hospital garb. Re-wrapped the baby in the hospital blankets, she swaddled them securely. Then she held the baby again snuggly in her arms.

With her fingers she stoked the baby's head and bent down to kiss her. She looked over at Steve, "Want to touch the face of an angel?"

His eyes filled with tears. He came to the bed and stroked the forehead of his daughter. Bending over, he planted a kiss on the baby's head. He was then overcome with emotion and quickly exited the room into the hall.

He sobbed heavily as the nurse and two nuns entered to take the baby away. "Oh, God. What have I done? What have I done?" he questioned in agony knowing he would never again see his youngest daughter.

The nurse and nun quickly wheeled the bassinet down the back hallway and into a waiting elevator. Steve tried to collect himself, blowing his nose on his handkerchief. He returned to Nora in the room. Her side rails were down and he sat down next to her on the bed and laid his head on her chest. This time, it was he who sought her stoic comfort. She cradled his head against her chest as he sobbed softly.

"It's okay. She had our love, our kisses and our blessing. She's our angel and our gift. I am sure she is going to a couple who will love her like we do."

"My dear, strong, Nora. I'm so sorry I put you through this. I am so sorry. Please forgive me." He nestled his head in her bosom. She wrapped her arms around him snuggly.

"I already have, Steve. I forgave both of us, long ago. It hurts like hell, but it will be okay. Now that I've seen her, I know it. She has the face and hopefully the indomitable spirit of Jack Broussard."

Chapter 51

Nora stepped out of Humble Oil van and onto the sidewalk of Union Station in downtown Dallas. Shivering, she wrapped her jacket around her small post-partum bulge as it was cold and blustery. She wasn't sure if it was the stiff breeze or her final moments with Steve that sent chills down her spine.

"Do you have your ticket?"

"Yes. You gave it to me, already."

"And your bags. Did I get all of them?"

"Yes, Steve. They are all here." Nora smiled. There were only three. She knew his mind wasn't in what he was doing either.

"It's still early. Let's go inside for a coffee," Nora suggested.

"Yeah, okay. Or a stiff drink. I'll go park the van."

Nora waited for him on the sidewalk of the station. She could hear the locomotive whistles as they pulled in and out. Dallas was a busy way station for many of the commuter lines connections. Steve joined her and took her hand as they walked inside.

At this point, she was handling things better than he. Steve had been a nervous wreck ever since he helped her check out of the hospital. Nora had accepted her fate. She was anxious to see her children and get on the road. Far, far away from Tyler and Texas.

They walked to the café inside the terminal. Coffee. It had all started with coffee, Steve thought as he brought her a cup of strong black java. So many years ago. He put cream in his and a little sugar stirring it nervously.

"So you will be leaving today, then? On that drive?"

"Yep. My train gets to Tyler at about eleven. Once I get the kiddos loaded, we'll leave straight away. I plan to take a different route back. I'm going to over to Vicksburg and then head down. That way, the kids will get to see parts of historic Mississippi. I think it will be pretty late in the afternoon when we get to Shreveport. So I may stay there for a stopover."

"Guess it will take you a couple of days then."

"Yes. More than likely."

His gaze rose from his coffee to look at her face and meet her eyes. It was hard to believe that they had been through so much in the last year and a half. Star crossed lovers.

Nora asked him about his plans, "So you'll be flying to Houston?"

"Yep. Should be back to Tyler by Friday." He was flicking the coffee stirrer in his fingers. God, she was gorgeous. He would miss her with all his heart. She sipped her coffee slowly. Resolutely.

He reached over and touched her arm lightly. "How did you do it? How did you get through it? What made you change your mind?" He was full of difficult questions.

"Several powerful forces in my life. Charlene. My children. Jack. And Gia."

"Gia?"

"The mysterious woman with the exotic eyes. From the shop in The Quarter."

"The woman who gave you life."

"No, that gave Nellie and Jack a life."

He was in awe of her stoic grace. "Nora, you know that part of me will always love you."

"I realize that. I feel the same, too. Our timing just isn't right," she responded in her sultry, classically Nora voice.

"No, I suppose not." He couldn't take his eyes off her. These were to be their last moments together.

"Come on. They are boarding my train." She took his arm and he walked her to the outdoor train platform. The Texas Eagle was silver and painted with red and blue accents. Steam was coming from beneath the engine car.

The engine conductor was making his calls. "All aboard. All aboard the Texas Eagle. Eastbound. Greenville. Mineola. Tyler. Longview. Shreveport. Alexandria. Baton Rouge. New Orleans."

This was it; they were at the steps to board. Nora turned to face Steve. "Thank you. For being there. For helping me and my children get through this. I know it was extraordinary."

"I wouldn't have had it any other way," he held her hands tightly. He didn't want to let go.

At the foot of the steps, she reached up to kiss him on the cheek. But before she could, he placed his hands on the sides of her face and kissed her passionately and deeply. It startled her at first and then she felt her body meld into his. He kissed and kissed and kissed her, not wanting to break free. Their heads moved and their lips united in futile desire and desperation. Tasting each other. Touching for the last time. It was Nora who gently broke free. "I have to go, Steve."

"Nora. I'll always love you," he expressed earnestly.

"And I will always love you, too. My instructor pilot." She pulled away from him and waved. She forced herself to smile. And hoped he didn't see her lip quiver. "Bye, bye now."

Nora turned and left him standing on the platform, helplessly watching her depart. She stepped on onto the stairs and into the compartment doorway without looking back. A bellman helped her find her seat. Steve moved along the train until he could see her seated. She almost wished that he would just leave. Prolonging it was painful. She turned to wave and then looked straight ahead.

Inside her gut was wrenching in heartache and pain. She bit her lip, determined not to cry. She could feel herself breathe. Moments in time stood still. Slowly she felt the train begin to lurch forward. Steam rose from the undercarriage as its wheels squeaked on the metal rails.

Nora saw his image become smaller and smaller until they were away from the platform and station. Steve had still not moved. Nora looked forward out her window. She could no longer bear to see him on the platform.

The sun was glistening radiantly on the sky scrapers of

Dallas. Traffic was rushing by on the streets. Nora looked up and saw the red Mobil winged horse on top of one of the buildings. Pegasus. It was lit up in bright red neon, even during the day. She looked towards clouds the sky, the ones in which she had soared, feeling so free, only months ago.

So much emotion. So much pain. Her children. Steve. Her baby girl. Her angel. Who would her take care of her? What type of people would they be? Nora turned to look back in the direction of St. Paul hospital. She took out the Polaroid picture of the baby that Steve had taken. Her emotions overcame her. Choking them back she whispered, "Oh, God . . . Jack, give me strength." Not being able to bear more, she quickly put the photo back in her wallet. The train was rumbling over the tracks, increasing its speed. It was over. It was done.

Taking stock in her decision, Nora knew she had done the right thing. For her four children, especially Kayce. For Steve and his wife. Even for herself. The turbulence had subsided. Navigation of a new start to life had to take over.

Attempting to edge out the heartbreak of forsaking her baby daughter, she forced herself to not to turn her head. It was time to begin a new page in life's journey. Looking ahead towards a new future was the only way she could cope. Defiantly, Nora shut out the pain of Dallas, Steve, and the child she was leaving behind. She completely severed the chapter on her love for Steve. As train picked up momentum and left Dallas, she reached up for the window shade. Pulling it down, she symbolically closed this period in her life forever.

Jeanette Vaughan is well established as a writer and story teller. Not only is she published in the periodicals and professional journals of nursing, but also in the genre of fiction. Out on her sheep farm, she has written several novels and scripts. She is the mother of four children, including two Navy pilots. She lives in a Victorian farmhouse out in the pastures of northeast Texas with her sheep, chickens, donkeys and sheep dogs.

Follow me online here:

Blog: www.jeanettevaughan.com
Email: jeanettevaughan@ageviewpress.com
Facebook: www.facebook.com/AgeViewPress
Twitter: www.twitter.com/VaughanJeanette
Goodreads: www.goodreads.com/Jeanette_Vaughan